1st ed

ECHOES

ECHOES

CARTER KAPLAN

international authors
brookline, massachusetts

Published by International Authors: Brookline, Massachusetts.

This is a work of literary experimentation. Any resemblances to actual persons or institutions are unintended and coincidental.

ISBN: 978-1721136599

Library of Congress Control Number: 2018906956

Kind thanks to M-A Berthier and Michael Butterworth
Cover art: Lee Talley. Cover titles: Joel K. Soiseth
Bronson Bodine portrait by Bienvenido "Bones" Bañez, Jr.

THE **INVISIBLE TOWER** TRILOGY

ECHOES

THE **ADVENTURES** OF **BRONSON BODINE**

VOLUME I

CONTENTS

PINS AND NEEDLES

BRONSON BODINE LEANED his powerful shoulders through the tower window and joined the gargoyles glaring out over the ragged mountains. He was above the freaks now—the lawyers, the doctors, the journalists, the film and television producers, the educational programmers—so high that the sun burned like a white hole in the sky, and the half-moon could be seen in detailed magnificence. The shadows of the lunar craters and the peaks of the mountains rising through the twilight of the terminator appeared closer than the features of the earth itself. The sky from this height was joined with space in a pure dome of bright, liquid purple—a drop of clarity hanging over the shadowed landscape in a vastness that radiated as deeply inward as it did toward the heavens. Below, the mountains rolled out as if viewed through the wrong end of a telescope. Like flat pieces of stage scenery, the ridges overlapped each other, hiding the pinelands, meadows and lakes in the valleys below.

A single yellow road wound up the mountainside to the castle. It curved from side to side and then spiraled around the mountain five times as it tightened toward the peak. Up the road a black Rolls Royce crept slowly. Dazzling stars of light turned around its chrome ornaments. Its windows flashed in the sun.

"Bronson," said a young woman sleepily.

The silhouette of his naked form turned inside the window. No matter how much light streamed in through the window, it always felt like night in

1

this room. The motes hovering in the air around the man flared like stars. She was sitting up in the four-poster trying to light a candle. Her lids hung heavily over her large eyes as she fumbled with the matches. She had broad cheekbones, a narrow chin, and a pointy English nose. Thin blonde hair hung over her face, draped gracefully down, twisted around her crossed legs and joined with the rumpled sheets. It was easy to imagine she had sent forth roots and was growing from the bed. She set the candle beside a half-empty bottle of *Caparzo Cà del Pazzo* that stood beside the bed on her moondial.

Hanging from the walls, framing girl, bed and moondial in a grotesque diorama, were tapestries patterned after Hieronymus Bosch's "The Garden of Earthly Delights." The panel depicting Earth hung from the wall behind the bed. Paradise was on the left wall. On the right, with seams cut through it to accommodate the door, beckoned Hell.

On the outside wall, with a rectangular opening for the window, hung an arabesque tapestry sporting designs that would not bear scrutiny. The elaborate patterns seemed to crank and spin in three dimensions, and if stared at for any duration they left a photonegative shadow in the viewer's eyes that remained for some time.

The young woman lit a cigarette, looked up at the man, and then turned rapidly away as if the arabesque patterns or the morning light was too much for her eyes.

"It is time," he said, studying her. "I am leaving."

She sucked on her cigarette, her eyes staring forward. "Stay."

He looked away. "I've already decided."

Neither of them heard the bee outside the window.

"We could have it pretty good here for a long long time." She ashed on the sheets, her sudden gesture reflected the activity of a strong and rapid mind.

He agreed. "But that's not why I came." He took his jeans from the floor and slipped into them. She watched him button the front over his naked pelvis. He finished and then looked at her. His eyes were a piercing blue, bright, cruel, wonderfully vast. "If we stayed here we'd end up like them."

She sat quietly with one hand squeezing her forehead. After a few moments she took another drag. "That's not the issue though." She finished exhaling. "Is it?"

"I'm twenty-three," he said calmly. "You're fifteen. That's an issue."

"That's a copout." She sighed contemptuously and flicked the unfinished cigarette into the corner where her pet rhinoceros beetle paced up to inspect it. She stared at him. "I'm talking about you. Just you and what's best for you. Where do you think people like you can go? Do you think there's anything out there as good as this? Nothing's going to happen, you know, like finding a grail."

His large eyes narrowed and he looked very arch. "The finding is in the looking."

"Isn't that what the cowboys of the round table said before they bushwhacked America?"

He smiled at her. He was going to miss her precociousness. "It's unfortunate you had the wherewithal to run away from boarding school. They could have helped you there. You are much too secure for this world."

"I'm too secure?" She cursed. Look at those pimples on your shoulders. Physician, heal thyself."

He felt a pang of lust echo up his spine. It passed. He sat at the end of the bed and gazed toward the window.

"Bronson." Her voice was irresistibly sweet, perfectly clear and delicate. He looked back and she nodded toward the shelves holding his books, volumes of Poe, Bierce, Verne, Lovecraft and Huxley. "For pitching a little hay and playing tour guide, Krugan treats you like his own son."

"Perhaps it's how he treats himself that concerns me." He turned back to the window. The walls mixed around it. "Remember when he torched your butterfly cape? Magic has a disturbing tendency to take on a life of its own, and in a very unhappy way."

"Is the government of any country you could go over to worse than Krugan?"

He turned back and saw her framed in a swirling trellis. He piously intoned "America" and sighed meaninglessly, but he felt suddenly bitter.

She looked at him coldly. "Do not patronize me." She lit another cigarette. For all her stiff upper lip she was now very uneasy. Emotions were things she usually controlled—except with this man. She nodded suddenly. Her eyelashes swept through space. "You are a puritan, deep down; which is to say you're ferocious. That's it, isn't it? It's been years since you left but America is still part of you. Even worse, it has become for you a myth. Indeed, and you complain of magic?" She studied his reactions, which were sphinxlike, yet to her revealing enough. "It's the ferocity—yes? The horror, the dread, the pathetic, sorry-for-yourself shock of being alone with only yourself to see you, to feel you, to love you. All those pathetic visions of the world in blazing flames, with yourself as reflecting silver avenger. Better than sharing yourself with me. It's easier."

Deep furrows sank into his face. He leaned forward and swept his shirt off the floor. Beneath the shirt was a Walther PPK. He checked the magazine and slid it back up the grip. "No," he said, standing and pushing the pistol into his back pocket. "Life here is truly beautiful, in an hypnotic sort of way. But it is not my choice of life. That's simple enough, isn't it?" There was no further reason to argue with her. He tugged on his shirt so that it hung over the gun.

"I should tell Krugan you're up to something," she said.

"Stay out of it." He kneeled down and felt for the leather straps under the bed. He pulled them out.

She studied him as he approached. "Have you come to your senses, darling?"

He tied and gagged her, his large, powerful hands working gently but with a strength that was driven by an explosive capacity for violence. She had seen him strike bricks with such force that they splintered into fragments, and merely moving his fists inches. That power went deeply into something else, something that was using him, using her. Before she had found it delightful, but now it frightened her and with her characteristic prescience she wondered where he would be in the world when he looked into himself and suddenly discovered what that force really was.

Her teeth chewed uselessly against the gag. She refused to look at him, then through her teeth called him "coward" as he climbed off the bed and stepped back.

"Ouch! Damn!" He picked up his foot and pulled a pin from his heel.

2

ONE OFTEN STEPPED ON PINS and needles in Casa Fuld. Prince Krugan had forbidden the wearing of shoes within the ancient walls, and his wife, Gertrude, sprinkled the pins about liberally. They gathered especially on the stairs and short landings that separated the castle rooms, none of which occupied the same level. Electromagnets had been installed in the ceilings some years before, but they had never been quite powerful enough to draw the pins all the way from the floor. Krugan brought in step-up transformers from outside the country, but the Austrian authorities, weary of such equipment in Prince Krugan's hands, had confiscated them.

Krugan explained that Gertrude sprinkled the pins and needles about to prevent her father, the great globalist poet, Loomis the Exile, from haunting the hallways. But Bronson had never been convinced that Loomis was completely dead. In fact, Bronson knew that Gertrude was simply careless with her sewing.

But whether or not Loomis was dead, his presence was not unfelt.

"*Ach, nein, nein*. He cannot be dead," Gertrude would say, snapping her teeth together like a Carmelite. One of her uppers was a carnelian and she liked to tap it with the tooth immediately below it to produce a wavering liquid clicking. She was blind and this was how she found her way, by echolocation.

"*Mein Papa*, Loomis!" she once hissed at Bronson. "He was the vessel of Western Civilization before him. His teachers put the minds of past poets into his own—ah so, you see?—to prepare him for his great labor. The mind of Loomis then passes into our own. But his teachers did not care for their experiment. They had for Loomis no sinecure at the universities. No chair—pah!" and as she said this she made a motion as if to spit into invisible faces, and then with her knuckles she laid into the stone wall. "This is his sinecure." And, clicking, she walked off. Her sewing shook in her bony hands and the pins dropped behind on the stone flags.

Krugan happened to be nearby hiding behind a tapestry when she said this. After Gertrude had disappeared through the door at the far end of the passage, he emerged and accosted Bronson.

"Poor woman," he said, shaking his head. And out of habit he reached for the heavy-duty knife switch on the wall. He threw it. A few sparks crackled from the contacts and the ceiling began humming. But the pins remained on the floor.

"Have you read Ezekiel 18?" asked Krugan in his tired Russian voice. "*The fathers have eaten sour grapes, and the children's teeth are set on edge. As I live, saith the Lord God, ye shall not have occasion any more to use this proverb in Israel.*"

Bronson shrugged. "I don't recall—"

"Bah," spat the prince. "I thought you've been up to Cambridge?"

Bronson shrugged again, this time smiling. "That's just an overcoat I follow around."

The statement was innocuous enough, but Krugan eyed him suspiciously, then turned and rapidly marched away. "Inscrutable." Krugan cleared his throat in tones of exasperation. "But I am making progress with you, admit it!"

Now, several weeks later, Bronson was walking through this same passage when Krugan came up to him.

"I have important guests coming, Bronson. Will you light the boiler? We will need much hot water."

Bronson nodded. "Gertrude was working in her father's study last night. Shall I straighten up?"

The exiled Russian prince put a friendly hand on Bronson's forearm. "That won't be necessary. These are not literary guests."

"Oh?"

"Business." Krugan started to move off, then turned. "By the way, where is little Shadow?"

Bronson put his hands on his hips to confirm that his shirttail was covering the pistol in his back pocket. "She's tied up at the moment."

Krugan nodded. "Very well. When she is through, have her go to the kitchen. Much cooking today."

Bronson smiled. "Ah, a large party, then?"

Krugan nodded impatiently and moved off.

Bronson ran a cold finger over the cleft in his chin. He was really going to give it to Krugan, pitch him against the stone wall of his own deceptions and break him down once and for all. In the past Bronson's targets had been abstractions—industries, institutions, distant ships, or far flung aircraft that were little more than glowing points on a radar screen. This was different. This was psychic, and it was taking on a life of its own.

He pushed the fingers of both hands through his thick black hair and set off for the boiler room. At several points along the way he stopped and, raising his fist to the wall, rapped out the rhythm of the first three measures of the second movement of Beethoven's Ninth Symphony. Tap-tap, tap-tap, bang-bang-tap-tap. *Molto vivace!*

After lighting the boiler he climbed the steps to the main hall where he found little Precious, little Shadow's identical twin sister. Little Precious sat on a paisley ottoman as she threaded needles for Gertrude. Above her on the wall hung Giorgio de Chirico's "Mystery and Melancholy of a Street." The oranges were quite active in the light from the sun, which slid through the open window on a dazzling angular beam, a geometric essay in three dimensions crossing obliquely through space to ignite the flat painting, in which form and impression suspended like particles of a frail consciousness.

"Precious," he said.

She looked up at him. She completely lacked the wit or poise of her twin. "*Ja?*"

He kneeled by her. "We're playing a trick on Krugan today. We want you to pretend to be Shadow, okay?"

The little girl stared at him through round eyes. "But Gertrude will know it is me because I am threading her needles?"

"That's fine. You look almost done."

She wet a thread in her mouth and pulled it out slowly. "Does this mean you're going to stroke me the way you stroke my sister Shadow?" She placed her hand against his cheek; pinched between her thumb and forefinger was a needle. Though she was physically identical to his lover, the idea of intimacy with Precious repulsed him.

"No," he quietly said. "We are simply playing a game." He stood. "I left one of Shadow's dresses in your room."

Her face was disturbingly blank. "Which one?"

"The blue mini-dress."

"*Ja, ja.* Okay," she said, and she went back to her threading.

For a moment the prospect of being attracted to Precious in Shadow's dress seemed frightening and ominous. Then he realized he was being ridiculous. He patted the gun in his pocket for reassurance, then went out the main entrance.

That strange brilliant sky greeted him. All the world appeared far far beneath it. He stared toward the barn and across the mountains. The closest peak was less than a mile away. Between the two mountains was a saddle-shaped meadow covered with yellow flowers. They flickered in the wind. Above the meadow, a hawk floated with precarious ease. It slipped left and right and swiftly shot up with a current that drew Bronson's eyes to the

7

castle's gray walls. To the left were the three towers. They were connected to each other and to the main hall by arched buttresses. Ponderous and oversize, the buttresses suggested some kind of stone viscera or a crystallized skeleton. Indeed, inside some of these structures were hidden passages that were a favorite playground of his and little Shadow's. The highest tower housed the study of the dead poet, Loomis. The tower of medium height was empty, having been gutted by fire during the Second World War. In the shortest tower was his own apartment—and Shadow stood there gagged, framed in the window, hands stiffly held behind her back. She was staring down at him, her pretty form presenting a startling contrast to the gargoyles sitting on the ledge to her left and right. Her thin yellow hair blew to and fro in the changing wind.

He glared up at her and wondered why he didn't think to tie her to the bed. But she was gagged and her hands were firmly behind her back—even tied at the elbows—and the door was securely locked. The door was quite thick enough to muffle her kicks. And as for the hidden passage, he was sure she would be unable to open the trap door. He waved—a gesture falling somewhere between a salute and a warning. Her eyes registered him without emotion, then she disappeared into the blackness of the apartment.

He turned and followed the progress of the Rolls Royce he had been watching earlier. It was above the terraces now and slowly winding up the third circle beneath the peak.

He hurried to the barn, swung the door aside, and went in. A few chickens bobbed up to check on him and then tottered off. The quiet inside the barn, contrasted against the wind whistling around it's corners, was as deep as his reflections. Little Shadow was wrong. It wasn't ferocity, it was integrity. He was beginning to feel his old self again.

Ten minutes later the black Rolls Royce eased up in front of the castle. Bronson took a pitchfork and began scattering hay into the cow's stall. He appeared intent on his work but remained attentive to the motion around the Rolls.

A bald Tutsi—over seven feet tall and as black and shiny as the automobile—emerged from the driver's door. He wore a dark business suit of a conservative, Central Asian cut. He was also wearing spurs. After adjusting his suit coat over his shoulders, he opened the double doors on the right side of the car.

Four men emerged and, blinking at the sun, put sunglasses over their faces. They were dressed like the Tutsi. Two of them were obviously from the Middle-East. Another, with a wedge-shaped face and a pronounced overbite, had a prim English look about him. Stepping proudly toward the castle, he put on his bowler and gave it a sharp tap. The last member of this party was either a Prussian or a Russian. Arrogant, stiffly contemptuous of those around him and sporting his shortly-cropped blond hair like an edged weapon, he glanced around with the bearing of a disinterested vulture, at once repelling and impressing Bronson with his height, his solid build, and his hostile countenance. He spied Bronson, stared at him a moment, reached to adjust his bowtie—the gesture itself was innocuous but somehow vaguely threatening—and then he followed his companions to the door.

Something distracted Bronson's attention. He glanced over at the tower: Shadow was staring down at him. Her lovely breast buds, pink and sharp, fluoresced in the sun.

Then Krugan was opening the door to admit the visitors. Krugan was wearing his old threadbare tuxedo. Over his shoulders and fastened below his collar with a chain of green copper there hung a black velvet cape with a crimson lining. Krugan had jet-black hair that was gray on the sides. With the sun beating down and washing out his strained and pallid face he seemed very much the Hollywood vampire.

Smiling broadly, clapping and rubbing his hands together, he had the visitors remove their shoes outside the door. As they picked up their shoes and walked in, he glanced over to the barn and waved for Bronson to join them.

When Bronson entered the castle he stopped and stood with the group, now staring at the Tutsi, who, bending his long body over, was strapping his spurs around his bare feet. And what strange feet they were. The Tutsi's toes were over-large, gnarled and twisted. Evidently the man's feet had been deliberately broken many times until the phalanges were enlarged and calcified into heavy knobs. Bronson was afraid of no man, but he respected a problem when he saw one. The Tutsi walked about upon shillelaghs. Shillelaghs equipped with spurs!

Bronson glanced up to discover that the tall Russian with the bowtie was also studying the Tutsi's feet. The Russian slowly shifted his gaze until he met Bronson's eyes. The two men regarded each other and by their

9

expressions shared a sort of speculation. What it would be like to scrap with the Tutsi?

Then Krugan took Bronson to the side. "I want you to open the west wing, and could you and Shadow give up your tower for a few days?"

Bronson stared blankly at the prince. "I guess so—of course."

"Good. There are more coming."

"Excuse me," said the Englishman. "Krugan, was that a mannequin I saw in one of your tower windows?"

"Eh?" The prince narrowed his eyes suspiciously.

"Perhaps it was Miss Shadow," said Bronson. "She wanted to change. She might have glanced outside when she heard the car approach"

"My niece," agreed Krugan, and he placed his hand on Bronson's shoulder. "Please, gentleman. Allow me to introduce my assistant, Bronson Bodine."

In turn, Bronson took each of their hands in both his own. They watched him with guarded approval. One by one raising each of their right hands, he quietly kissed the top of his own. He did well. Here was a young man who knew something of the old ways. Bronson nodded at the group and departed, his head thrown back and his big arms hanging wide.

The blond northern European, a bit taller and a year or so older than Bronson, watched him walk away and then muttered something in Russian.

"What does he say?" asked one of the Arabs.

Krugan smiled. "Mr. Yurchenko is suspicious of young, athletic men."

The second Arab said, "Tell Mr. Yurchenko that he is young and athletic as well." They all started laughing, and then the Arab added: "But we will not hold that against him."

As the assembly exchanged polite remarks the Russian took the opportunity to train his measuring eyes once more upon the Tutsi.

"Gentlemen," laughed Krugan, grasping the edge of his cape. "After you refresh yourselves: croquet on the mountainside!"

Meanwhile, still bound and gagged, little Shadow was dropping through the trap door beneath the bed. An oak beam knocked the wind out of her and as she lay gasping in the darkness she experienced a vision of fire breathing locusts descending from the sun, dark hills, barbwire, concrete ribbons.

Trailing black smoke and rippling bands of heat, the big transports, their propellers throbbing, their wings gently dipping left and right, hurled from the runway and climbed out over an obscure Luxembourgian airstrip.

3

PRINCE KRUGAN REMOVED HIS cape and hung it beneath the unusually large goat head on the fifth wall of the pentangular room. Two hooks beneath the head held the cape by the shoulders and so provided the goat with an empty body. With a flourish, Krugan smoothed the cape several times, and then, with ritual precision, he slid his bare feet along the lines and vertices of the pentagram, which, with red chalk, he had moments before finished labeling. The pentagram itself was permanent, laid out in a pearlescent white paint, and re-labeled each time Krugan cast a new spell.

Standing around the pentagram, Krugan's guests viewed the proceedings with mixed impatience and wonder. The Englishman licked his front teeth with amusement; the tall Russian, head tilted forward, shifted his gaze back and forth morbidly; while the two Arabs, uncomfortably nursing a blasphemous curiosity, reacted to each stage of Krugan's preparations with barely audible grunts and hisses.

Krugan was unfolding a white undershirt at the center of the pentagram when four new men, led by the Tutsi, entered the five-sided chamber. Three were Turks of the new order. They wore dark sunglasses, yellow suits and tasseled fezzes. The fourth, tall and sunburned, with silver sideburns and a pock-marked face, revealed himself to be an American when he undid his long overcoat. He wore a bolo tie with a large black scorpion preserved in the transparent slide-clasp. It bobbed up and down when he saw the pentagram beneath Prince Krugan's feet.

The original guests entreated these newcomers to remain silent and nodded for Krugan to proceed.

The prince cracked his knuckles. "Welcome gentlemen. You see at my feet an undergarment once belonging to a young American, a professional critic of contemporary poetry, now living in the south of France, who recently, at a not-unimportant social occasion (which prudence forbids me to name), I say, this fellow had the temerity to insult the memory of Loomis the Exile. Loomis, as some of you gentlemen know, was my wife's dear father who ascended to higher planes several years ago."

Krugan kneeled on one leg before the undershirt and manipulated the air above it with his left hand, as if feeling the contours of unseen energies. An intense, sharp expression suddenly came over his face. He blushed red. His eyes fixed in an angry stare. His head began vibrating. From the sash around his waist he drew a green twig that mysteriously ignited at the end. The flame flickered and then *bent down*, and the staring audience was confounded to understand the nature of what they half-knew had to be a parlor trick. Krugan pushed the inverted flame toward the undershirt. The twig followed after the flame, curving down as it was brought closer. Drool appeared on his lips as he pronounced a guttural name, whereupon a lattice of silver energies enveloped the undershirt. The energies shifted, and then all disappeared, replaced by a sphere of barely-perceptible blue light that expanded from the center of the pentagram and pressed out to swallow the room.

One of the Turks stepped back as the edge of the sphere neared him. But then he cried out and picked up his foot.

He had stepped on one of Gertrude's pins.

4

BRONSON PULLED HIS FACE from the hollow goat head. It was dark between the walls.

"Syd," he said.

"Yeah?" hissed a thin, handsome man with long, reddish-blond hair. "What'er they dew'n 'n thar?"

"Krugan just torched a shirt. Four new guys just came in."

Syd Reilly kneaded his hands. "Four more, huh? I hope Vitaly can keep 'is cool."

"Of course he can."

"That temper a'his."

"Don't you think these people have tempers too?" Bronson stuck his face back in the goat's head and peered through the mouth at the tall Russian who was just then tugging at the ends of his bowtie.

"Bronson!" hissed Syd. He pulled his friend back. "Y'hear that?"

There was a clicking sound approaching. Bronson hesitated a moment—then he was sure it came from somewhere between the walls. "C'mon." They quickly moved off.

A few minutes later a naked girl, gagged and bound, blonde hair trailing to her waist, shuffled up to the wall behind the goat's head. She dropped the stones that she had been tapping together, put her face into the goat's head, and then moaned and cried as loudly as she could against the gag.

But the men on the other side, excitedly lauding Prince Krugan for his metaphysical demonstration, were deaf to little Shadow's pleas.

"Tell me," said the Tutsi. His spurs jingled as he shifted his weight. "What effect will your spell exert on the victim?"

"*Subject*, you mean," corrected Krugan. "And I am reserved also in the use of the word 'spell.' But to answer your question," he raised one eyebrow, "within a fortnight the subject will be afflicted with a perirectal abscess."

Surrounded by "ooh's" and "ah's", the prince led the group to the adjoining chamber: a dining room where a great feast had been laid on. In the center of the table, impaled vertically on a medieval two-handed sword, was a succulent roast lamb, expertly coaxed by Chef into the zenith of succulence, with sweet juices dripping slowly from its sides in glittering rivulets both as attractive and as sublime as Alpine springs. Arranged around the shimmering lamb were breads, sauces, cheeses, tureens of soups, and tall crystal vases like tree trunks with peacock-feather branches. At either end of the table were round plates piled with olives, grapes, peppers, cashews, and small oily onions. By each place setting was a little pot of honey, iced water, hot tea and an empty wine glass. The silver and crystal seemed to take on a life of its own, reflecting the flickering flames of the four reptilian candelabra standing at each corner of the room. The guests clapped and rubbed their palms together to behold such a feast, which brought pleased looks to the eyes of the shriveled old servant standing at the far end of the room with a dusty bottle of vodka cradled in his hollow chest. His long, dried-out fingers tapped irregularly against the bottle like the legs of an entranced spider.

Krugan moved around the table, inviting his guests to sit and begin. After the Russian fashion, he went up to each guest, welcomed him to the table and hinted at the surprises and entertainments to come. "Welcome, my dear friend… you are especially invited to inspect my new diagrams… sestinas are your favorite, is it not so?… after desert, my collection of hats will be brought out for your inspection… what, my friend, a ghost story? Ha, ha, ha. Yes, of course, I promise!"

Krugan sat and the servant came around with the vodka. No teetotalers themselves, the Muslims cheerfully joined in. Toasts were made, oaths were remembered. Cheers and laughter shook the room as the lamb was cut and served.

As they satisfied themselves, the conversation once more turned upon the subject of magic. The American, pointing around the table with his fork, insisted it was the art of power. Amiably disagreeing, one of the Arabs suggested magic is the love that's to be found in a good horse, or the sound, at night, of the breeze shifting across the sands of the sleeping desert. Not disputing this, the Turks were anxious to clarify precisely what the Arab meant. After momentary debate in their guttural language, they unanimously agreed that magic was the harmony of eternity in conflict with the instantaneous crescendo of sexual climax, which, cast in polyglot strains of Arabic, Russian, and English, prompted much emotional dilatation amongst the diners.

"Yes, yes, well," the Englishman said, rocking his head back, and by this gesture of confidence gaining all their attention, "It all happens in-between the center mark."

"Are you talking about magic, or are you talking about poetry?" sniffed the American.

Yurchenko, the Russian, made an observation and one of the Arabs entreated Krugan to translate.

"Very well." The prince nodded. "Our young friend asserts that magic is as distinct and as related to poetry, as poetry to music, or music to magic, but all three are identical in their task of opening to man unknown realms beyond his reason, and so enable him to perceive obscure forces."

The Englishman, following this carefully, raised his knife. "*Subdue* obscure forces."

The American agreed as he set his napkin on the table. "Whatever magic yields or promises, it can't trespass into our day–to–day understanding and the physical arena in which we operate. If it does, well, then it's no longer magic. It's creative imagination, or maybe guile." He cleared his throat and the scorpion bobbed up and down.

The tall Russian, straightening his bowtie, smiled.

"You understand me?" asked the American.

The Russian cocked his head while the American repeated the question.

"He understands some of what you are saying," said Krugan.

The conversation continued along similar lines: assertions, explanations, dismissals, further suggestions. Then Krugan was asked for his own views.

"I want to say," began the prince as he lit an unusually long cheroot," that we are bound by an irrevocable chain of events—a linear, dialectical, adamantine, crystalline cosmos of happenings. Magic is the magician behind the magician who flees this implacable succession of events. Magic is the desire and the liberation from restraint and the hazard of circumstance. Pure integrity." He motioned for the servant to carry the cigars around the table. "If you will, magic is the harmony of the spirits—and I do mean spirits as *plural*—in matter. It is the balance between past and future. The father survives through the son and on and on. Rebirth. Immortality."

One of the Arabs raised a crooked finger. "Do you mean the rebirth of the soul? Or the preservation of personality through language?"

"My dear friend." Elegant and languid, Prince Krugan leaned up against the table. "That is a question of faith. I know only magic."

Everyone agreed that this was very good.

Suddenly there was a thump above them. Plaster cracked and fell over the table. A hole opened in the ceiling and little Shadow, bound and naked, fell down upon them. The impression was silent but explosive. Her mass thrust away the cut and torn lamb as she slid upon the two-handed sword at the center of the table.

5

LITTLE PRECIOUS PUSHED the heavy door before her, slowly moving its mass on the grinding and creaking hinges, and she listened selectively to the echoes of her motions racing to and fro through the corridor and the room before her. Hesitating a moment to look around, she entered the high tower chamber that had formally been the study of the poet Loomis. Gertrude sat at the desk sorting through her father's papers. She turned as the girl approached and began clicking her teeth. "*Ah, Liebchen!* Is that you, Little Precious?"

The girl went up to the woman's chair and put her hand on the armrest.

"*Ja, gnädige Frau*; but how could you tell through your blind eyes?"

"I could hear your feet. You step more lightly than your twin."

"But if you could see me, you would think I am Shadow, for I am wearing her dress."

The woman reached out and fingered the fabric. "So you are. Are you playing tricks with the guests?"

The girl shook her head. "Krugan shooed me away when they arrived."

"Little one, be careful of your disguises. Us women have a tendency to become the roles we play." Gertrude laughed and turned back to her father's papers. The girl watched the woman turn the papers over and arrange them.

"*Gnädige Frau*, how is it you can read these papers?"

The trace of a smile tugged at the woman's lips. She didn't look up from the papers. "It is because I am only blind to what I do not wish to see. I have what is called hysterical blindness."

"Hysterical blindness?"

"*Ja*." The woman turned her blind face to the girl. Her eyes rolled up. "Krugan hides in his magic. I hide in my disease. Where do you hide, little Precious? In your youth? In your virginity, perhaps?"

The girl clutched the ends of her long blonde hair and crossed her arms so as to pull the hair before her chest. "How is it that you can see your father's papers?"

Gertrude sighed and then, hearing a noise, picked her head up. "What is that?"

The girl turned toward the fireplace. There was scratching within.

"Someone's in the fireplace," said little Precious. Gertrude starting clicking her carnelian tooth.

A cloud of soot rushed from the fireplace and two men fell out on the floor.

"It's Bronson," said the girl, "and some man with long hair."

The two figures on the floor shook themselves and stood up.

"What is this, Bronson?!" demanded Gertrude. "Who is with you?"

"Forgive me, *Gnädige Frau*." He drew his PPK as he and Syd Reilly ran from the room.

They tumbled down the spiraling staircase until they came to a door that opened into the short corridor leading to the adjoining tower. They ran through, swung a second door aside, and then stepped into the hollow tower. It was a quiet, musty silo, illuminated by a single yellow bulb over the doorway. Long vertical scorch marks, many decades old, blackened the walls.

Bronson plodded across the dirt floor, kicking up dust with his bare feet. He pointed to the base of the wall. "Move these two stones. I'll get Vitaly."

While Syd began struggling with the stones, Bronson pushed open a panel that led to the newer section of the castle. He went through the opening and found himself in the darkness of a long vaulted corridor. He ran down it.

At the same moment, up in the study, paratroopers smashed through the windows, leveled their Sigs. The women raised their hands instinctively, but the action of the fingers squeezing the triggers had been decided weeks before, and Gertrude and little Precious were transformed into lifeless dolls dotted with perforations that gaped as round openings a brief few moments before erupting into dark crimson blobs that swelled across their clothing.

"What was that!" Krugan cried out in the dining room as he glanced about for the source of the muffled gunfire. The guests, already horrified by the impaled form of little Shadow, drew their pistols.

"Order!" demanded Krugan. "Mr. Yurchenko, accompany me. *Prosim! Prosim!* The rest wait here. We shall see what happened."

Several of the guests objected.

Bronson rushed in. "It's the death squad! Commandos!" Then he saw little Shadow's form elevated high above the table, the sword running up through her torso. She—it—was a thing now, a lifeless ghoul, unmoving as a memory but for the dark purple grume that was oozing slowly down the sword and falling upon the ruin of the lamb. Her facial expression? Her eyes were narrowed skeptically while inside her mouth her tongue was thrust firmly against her cheek. He held his hand up before the sight, as if blocking the rays from a source of intense illumination.

Krugan was cursing. "Remain calm! There is an emergency tunnel. Return to the magic room. Tear the goat head from the wall and the passage shall be revealed. Proceed to the right and I shall join you." He pulled a black Heckler & Koch G-11 automatic rifle from beneath the table. "But first I must save my family!"

The old servant shuffled in. "Prince Krugan, intruder alarms are going off all over the castle!"

"Indeed!" growled the prince, and he stormed off.

"Vitaly!" Bronson grabbed the tall Russian by the shoulder. "This way."

While the guests pressed into the pentagonal room, Bronson and the Russian ducked through the servants' entrance. Alert to this, the Englishman and the Tutsi followed.

Bronson turned and called back to them. "We're going to help Krugan. Follow the others to the goat head!"

Sensing something, the Englishman drew his Glock 10mm pistol, but only to be shot through the eye by Bronson, who held the smoking PPK in his right hand as, shaking with disbelief, he observed the effects of his marksmanship. The Englishman clutched at his face and did a strange little dance that continued even as he fell to the floor. The dance became suddenly more excited until, abruptly, the Englishman froze.

"My God, Bronson!" The Russian stood in horrified fascination.

"You speak English!" roared the Tutsi. He bound at them, spurs jingling.

Bronson fired at the Tutsi, but the giant proved a more evasive target than the Englishman. His long body dropped down and, twisting on his heel, the Tutsi's giant hand came up and slapped the pistol out of Bronson's fist.

The Russian swung out with his right arm but was knocked back with a jab from the Tutsi's elbow. Bronson caught his friend and kicked out at the giant's long legs. But a broad black hand reached out to easily intercept Bronson's foot and push it away, and the same hand flashed forward and palmed Bronson's head and drove it repeatedly against the wall. Bronson's head throbbed with each sharp crack. Lightning stabbed through his brain and each impact was a glimpse down a tunnel to blacker and blacker worlds. Then the Tutsi lashed out at Bronson's legs with his club feet. Bronson felt a blow against his shin, and then the spur came back and dragged against the fabric of his trousers, which just barely protected his skin. Bronson hissed and with a sudden explosive thrust launched his palm against the Tutsi's nose and broke it instantly. A flood of blood gushed forward and ran down the Tutsi's mouth and chin.

Now the Russian dived into the Tutsi's waist. Both growled madly, and the Tutsi's head shook violently against Bronson's hooked fingers as they raked down the Tutsi's face. Bronson found the Tutsi's lower lip and clutched fast, savagely twisting the soft tissue and yanking the lip down until a burst of purple blood erupted around the giant's lower teeth. With animal grunts, Vitaly snapped his shoulders explosively as he threw his heavy fists into the Tutsi's ribs, each impact sounding like an axe biting into the trunk of a tree.

But they were fighting a tiger. The Tutsi violently shook his body and jabbed at the two men with his powerful hands. His spurs lashed out at their legs. For several moments the three men were clutched together in a bundle of limbs that thrashed in every direction. The men slammed violently into one wall and then the other. Heels rocked back and kicked forward. Fists on the ends of cruel arms snapped back and forth with explosive force. Grunts and hisses accompanied the shoving, yanking, jabbing, hammering, biting, clawing. Several times the Tutsi's kicking feet met the stone wall and the crack of the impact was like the report of a pistol.

The battle dragged down the corridor until the men dropped to a short landing. On the wall was one of the heavy-duty knife switches that activated the magnets in the ceiling.

Crying out, Bronson shoved the Tutsi's arm into the switch and slammed the handle down at the contacts. There was a tremendous *snap* and Bronson and the Russian were thrown to the floor. The Tutsi fell back against the wall, his chest swelling out and then pushing violently upwards. His long legs bent at the knees, and he rocked up on his clubbed toes until his enormous body formed an arching sculpture of pain. The wet of his eyes, his saliva and his blood began to steam, and the ghost of some wild thing that had been a man seemed to mist upward with the vapor.

Bronson and Vitaly stood up and stared silently as the Tutsi, arm clamped firmly in the switch, fell down upon his collapsing legs. The giant's dead form dragged its head down against the stone wall until the ruin of the body unexpectedly ceased its ghastly motion. The switch held the arm fast, and the Tutsi's open-eyed expression, his conservative business suit, the long body, the broken feet tucked under the giant legs, the torn and purple mouth—the thing was like some pantomime of a gentleman who had dropped to his knees to demonstrate an acrobatic dance caper, but who now kneeled with his arm thrust out in a gesture of knavish foolery, as if waving with sudden and fond recognition at the Angel of Death.

The Russian then looked at his arms. "Ooch! Ooch!" There were pins and needles stuck all over them. He began pulling them out.

Bronson was also covered with pins and needles. He tore them out and dropped them—but at this distance from the magnets they flew up and stuck to the ceiling.

"What happened?" said Vitaly.

"Our intensions were uncovered. Commandos are all over the place."

A distant burst of machine gun fire rattled in confirmation: the unmistakable staccato of men murdering other men.

"Maybe they found Krugan," Bronson said grimly. "Come on."

They ran down the corridor and found the panel that led to the gutted tower. Inside, they found Syd backed against the wall beside the door. Bullets suddenly ripped through the wood. Chips and splinters flew through the air and dust was thrown up from the floor. Behind the door came the frantic voices of commandos calling in Persian.

When Syd saw his friends he let go a string of garbled profanities. Then, knees bouncing up to either side, he bound across the floor and dived through the hole in the stone wall. His friends dived after him. With crocodilian motions they slipped rapidly though the small tunnel.

The tower wall was seven feet thick and as they shoved through the tunnel they could feel the ground turn from hard dust to soil and dirt. Then they were out and standing up beneath the stars. In the darkness the tower wall stood above them like a cliff.

They could hear the commandos calling to each other. Two Hughes helicopter gunships were closing on the mountain with their searchlight beams reaching for the castle walls.

"Look!" hissed Syd. "Those are American choppers!"

Bronson hacked and spit. "Doesn't matter." He followed the course of the helicopters as they swept around; their throbbing soon echoed against the far side of the mountain. "Once again we're caught in the crossfire of competing ideologies, and with nothing to show for it."

Vitaly fingered his bowtie. "I've got pictures of them. That might be worth something."

"Don't deceive yourself," said Bronson with uncharacteristic impatience. He pulled a pin from his shoulder. The throbbing was growing louder again. The helicopters came around, passing slowly now, and the men ducked into the shrubbery. They were well hidden and watchful as the pounding machines began to drift around the castle, their searchlights carefully playing against the commandos on the rooftops and stone towers.

"We were betrayed," hissed Bronson.

"The Bilderberg Group?" suggested Vitaly.

Syd didn't think so, then his eyes widened. *"L'Aliénation Internationale?"*

Bronson was listening to the helicopters. The throbbing rotors beat the air, calling forth pictures of distance and motion. The shuffling vibrations lowered in pitch and it was time to flee. Bronson shook his head. "No, it was youth."

They ran down the mountainside.

EDDIE ALLAN'S
MYSTERIOUS
MANIFESTO

ALL IS INFORMATION. All. If not, then explain Man's wandering into outer space while men pursue play-acting. Why is the strait between these two continents so neglected? It is because information is terrifying. Information is omnipotent, ubiquitous, hostile to knowledge. Information is the dragon's not nonhuman face. It is the horror mode.

I am not addressing the simple prestidigitation of social symbols, though that is part of it. Nor do I claim that events, constructs, and numerical figures are externally veneered by the internal structure of their significance. Everyone is familiar with the rumor that tyrannical DNA camshafts order our forms and drive our beings; or the claim that people are merely tape recorders that echo recombinations of what they have experienced, and that the patterns of these recombinations are themselves only echoes. Most emblematic of the focus of my own concern is the notion which considers evolution and the female's dependence upon the male of the species in this ingenious fashion: women have evolved into what they are and appear as they do because they aspire to the equation of beauty—deranged by fifty centuries of civilization—that haunts the male nervous system. Such a storm of speculation this precipitates! With what camshaft does beauty affect its manipulations in the material world? We all understand the operation of slogans, flags, carnival midways, and so-called "hooks" in popular songs. But how do such mechanisms enable a televised demagogue to infect the populations of entire continents with mimetic contagion? From where in our finely-tuned clockwork cosmos comes the will to create miniature gardens? What is a monument? How does a monument differ from a ruin? When you think about information are you really thinking about language? Aren't there institutions to deal with all this? From whence comes the desire to consult an expert on such matters? But these problems are not to be wondered at, for information is inimical to conscious identity. So why try to understand something that does not agree with you? It is much easier to simply dislike it back, however fruitless and unprofitable. Better still: ignore it. I have always considered anger and hatred to be left-handed forms of flattery. If you really want to defeat something, destroy its image. How else was it possible for [redacted from manuscript; substitute code phrase "apple" etc.] to defeat the informants and at the same time become the apple of the law giver's eye? Which reminds me of the Keltic monks of old who cast themselves upon the North Sea in simple open coracles, heedless of wind and waves, much less their destinations. The bard Amhairghin wrote:

> I will fade into something
> Nothing is too bland
> But that is how it looks those times
> When I am
> Bland

I do not like telephones, I expect nothing from computers, and I revolt at the thought of everything about information being made easy! These vast communications bureaus operating under the cognomen "Network," while promising to accelerate the accumulation of wealth, are in actuality hastening the process of apocalypse. They are over-rationalizing the horror mode and are going to grind us in a crucible named "You cannot because you will not because you are too busy watching." The *Times* crossword, remember, is enjoyable precisely because it is full of blanks. It provides something to do rather than something to be filed away.

Next item!

I am convinced I would admit these things even if I had arms, legs, hair and smooth skin. And I am not afraid to confess that because of these handicaps I would have committed seppuku long ago except for the knowledge that my mother would somehow gain by it. She has a tremendous capacity for exalting in drama, a real flair. In this way my stepfather agrees with her most of all. I shudder to think of the countless hours he has spent scrutinizing our family's problems. Somehow it has conjured within him a bizarre taste for intrinsic traumatology. John sees people as he needs to see them rather than as they are. When he sees people he sees information—or he sees nothing at all.

In fact, it was John who first suggested to me that unseen international forces—known only to narcissists and intersectionalists—pressure us into forming family groups. It was stern medicine. I now consider this revelation as important as another breakthrough I made at close to the same time: the realization that I would never experience physical love with a woman. Indeed, not only am I without limbs, skin and hair, but I also lack, ahem, a *poignant plexus* as well. All that is left to me is information and the study thereof: *espionage*.

If I am to be remembered by history, I hope it is for my development of a new breed of secret agent and the cause he stands for. I like sometimes to use the term "super-agent" because his cause is himself. In this sense he is an over-spy, an operative of the Invisible Tower. At the present time he exists as a phantom in my mind, a Platonic ideal; though, for all his invisibility, he is no less clear to my imagination. Tall, virile, gentle, wise, kind, ruthless, uncontrollable, quiet, brilliant, keenly reflective, able to kill with a single blow of his mighty fist, a marksman, fighter pilot, submariner, astronaut, prophet, vegetarian, scientist; he stands erect, head back, gazing out morbidly from beneath his beetling brows, cool as moonlight, his keenness kept sharp by the icicles-of-doubt shattering at each thunderstroke of his unyielding heart. I remember his many prototypes.

These were agents and couriers who carried about with them their psychological complications in lieu of secret documents. When these spies tangled with each other it was as much to exchange or release their childhood fears as it was to accomplish some mission for their governments. As time passed and my agents infiltrated key administrative positions in the world's information bureaus, I was delighted to observe that the quest to act out fears and the government policies themselves were beginning to blend. I have always claimed that history is a cyclical process, though the flow of information across the centuries is quite plainly linear. More importantly, the progress of any literate species is invariably the story of compartmentalization: psychological, social, economic, and political subdividing. We are breaking up. The neophytes point to Machiavelli and *The Prince* and say "Ah ha!" thinking they have discovered some significant benchmark in the history of ideas. But we can be very sure that the sixteenth century Italian despots, upon being presented with the work (which is thoroughly unadventurous in approach, manner and medium), were quick to casually shrug and say, "So what else is new?" So information supersaturation shouldn't come to anyone's surprise either. Eleven-year-old murderers, victims' rights groups, babies found in drain pipes, civilian patrols, sordid talk show confessions, vulgar academicians, domestic violence hotlines, military interdiction, international arms rings, crimes of passion, sins of patience, etc., etc., certainly indicate the presence of some complex, variegated and horrible phenomenon. But, as in the sixteenth, sixth or any century, there is always something going on that can somehow be integrated together and labeled a whole. We in the business of espionage describe this construct as the articulation of fear and ambition through mass hallucination. This is how information displaces knowledge and manifests itself upon the world stage. I studied this phenomenon over the course of seven years and published my findings under the title *Spy Envy: The Geopolitical Ambitions of the Collective Id.*

I was careful to adhere to proper procedure and considered the phenomenon in terms of folklore, dialogical synoptics, the epidemiology of synthetic archetypes, linguistic auto-catharsis, psychic driving, sensory deprivation, and even as distortions of infantile and intrauterine experience. Nothing is so gratifying as having one's suspicions confirmed. My theories passed all these checks. I had hit on something, all right. But my spectacular insight was then made bitter by the cool reception I received from the information authorities (who are thoroughly unadventurous in approach, manner, and even in the architecture of their self-inhabited museums). Everyone knows about specialization, professionalization, departmental empire building, etc. They are quite remarkable, their organizational muscle, their capacity for hypocrisy, their pitiless spite. They said I failed to draw enough background scholarship into my argument! My only answer to the pill bugs that form such agencies is to tell them: "What a sordid sequence of serial selves describes you—phew!" As a full-limbed boy—assiduously working in collaboration with my good friend Mikhail Bakunin—gluing horseflies to little airplanes folded from very thin paper was an important activity. We did this in the school cafeteria with the smell of sandwiches, saliva and garbage deflowering the air, and the horseflies nipping at the tips of our fingers.

Seventh grade was probably my best year. Mikhail Bakunin, what a trump! We were what used to be called "boon companions." Together we formed sort of a mad-scientists' club known affectionately by our admiring teachers as "The Insectonauts." We both dated a Chinese-American mathematics prodigy named Julia "Choosy" Choo. Even after my fiery dismembering in boiling oil, we continued to frolic after school in Choosy's TV room with the stiff-moving animation of *Marine Boy* casting its emerald glow against the walls. Those afternoons we spent together made adolescence endurable for me. That Mikhail tolerated the presence of my grotesque form during those cartoons-n-capers is laudable. And Choosy deserves to be commended as well for the way she would instantly respond to my requests for snacks and soda pop, even during the best parts of the show. How fortunate I was to know charity at such an early age. And, unbeknownst to me at the time, I was moving from the prototype to the Mark I in my quest for the Tower agent *par excellence*. Mikhail and Choosy were people who could do for me what I could not do for myself. This quality cannot be created in people by an outside force. It is something that you must go out and look for. Anyone may be coerced into becoming a spy, but the Tower agent *par excellence*, ah, he is handed down by the gods! My life's task shall be to identify him, nurture his genius, and provide him with any and all facilities that may be necessary to allow him to fulfill his self-discovered task.

Hold these words no more than six inches from your eyes. We are going to annotate everything. This document is to be used as a charter for the formation of an *Institute of Disinformation*. Quote from it freely, always footnote conscientiously. We must convince the children of the directorial classes—professionals, advertisers, publishers, museum curators, scholars, educators, entertainment producers—that they are insignificant elements in a resource pool of brutish human laborers. "Oh my God, I'm a white-collar proletarian!" How's that for the midnight cry of an intelligent and sensitive young person? Health, emotional stability and the dreams of adolescence are very important, but first we'll consider the alternatives. Ours is a quest for horror. It's not spooky, it's not poison. But can we resist the vanity of wealth, or repudiate the traditions and orthodoxies of our procreative oath? Infinite embryonic ley lines wait for the intervention of the spirit of the cosmocratic continuum; motion picture invitations to join the present are refused. How much longer must tears be shed over a body politic unable to understand the bureaucracy, and whose entire social consciousness is embodied in a conditioned response to a handful of adhesive labels? The modern savage is not driven by emotion, but by the tingles of information stimulus. The modern Roman does not carry a sword, but sits before a computer. Knowledge is the Gaul they would torch and plunder. But only *they* can age and die. Our own wrinkles are webs in our eyes, an emerging Hegemony, a Network amongst the stars. By the Spectrum beneath our tongues, I say, "We reign secure!" Such thunderbolts of awareness are enough for us, the rest we may discover in the clever interweaving *activity* of some Hopi's softly scattered sand, then we shall deftly ascend to our tower over and over again chanting "Let us not perfect nor embellish what is opposed to us!" until the words lose their meaning.

CIRCUMJACENT
CIRCUMSTANCES

"MOM, I JUST SAW it again!"

The open carriage clicked down the steeply inclined tracks while its dozen passengers leaned back against the slow-motion sinking that took them deeper and deeper into the Niagara Gorge. Ahead the Horseshoe Falls thundered with mechanical monotony—the combined crashing of trillions of tightly linked atoms of helium and oxygen, each molecule itself a tiny clear pebble of electro-chemical presence.

"Mom!"

The mother was leaning forward to catch a glimpse of the budding breasts of a pubescent maiden in the bench two rows below. The young girl's white cotton shirt was creased open around the neck. The girl shifted and the view was closed.

"Mom!"

The mother turned an empty face to her son. At the age of twenty-seven she had lost her left breast to the surgeon's knife. That had been four years ago, or was it five? "Yeah, honey?"

"I saw it again." The boy pointed at the edge of the Horseshoe Falls. "It had long metal legs."

She smiled and followed his pointing hand to the falling cliff of water. It was a color not unlike the yellow-green yolk of a hard-boiled egg. And it was pounding, frothing, roaring, sizzling, dropping, and yet not moving—an example not so much of nature's majesty but of inattentive matter. All that water just dumping, she thought. Dumping, dumping, dumping, dumping, dumping.

She stared at the boy. "I don't see anything." She smiled nervously. She was afraid his overactive imagination was unhealthy, his ADHD. But his ADHD wasn't her fault, the school psychiatrist had said so as he wrote out the prescription with the twitching principle looking on impatiently. It wasn't anybody's fault. The psychiatrist himself had said the cause was "inattentive."

"It slipped back under the water," he explained with a dull—but not too-dull—excitement. "It looked like a sub. It had a glass nose. Its tail poked out by the edge, and it had a propeller. It had a fin on its back, too, and metal legs."

She was terrified she was going to have an anxiety attack. "Here," she said as she went through her purse. She gave him some gum.

He smiled.

She forced a smile.

"I bet it was the dirty Russians!" He chomped up and down on the gum.

"Oh, it was nothing." She patted his thigh.

He pushed her hand aside. "Or the cheatin' Chinese."

She shook his knee. "Shhh. You didn't see anything."

"Or maybe it was the deep state!" Then with a precision and prissy omniscience some might attribute to complex Oedipal dynamics, he eagerly pronounced: "Or Muslims."

She wondered if had he spoken a little too loudly. Did anybody hear? What must they be thinking? What kind of mother does he have?

"I *did* see it, Mom."

"Miss—" a man with a whiney, know-it-all voice leaned forward on the bench behind them. He was somewhere in his thirties, speeding headlong across an empty dry lake bed towards an encounter with the "Cash Your Paycheck Now" boutique. A bee stinger with a little white glob of insect guts dangling from the end was stuck in his bald scalp. There was something smashed—like the essence of *smash* itself—on his boots, though it must be said his nails were trimmed, and his camouflage T-shirt and blue jean trousers were unstained.

One side of the mother's face screwed up into a frightened smile, while the other side remained blank.

"Miss," he said again. "Your boy's right. There is something up there. I caught a glimpse of it myself. Something out of this world." He had pegged her for a *Lonely Single Mother Type Four* when she first boarded the carriage.

"See mom, I told you."

She sniffed something that smelled like—what? Bugs? She smiled nervously and faced forward.

"Do you think it was the Chinese?" asked the boy. Obviously the stranger was an authority on such things.

"Eh." The man pinched his nostrils several times and then rubbed his hand against his trousers. "Could be, buddy."

"Wow!"

The man continued. "But like you said before, it could be something even worse. There's secret bases all over the world, everyone knows that. Jet bombers buried under Mount Rushmore, robot labs in Disneyplace, antennas in the Statue of Liberty, cameras in space. Why not a sub base behind Niagara Falls?"

"Do you think?" the boy's mouth sprang up and down on the gum.

The man slowly passed his hand through the air. "Obi Wan Bin Laden is everywhere."

"Wow!"

"Kid, I been all over this planet and I seen a lot of things." The stranger put his arms on the edge of their bench. He pushed his right elbow against the mother's back. "I bet it's a lab, or maybe a missile base. They could fire the missiles right through the waterfall—woosh!" His gesturing hand fell on the boy's shoulder.

"Wow—" The boy imitated the man's gesture. "Woosh!"

The mother was frozen stiff, terrified to pull away from the elbow softly pushing against her spine.

High above them, a telescoping elbow of bright steel momentarily emerged from the thundering water, then was as quickly withdrawn.

THE WIND HAUNTED BY ITS OWN GHOST

THE PICKLED THING ON THE examining table wasn't human. But then again, it couldn't actually be said that it was non-human. We all have different ideas about what makes something human. Some stress the importance of being well-groomed. Others stress the importance of a high moral character. Still others reject such approaches as philosophical and boring. They like to tackle the problem empirically—that is, they emphasize those characteristics about which there can be no argument. And, never squeamish, they go right to the essence of the problem.

Bronson Bodine took a stainless steel probe from the instrument tray and inserted it beneath the horizontal genital flap at the base of the thing's pelvis. His eyes winced, not with distaste but with interest. He saw no scaring or distention, no evidence that the thing had ever given birth or even laid an egg. "At this point," he pronounced, "I wouldn't be surprised if it turned out to be an hermaphrodite."

Several voices in the dark laboratory hummed their acknowledgement.

Twisting the examining light, Bronson passed his hand down one of the thing's very human but grossly curved thighs.

"Rickets was my first impression," said a voice in the darkness. The voice was an electronically amplified whisper.

Bronson concurred. He ran his hand over the bulbous knee. "However, it seems very strong. The kneecap, for instance." He grasped it like a doorknob and roughly twisted it back and forth. "It is very stout and firm." He took a shiny hammer from the instrument tray and struck it. "Sound hollow?"

Heads tilted in the darkness, not answering. Bronson replaced the hammer and continued his examination of the leg, pulling his hands down the calf, feeling for anything significant.

The feet were quite human, except for the toes, which, like the fingers, were smooth, jointless tentacles. Each tapered to a hard conical point. Bronson manipulated one of the toes and found, again like the fingers, that it moved freely in all directions. He took a curved scalpel and scraped away the flesh. Inside he discovered a white core of cartilaginous material resembling a thin rod of nylon.

"You are ready to begin the dissection?" asked the amplified voice in a cautioning tone.

Bronson nodded his handsome face. His pointy, black beard and deep-set, icy blue eyes seemed more the features of a Don Juan than an anatomical investigator. "Yes. I would like to begin, if there aren't any objections?"

"No," said the amplified voice. "I hesitate only because I am still dazzled by my first impression. I would like to look at it once more before we mutilate it."

"Of course." Bronson raised the examining light until the corpse was completely illuminated in a cone of bright blue-green. Questions of humanity aside, it had two arms of unequal length, and two bowed legs. Each of the limbs ended in five tentacles of identical length. A single horizontal flap that swung forward, running laterally at the base of the pelvis, was the sole orifice in the lower body. There was no anus. The head was small-jawed and pear-shaped with the larger end at the top. Its features seemed adapted to an aquatic or semi-aquatic existence; it shared something in common with both a small-featured choirboy and a sea anemone. The slanted eyes contained multiple pupils—tiny but complete in every way with individual irises and lenses.

Above it now, casting a shadow through the cone of light, swung the armless, legless, fire-scarred torso of Eddie Allan. The little jars, sacks and bottles under his hollow pelvic cavity jiggled together as he moved.

"Are there any m-more of these things?" asked a third voice in the darkness. It was Nabnak Tornasuk, Bronson Bodine's field assistant. He was one of the newer agents in the Invisible Tower. His stammer betrayed a touch of understandable apprehension.

Eddie Allan lifted his bald head and, with his support wires squeaking through the pulleys above, rotated to face the Eskimo. "That is unknown at this time, friend Nabnak. Perhaps the results of the chromosome test will provide us with some insight." A small black amplifier the size and shape of a pocket radio was strapped crookedly over Eddie's mouth, making him appear, with his charred cheeks and forehead, frightfully tragic in the Eskimo's eyes.

"What exactly are the possibilities?" asked Nabnak.

"There are four possibilities," stated Bronson as he moved around to the other end of the table. He picked up the thing's anemone head and fingered the frog-like ear diaphragms behind the multi-pupil eyes. "First," he said, "it might be a mutated *Homo sapiens*—in which case it is going to be difficult, with what we have here," he raised the head of the corpse, "to determine if the mutation was natural or induced in a laboratory."

Nabnak's eyes widened. The prospect of infiltrating a laboratory of mutation-obsessed madmen was as compelling as it was frightening.

Bronson continued. His tall stature, broad shoulders and confident, even tone made his observations seem particularly well considered and authoritative. "The second possibility is that the organism, let's call it 'X', is genetically—"

"*Gaea*," interrupted Eddie. "Grand Anthropomorphic Enigma. G.A.E.A. I'm sorry, I have already named it."

Bronson shook his head. "No, I quite like that. *Gaea*: the primordial goddess of the Earth. Very good." He eased the anemone head back on the table. "Again, the second possibility is that Gaea is the product of genetic manipulation. Perhaps it was created in a test tube and then placed inside the womb of a human host. Then, third, is the possibility that Gaea was assembled like Frankenstein's monster from pieces of human corpses or— as is more likely in this case—from parts taken from living donors."

"Why would someone want to build an hermaphrodite?" asked Nabnak. His heavy forearms were folded before his chest. One of his hands reached up to pinch his chin.

"An excellent question," said Eddie, still hanging over the Gaea. "May I qualify it, however, by asking another: How could a person or institution benefit from building an hermaphrodite?"

"Or a race of hermaphrodites?" suggested Bronson. They looked around at each other and he continued. "But we must not overlook the possibility that Gaea is a completely independent species—*Homo enigmus*, if you will—and what we have here is an example of that species, lost somehow in our *Homo sapiens* world. By the pale color of the skin and the multiplicity of pupils, I would venture to guess that the Gaea race leads a subterranean existence. The many pupils would certainly be helpful in the darkness."

"The anemone-like projections on the head," suggested Nabnak, "might serve as feelers to keep them from bumping into stalactites?"

"*Cgh-cgh*—just so," Eddie said through his amplifier. "It is interesting, however, that you compared Gaea's feelers, as you call them, to the tentacles of an anemone. Gaea was found in the bilge of a supertanker that was laid up for some time in the Persian Gulf. Perhaps it is an aquatic organism?"

Bronson slowly disagreed. "No… well, perhaps amphibian. These eyes don't appear to be constructed to operate under water."

"I am curious about its capacity for language," said Nabnak, an amateur philologist. "Let's have a look at its larynx."

Bronson fingered its head. "You mean the language centers in its brain, don't you?"

Nabnak shook his head and made a dismissive gesture. "The capacity for speech is mechanical. You see, I'm interested in the Gaea's physical capacity. Mental capacity isn't that important. It is my theory that language operates independently of will."

Bronson took the suggestion personally. "Nonsense!" He shook the thing's head so that its anemone tentacles rocked and quivered. "It's in here. Language is a tool of the will."

Nabnak shrugged at this. "Rather, we are the tools of language. The larynx is the prime indicator of linguistic capacity."

With his fingers drumming against the Gaea's head, Bronson again pooh-poohed Nabnak's theory.

"In the interest of science," Eddie said matter-of-factly, "we should consider the question from the perspective of both theories."

While not willing to give up their positions, Eddie's advice worked like a charm, and that pleasant affection that characterizes the Invisible Tower was restored.

Or was it?

Nabnak cleared his throat and repeated his original point about language, rephrasing it in a way that patronized Bronson's sensibility. Indeed, Nabnak suggested that the concept of human volition, as it is represented in the latest linguistic theories, was a "starry-eyed" notion. Bronson listened cheerfully, but adhered to his position. Nabnak pressed his index finger against his upper lip and stared at the thing on the table. Bronson sighed with frustration. Nabnak crossed his arms over his chest and said, "Hemm." Bronson gave every indication of his willingness to concede, then suddenly glared up at Eddie.

Several minutes of this had passed when a rectangle of light opened in the darkness. The silhouette of a figure wearing riding pants and a broad brimmed Smokey-the-Bear hat stepped into the rectangle. The figure grew larger as it advanced toward them and revealed itself in the examining light: a tall, well-scrubbed officer of the Royal Canadian Mounted Police. Boots tapping softly together, he gave the brim of his hat a quick, efficient pinch. "Mr. Allan, sir."

"Results of the chromosome test?" asked Eddie.

The Mountie nodded. "Ready, sir. Twenty-seven pairs. That's a checked and confirmed figure."

"Not twenty-three!" exclaimed Bronson. "Then it is true. A new species! Gentlemen, may I present *Homo enigmus*." He yoked its forehead between his hands. "I can't wait to see the brain."

"Still," began Nabnak, "if you could just start with the larynx. I could rush over to the linguistics laboratory and compare it—"

"*Cgh! Cgh! Cgh!*" coughed Eddie through his amplifier. "Gentlemen, please. Consider the broader picture. We are dealing here with an in-dependent race who must by necessity possess a highly sophisticated culture." He gazed down compassionately at the Gaea. "This being may have once loved, sang, danced. For you to eagerly gloat over its corpse, excitedly express your desires to cut into its *boe-dy*—" The suspended ash-man shook his head. "Tut tut, gentlemen. Decorum, at the very least, if you please."

Bronson looked at Nabnak. Nabnak looked at Eddie. Eddie swayed slightly in his harness.

"You are right," said Nabnak.

"Of course, of course," admitted Bronson. And after a few moments of silent soul-searching he added, "Sorry about the toe, Eddie."

But it was forgotten. The magnanimous ash-man easily forgave their admirable—albeit hasty—enthusiasm, and then brought up the question of making contact with the new race.

"But where are they?" said Bronson. He paced slowly around the cone of illumination. "At what point over the ten-thousand mile journey of the supertanker did the Gaea slip into the bilges?"

"At sea," began Eddie, "the bilge pumps would be constantly running, preventing any influx of debris or *boe-dies* from the sea. While—"

"While at port," Bronson finished the thought, "the bilge pumps are shut down to prevent oil from slicking the harbor. The bilges on such ships are invariably contaminated with oil." He stopped pacing. "I think we can assume that our specimen of *Homo enigmus* swam up one night and crawled in through the bilge effusion ports."

"Very good," said Eddie. "Once in the bilge it was overcome by noxious fumes and expired. The origin of *Homo enigmus* must therefore be the Persian Gulf region, somewhere in the vicinity of the offshore terminal which serviced and loaded the tanker."

It was time for action. Bronson moved through the darkness to a table where, earlier, he and Nabnak had placed their field equipment. Nabnak joined him and they strapped on their utility belts and shoulder holsters. Metallic clicking and snapping noises filled the darkness as they checked the magazines in their .52 caliber automags. These big, vented handguns were chambered to fire a wide variety of ammunition, from poison mini-harpoons to plastic mob mollifiers.

"Well, Nabnak," laughed Bronson as he slapped the big automag into its holster. "So much for a diplomatic appearance!" They both wore black Nehru jackets, silk genie pants and high-heeled combat boots.

The short, squat Eskimo rested his hands upon his utility belt. A clever smile lit his face. It was refreshing—and reassuring—to see Bronson in a light mood before a mission of this type.

"Farewell" is a word not often heard in the Great Game. After exchanging almost sinister smiles with the suspended ash-man, the two scientist-spies turned and ran out the door.

As the clacking of their boots dwindled down the corridor, the Mountie looked up and asked, "What about the corpse?"

Eddie had to give this some thought. Above him the squeaking pulleys seemed to echo the machinations of his brain. Then, after a protracted spell of amplified throat-clearing sounds, he observed that, not knowing the funeral procedures of *Homo enigmus*, it would be appropriate to hand over the corpse to the taxidermist and have it preserved until such time as contact with the Gaea authorities was established and arrangements could be made to return the body (Eddie said *boe-dy*, rhyming with toady) in a manner appropriate to Gaea customs.

"Until then we'll keep it in the menagerie," he concluded earnestly, proving that profound humanity and scientific curiosity can beat together in the same breast; for who could question the scruples of Eddie Allan, gentle mastermind of the Invisible Tower?

2

THE AEROSPATIALE *MANTEAU RAIE* skimmed unnoticed over the black water north of Muscat. Side by side in the cockpit, Bronson Bodine and Nabnak Tornasuk operated the craft with mixed feelings of appreciation and apprehension. The moonless night was a boon to their enterprise, but rushing along at four-hundred knots in pitch darkness knowing their wing tips were scarcely four feet above the waves was more than a trifle disconcerting.

The *Manteau Raie* was a hybrid of airplane and hovercraft, supported and stabilized over the water by a cushion of air scooped under the fuselage. The craft was delta-shaped, with the pointed end aft. The wings swept forward and drooped to a negative anhedral of thirty degrees, though their position was variable to accommodate changing sea conditions. Rising from the rear of the fuselage was short fin that supported a horizontal stabilizer with a pronounced forward sweep. At the ends of the stabilizer, housed in bulbous nacelles, whined two General Electric TF34-G-100 high-bypass turbofan engines generating a combined thrust of 18,130 pounds. This particular craft, stripped of armaments and lead shielding, weighed a mere 15,000 pounds.

Bronson kept the throttles well back, quite aware that an application of too much power would raise the craft from the stabilizing surface effect and send it tumbling through the air, finally to crash into the sea.

Nabnak was using a circular slide rule to check the fuel consumption figures given by the navigation computer. After checking the figures a second time, he nodded to Bronson and slipped the circular calculator into the sleeve on his boot uppers.

"You're having doubts about the navigation computer?" asked Bronson.

Nabnak cocked his helmeted head. "Let's just say I want to make sure there is enough fuel to get back."

"The Persian Gulf isn't my choice for a vacation either." Bronson checked his watch and then saw the ECM warning light flash on.

"ECM," stated Nabnak coolly. But, as quickly as it came on, the warning light winked out. "What do you think—radar sweep?"

Bronson shrugged. "Perhaps we passed over a submarine transmitting to its home base."

Nabnak shifted against his straps. Too much about this mission was unknown. He was second-guessing everything. "This new race," he said, "*Homo enigmus*—it's just too incredible."

"The chromosome test was conclusive. Whatever the Gaea are, they are definitely part of the order of things—natural, if that word has any meaning."

Nabnak crossed his short arms. His muscles bulged inside the sleeves of his black Nehru jacket. "Being part of the order of things doesn't concern me, but rather *how*? The oldest human civilization we have any evidence of originated not far from where the Gaea boarded the supertanker. Did the Gaea race compete, in the beginning, with ancient humanity? Or, possessing some genetic science, did Gaea create humanity? And as the architect of our beginnings, does Gaea control our destiny as well?"

Bronson was ominously quiet for a few moments. Finally, he made a startling confession. "I did not want to alarm you earlier, Nabnak, but I must share with you a feeling I have had ever since we walked into the lab and saw that thing—"

"*Them*" Nabnak said, by which he meant Eddie Allan's relatives and their operatives.

"Well, yes." Bronson hesitated. "I wasn't sure how you felt?"

"A trap. Yes, I've considered it."

Bronson found it difficult to press this next question. "Will you?"

Nabnak swallowed. He knew too well what Bronson implied. For an instant he could almost feel the black capsule in his boot heel. Fortunately, there was the more immediate problem of operating the *Manteau Raie*.

They were approaching the Strait of Hormuz now and the ocean was smoothing out. Bronson lowered the wing dihedral by another five degrees, adding another ten knots to their already, at this altitude, tremendous airspeed. With subdued exhilaration Nabnak eyed the altimeter and airspeed indicator. "ETA," he announced, again checking the figures on the computer against his circular slide rule, "seventy-three minutes." He consulted the little clipboard strapped to his thigh and then twisted the grid coordinate knobs on the navigation computer. In the navigation display the Gulf of Oman slowly disappeared to the right as the Persian Gulf—from Hormuz in the east to the Euphrates Delta in the west—panned in from the left. A flashing orange dot, just breaching the strait, indicated their present position, while a green line, twisting in places to avoid military and geographic obstacles, traced the course deemed safest by the computers in the tactical command satellite in geosynchronous orbit 22,300 miles above them.

"I have a notion to take her in on our own heading," said Bronson dryly.

Nabnak was quite willing to follow his friend's instincts. "Switch over to inertial?" he asked, glancing out at the darkness beyond the windshield.

Six-hundred miles to the west another pair of eyes were looking into the darkness. Commander Pelican Montieth stood at the extremity of one of the four quays that radiated out from the steel island. There was only one tanker in now, taking on a load of oil pumped from the shore refinery fifteen miles to the south. Somewhere in that direction also lay the city of Kuwait, blacked-out to encourage the belief among the citizenry that their security was threatened.

Montieth was attached to the United Dictatorships group that regulated the sale and distribution of munitions to the six major states bordering the gulf. It wasn't a bad assignment. United Dictatorships certainly had worse places to send its people. Central America was said to be an absolute bore. Of course, no place was uncorrupt, but the corruption here was somehow unsullied. Perhaps it was because of the fantastic amounts of money involved, or the clean-cut corporate way affairs were conducted? Whichever, what mattered to Montieth was that he had found an orderly place to bring up his children; and his wife so enjoyed their obsequious Bangladeshi servants. There was the so-called war, of course, but here in the Middle East there was such a quaint tenth-century complacency about it that no one took it seriously. Montieth had even seen the grudging eyes of aging mullahs brighten with ironical amusement at the mention of that splendidly ridiculous word, "jihad."

But it was a great risk he was taking now, and Montieth struggled with himself in the darkness to convince himself of his foolhardiness. He had put his position, his family, perhaps even his self-respect in jeopardy. A voice within argued, pleaded, and then demanded that he turn his back on this affair. But the more sensible and frightening the reasons became, the more resolute was his determination to aid the brave agents from the Invisible Tower. He knew that it was United Dictatorships and only United Dictatorships that allowed him to live as well as he did. But his feelings drove him to a greater loyalty. In the final accounting, no man can place personal comfort before his duty to science.

It was ten minutes past eleven p.m. and dark clouds were rolling across the stars from the west when Montieth heard the dull whistle of the *Manteau Raie*. He blinked his flashlight in the direction of the sound, waited a full twenty-seconds, and then blinked again.

The craft's red and green navigation lights flashed once as it swept toward the steel terminal. The whining of its engines lowered in pitch and Montieth heard a sibilant splashing as the craft bellied into the water. And then out of the darkness, its wings folding upward, Montieth spotted the *Manteau Raie* sliding across the water toward him. Light from the terminal reflected against the canopy as the craft came alongside. The flames in the enormous engines went out and the canopy raised between the spinning compressors. A short, helmeted figure stood up on his seat and tossed Montieth a line. Montieth tied it off while the two men from the craft scrambled up the steel girders.

"I often get angry watching television," Montieth said. His hand hovered over the handle of his pistol.

Bronson Bodine removed his helmet. "Then you should shut it off."

Montieth advanced, reaching out his hand. "I always fear I've got the previous day's password when I go through this sort of thing at night." His voice was attentive and precise, and he sang his vowels happily. He was clearly English and not merely British, although such distinctions were overlooked, as point of principle, in United Dictatorships.

Bronson shook Montieth's hand once and firmly so that he instantly gained Montieth's respect, loyalty and affection. If it wasn't gauche, Montieth could have been moved to say "ready for the bash," or "cracking good to be on the team," or something equally keen and gung-ho.

Bronson indicated his companion. "This is Tornasuk."

Nabnak took the Englishman's hand. "I sometimes hesitate over the password myself."

Montieth was a perceptive judge of character. These were good men—but dangerous, just the same. He led them down the quay. Occasionally the sheet metal decking depressed beneath their feet and made a dull bang.

"Our *Manteau Raie* will be all right here?" asked Bronson. He hooked his thumb over his shoulder.

Montieth, smiling pleasantly, nodded. "Oh, yes. The Arab engineers who operate Offshore Terminal Double-Twelve are socially quite impossible, but only too willing to cooperate with United Stations." His manner became more serious. "I suppose you have heard another of those mutants has been found?"

Bronson stared at the Englishman. "No."

"Close to here," said Montieth. "Washed up along the shore south of the Euphrates Delta. Rumor is the marshes are full of 'em. Terrifying to imagine being out in those horrid reeds, dodging unseen bullets, smelling the enemy, then coming up on one of those devils. What do you chaps think they are?"

Bronson said, "Ask me when I've returned from the marshes."

Montieth stopped walking. "The fighting's grim there, my friend!"

"What better cover for our activities?"

Montieth balked at this, prompting Bronson to tell what he knew of Gaea genetics and anatomy. While Bronson presented his little lecture, Nabnak peered over the edge of the platform and examined the struts and cross-braces supporting it in the water. He turned again as Bronson concluded:

"So you see, it's absolutely imperative we make contact with this race."

The Englishman agreed. "I strive to keep a low profile around here, but I'll try to put out an ear for something more on those rumors."

"I need your most recent reconnaissance reports of the area," said Nabnak.

41

"Reconnaissance reports?" Montieth shook his head. "People intelligent enough to write reconnaissance reports know enough to stay out of the marshes—no offense intended."

Bronson put his hands on his hips. "None taken. Can you find us a guide?"

"No problem. When do you plan to depart?"

"Soon as possible."

Montieth paused to register Bronson Bodine's pluck. "Can you wait five, six hours? I'll have to wake someone up who will have to wake someone up, and so on—unless I can get a guide released from quarantine."

"Fine." Bronson gazed down toward the center of the terminal. "We'll need a rubber raft too. Motorized." He made nervous fists. His knuckles cracked.

Montieth nodded his head in a dependable manner. "Very easy." He noticed Nabnak was bouncing on his heels. "I have arranged quarters for you. I'm sure you'd like to rest?" Montieth took a step toward the central terminal.

"No," said Bronson. "Go ahead. We'll meet you back here."

Montieth felt it only proper to insist. "You're quite welcome. Come along. What can you do out here for six hours?"

Bronson and Nabnak looked at each other. The Englishman failed to realize that the struts and cross beams supporting the terminal formed just the sort of monkey bars that Tower agents dream of.

Bronson winked. "We'll be climbing around."

"Yeah," said Nabnak eagerly. "We're enthusiasts."

Montieth accepted this without making inquiries. Altogether he was an unremarkable sort of person.

3

"CAN YOU SEE WHERE we're headed?" cried Nabnak over the howling wind.

The rain slashed at their eyes. Waves rolled over the tiny raft's sides. Bronson shook his head as he worked to keep the faltering outboard from quitting completely. Nabnak looked around them. Water streamed down his face, down his back. In the hazy light of early dawn he could make out the gray tops of the waves boiling around them. The Kuwaiti coast guard vessel that had dropped them off was out of sight now, charging away from shore into the relative safety of the gulf.

Bronson drew a compass unit from his utility belt but Bubu, their fourteen-year-old guide, clapped his hands over it and shook his head. He mumbled something in Arabic.

"He says the GPS will not work," said Nabnak. "He says there are certain corks—buoys—in the water which make the needle point the wrong way."

Bubu glanced anxiously in every direction, and then pointed into the wind. Bronson narrowed his eyes at the stinging rain and turned the raft. They heeled up on a wave and slapped down the other side. The next wave flooded over the bow and pushed them down. Bronson twisted the little motor and the raft rose through the swell and slid forward. Water streamed from the sides. It was slow going. Bronson continued jockeying the raft back and forth on the waves, shouting for Nabnak to shift his weight as the water leaped and fell around them. The little outboard put up a fuss but didn't fail to move them ahead. Then Bubu was chattering. A vague patch of gray was visible in the gloomy distance. The boy hopped forward and steadied himself on Nabnak's shoulder. They made a strange, cozy picture with the dark clouds overhead and the rain swirling around them.

Soon they could make out the outlines of what quickly became clumps of reeds whipping back and forth beneath the slashing rain. As the agents neared the reeds the waves became less severe. The little outboard finally ceased its coughing and drove them forward at an acceptable clip. Bronson steered for one of the narrow channels leading into the reeds.

They entered cautiously, wary of the distant crackle of rifle fire that rose and fell with the wind. It was impossible to guess the location or distance of the fighting, but death could be felt like the stinging water creeping beneath their clothes. Bronson decided it was prudent to shut off the motor and proceed with the oars.

Nabnak drew his automag and watched their progress as Bronson rowed. The rain still rattled against the water, but as they moved deeper into the marsh it began to slow. They found themselves in a somber, yellow-green dream world. Around them the reeds raised like the walls of a maze. They pulled in deeper and deeper but the endlessly winding water channels remained the same. Bronson's head twisted around on his shoulders, ever on the alert as his powerful arms pumped the oars. At length the rain slowed to a drizzle. Steam rose off the water where the little rain drops created a myriad of rippling silver circles.

"I'm itchy," pronounced Nabnak, unable to contain his discomfort any longer.

Bronson was also feeling the sting of wet clothing. They undressed, retaining only their fashionable European briefs, their high-heel combat boots, their utility belts, and the shoulder holsters for their stainless steel automags. Nabnak's automag was loaded with depleted uranium shot, as was indicated by the red tape across the bottom of the magazine. The blue tape on the magazine in Bronson's weapon indicated mercury-filled exploding rounds.

Bubu, already fascinated by the Eskimo, was now amazed by both agents' strange, minutely defined musculature. Each muscle on their bodies rose independently of the others and was itself crossed with steely sub-divisions. To Bubu it almost appeared as if their skin had somehow been removed, exposing their inner pistons, pushrods and steam lines.

Bronson was in many ways equally amazed with Bubu. "This boy has the face of a man. What do you make of those wrinkles? Look at those folds down his cheeks."

Nabnak smiled at Bubu. "He knows you are talking about him."

Bronson forced a smile and drew a Hershey's kiss from his utility belt. He tossed it to Bubu. The naive and eager look on the boy-man face presented a startling contrast to the reality of their situation. Bronson frowned and resumed rowing.

After a few minutes, a modulated electronic purr came from the radio set, and then: "My countrymen provided me with a personality I could call my own... My countrymen provided me with a personality I could—"

Bronson picked up the microphone. "But I rejected it. Go ahead, Montieth."

The confident voice of the Englishman came clearly through the radio: "Intelligence report just came across my desk. Network operatives are in your area. They are supposed to be filming an archeological documentary, but perhaps they are looking into your problem. Leader has been identified as Dan Either, over."

"How long in area, over?"

Montieth hesitated. "Sorry, thought I heard something in the corridor. At least a week. That's it, over."

Bronson exchanged glances with Nabnak. "Well done, Montieth. Thanks, out."

Nabnak was shaking his head. "Dan Either, the news anchor! Now what are we going to do?"

Bronson shrugged. "Let's call him up. Hand me the code book."

Nabnak tossed him the torn blue manual. Bronson looked up the Network scramble code and password for that day. Then he reset the radio's scrambler and raised the microphone. "Rustbelt goontown pride... Rustbelt goontown pride..."

The radio soon answered. "A real upscale place to raise your kids. Go ahead, guy."

"Yeah," Bronson said, getting into the Network idiom. "Guy, I was taping a war-boy docu, but the little dudes crashed the party. My people are bored. I'm in big need for a new beginning."

"Oh, wow. Just hold a sec, guy," said the radio. Bronson and Nabnak exchanged on amused glance. The radio crackled back on. "We're the ones to look for. Is your RDF cool?"

"Check."

"'Kay, guy. Home on 27.05. You will be."

Bronson nodded. "Sweet. Throw some pink things on the barbi."

"Oinkey dokey. Yacht quick, out."

Bronson hit the scrambler bypass and tuned to 27.05. The mini-loop antenna inside the radio quickly located the signal and a bearing appeared on the dial.

"Here." Bronson handed Bubu a leather-covered tube and pointed for him to give it to Nabnak. The tube contained the most recent map of the marsh. Nabnak opened the tube and pulled out the map. After checking the corner, he flipped it over and unrolled it on his lap. He pointed at a red circle. "They could be at this archeological site," he said. The boy began chattering. "But Bubu says the map is wrong."

Bronson said, "We'll find out soon enough." He started the motor. "Get me through this maze."

With Nabnak directing him, Bronson steered the raft through the marsh. They were bent over in the raft, their weapons drawn. Rifle fire echoed ceaselessly in the distance.

Soon they entered a broad expanse of water ringed with hundreds of inlets from the reed marsh. In the center, ringed with reeds, was an island shore three-hundred yards across. They motored around it, maintaining a distance of fifty yards from the reeds until they made out the camouflaged profile of a long, sleek patrol boat.

"It's a T-68," said Bronson, recognizing the configuration; "a Danish Willemoes class: nearly as large as a frigate. Network operates six of them."

Bronson turned the raft toward the large craft. A sailor at the bow waved his arms to catch their attention, then pointed to a little channel that led into the island. The sailor raised a walkie talkie as they passed under the bow and steered into the reeds.

The channel curved along for thirty yards until they were once more out in the open. Before them stretched an expanse of steaming brown mud. The raft quickly slowed, stopped. The motor quit.

From the edge of the little channel a narrow plank walk reached across the mud to a wooden platform about thirty yards away. Dan Either, wearing a white safari coat and holding a drink, stood surrounded by technicians, bikini-clad hangers-on and a squad of sailors, some of whom wore muddy waders. Many carried submachine guns slung under their arms.

Dan Either raised his glass and called out to his new guests: "Hey, guys! You thirsty?"

Leaving Bubu with the raft, Bronson and Nabnak trudged through the slippery mud to the plank walk.

"Yo, big guy!" said the notorious Network agent, evidently impressed with Bronson's tall and solid form. A look of sly recognition appeared on his face, but he had never seen Bronson and did not know who he was. He nodded for one of the girls to prepare drinks for the newcomers. "You," Dan said excitedly, raising his palm over his head, "You did *Does Your Baby Have a Terminal Disease?* Right?"

"No." Bronson shook his head modestly as he strode up. He raised his hand and exchanged an enthusiastic "high-five" with Dan Either. "Hey all right! But no, gee. Maybe you're thinking of my *Steps You Can Take to Prevent Your Baby From Getting Sucked Up In A Tornado?*"

"Was that it?" Either, not unimpressed, took the drink the girl prepared and passed it to Bronson. "Anyway, guy, that's real class the way you told the truth there." He sipped his drink and drunkenly smiled. "Anybody else would have taken the credit. But anyway, big guy. Gosh." He took a step back and shook his head at the way Bronson and Nabnak were dressed. "We just don't have a pool. Or—He! He!—do you guys do a mud wrestling thing on the side? Ha! Ha! Ha! Ha!" He turned around and exchanged a "high-five" with a nearby technician.

This disturbed Nabnak who as a dedicated Tower agent was rather fastidious about the "high-five" gesture, which was looked down upon as a circus contortion of some kind. It had been humiliating enough when Bronson exchanged it with Network agent.

"Yo, guy! Something the matter?" asked Dan Either, looking at the Eskimo narrowly.

Nabnak swallowed. He realized that he had forgotten that old college adage which says:

Discretion is the Better Part of Valor

Fortunately, Nabnak thought quickly on his feet. "Our camera crew—" he paused for a moment and stared blankly ahead to build the effect "—all gone."

Dan shook his head sympathetically and snapped his fingers for someone to hand Nabnak a drink. "Hey, guy, forget that mud wrestling crack. It was just a crack." He turned to Bronson. "So what happened?"

Bronson lied admirably, weaving together a story of sex, violence, graft, blackmail, betrayal, jealousy, despair, revenge, cruelty and murderous emotions gone out of control. The gathering of Network agents sighed apprehensively as he concluded, while Dan Either, knowing their reaction put him on the spot for a better story, poked his index finger into his collar and tugged away.

"Can you believe it," began Dan, nodding toward the center of the mud field. "Two weeks ago I get this call about some freaky temple that rose out of the mud in the Middle East. Cool. We hire a gunboat, sailors, film crew, and come down here. 'Wow!' I said when I got here." He turned to the blonde at his elbow. "Didn't I say 'wow,' sweetheart? Well, anyhow, you should have seen it—right off a D. W. Griffith set, with snakes and squatting demons and frog women carved all over this weird ancient structure. *It was news.* We set up to go ahead and film: make a docu and then maybe an art thing with the girls. Then all these bow-legged, squid people squeezed out of the temple and ran at us with knitting needles. We must have iced fifty-million-thousand of them. And, well, we were pretty grossed out after that; and by the time we felt like taping again the screwy temple starts sinking in the mud!" Dan shrugged, spilling some of his drink. "Hey, big guy, so what could I do? The party was totally over."

Bronson shook his head. "Oh, guy! Way too bad. But, um, what happened to the temple people?"

Dan fixed an eye on him. "All sunk in the mud, drawn down like they were pulled by a magnet. Just like the temple."

"And you didn't get inside the temple at all?"

"Ah," Dan wrinkled his lips in an appraising sort of way. "There's like this hole still there now, big guy. Over there in the mud, you know?"

Bronson shrugged. "So let's take a look."

Dan Either the shrewd Network agent nodded. "You want me to go over there, you gotta let me record you crawling down that hole."

Bronson laughed. "If it looks like news, you'll have to fight me to keep me out."

Dan shook his finger at Bronson. "Big guy, you are real people." He raised his voice. "All right boys and girls! Break out the cams. Someone get a rope. Big guy is going to do some spelunking!"

After pulling his waders on, Dan led the entire company across the mud to the rim of a crater. It was nearly fifty feet across. The entire company gathered around it in a ring. At the bottom was a dark hole just big enough for a person to crawl through. The mud was slowly slipping into it.

"Give me the rope," said Bronson. He directed a sailor who staked the rope's end into the mud, and then threw the coil into the crater. It played out, disappearing into the hole at the bottom.

"We do this under one condition," Bronson said, testing his weight on the rope.

"Sure, sure," said Dan.

"If we don't come back, I want you to take care of the boy we came with."

Dan waved his hand through the air. "No problem. I got this hat with a big tray screwed on top. He can carry drinks on it wherever I go. Job for life." He raised his hand to make the okay sign. "'Kay-'kay?"

Bronson laughed. "'Kay-'kay!"

While cameramen *splotched* and *sukplitched* in the mud around him, Bronson took the rope and lowered into the crater. Nabnak started behind him, but Dan stopped Nabnak and shoved a radio mini-cam into his hands. Dan said, "The light wastes the batteries fast, so make sure you take pictures of something special, huh guy?"

Nabnak took the camera without saying anything and climbed down after Bronson. At the bottom of the pit, kicking the edge of the hole with their boots, they appraised the situation. They conferred for a moment, exchanged nods, and then lowered themselves into the darkness.

When they were completely swallowed by the hole, Dan Either turned a disbelieving face to a brunette in a pink maillot. "Did you see that! I can't believe these clowns! Are they jerks, or what?"

At the same instant, Nabnak was looking up through the hole at Dan Either. "I can't believe that clown. Is he a jerk, or what?"

Bronson was drawing a flare from his utility belt. "Ignore him, he's just a newsman."

They stood on the roof of the temple Either had described. Mud covered most of its walls and had swallowed half the roof. The mud was slowly but perceptibly oozing between the columns and into the entranceway. A peculiar scent like dried oil or electrical machinery rose from the entrance and mixed with the stale smell of damp earth. Beneath their feet they could detect a faint throbbing vibration while around them the mud shifted slowly and made a sliding, sucking sound.

Bronson lit the flare and the gray light from the hole above them was replaced by a wavering orange glow. The full extent of the mud cavity became visible. Nearly the entire temple had been swallowed, and the two agents sensed that the mud might collapse around them at any moment. They had to proceed rapidly.

Bronson dropped from the temple roof onto the ramp of mud which was slowly oozing into the entranceway. His feet slipped when he landed, but through a miraculous twisting of arms, neck and back he managed to remain upright and skidded forward into the temple. Nabnak discarded the camera and sprang after his companion. Slipping awkwardly in much the same way as Bronson, he plunged into the temple and skidded to a stop on the stone floor.

Inside was a short passageway some twenty feet deep. The walls, ceiling and floor were encrusted with calcite deposits that glittered in the flare light. "And what is that?" asked Nabnak.

At the end of the passage on the wall was a beautifully carved but grossly elongated representation of a Gaea hermaphrodite undergoing some sort of division. Its body was split apart at the waist: male to the left, female to the right. The two heads were thrown back in an expression of frightening ecstasy, their mouths agape as if screaming in a silent and meaningless duet.

"Maybe *Homo enigmus* reproduces by fission?" suggested Nabnak. "Like the amoeba or the paramecium?"

Bronson said nothing but moved with pantherish steps to study the figure more closely. He halted suddenly. Before the statue and running from wall to wall was a rectangular pit measuring three feet by ten. A warm, dry draft carrying that peculiar machine scent rose steadily from its black and yawning depths. The pit had about it the uncertain aura of bottomlessness.

Bronson lit a new flare and dropped the old one down the pit. The orange glow raced down the sides of what was revealed to be a deep stone shaft. The glow dwindled, becoming a spark, and then it was swallowed by the black void.

"I counted twelve seconds," said Nabnak. He made a quick calculation. "It's at least fourteen-hundred feet deep."

Bronson knelt down and felt the stone lining the shaft. It was grooved like corduroy fabric. "How do you feel about climbing down?"

Nabnak nodded back at the mud slowly sliding through the entranceway. "The problem isn't so much the climb as the time we have left. We're taking our chances as it is."

"Still," said Bronson, "can we afford not to exploit this opportunity?" He stared earnestly at Nabnak." Who knows what we will find, what we may learn? Perhaps we could gain insights of such profundity that we would be moved to never return. It is staggering, isn't it? Think of the knowledge the Gaea have accumulated over the centuries. Are they the long time masters of Man's pitiful, surface dwelling civilizations? Do they possess the knowledge by which we may transcend the limits of our socially-instilled preconceptions and so enter into realms of consciousness greater than our limited senses can perceive? Do they know the secrets of substance, love, truth?"

"Ah," sighed Nabnak as he considered the possibilities. "Go on."

In the wavering light of the flare Bronson's bearded face shone with diabolical charisma. "I believe life is a change in destinations, the evolution of material tyranny into a dream of will and forgiveness. When change calls there are worse things than to follow."

Nabnak was deeply moved, and he wondered why. Was it the mystery of the pit? The strange beauty of the Gaea statue? What was it that caused this curious welling of expectation, this dangerous enthusiasm?

It was decided. Bronson took a spool of tape from his utility belt and secured the flare to his boot. Then, bracing himself by placing his feet on either side of the shaft, he lowered his body into the pit. Nabnak followed in beside him and they began descending. The grooved face of the stone was ideally suited to their purpose. Their boots gripped easily and they found they could move down rapidly.

Occasionally they felt the shaft shudder, and as they went deeper and deeper the oily, machine smell became sweeter until it resembled the ozone scent that follows in the wake of a thunderstorm. They also experienced strange visual sensations. These were so subtle and varied as to be indescribable, but the most profound were flare-lit images of their own selves climbing down between the walls, over which strange angular scratches floated by, like vitreous floaters or some forgotten ancient alphabet. Then everything would again be crisp and clear and normal, except for the lurid glow of the flares and the shaft stretching into the blackness above and below them.

They had been climbing for nearly an hour when Nabnak announced the sides of the shaft seemed farther apart. "I believe the walls are diverging."

"Are you sure?" asked Bronson.

"Yes. My legs are shorter than yours. If it angles out anymore you should feel it as well."

They began descending again and Bronson indeed detected the shaft's expanding geometry. "You are right. I can sense it, too."

Nabnak shifted his legs around. Climbing through the wider shaft put a strain on his ankles. "Do we go on?"

Bronson answered by dropping a flare down the shaft. The light dwindled rapidly, becoming a winking red spark. It disappeared.

"Eight seconds," hissed Nabnak. "That's another seven-hundred feet."

"It's all right," said Bronson. Sweat glittered on his arms and chest. "We will make it."

They resumed climbing; but after another twenty minutes the walls were almost five feet apart and they found it necessary to shift so that the entire lengths of their bodies stretched between the walls. Facing down, Nabnak walked with his feet against one wall while he pressed with his hands against the other. Bronson lowered himself in a reclining position, pressing his weight between his feet and upper back. But as they lowered further and the walls drew farther apart, Bronson had to turn around and descend like Nabnak with his body stretched between the walls. The muscles of his arms, legs and back strained against the pull of gravity. However well-conditioned, the human body was not made to support itself in this fashion. The agents groaned and wept against the pain that tore on their limbs and twisted the discs in their backs. Sudden eruptions of perspiration rolled off their bodies and dropped down the shaft.

"Bronson," gasped Nabnak who was now effectively on tip-toe "I can't do—" he forced a swallow "—It's too wide, too wide—"

Bronson shifted to Nabnak's side and instructed him to push forward with his hands. Bronson grabbed Nabnak around the waist with his arms. Nabnak relaxed his legs and the relief he felt in the small of his back gave him new strength. They began descending once more, pressing their combined weight between Bronson's legs and Nabnak's arms.

Deeper and deeper they went, but the walls continued to separate and Bronson had to pass Nabnak up through his arms until he held the Eskimo successively around the hips, the thighs, the knees, the calves, and then the feet. Soon it was necessary for Nabnak to stand on Bronson's shoulders. Sweat poured from their faces, which were contorted in screams of silent agony. The pain twisted at their backs. Their lungs wheezed and cracked like dry leather bellows. Complete darkness surrounded them, their flares having burned out many minutes ago. They perceived themselves as mere nerves in the darkness. Straining, sweating, quivering nerves. And when it seemed as if their spines were going to snap out of their backs, the walls widened beyond their ability to press between them. With a desperate effort Bronson took Nabnak's boots in his hands and pressed the Eskimo forward. "Your head, friend Nabnak, press your head against the wall—"

Nabnak's hands slipped. They fell.

"Oouf!" They both grunted. There was a strange protracted silence and then they both laughed aloud. It had been a mere fifteen-inch drop! Without realizing it in the darkness, they had climbed to within fifteen inches of the bottom of the shaft!

Bronson lit a flare. Next to them were the butts of the flares they had dropped during their descent. The Tower agents stood up and reached for their canteens. As they sated their thirst, they looked around them.

From the base of the shaft extended a narrow tunnel curving gradually upward and to the right. It was lined with closely-fitting stone tiles, and they quickly perceived the dimensions of the tunnel were remarkably square and regular. Everything was covered with a uniform layer of dust. Running along the ceiling, walls and floor were parallel strips or bands, about six inches wide, and leading off into the darkness. The strips were filled with a multitude of cluttered depressions that were evidently some form of writing. A pair of these bands ran on either wall below the low ceiling; on the ceiling were two bands, each set close to either wall; and directly under either band in the ceiling was a band set into the floor. There were eight strips in all, four on each side of the tunnel. Something about their configuration suggested tracks. They ran along with the tunnel into the darkness beyond the light of Bronson's flare.

Nabnak ran his hands across the strange writing. "This has been set in clay."

Bronson explored the writing with fingers not so expert as Nabnak's. "Can you make it out?" said Bronson.

"I don't know," answered Nabnak. He was intrigued. "I think so." He drew a small whisk broom from his utility belt and swept the dust from the obscure characters. An expression of delight seized his face. "I thought so: cuneiform."

Bronson raised his eyebrows. "Cuneiform?"

"Of course." Nabnak chuckled triumphantly as he brushed away more of the dust. "This is wonderful: easily the most important archeological find of the century. The boys back at the American Oriental Society will be just green." He trained his whisk broom against the second strip on the wall and then the strip above his head. Breathing deeply, he translated a particularly intriguing line: "*And the wind shall be haunted by its own ghost as the trees bow to make it so.*"

"A peculiar idyll," said Bronson with subdued astonishment.

"Indeed," agreed Nabnak. He surveyed the writing, his hands high on his hips. "This is cuneiform, the ancient wedge-shaped writing form invented by the Sumerians and later adopted by the Assyrians, the Babylonians and the Hittites. Of course, now it seems it wasn't invented by *Homo sapiens* at all, but by *Homo enigmus*." Nabnak placed a hand on each of the two wall strips.

"Remember how the Gaea we examined had one arm shorter than the other, and all those tentacles on its head? The explanation that occurs to me now is that it had adapted to wandering through these corridors—its hands placed *so* against the strips in the wall, it's feet over the strip on the floor, and its head tentacles reaching up against the ceiling strip—reading the cuneiform like Braille as it moved along."

Bronson dwelled upon this a moment. "The completely literate animal, living underground and subsisting not in the light of the sun but in the light of knowledge."

"I wonder," said Nabnak. He resumed brushing dust from the strips.

Bronson lit another flare. He noticed there were no footprints on the dusty floor except for Nabnak's and his own. "Listen," he began. "I'm going on ahead to find another way out of here. You stay in this area. I don't know how far these catacombs stretch; but in any case, I'll be back in five hours."

"What if you run into the Gaea?"

Bronson cleared his throat. "I'm beginning to suspect they were wiped out by Either and his news crew. Then again, perhaps they live in some other section of these catacombs." He checked his automag and re-holstered it. "Do you have enough flares?"

Nabnak nodded, wiping his dusty hands on his briefs. "Promise me you won't try climbing down any shafts alone."

"Wouldn't dream of it." Bronson pulled a phosphorescent ink marker from his utility belt and set off to explore the Gaea labyrinth.

It felt good to be moving again. As he turned down the tunnel inter-sections he blazed the corners with a quick, confident stroke of his marker. The tunnels ran for miles, some curving gradually, others elbowing and turning back on themselves or splitting at multiple forks into parallel tunnels that inexplicably rejoined further on. In places he came upon narrow shafts, similar to the shaft he had descended with Nabnak. Some of the corridors curled through the Earth in great coils and then ran straight for miles. Still others came to dead ends or narrowed into flat vertical cavities where other tunnels converged, forming a wall of openings. On the floor of one of these confluences he found a quiver filled with thin metal skewers—evidently the "knitting needles" described by Dan Either. Curiously enough, the quiver was free of the dust that coated the tunnels; this again suggested to Bronson his theory that the Gaea inhabited some remote section of the labyrinth. But there were no footprints in the dust that covered the floor. How did the quiver get here? He replaced it carefully and moved along.

He had been traveling for some time when he came upon the stiffened crystallized form of an *Homo enigmus*. It was frozen in the pose Nabnak had demonstrated earlier. It's jointless fingers were coiled over the two strips in the wall, while its head tentacles extended upward, pushing against the ceiling strip. Bronson raised the flare to the creature's mummified face and with an even stream of air from his pursed lips blew away the coating of dust. It lifted off and flew away cleanly so that a delicate countenance wearing a very serious and earnest expression was revealed. The tunnel's dryness had done a proper job of preserving even the color of its skin. The creature's multi-pupil eyes were clear and only moderately distorted. It was strange to think that it had died this way, simply moving along, reading, and then sudden death, stiffness. Bronson wondered if that was possible. And how old was it? Did it perish five-thousand years ago? Ten-thousand? Or had it frozen here recently, drying quickly over a handful of months?

He photographed the creature and took a skin sample. Then he spotted some sort of drawing—the first he had come across—beneath the Gaea's tentacular feet. He kneeled down to examine it.

While he brushed off the diagram, Bronson entertained himself with notions not altogether conventional. In these dust-filled vertices he saw aggregate elements of a subsuming presupposition. He imagined himself returning with the drawing to the surface to confound the scientific world. Here were idiosyncratic systems and complexities that plunged far deeper than the puny equivocations of university learning. Premonitions of cataclysm and change erupted in Bronson's brain. Autonomous associations recapitulated themselves. His tongue rolled over in his mouth. It was evidently a diagram of some kind. Perhaps a map of the labyrinth? He looked for a tunnel pattern he might recognize, like the large spiraling coil he had walked through an hour earlier. But then it hit him. It was an electrical schematic diagram.

Bronson sat back on his ankles and took a deep breath. *Homo enigmus* stood before him in all its mummified grandeur, as sullen and as proud as a wreck.

Reluctantly, Bronson yanked at the thing's brittle legs. The knees tore apart like knots of rotten straw. He pulled the feet up off the diagram. Affixed by the stiff hands and anemone hair dried to the wall and ceiling, the body remained hanging in place. Bronson rubbed the crusty remains of the feet off the diagram.

It took a few moments to put the riddle together, but there it was. The entire labyrinth was an electrical battery, or, more specifically, a capacitor built to store up a charge over the centuries, perhaps collecting energy from the rotation of the Earth or the bombarding thrust of the solar wind. The frozen Gaea was probably a technician of some unknown rank who had been electrocuted. But what was the purpose of this enormous electrical device? The raising and the lowering of the temple occurred to Bronson. But there was something more, something to do with the sudden appearance of the Gaea and the ancient dust covering the walls. Had he stumbled upon an ancient paleoanthropic time machine?

A sudden impulse made Bronson lean up and look into the darkness. He had the feeling he was being watched. He hesitated. "Nabnak?" he said.

There was no answer, but the feeling remained. He smelled something. His heart suddenly pounded. He drew his automag. What was it? What was different? All his senses were heightened. His nostrils dilated. What was that smell? And then relief flushed through his body. It was fresh air cutting through the dry ozone atmosphere of the catacombs.

He moved forward in the direction of the fresh air, his fingers tingling as his system burned off adrenalin.

Bronson found the air source about four-hundred paces beyond the stiffened Gaea. He marveled at his ability to have picked up the stream of air from so far away. The air was coming from an elliptical opening in the roof of the tunnel. There was a similar opening in the floor twenty yards further up. Both openings had a mean diameter of about thirty inches—quite large enough to crawl through. Evidently this was the empty shaft of an oil well abandoned after an unsuccessful search for petroleum. If only the riggers had known what they had drilled into instead!

Satisfied that he had found their means of escape, Bronson set out to find Nabnak. He moved at a brisk pace following the glowing arrow marks he had left on the walls. Occasionally he ran with the flare held over his head. Other times he walked in the pitch darkness, an unlit flare ready in his hand and tempting him to fear the nothingness around him. He was unfamiliar with the pattern of the tunnels and was suddenly startled when he came upon the orange glow of another flare and the short, muscular profile of the Eskimo examining the wall.

"Nabnak!" Bronson called. "I've found the way out."

"Excellent." Nabnak was unstartled by Bronson's sudden appearance. "But, to tell you the truth, I could work down here for years." He gazed at the writing on the wall and shook his head in admiration. The inscriptions refused to give up their hold on him.

Bronson was happy to see the interest and enthusiasm in Nabnak's face. "It certainly is amazing, isn't it? But now I have returned to confound you again." He wiped his beard and pushed his hair back across the top of his head "I found the shaft of an oil well running diagonally through one of the tunnels; about three hours from here."

Nabnak folded his arms and turned to face Bronson. "Diagonally?"

Bronson explained how a single oil derrick could drill a multitude of wells, causing each one to radiate out in a different direction. "It will be a tough crawl, and we may find ourselves pausing to nap in it, but I think we'll get up and through it to the surface." Bronson raised his mighty arms and rolled his shoulders. He was anxious to begin.

Taking one last admiring look at the figures he had brushed clean, Nabnak motioned his friend forward and they began walking.

"Remember," said Nabnak, "when we were examining *Homo enigmus* in the lab, and I suggested language operates independently of intelligence or a controlling will?"

Bronson remembered very well the argument they had over that suggestion. He shrugged. "I think so, vaguely."

"Well you see," said Nabnak. "I don't think this was necessarily true of the Gaea. They were very organized, very systematic. In fact, along these walls is the total knowledge they were able to derive systematically from their observations of the world."

"I was right then. They were a race who dwelled in a world lit purely by knowledge."

"Well, maybe. It might be that they were very limited when you compare their knowledge to Humankind's. They were in complete control of language and were too logical to let language control them. But their knowledge, you might say, was only empirical, like fossil imprints or catalogs of photographs. They lacked a capacity for irrationality and thus possessed no knowledge of the irrational."

Bronson lit another flare. "Go on."

"There came a time when the Gaea race understood that their knowledge was incomplete. So, approximately seven-thousand years ago, they took some of their own people, split their hermaphrodite bodies into the forms we call male and female, probably to more efficiently generate irrational knowledge, and put these new creatures up on the surface. So began the human race."

"So what are you saying?"

"Well," Nabnak thought a moment. "For instance, do you remember that old theory about a room full of apes pecking on typewriters; how, if left at it forever, they would eventually type up all the classics of civilization, the epics, the poems, the novels, the histories, and all the great works of science? In a figurative sense, we are those apes." He put his hands behind his back. "However, since we are more imitative than apes, it hasn't taken us as long to complete this great task."

"Remember it thus unto your children," said Bronson Bodine, and his laughter echoed through the catacombs.

APE AND
SUPER APE

THE LOCK RELEASED WITH a shrill electronic squeal as the hissing door slid swiftly to the side to admit Elvis Aeterna, henceforth known as "the tenant." He was not tall, but neither was he short. His brown hair was of average length and his medium build was fully inconspicuous, even as he moved around alone inside his apartment.

He lived at the two-hundred-twelfth level, which was not quite as good as living at the two-hundred-fourteenth, but better than the two-hundred-eleventh. Of course at the end of the day the discrepancy between the two-hundredth and the two-hundred-fiftieth were not really important. Basically, the only differences were color schemes and window sizes. As you ascended through the two-hundreds the windows became smaller while the colors became more adjustable.

He dialed through glittering shades of amethyst, and then lumbered up to the window in a slow-motion blur of swinging blings and projected re-flections.

The philosophy behind window sizes was some brittle relic of a brittle past. It was thought those living at the lower levels should have windows so they would from time to time remember (yet not clearly see) where they had been. The best interrogative simulcasts recommended ten minutes window

59

time per day, Monday through Saturday, with twenty-minute vigils on Sundays or upon receiving news of the death of a friend or relative.

The tenant pressed his face against the perspiring glass. The window was a foot wide by fifteen inches tall, set into a deep niche in the side of the building so that the ground and the tops of the shorter buildings were blocked from view. It was another typically gray, overcast day. Helicopters skidded along just below the clouds, chemtrail nozzles retracted but poised for emergency deployment. One helicopter was lighting on the peak of the nearby school building.

"School days, fool days," mumbled the tenant as he craned his neck to look down at the pyramidal structure. He shook his head. How many? Even in the past month? Fifteen? Twenty? Twenty-five? The school was a notorious center for suicides. All those adolescents gathered together and forced to sit still for endless, tedious, protracted periods, their hormones boiling, their young muscles quivering as musicians badgered them into conformity. It was torture, plain and simple. Dancing on thick rubber pads? Running races at the end of safety tethers suspended from tracks on the gymnasium ceiling? No wonder students so frequently found their way to the heliport and hurled their bodies down at the tiers below. But then again, there was a shortage of apartments in the one to seventy-five post-school levels.

The tenant shook his head. If only the students were given something to help them cope. In the old days the vocational therapists had looked the other way when the students sold each other Enhancer. School had been nearly tolerable. But then it was decided by some know-it-all (probably a group of educational futures brokers or commoditized phenomena regulators, or perhaps some combination of both) that Enhancer reduced the quality of the Career-Orientation-Motivation-Factor (COMF) in the children, and Enhancer was replaced by a drug called "Attention Retention," or "AR"—or as it came to be called in the city's vulgar vernacular, "Butt Binder." Yes, it was a horrid phrase. Fortunately, however, some perceptive educational futures broker was quick to recognize that the phrase was an instance of political impropriety—that is, it was not in the interest of the ruling elite, up there in the higher stories. Ergo, the phrase was duly proscribed. The tenant had learned about it viewing the interrogative simulcasts. The blockage AR produced in the large intestine effectively immobilized the students while stimulating their visual and auditory sensitivity, so that the schools were filled with students agonizing at their desks, groaning against their bowels for a form of relief that was impossible, even when the bell rang. The only escape they knew was to lose themselves in their studies. True, the Attention Retentive compound augmented the learning process but Enhancer obviously produced happier citizens. In any event, this was the logic of the system. People wanted enhancement, but enhancement was possible only through ascending into the higher stories, and to get there people had to study.

To the right and just behind the school stood the Oracle Time and Life Company, the entrepreneurial breakthrough of the century, formed as it was by an alarm-clock manufacturer and an insurance salesman (the latter said to have been living at only the ninety-second level at the time), who came up with the idea of insuring time: an idea that was physically realized in the underwriting of time pieces. It was one of those cases of being in the right place at the right time. Six months after Oracle was formed, a grassroots movement materialized to demand both the standardization of time and the establishment of government-imposed specifications for chronometer con-struction. As Oracle patents and Oracle publications had already defined the field, it came to nobody's surprise that Oracle was the first to produce the certified timepiece. Then, in what came to be known as the "Hour-glass Massacre," the leaders of the grassroots time movement were deposed, Oracle went public, the stock sky-rocketed, and laws were written requiring all clock owners to have their time pieces insured. Public demand, like public interest in the company's stock, forced the state to make Oracle the sole temporal underwriting licensee. Time insurance became the economic basis of the city. And in a few years the riffraff were cleaned out, leaving the city inhabited solely by Oracle Time and Life stockholders.

The Oracle building, like the school building, was dwarfed by the high-rise apartments that rose around the two public facilities like redwoods marching around young oaks. In the riot of the city, these buildings—like the big trees in plasma screen forests—were king. It was here in the apartments that the people lived and strived and dreamed.

What could be better, thought the tenant, than moving to a higher story? He gazed at one of the nearer apartment buildings, mentally reviewing the trappings of the various levels. One through one-hundred: one-quarter wall plasma screen, twenty-five channels, fifty-hour work week. One-o-one through one-ninety-nine: one-half wall plasma screen, seventy-five channels, new carpeting and furniture every week. Two-hundred to two-ninety-nine: full-wall plasma screen, two-hundred channels, limited decor dialing, forty-five-hour work week, domestic companion clone. Three-hundred to five-ninety-nine: two, three and four wall plasma screens, universal satellite access, four metric month work schedule (four on, six off), child option, no windows, travel permits. Six-hundred through—? How high did the buildings go? No one knew, but there was a feeling—more than a legend, less than a belief—that immortality itself was reached in the highest stories.

The tenant knelt beneath his window and attempted to glance up at an oblique angle. No. He couldn't see much past the five-hundredth level. But it did not matter. If he was going to get up there someday he would; growing up with Enhancer, he had learned to control his expectations. Kids these days with their darn Attention Retentive were too anxious to get to the top.

"Hey Babe," he called, resolute in his maturity. He turned from the window. "Hey! Baby, where are you? Come here."

There was no answer but then he didn't expect one. "Hey, Babe. Get your topographic in here."

Again no answer. Where was she? It felt odd. She should have been there by now. He knew he should have kept her in restraints, or at least locked in her terrarium. All the simulcasts said so. He was just too kind-hearted.

"Golly, Babe." His mind reviewed the shenanigans she had pulled in the past—getting into his shaving kit, cutting her hair, the messes she had made in the kitchen. And then he thought of the old Babe, the one he had acquired when he first moved to the two-hundred-twelfth floor, how she locked herself behind the watertight door in the jungle room and set the two faucets running and running and...

"Oh, no! Babe! Where are you?" He raced toward the jungle room and looked in.

"Arraaagh!" She had been into his shaving kit again. There was cream all over the mirror and ringing the toilet seat—but no Babe. He turned and raced back to the living room, where he knocked over an ornamental stool, sort of a corrugated tube of elastic green gelatin. The stool collapsed beneath his foot and then shot to the side as he kicked it away; then he stared a few moments as it began to swell back to shape. What was it about the thing that made a person stare? Then, shrugging it off, he skipped merrily and jumped on the couch, bouncing up and down and calling, "Babe! Babe! Babe! Here comes Elvis-boy!" As he bounced he removed articles of clothing and flung them around the room. He sprang off the couch and landed in the high speed whirlpool between the couch and the main plasma wall. But the bottom of the whirlpool was full of silverware—she had dumped it there, obviously. Now he was angry. He pulled himself out, dripping a trail of fast-evaporating nu-water across the floor, and stomped into the kitchen.

"Baby Babe!"

There she was standing in her black bra and grab-cord, swaying slowly with a childish grin on her face staring into the humming microwave oven. She was a tall, well-built girl, a perfect picture of healthy babegineering. Her long transparent hair was dyed silver at the ends. On her chin she wore a long pointy cup that was shaped like the toe of a Persian slipper. She was watching a metal coaster spark and crackle in the microwave oven, and, wouldn't you know it, she was drooling!

"Oh, Babe," he sighed with exaggerated concern. He walked over, turned off the oven, and then—when she reached again for the orange button—he gave her firm round buttocks a resounding spank.

"When will you learn?" he said.

She said nothing. Indeed, she lacked the ability to speak. She stared at him pitifully like a three-year-old, slightly hurt but rather more confused by his anger. He knew of course that her pouting was a ruse. She had all the intelligence of a six-year-old, and though she couldn't talk and responded only to fifty or so words, her pouting was, outside of disrobing and per-forming a jungle jig, her only means to divert his attention—all of which, after studying her manual on Babestream, he clearly knew.

"Oh, Babe. You have been naughty again. I don't know why I don't lock you in your terrarium!"

She moaned and pressed her large, full breasts against his arm. His eyes looked down and, in a sort of flash, he suddenly recalled the words from a fascinating edutainment feature he had recently viewed; something like, "The eyes saw and the spirit went along for the ride." For several moments he stared, as if in a stupor.

"Enough, enough," he suddenly said. "Don't let me catch you in the kitchen ever ever again." His voice became fatherly and perhaps a little precious as he began shaking his finger at her. He pinched and no-no'd the end of the slipper toe extending from her chin. "No kitchen. No! No jungle room. No!"

She smiled sensually but without warmth. It was another of the handful of expressions her creators had given her to work with. He understood how she was using the signal, but that didn't prevent him from grasping her waist with something other than paternal concern.

"You just don't understand—very little anyway. Now, Babe, I want you to go to the jungle room and wipe off the mirror and the potty seat. There's shaving cream all over in there. Go on."

She stared dumbly, then stuck her thumbs in her grab-cord and snapped the elastic several times so that it *thwacked* against her smooth milky-white skin. Seeing he needed to take control of the situation, he grabbed her hand and marched her in the direction of the jungle room.

But in the living room she inadvertently kicked against the elastic green gelatin ornament. She lifted her foot from it and started up with strange vague confusion as the ornament began to swell back into shape. She never liked the look or the feel of the thing. Actually, she was quite frightened of it. As he watched, her reaction suggested to him an enhancement response. Notwithstanding the ornament's elastic properties, she seemed to imagine the green material was stuck to her feet. She began to make her mute panic sound, which was very similar to the bark of a dog with clipped vocal cords. For a moment he envied her mild state of hysteria, but at the same time her disaffection needed to be attended to. Her hoarse barking continued.

He stared philosophically at her feet and shook his head. What to do? He considered getting the vacuum to create a distraction that would snap her out of it—she liked the vacuum, just as she liked cleaning—but then he considered more carefully and decided the matter: he led her to the whirlpool and made her dip her feet in the artificial nu-water. This stopped her mute barking. For the time being.

They resumed their odyssey to the jungle room. He could tell it was getting near time to get the wall moving. There was just so much of this he could take!

In the jungle room he made her fold her hands and watch as he wiped off the mirror and the toilet seat. "Isn't that nice and clean now?" He turned her round, pushed her to the jungle room door, and gave her a light spank intended to direct her toward the big couch.

"Watch!" he cheered, like it was some kind of reward. "Watch! Watch! Watch!"

She slinked over to the couch and lay down on her belly. The cleavage of her pretty hams was divided neatly by the black grab-cord. Sensing her chin cup wasn't exciting his attention—and it was after all a mild but uncomfortable distraction when watching the wall, she pulled it off with a pop and sent it whizzing through the air.

The tenant thumbed a button on his remote and dry ice fog came pouring through thousands of tiny pores in the coach. The mist jetted out rapidly, erupting suddenly into a turbulent cascade that flowed lazily to the floor. Some of the fog licked up in little curves around Babe's body, rising and swirling with the heat given off by her skin. He picked up her ankles, sat down, and then lowered her feet across his lap. Shuffling under her slightly, he put his feet up on the coffee table. He thumbed the remote, and the room lights dimmed automatically to the pre-set level.

The wall was always on. A room with a one-wall plasma screen felt as empty as a bout of unexplained anxiety, or worse. Up to this point the wall had been displaying a vague checkerboard plane beneath geometric shapes flying in every direction, chasing each other, flying in formation, assuming kaleidoscopic patterns. The tenant began flipping through channels and then held the button down. Twelve channels flashed by per second. The tenant allowed himself to be entranced by the fleeting images. Every fourth or fifth image registered in his consciousness until it was knocked away by another image. He sought to avoid the memory of what had passed. As the images flashed by he felt himself drawn closer and closer to the present. He had once seen a simulcast devoted to the phenomenon: *Exist Now*. There were many benefits to "watchnotizing yourself," as it was called. It was cognitively diverting, visually stimulating, relaxing, and completely undemanding. He sat there as the images flickered by: daffodil, race car, woman's face, laughing child, helicopter, snowy field, dark blue, rabbit or duck (it was a kick in itself when the interpretations blended together), pencil, pouring water, soldiers, golf swing, riots in a cloud of gas, stopwatch, fireman, bearded man, stars, zoo cage, angry woman, explosion, flugelhorn, tight belly, praying monk, tongue licking teeth, finger ring, matador, orange dot, bearded man reaching out, naked bodies, plane crash, bearded man shaking his head, forest, a frog kicking in nu-water, mountain range...

After a few minutes he had reached that state called "Ready-to-think, perchance to dream." He switched to a news channel and set down the control.

Toddlers lined up for group aerobics... the microwave network was being enlarged... an escalator rider described his many phobias... There was nothing new on the news. There never was. Except for the occasional metaphysical speculations concerning the outside world, it was all one homogeneous bore. Oracle had elevated the city above the news.

A bearded man reached toward him. He blinked.

He picked up the controller and found a Western. Westerns were the tenant's favorite fantasy package—they were so scientifically plausible. Of course the gun was a physical impossibility, every phase-three physics student knew that, but the Western did suggest some interesting sociological possibilities.

A bearded man was reaching out. Was he handing the tenant some Enhancer?

The tenant blinked his eyes and pushed Babe's legs off his lap and sat forward. A Babe commercial was coming on. It was a new one. An unseen narrator with a rather tawdry Australian accent described what was going on as it happened:

"She emerges from the sea, riding on the roof of a scarlet sporty car with B. E. A. S. T. written across the grill. She wears a lovely purple and scarlet one-piece with low back. You can easily make out her darling bottom. She holds a can of foaming soda-pop just for you which she tries not to spill as she dances on the car's hood— Hey! Looking good! As the car drives on the beach, more lovely Babes enter from the side just for you and dance in unison, flanking the dripping car as the tempo builds into a crashing crescendo! And the Babe song follows as the dancers run into the sea while the first Babe stands up on the hood of the Beast. And—what is this? What is this! Wait for it! Wait for it! Is she is about to sing? Oh, no! It's the all-new Talking Babe!

Bay-abe— Bay-abe—
Mystery and wonder
A song from the sea
With you I'm free!

Bay-abe— Bay-abe—
Booty and plunder
I'm followin' you
Tell me what to doooooo...

The tenant rocked back and forth, blushing, laughing, laughing, laughing. How wonderful! How mysterious! How dear! And then he shivered spasmodically and cried out at Babe: "Hey! Isn't that music the theme song from *Flipper*? Ha! Ha! Ha! Ha!"

The images were replaced by a solid dark blue field, and then in big block letters the screen said:

YOU KNOW WHAT TO DO!

And the tenant did.

In one fluid motion he pushed Babe's legs off his lap, stood, grabbed her by the wrist, pulled her up, pushed her over to the iris in the wall by the screen, pulled a lever, watched the petals of the iris dilate, then pushed Babe into the opening and sniffed with something well-nigh horror as he viewed her clutching the rim of the opening with her fingers; and she looked up at him one last time with an expression communicating confusion, panic and then sudden loathing. Gritting his teeth, he pried her fingers loose so she slipped down the long metal chute, the echo of her banging body dwindling along with her garbled cut-vocal-cord dog bark—all sending exhilarating shivers up and down his backbone as the petals in the iris quickly shut again to forever silence the wretched music of her fall.

Then there was a wonderful squealing sound. But what was it?

It was the door!

The shrill electronic squeal once more electrified the room as the hissing door slid swiftly to the side to admit the all-new talking Babe!

She looked exactly like the old Babe. Exactly! But could this one really talk?

"C-c-c-c-can you really talk?" he asked.

"C-c-c-c," she said, mocking his stuttering, and then said: "Can the small talk, Elvis! Let's get to know each other!"

He blinked his eyes at her. "How do we do that?" A million thoughts went racing through his head. "I mean, how do we *really* do that?"

She was wise. "By sharing. By doing things together. What do you like to do?"

And it was like love! She really was wise! But of course she should be, and why not? He shrugged matter-of-factly. "Mostly, I like to stare at the wall."

And that's just what they did. Adjusting her grab cord efficiently and without modesty, she lay down on the couch and, anticipating the routine, raised her shins so he could sit under her feet. He unflinchingly took his place, and in a snap he was sitting with his all-new talking Babe with her feet over his lap. She popped the Persian toe cup off her chin and sent it whizzing across the room. There they were like snug old friends watching the screen as culture and images and shades and suggestions and intimations and hints and paranoia and strange insights and peculiar disclosures and obtuse inscrutable surprises flickered by as fast as time itself.

Suddenly the screen went dead.

Completely blank.

It was like facing an empty refrigerator. He picked up the controller and jabbed the buttons.

"Golly," he said. "Now what's the matter with this clunky thing?"

Then the screen was flickering once more. Two men faced the camera. Behind them smoke drifted across a blue wall. The tenant assumed the men stood in a plasma studio.

One of the men was tall and handsome, sort of like a big cowboy, but he wasn't wearing a hat. He had brilliant blue eyes; his thick black hair was combed back from a broad and lofty brow that obviously marked him as a man of lofty thoughts and still higher—indeed, *flying*—principles. An exquisitely formed beard trailed down to a point, while the tips of his mustachios were twisted upwards in some vague indication of mysterious ecstatic energy. The beard was familiar. Where had he seen it before? The other man was at least a foot shorter. His skin was dark. He was very broad and muscular—even his face was muscular. He had slanted eyes and, the tenant realized, he was an Eskimo. But weren't they make-believe?

Both of the men had a grim look about them. They were angry but at the same time very cool; once again the tenant was reminded of cowboys. They both had big pistols, but the pistols were much larger than six-shooters, and the men wore their holsters under their arms rather than on their hips. A sparking wire fell behind them and a flashing light reflected on a blue wall before fizzling into nothing. The man with the beard began speaking. His voice was soft but rumbled with authority:

"My name is Bodine, Bronson Bodine. I represent the Invisible Tower, a non-aligned intelligence agency dedicated to the cause of Tremendous Overpowering Weird Esoteric Revelations. Here with me is my associate, Nabnak Tornasuk." The Eskimo folded his enormous arms and glared at the camera so that his menace seemed right there in the room. The tenant took it personally.

The big man with the beard continued. "We have entered your city and taken over your communications to let you know the truth about who you are, where you are, and to reveal to you the identity of your master—"

The tenant was snapping buttons on his control, but the two men from the Invisible Tower were everywhere. They had taken over all the channels.

"You dwell in an experimental city," continued the man with the beard. "The insane scheme of an eccentric trillionaire, John Allan, who is manipulating you to gratify his grotesque need to impose a scientific explanation upon everything. Whenever you feel *they* are getting you down and forcing you to do what your heart cannot bear, it is John Allan. He is worse than a tyrant, more diabolical than a Hitler, possessing a greater ambition than Alexander, for he doesn't want or need you. It merely interests him to see how dreadful you can be. This is the reason why this city was created. Oracle is not real. You see—" The man with the beard raised his hands and squeezed them into fists. From one of the fists an index finger burst forth and it pointed at the tenant. "You have been created from the genetic material of Americans. This city of yours is located in the Rocky Mountains, in the state of Utah, eighty miles east of Salt Lake City; which, incidentally, is a real city." He cleared his throat. "The last three generations of your history have taken up a mere seventeen months in our history, the history of the outside world, the real world. By stimulating your pituitary glands—as he did to the glands of your ancestors—John Allan has ac-celerated the turnover of your generations. Subliminal teaching methods and

69

memory implants have allowed your minds, such as they are, to develop along with your rapidly maturing bodies. Having successfully created the illusion of your history and your identity, now John Allan's purpose is to study your behavior in real-time patterns. Thus recently a deceleration has taken place. Your origins are indeed bizarre, yet many of you could still lead normal lives—"

There was a strange glitch in the image, and the big man with the beard seemed suddenly closer, as if he was in the room. He continued, his voice stronger now and with a sharper edge: "—initial reports indicated there actually was a city, but upon arriving at the location we discovered a small automated laboratory complex. There were no security measures to overcome, which initially aroused our suspicions, and after some hesitation we penetrated the complex. Inside, we discovered some kind of organic material in a transparent canister. It looks like a brain and a spinal column. After examining the computer database, we've identified a complex artificial intelligence paradigm generating what we think is an illusion of the sprawling city we had expected to find here. We are now seeking to make contact with the organic material to which the computer is connected, but so far the A.I. is adapting to our inputs in order to maintain the illusion of the city—communication—probable distortions seeking to maintain—" There was another glitch in the screen, and the big man with the beard retracted into the screen and assumed a two-dimensional appearance. He continued, "Your DNA was taken from Americans: forthright, independent, courageous, honest, vigilant. Your ancestors tamed a continent in the name of justice and equality and the right of each individual to fulfill his or her self and find happiness." He paused and blinked his glorious eyes and held out his hand. The tenant blinked. The hand reached right out of the screen. It was just like Enhancer. It was just like talking to Moses! The tenant licked his lips and chuckled softly as the bearded man continued: "The land, the living rivers, the sheltering forests, the rich pastures, the great prairies, the tall mountains—and—and—" The bearded man let his hand drop. He appeared to be considering a sudden doubt. He turned to face his Eskimo companion. "Nabnak, I don't know how effective this has been? I wonder if—"

"Bronson?" The Eskimo studied his doubtful colleague. There was unease in both of their expressions, but also an objective and clinical coldness.

"Perhaps righteous indignation got in the way of my better sense?"

The Eskimo shrugged. "Well, it was a good speech."

"Yes," said the tenant, somewhat perplexed, wiping his upper lip. "That was a good speech, *I think?*"

The Eskimo was nodding. "Now that you bring it up. I guess there is cultural contamination to consider, as well as biological. You are right—" Again there was a glitch, the Eskimo suddenly appeared in the room as a three-dimensional figure. He continued: "Although the organic material suggests a human brain and spinal column, I remain unconvinced it meets our criteria for passing as a human being—" Anther glitch, and again the Eskimo appeared as a two-dimensional figure framed by the screen. He said, "They are not real people. Not anymore."

The big man with the beard thought a moment. He nodded. "We will need to sterilize the entire sector."

The Eskimo caught sight of the camera in the corner of his eye and nodded for his associate to consider it.

The bearded man turned from his companion to face the camera. He smiled pleasantly. "Just a show folks—um, folks at home, did we have you going there? None of this is real, of course." He winked. "One way or another, we'll get you out of here."

The Eskimo slipped out of the frame.

The bearded man turned his face, and his eyes moved to follow the Eskimo's movements. The tenant looked around his apartment. For a moment he thought he could see the Eskimo moving in his living room.

The screen went dead.

"Just a show? Not real?" The tenant threw Babe's legs off his lap and stood up. He was having a hard time getting in touch with his feelings. "None of this is real?"

He brought his hands together and pushed them across his chest. "What kind of Western was that? The city is all and all is the city. Outside is fog. Everyone knows that." He pointed an accusing finger at Babe, who stared dumbly at him from the couch, licking her teeth.

"It's real," he said. "Really real!"

"Are you freaking out?" she said, somewhat bored. And then she shook her head as she mused aloud: "Ugh! Don't tell me they've set me up with a sensitive one."

He started breathing heavily. He was exhilarated. He suddenly grinned. "By gosh!" he laughed, affecting a British accent. "What a trah-men-dee-ous shooooooowww! I hammm indeed very much trah-mah-tized!"

She leaned forward so the transparent hair fell across her face, her lips forming an attentive "O"—some sort of pantomime reflecting his funny put-on accent—and as she stared at him through the light-catching strands hanging over her face, she registered an agreeable thrill promising that there was more to this sensitive guy than met the eye.

"It woss just a shoooow, woss it not, dahhhling?" He laughed as he skipped over to the little window and kneeled. He pushed his face against the lower corner of the glass so he could look up and see the upper stories of the nearby high rises—just where they were cut off by the clouds. A series of staccato glitches put out the sky, revealing nothing.

2

BRONSON BODINE, NABNAK Tornasuk and Syd Reilly had been in the pit for three weeks now. Around them the prisoners were lumbering aimlessly, sometimes looking above them to view the concentric terraces stepping up to the edge of the disused Brigham Young open-pit copper mine. It was a maximum security prison now, populated with the refuse of society—the misfits, the rejects, the criminals, the addicts, the broken, the poor, the heirs of generational dysfunction, the alienated masses who had been cast into the pit to fend for themselves, to scrape and struggle for survival, to create what civilization they could. Syd Reilly was wandering among them, nursing the sick, encouraging the despondent, distributing copies of the Manifesto. He read it aloud to those who could not read. Several times Syd encouraged the formation of small groups of men and women, who shuffled together to stand below him, and they would direct their ragged stares up at his lanky silhouette gesturing passionately from the edge of the next terrace. With long golden hair blowing wildly in the wind, he led them with a voice hoarse with desperation. Over and over he had them chant:

"Let us not perfect nor embellish what is opposed to us!"

Bronson had thought visiting the pit would be an interesting adventure. He wasn't so sure anymore but he wanted to see it through, just in case. Not as enthusiastic as Syd, he nevertheless attempted to communicate with several of the inmates, but it was no use. The prison was a beehive of multiple personality disorders, bipolar enthusiasms, psychotic splits from reality, paranoid delusions, sociopathic predation. Even those who seemed to understand where they were, those who assured themselves "I am getting out of this place someday," or, what was even worse, "I am somebody," consistently demonstrated themselves unable to comprehend the simplest explanations Bronson offered to reveal to them the true nature of their situation. They were creatures of the ahistorical ether, transitory fabrications somehow consumed by the same burning substance that formed their lurid and shifting identities, as alien from reality as dissolute figments in a dream. Meanwhile, Syd Reilly's attempts to explain the Manifesto became bizarre and grotesque, indeed comic in a ghastly sort of way.

"No one's getting out of here," said Nabnak. They are fooling themselves. There is nothing else to do. Let's get out of here."

Bronson wasn't quite ready. "But that's what I came to explore. What does it mean to want to leave, to dream of escape, but to never really get out? And to go on like this forever?"

3

EDDIE ALLAN SAT QUIETLY as Bronson and Nabnak recounted their adventures in Utah. "Your exploits are quite striking," said Eddie, who without limbs or lower body cavity was prevented from getting out and seeing the world for himself, except for those brief episodes in which he slipped into a genetically engineered body and ventured from his cave to view the outside world—but, alas, only to find himself in a race against time as the body began to cease functioning, usually in less than a day. "I am reminded of another experiment conducted several years ago by my stepfather John Allan: the 'Monkey Box Experiment.'"

"The Monkey Box Experiment?" asked Nabnak. "What happened?"

Bronson was also curious, yet still feeling a bit distant after his experiences in Utah.

Eddie called upon a Mountie to fetch the following report. It was written, as Eddie explained, by the subject of the Monkey Box Experiment himself. When the Mountie returned, Nabnak took the report and read aloud:

Ape and Super Ape

There is a man and a monkey in a box. I am the man, but I experience only the monkey's sensations. The monkey experiences mine. We both wear cybernetic interface radio caps to make this possible. Mine is bigger. Both are conical, with short aerials at the top.

I used to strike the monkey even though it hurt me. I used to throttle him until his eyes watered, and then beat him around the muzzle for good measure. I would stomp on his tail and bend his arms behind his back and flick his eyeballs with my fingers. Such was my loathing.

Monkeys make mistakes. Monkeys make too many mistakes. Monkeys are stupid, filthy creatures. And I felt it all. I felt stupid. I felt filthy. I felt like a monkey in a box with a better man.

Then the doctor gave me three choices.

One: I could leave the box and be free. But I would still experience the monkey's sensations, i.e. be a monkey in a box.

Two: I could stay in the box and try to live with the monkey watching me through monkey eyes.

Three: I could "neutralize" the monkey and see what happened.

I tried the first choice. I left the box. But, alas, I was still in the box. In time I couldn't even smell myself anymore. I went back in. There I was again, looking down at the filthy monkey with disgust.

I tried the second choice. I tried to live with the monkey. Even though I had been frustrated before, I tried to make it work. I told myself that living with the monkey was my own choice. Yes, however bad it was being alone in a box with a monkey, well, at least the decision was mine. But a monkey is a filthy stupid thing. A pest. I stretched out his little arms and lifted him. It became hard to breathe. But I knew *I* was breathing.

I tried the third choice. I put the monkey face down on the floor. I placed my right foot across his filthy buttocks. I placed my left foot across his back. My entire weight was now resting on the monkey. It hurt. It was difficult to breathe. But I knew *I* was breathing. I slowly shifted all my weight to my left foot and bounced. The monkey's rib cage compressed. The pain in his diaphragm was hot and tight and moist. This is the only way to make a monkey sweat. Suddenly his ribs went all rubbery and they folded together.

I emerged from the box shaken. The doctor explained that I was part of a control experiment. That cleared up the mystery.

But the cap was still on my head. I sighed. It was only monkey heaven after all.

"My goodness," exclaimed Nabnak as he finished the report. "How extraordinary."

Eddie nodded his fire-scarred head significantly. "Another example of how far my stepfather will go to provoke a chilly response to the human condition."

"Oh, I don't know," Bronson said, without emotion, without significance. He looked around the dark cave, master of himself, master of all he surveyed.

PATIENT **ZERO**

1. Coordinate Inversions

Let the vertical axis X = EV (emotional value)

Let the horizontal axis Y = MV (memorability value)

Let the axis of depth Z = CV (crisis value)

Let the spatial point of intersection (or "Singularity") represent a scale of infinite regression embodying CPA (coefficient of political affect) as conveyed in the expression S = CPA

Now plot coordinate values for X, Y, Z, and assign S for each discernible public event in the following sequence group:

> "Hail the monster truck!" or so they cried as the roaring mechanism snorted the winds of Hell and crushed the puny automobiles of Man beneath the rolling black hammers of its knobby tires. The roofs folded in as metal cracked, blistered, splintered, and detonated. Clouds of rust sputtered, blew forth and swelled in swirling glory. Glass flew out in bursts of glittering dust and shimmering fragments. Tires popped. Engine blocks laboriously groaned and creaked with stilted distress. Frames buckled. Axels snapped. A Milky Way of flashes swept across the arena. Righteous fists punched the air. "Yo! Hail the monster truck!" The great machine roared with

hoarse authority, then rumbled into idle so all could hear the rotating full-race cam drive the monster Chevy power plant to throb with orgasmic intensity: *wob wob wob wob wob wob wob wob wob wob wob wob wob wob wob wob wob wob wob wob—*

The attenuated voice of the Grand Announcer scratched in to say the night's attendance had been tabulated and 73,000 truck fans were present, a Pontiac Silverdome record for a motor event. "Yeah!" filled the air. "Ar! Ar! Ar! Funhouse! Yo! Sick! Right-on!" The monster truck answered the cheers of the masses: *wob wob wob wob wob wob wob wob wob wob—*

Tower agents Bronson Bodine, Vitaly Yurchenko and Nabnak Tornasuk walked upside-down across the roof. Terrorists, perhaps? Quaint notion. To those drawing their life breath from the miasma of global espionage, they were something far more sinister. They crept along the wall, away from the roofs of the press boxes where they had been hiding since that afternoon. Bronson Bodine led the way, and as he moved forward, kicking his elaborate boots into the ceiling, he represented a kind of alternative Grand Announcer commenting on their surroundings, now describing the chemistry of fuel mixtures, then speculating upon the identity of the Grand Announcer, then explaining—rather dryly but with that winsome touch of Bodine irony—that the Silverdome was roofed-over with a flexible polymer derived from a quality GMO corn product formulated by the technology of *tomorrow*, notwithstanding the certain fact that this was *today*. Like their spirits, the roof floated on the air pressure inside the great arena. His friends grunted unevenly at his witticisms, their attention focused on their inverted situation and their walking gear. Barbed spikes mounted on the agents' boots poked in and out of the fabric as they marched across the floor of the inverted world. They controlled the spikes with rubber squeeze bulbs hanging from the sleeves of their camouflage jumpsuits. Earlier, they had taken ZR-7-12, a compound that lowered their blood pressure to prevent inversion narcosis and unconsciousness. Unfortunately, it also elevated the propensity of the human brain to construe allegorical associations—not so much hallucinations as *ideas*, which are even worse because their reality is based on reason itself.

Bronson nodded "up" at the crowd and the activity on the floor. "I'm experiencing Rome flashbacks. It's the ZR-7-12."

His trusted companions turned their vein-webbed faces to view the crowd. The dirt floor, broken cars, and steep, undulating stands presented a strange contrast to the smooth bowl of the dome curving out and "down" before them. The caterwaul of the crowd spun around the arena to beat upon their eardrums, and their crown chakras crackled with ecstatic flashes of stunning insight and degenerate illusion.

Bronson halted and glanced down to see his boots clutch the roof. Air whistled through the punctures made by the spikes. He was tall and broad, slightly thinner through the waist than Vitaly, who was also a bit taller. Nabnak, just five feet tall, was much shorter than either, but he was also broader across the shoulders. He out-weighed them, could out-climb and out-run them, and he did a fair job of holding his own against them in the ring. And this never ceased to confound Vitaly, who had been raised by a tough Brooklyn boxing promoter. But Nabnak's drive was understandable. While Bronson, with his black Edwardian beard and icy blue eyes, had been blessed with a compelling testicular virility, and Vitaly, fair and soft featured, shown with self-assured calm, Nabnak struggled on with something of the fairy tale tragedy of a beautiful soul buried inside the squashed hulk of an ogre. He hooked his big thumbs under the straps of his knapsack. "Bread and circuses," he agreed, not so much with moral feeling as with abstract clinical interest. He spoke with the slight trace of an Inuit accent, though rest assured he had been to the best universities.

"I've been concentrating on getting used to *up* being *down*," said Vitaly. He spoke with the flat articulate monotone of a suave and cultivated New Yorker.

"Concentration will not shield you from the Empire," said Bronson with facetious gravity, demonstrating that he didn't let his delusions get in the way of enjoying a jest. At the same time, the crowd was roaring "good-bye" to the monster truck as it rumbled off to its lair beneath the stands. Bronson checked his thirty-two function spy watch. "Our Eddie Allan has about had it by now."

Nabnak checked his own watch. "They should bring him out soon—if they'd hurry."

From below came a sputter and the grind of gears, then the familiar sounds of metal snapping and folding together, the hiss of shattering glass. Lumbering yellow bulldozers were pushing dirt over the smashed cars as if to mold some strange ziggurat of ruin; soon they had created a steep, fifty-foot tall earth mound in the center of the arena.

The three agents glared with bulging eyeballs. Vitaly raised his watch. He studied it for a few moments, counting silently with his lips. "All right, this is it… Now! Watch for the helicopter."

Bronson aimed his hand to the spot where the dome was highest above the floor. There, just fifty yards away, three round depressions pushed into the taut fabric.

Far below, the object of their mission was ushered into the arena. Two burly members of the Certified Brain Authority tastefully garbed in long white lab coats prodded the stumbling fellow along with their chrome plated ice-tongs, which they raised high above their heads and snapped—*Tink! Tink! Tink!*—to delight the fans as much as to exercise the exuberant authority of the discharging energies coursing through the accredited ley lines of their official presence.

They had put a square-cut wig on him, a false beard, a philosopher's tunic, a laurel wreath, and they made him carry a sign that read "Mr. Know-It-All." And this was dear Eddie Allan! His stumbling became more pronounced, he fell dramatically to his knees, and so the brain workers grasped his tunic with their tongs and slowly dragged him up the death mound—a sort of "Golgotha of the Mind"—dominating the center of the arena. At the summit they threw him on his back and staked down his arms and legs. The Grand Announcer called for absolute quiet, and the brain workers finished by sticking the sign in the ground above his head. A few brazen voices in the arena, unabashed by the Grand Announcer, jeered and laughed. The rest of the crowd followed, timidly at first, but soon the arena was buzzing together as one united hive of guffaws that wavered in and out of phase as the spirit of abject diabolism seized the sports fans and worked its merry capers.

"And now please stand for our Wild Warriors!" cried the Grand Announcer.

Sausage-dog cowboys in fashionable black leather were suddenly ripping across the floor on their smoking dirt bikes. Their black ten-gallon hats were set off with chromium studs that matched the studs on their black chokers and black leather vests. Below the waist they wore G-strings, studded chaps and knee-high boots with pointy chrome toes. The Homeland Security, Inc. anthem began pouring out of the loud speakers, and the fans stomped their feet as the Grand Announcer called their excited attention to the celebration of absolutely nothing.

"Comparable," observed Vitaly.

Nabnak stared at the bat-hung figure of the Russian. "What's that?"

Vitaly explained that the character of the great questions of political science was comparable to the character of the human race itself. "The expression of these questions, like the historical expression of humankind, will change, but the essential character of the questions remains the same."

"Which is?" asked Nabnak, intrigued.

Vitaly cocked his head thoughtfully. "In terms of both character and expression, I speak of the essential underlying absurdity of thought, which, if I may borrow from the Bard, is the true 'Undiscovered Country.' Ah, but what is this essence if not *substance* itself! If you will, substance—*substance*—is what the world stands upon. Long ago, in some sage and antique land, it was believed that the world reposed upon the back of an elephant, which itself stood upon a dragon. But what did that dragon stand upon, indeed, if not thought itself?"

Bronson saw that Vitaly's sudden burst of suppositional activity had been excited by the ZR-7-12. His response was to call his agents to resume their march across the ceiling to that precise point directly above Eddie Allan.

The folks in the stands remained insensible to the sinister spies creeping above them. They were too wrapped up in the drama unfolding on the hill. The leather-clad sausage-dog cowboys had by this time run over the "Mr. Know-it-All" sign and were working on Eddie's arms and legs. They flew up and down the hill on their motorcycles, bouncing across Eddie's knees, spinning their tires against his staked-out hands. One sausage-dog cowboy stood on the foot pegs flashing and roostering himself before the crowd, but in his bravado he failed to notice one of the stakes, and as he blazed by his front tire was abruptly arrested and the proud warrior launched over the handlebars. He skidded down the hill, gathering his balance as he slid, and once at the bottom he stood up smartly, stuck out his chest, and waved heroically to the fans. The crowd whooped and cheered. Halfway up the hill another sausage-dog cowboy was suddenly enveloped in an instantaneous flash. The bike flew one way, he another. The crowd cheered, thinking it all part of the show. Then more explosions erupted around the hill.

Still no one saw the camouflaged figures working above the shifting haze.

While Vitaly and Nabnak dropped miniature hand grenades, Bronson opened Nabnak's rucksack and, mindful of gravity, removed the winch. It was a simple affair: a spool wound with thin steel line, a small motor, and a battery. The battery stored enough juice for one attempt. There could be no hesitation or error. Bronson pulled with his thighs to squat against the roof. He pushed the winch against the ceiling and threw levers that punched hooks through the fabric to secure the device. He took the line and clipped it to the loop sewn to the back of his jumpsuit. Then he un-twisted his cat-like form, unzipped a flap in the front of his jumpsuit, reached under his left arm for his .52 caliber automag, and hauled the weapon out.

It was a big shiny angular thing, like a Colt 1911 but with a bigger grip and a series of vents along the slide that resembled the exoskeleton of an abnormal sea creature. He turned the weapon in his hand to check the colored tape along the bottom of the magazine. The tape was red, indicating loads of super-dense, depleted uranium shot. Bronson easily hefted the massive weapon in his gloved fist.

"You ready?" hissed Nabnak as he watched a cold and cunning expression emerge across Bronson's face.

"Yeah." Bronson grabbed the gun with both hands, yanked the slide back—and then he kicked his boots off the roof. He swung down to an upright position, and dangled spread-eagle six feet below the winch.

Nabnak pulled himself up with his thighs and grasped the winch control. He looked at Bronson swinging before him. "Ready here."

"Let her go!" And as Bronson said this he dropped thirty feet… fifty… passing through seventy feet he caught the sweet odor of burnt methane, rubber and steel… one-hundred, one-fifty, two-hundred… he flew down at the hill with the automag exploding and kicking back in his hands.

The first sausage-dog cowboy to be hit had torn Eddie's wig off and was fooling to put it on top of his hat. The depleted uranium shot blew through his chest, and a cloud of red mist swirled and sparkled around the crimson body as it somersaulted back several times and slid to a stop on the hill. Another sausage-dog cowboy lost his bike beneath him. It burst into flames as he flung forward. His face met the spokes of a second bike crossing his path, and little chips of flesh and the mist of blood inflated through the air in a cloud of inglorious horror.

Bronson landed solidly at the apex of the hill, not far from Eddie. The folks in the stands quieted momentarily, though not a few laughed at the rapid way Bronson had suddenly landed with his long legs flexing, his amazing physique dominating the scene, the gun exploding and bucking in the air.

Half-way up the hill, two sausage-dog cowboys pivoted acrobatically on their front wheels and roared back down to the floor. Bronson raised the big automag after them—but a third cowboy from the other direction was suddenly rounding the summit. He flung himself off the bike and cut into Bronson around the thighs. The automag went bouncing down the hill as the two men rolled together. As they slid to a stop halfway down the hill, the sausage-dog cowboy managed to end up on top of the big agent.

There was no time to struggle with difficult emotions, though Bronson was aware of the distasteful impression he had of tattooed skin pressing against his face. Bronson grabbed the wild warrior by his bleached white hair, looped the metal wire around his neck and pressed him up like a barbell. The tension in the wire drew the loop tightly around the tattooed neck. Nabnak was working the winch from above, and the loop closed together, slicing through the sausage-dog cowboy's illustrated flesh and—producing a sound that revolted Bronson—clamping tightly around the vertebrae in his neck. Warm watery blood bubbled out from either side of his neck and splashed across Bronson's face and chest. Of course it was an altogether disagreeable situation, but there was nothing else to do except get on with it. If only. Bronson tried to throw the cowboy off, but the wire had sunk deeply into the bone and held tight. Bronson rolled on top of the tattooed, blood-gushing sausage-dog cowboy and yanked several times to separate himself. It was no use. At the same time more wild warriors were approaching. Bronson glanced about for his gun. How was Eddie?

Nabnak slacked off on the winch and Bronson saw that he could get to Eddie. Crawling on his hands and knees, Bronson dragged the dead warrior along with him. A few more grenades dropped from above and the approaching sausage-dog cowboys, roaring up the hill on their dirt bikes, were blown through the air.

Bronson drew a knife from his boot and cut Eddie's straps. Eddie looked dead but of course with Eddie you could never tell, and anyway Bronson knew in his heart that he was not too late, and what else motivates such gallant men if not faith itself?

Meantime, he was attached to the dead sausage-dog cowboy. The winch motor wasn't powerful enough to lift all three men, yet the wire was irreversibly stuck in the dead man's vertebrae. Bronson's friends had run out of grenades and were firing down at the ground with their automags. The grenades had been a better deterrent, and again up the hill came the sausage-dog cowboys, who twisted the throttles of their dirt bikes with growling menace, and croaked out to each other some kind of absurd rooster call. For a split-second Bronson enjoyed the thought that they were a bunch of morons, but such amusement flashes by swiftly in the midst of battle, and Bronson Bodine was indeed in the midst of battle.

Near the hilt of his knife was a sharp hook; Bronson brought it against the wire above the sausage-dog cowboy's neck and yanked. The wire snapped and swung away, leaving the short section of wire connecting him to the completely useless corpse. Incasing the dead body, the ugly tattoos were particularly ominous and suggestive—and far more grotesque than the coarse and lurid images that had actually been rendered by the hand of the tattoo artist. Death had consummated the act of self-abasement that had begun when the sausage-dog cowboy—whoever he had been—first sat for the artist's needle. And here the thing was—death wrapped in colored designs, death in triumph, a fantasy of skulls and naked women and gothic visions that held meaning for a base and uneducated man, rendered in scarring ink, and proclaiming little more than the death of a retard. Suddenly realizing he was locked in a ZR-7-12 reverie, Bronson twisted round, unfastened the wire from the back of his jumpsuit, and sprang to his feet.

Nabnak lowered the wire to stop it from swinging and Bronson caught it. While a new wave of sausage-dog cowboys roared up the hill, Bronson rapidly twisted the wire around his left arm.

Bronson stooped down and caught up Eddie in his right arm. Eddie's limbs hung in odd ways, and as Bronson raised Eddie's body against his chest, he could feel that his dear friend's ribs were badly broken.

Then there was a sharp tug and he and Eddie shot into the air.

The wire bit into Bronson's arm and he cried out as it cut through the fabric of his sleeve and twisted into his skin. With all his might he flexed his arm and the wire held fast, gripped with a strength that few men possess: ten years of breaking two-by-fours with his forearms had prepared him well. But of greater import to Bronson was the possibility that Eddie Allan might be dying. The stinging wire was nothing to this!

As they reached the ceiling, Vitaly took Eddie and began examining his unconscious form. Nabnak helped Bronson turn and push his boots against the ceiling. The spikes punched through.

"Is he?" Bronson stared at Vitaly as Nabnak unwound the wire from his arm. The blood was soaking into the torn sleeve of the jumpsuit, but Bronson shook free from Nabnak's attentions.

"That arm—" began Nabnak. Bronson couldn't care less about his arm. His thoughts were of Eddie.

Again he implored: "Is he?"

The tall Russian was reluctant to conclude his assessment. "I do not think so."

Nabnak slashed a hole in the ceiling and the escaping wind ruffled the fabric. He climbed through and took Eddie as they pushed him up. Bronson and Vitaly followed. The agents crawled rapidly away from the whispering opening and stood up in the warm Michigan night. Detroit cast a dirty yellow pall across the southeastern sky.

"Out of one dome," Bronson wiped the blood and sweat from his pointy beard, "and into another."

Fifty yards away stood the big Mi-24, rotors spinning, strobes flashing—here was their way out, the machine that would sweep them off and away. The smell of warm exhaust surrounded the men as they rushed Eddie toward the helicopter. They piled in through the side door and the craft beat into the air. The five-blade rotor wheeled and throbbed as the twin 1,500 shp Isotov TV2-117 turboshafts whistled an angry duet.

Inside the helicopter, a wiry Indian with a stone face and a waist-length ponytail—it was of course Chief Lonetree—helped the men slide Eddie onto a stretcher. Nabnak unwound the oxygen line and taped it under Eddie's nose.

Bronson picked up Eddie's eyelids. "Adrenalin!"

Chief Lonetree handed Bronson a syringe, and with a snap the needle was piercing Eddie's heart. The plunger rammed down. "We're going to have to get him out!" cried Bronson as he took a pair of scissors to cut away Eddie's tunic. What was revealed was not good. The skin across Eddie's chest was pale and jaundiced. The seam around his neck was inflamed and ulcerated in several places. Bronson took a scalpel and, beginning at the seam, cut down the sternum to the body's solar plexus. The broken arms and legs started flapping.

"Hold him down!" Bronson rocked back and the scalpel fell from his hand. He took another from Chief Lonetree, but then suddenly froze.

Nabnak saw his friend's face go blank. "Bronson? Bronson! You all right?"

"It's his arm," said Vitaly. "He's lost much blood."

Bronson winced and shook his head clear. "No." He half-smiled. "Sudden *deja vu.*"

"*Deja vu?*" Nabnak twisted his mouth to the side.

"Forget it." Bronson made two transverse incisions six-inches long above the solar plexus. "Irrigate the clavicle seam!"

Nabnak took a squeeze bulb and inserted the tip at several points along the seam below Eddie's neck. Vitaly was busy tearing open plastic bags that held small jars, strangely-shaped stainless steel fixtures, and lengths of clear plastic tubing.

Bronson began manipulating Eddie's chest while Chief Lonetree swabbed up the light flow of blood seeping from the incisions. A funny stink came out of Eddie's chest, like molasses.

"The unicellular membrane has ruptured." Bronson thought a moment. "Nabnak, more irrigation. Chief, hand me the circular saw." The Indian passed it to Bronson. "Turn your faces."

Bronson laid the saw against the solar plexus, squeezed the trigger, and cleanly pressed the whirring blade up the right side of the rib cage to the clavicle. Red blood and fragments of bone sprayed around the cabin. The first cut done, he made an identical cut up the opposite side of the ribcage.

"It smells like I'm getting my teeth drilled," Vitaly hissed through gnashing teeth. He held a short length of rubber hose. From it swung a stainless steel adaptor.

"Everybody?" Bronson stared round at nodding faces. He called up to the pilot, a determined young Mountie. "Slow her down. We're going to drop a few things." The Mountie's wide-brimmed hat dipped in acknowledgement. The helicopter slowed. Vitaly slid the door open and downwash from the beating rotor roared into the cabin.

Bronson raised the sections of ribcage he had cut from the body's chest and flung them through the door. Then he lifted Eddie's trunkless torso from the oozing bowl of the chest. A green umbilical with purple veins joined Eddie to the body. Bronson revved up the circular saw and cut it away. Vitaly handed Chief Lonetree a tube and then slid the body out from beneath Eddie. The body went overboard and Vitaly shut the door; the cabin once more muffled the sounds of wind, whirring turbines, beating rotor blades. The men felt the helicopter pitch forward and accelerate.

Bronson positioned Eddie on his side and attached the rubber tube to the umbilical stub. To the adaptor he screwed a filtering device contained in a glass jar. Chief Lonetree tied this in place under Eddie's stumped torso with an elastic cord.

Working methodically, Bronson hooked up a half dozen tubes and pouches to the open end of Eddie's torso. The various vessels were filled with powders, liquids, nano-materials.

And Eddie's eyes opened.

"Get the mask off!" ordered Bronson.

Nabnak pulled the artificial beard from Eddie's chin and then peeled away the smooth, flesh-colored mask that covered Eddie's face. Beneath was revealed a melancholy countenance of scar tissue blotched with patches of white and brown. The armless, legless, organ-less, scar-skinned man picked up his head and gurgled.

Nabnak placed a black plastic amplifier over Eddie's mouth and fastened the straps behind his head. The amplifier was the size of a small radio.

"He begins to speak!" cried Nabnak.

Chief Lonetree was rubbing his thumbs across his fingertips with shamanistic intensity.

"*Cgh-cgh*—" Eddie raised his head. His eyes seemed to light up as he beheld his friends. "*Cgh*—Bronson, Nabnak, Chief Lonetree—*hocka hey*! And Vitaly. Where is Syd Reilly? Ah! Of course, he is flying the helicopter."

Bronson shook his head. "Syd is off on a mission. Officer Chipper is pilot."

Eddie strained to see forward. Bronson assisted him, and the limbless ashman called through his amplifier: "Greetings to you, Officer Chipper. And thank you!"

The Mountie turned around and tapped his hat with a salute so tight and smart-looking that, for a moment, he was the envy of the staring men. Indeed, Nabnak was inspired to return the salute as the other heroes once more fixed their attentions upon Eddie.

Eddie's eyes were smiling. "And thank you all!"

"We'll have you back up on your pulleys in no time." Bronson readjusted Eddie's position and began wiping him off.

"*Cgh-cgh*—that tickles, friend Bronson."

Vitaly raised a paternal finger. He had completely lapsed into his Russian character. "Now, Eddie, no more missions for you. Never again do I want to live through what past twenty-four hours have been. You have nice wax museum and cave. That is where you belong."

Nabnak put his hand on Eddie's shoulder. "I agree. Remember, if you need anything done, *we* shall do it for you. You must help us take care of you."

Eddie made a noise through his amplifier that conveyed reluctant resignation. Above him, Bronson worked patiently. Eddie knew that Bronson would never tell him what to do. Bronson would never scold him like he was a little boy. "*Cgh*—tell me, friend Bronson, what have you done with the *boe-dy*?" Eddie said "body" in such a way that it rhymed with "toady" and perhaps in this way he regarded the human body in the abstract, as a kind of obsequious servant.

"Over the side."

Eddie laughed. "*Cgh-cgh-cgh*. Imagine the looks on the faces of the people who find it."

Bronson shared a smile with Eddie. "Something of a surprise, I should think."

"*Cgh-cgh-cgh-cgh-cgh*."

Bronson had finished wiping Eddie down. He tossed the towel aside, ripped his sleeve away, took another towel from Nabnak, and wrapped the towel around his bleeding arm. The skin was cut and needed a few stitches, but nothing to bother a man like Bronson Bodine. "Was your mission a success?"

Eddie nodded. "Indeed, I have made an important contact—"

Officer Chipper called back to them: "Niagara Falls, thirty minutes!"

Bronson studied Eddie. "Contact?"

"Have you—" Eddie paused and narrowed his eyes. "Have you heard of Patient Zero?"

"The pale man?" said Vitaly, suddenly concerned.

"Yes, friend Vitaly."

"The man with the poisonous body?" Nabnak shuddered.

"The very one," Eddie spoke with dread. "The poisonous *boe-dy!*'

Chief Lonetree hummed an ill omen, and then hummed again.

The agents stared at each other with blank and empty eyes. Patient Zero! It was much to take in, and as they contemplated the import of the revelation each man became lost in a maze-like apoplexy of private horror. One by one they looked away with Acheronian dread into isolated voids of ego death, and they cringed wretchedly as their shattered psyches fell through infinite depths of black waste, appalling nothingness and ultimate self-exhaustion, altogether helpless before the whispering voice of Eddie Allan:

"Patient Zero is a geneticist who has been at the vanguard of germ warfare research the past ten years. His particular specialty is viral toxins. Six months ago he succeeded in synthesizing 977-K, an airborne virus that attacks the genetic control centers of the human nervous system. Symptoms emerge as soon as four days after exposure. Test subjects have exhibited intense psychosis, intolerable pain, and extremely violent behavior patterns—*cgh cgh cgh*—followed by death in forty-eight to seventy-two hours. Patient Zero has been infected but is somehow immune; however, as 977-K thrives in the open air, if Patient Zero were to be allowed to leave his safety capsule and exhale the virus into the four winds—"

"Omega," sniffed Vitaly. The others echoed him. "Omega... Omega..."

Eddie nodded. "I have discovered his location. The Submarine Science Patrol is keeping him in the New Aristotle Abstraction Laboratories. Now, according to my contact, Patient Zero has discovered the antidote for 977-K."

"So why don't they give it to him and destroy this 977-K?" demanded Nabnak.

"Did you say *they*?" Bronson raised his eyebrows with indication.

"Exactly," said Eddie. "Friend Bronson has perceived the major obstacle to reason. As usual, it is *them*."

Vitaly closed his eyes and slowly turned his head from side to side.

Bronson became dry and professional. "Do you have a plan, Colonel Allan?"

Eddie nodded. "Indeed, Colonel Bodine. Fortune has smiled upon us. Patient Zero is in need of an operation for an inguinal hernia. Naturally, the world's surgeons are not anxious to enter Patient Zero's safety capsule to perform the operation. If, however, we could place an agent—"

Bronson interrupted. "The agent will require surgical skills."

"As well as laboratory skills," insisted Vitaly.

Nabnak sucked in his cheeks. He was reluctant but understood his duty. "An anesthesiologist will be required."

Bronson shook his head. "Negative. Too many unknowns. I will go in and operate on Patient Zero—alone."

There was a moment of shock, mixed feelings, hesitation.

"I object!" Nabnak spoke forcefully. "You'll be exposing yourself to the virus. And even if Patient Zero has discovered the antidote, you cannot be sure you will get it in time. Do we even know it works? I must be allowed to go with you."

"Impossible." Eddie's electronically enhanced voice was patient but firm. "Bronson is right. He must go alone."

Vitaly did not like it at all. "It will be a feat in itself getting Bronson down into the New Aristotle Abstraction Laboratories."

Bronson thought a moment, shook his head. Suddenly he smiled. "We will take it to the source."

"Meaning?" asked Vitaly.

"*Cgh-cgh*-Congress." Eddie's wise and noble eyes gazed into each of the men's faces.

Vitaly frowned. Nabnak averted his eyes. Chief Lonetree stared back at Eddie and said nothing.

Bronson was resolved on the matter. He withdrew to the back of the cabin. Chief Lonetree followed with a needle, suture, and a roll of bandages to treat his arm.

"Don't look so concerned, friend Vitaly," said the little, limbless ash-man. "Bronson is the agent for the job. Now then, why don't you please help me into my flight suit. I don't want to be embarrassed in front of the Mounties when we reach the cave."

The two men stared at each other and listened to the dull throb of the rotor. It was a lonely sound, a tired sound. Finally, Vitaly pulled a three-foot long silver mylar sleeping bag from Eddie's equipment chest. With Nab-nak's help, he slipped Eddie's subtended torso with its jars and tubes into the "flight suit." Over the right breast was sewn a ring-shaped plastic cup holder; just below, a spring clip dangled from a chain. Over the left breast was sewn the patch of some old and faded organization that people scarcely remembered. The emblem read "NASA." Eddie's eyes lit up as they zipped him in. He began talking about a model airplane he wanted to buy, and asked if they would help him put it together.

Vitaly was reluctant to relax and talk about model airplanes. He drew his automag, grasped it by the barrel, and shoved it at Bronson. "Getting into New Aristotle is one thing, but getting out—you will need this."

Bronson took the big angry weapon and examined it. The tape along the bottom of the ammunition magazine was blue, indicating exploding rounds. "Getting out of New Aristotle?" he inveighed. "At this point I'm concerned about appearing before Congress."

Vitaly nodded at the heavy weapon. "Politically-oriented people have a deep psychic need to submit to symbols of power and death." A thin, ironic smile tugged at his mouth. "So put on airs."

2. A Political Prophylaxis

THIRTY-TWO HOURS later Bronson Bodine sprang to life in his Washington motel room. He ignored the camera on the ceiling as he rolled from bed, slipped out of his boxers, and stepped into the shower. The centipedes and garden slugs in the stall were not overly unpleasant, but the water was gritty and oily. Advancing into the next sequence, he prepared breakfast, which comprised a carrot, a raw onion, and crackers smeared with a distillate made from royal jelly and gorilla mojo. Not strictly the vegan diet most secret agents enjoy, but Bronson was careful about what he put into his body, and the mojo was not farm-raised but taken from gorillas found naturally dead by the roadside. As he sat down to his repast he switched on the television.

There was still no news about the incident at the Silverdome, and as he smacked his lips Bronson thought it a shame his fellow citizens were kept in the dark about the true extent of unauthorized intelligence activity taking place inside Americo's administrative margins. At that moment two news-men were arguing whether or not the news media was responsible for the poor turnout at the polls. Then came product and service advertisements: urban scarecrows, NASCAR psycho-drama, Rent-a-Fool, antihistamines, appeals for jihad donations, medical hard-luck stories, boner pills, freak-out bags, passionate calls to end the heartbreak of racism, then a lengthy, indeed revolving, public service announcement from the electric utility announcing austerity measures in the guise of an encouraging "Bold New Connection."

Bronson looked carefully at the screen. He was sure he could make out split-second messages between the advertisements: "You're Ugly... You're Lonely... Dreaming is a dead end... Looking for a job? Give it up... Let them feel over and under your underwear... Coughing? No Problem..."

He shut off the television and washed down his wonderful breakfast by sucking the oil from the top of a jar of unhomogenized peanut butter. Then he went over to the mirror. His hair and beard were rather too long and thick to appear before Congress, that was obvious. His solution was to grab the peanut butter jar, pour what was left of the oil into his hands and use it to smear down his unruly tresses. He entertained mixed feelings about the effect, but there was a job to be done. He twisted a bit of the oil into the tips of his mustachio and beard. That did the trick, and he smiled as he admired himself in the mirror. Ah, but was *he* slicked down? That is, was his *brain* prepared?

Bronson hesitated. "Am I one of the tinfoil cap crowd?" He frowned heavily but then saw he was being hard on himself. After all, it was D.C. and even a strong-minded person could get caught up in the twinkling decrepitude of the deception. He unscrewed his toothbrush handle and out spilled a tiny triangular lozenge, the famed TT-21 mental prophylactic and perception wipe. Bronson eyeballed it closely, then ate it with an impulsive gulp. He felt better for talking the precaution. Things might seem a little weird for the next forty minutes as the TT-21 began working, but the side effects were temporary and he would be razor-sharp by the time he appeared before Congress. His thoughts would be his own, and that was the important thing.

He went to the closet door and slid it to the side. He had brought three uniforms with him. There was a Pittsburgh Steelers football uniform, an Air Force Colonel's uniform, and the scarlet jumpsuit of the Submarine Science Patrol. He finally decided upon the Air Force uniform since it was the least flashy. He thought it might be best to catch them off guard when he threw his fit.

Spies dress rapidly. He left the motel showered, slicked and shining, toting with him his .52 caliber automag and a twenty-seven by thirty-six inch artist's portfolio. Once out beneath the fat wobbly orange blob of the sun, he could tell the TT-21 was beginning to work. He raised the shiny automag and flagged down a taxi. It was a glossy 2027 Ford Country Estate Wagon with armor plating and shimmering springwire wheels—not very smooth castors to ride on but how they did resemble wire whisks! Toward the rear of the roof was a glittering clear bubble that housed twin .50 caliber machine guns. For an extra fifty bucks in blue scrip, Bronson sat in the turret and shot at the hydrogen filled barrage balloons that hovered over the city like a school of black whales. The taxi driver raised his fist and shrieked each time a flaming balloon flopped down: "There is no technology that can defeat a golf bag!"

The taxi roared up Constitution Avenue and then skidded with a shower of sparks onto Henry Bacon Drive. The metal wheels muddled in beautifully as the taxi bumped and twisted over the bright lime turf of the National Mall. Bronson had the cabby establish an orbit around the Zeitgeist Memorial, and deep inside himself he felt the splendid pull of right-wing extremist anxieties that were poignantly bizarre. When the expanding streaks of silver light at last appeared and smeared down the vault of the sky, he lowered the twin .50 calibers and chiseled into the granite effigy of Tomorrow's Zeitgeist as it slid off its regal cathedra. The bullets blasted away sharp bits of stone to reveal the form of a deeply frowning one-eyed octopus exuberantly bursting into green and poppy flames that danced and interlocked with the pulsating parallel beams of orange sunshine; and deep inside that fountain of shimmering lights and shining colors the silhouettes of the tentacles hypnotically swayed and cast long jagged shadows across the National Mall, some so black and dark they described chasms that plunged deep into the earth.

Bronson was fumbling with the machine guns and felt a sudden shock of alarm when he looked up and saw the stoplight, but then as the light plunged from red to green there was a flush of relief that restored his sense of gusto, and thus like a confirmed rumor the taxi roared into the unknown, at last turning off into a roundabout: the cabby tootled his horn in dignified triumph, and as deliberate as original light itself they were beaming across the Arlington Memorial Bridge. Bronson threw the cabby another twenty, and they rammed through the gates of Arlington National Cemetery. As the gates tumbled away and in Bronson's imagination turned cartwheels across miles of bucolic landscape, the taxi found the section of Arlington set aside for the Hessians, and here the vehicle bumped up on the lawn and turned a few doughnuts among the Maltese crosses, tossing them up through the air so they spun around for what could have been forever. But when an Apache helicopter gunship opened fire on the taxi, Bronson and his tireless driver (teeth clenched identically in both their mouths) blasted out of the cemetery. After a few close calls with opposing traffic, they managed to get the vehicle on the freeway to the Pentagon.

A few minutes later they screeched up to the prodigiously grand and venerable building. Bronson pulled the emergency strap and the plastic bubble popped up, rolled ingloriously across the metal roof, then fell against the ground with a hollow whack. Bronson grinned as he leaped from the turret. He tossed the cabby a fifty and goose-stepped away, easily keeping his balance on the oddly-tilting pavement. He scrunched his eyes closed several times while he marched closer and closer to the stately edifice, and as he collected his thoughts he was rather surprised to be here so soon. Something he just couldn't seem to recall was wearing off, and just in time.

Two Marine guards at the doors saluted as Bronson approached. He stomped to a halt and returned their salute, but found he was at a loss when he needed to remember how to talk. One of the Marines asked if he could help Bronson with his large portfolio. Bronson smiled and lifted his sleeve to show the portfolio was handcuffed to his wrist. Nodding discreetly, the Marines grabbed platinum rings and slowly hauled the splendid doors to the side. The first responder had arrived.

Inside was a murky and cavernous foyer. The ceiling was nearly invisible five stories above. Walls and flag stones, benches, the reception desk—the edges of the sparse interior fixtures were outlined in salt and pepper granite.

The doors shuddered as they closed, and from a single casement far above the tall agent streamed an angled shaft of blazing, mote-filled sunshine that fell upon the floor to illuminate an elaborate marble mosaic depicting the Pentagon's sister bureau, the United Dictatorships building in Nueva York City. Arrayed around the sweeping modernist erection were scenes featuring the great figures of world mythology. One panel showed Odysseus returning home after years of wandering to now behold his faithful dog Argos, who, upon seeing his master at long last, slipped into the shadowy mists of death. A similar panel depicted great Hades, god of the underworld, feeding his three-headed hellhound Cerberus a bowl of Purina Dog Chow, while yet another panel depicted John Rawls feeding Ayn Rand a bowl of warts, corns and toadstools that had been cut out of the feet of Slavoj Žižek.

The heels of Bronson's patent leather boots contacted the mosaic and, clearing his throat, Bronson delighted in his suave motion and his tall form as he soared over to the broad and proud reception desk. His sweeping approach was heralded by the enthralling *cha-cha-cha* of his footsteps, and he gazed ahead—both through physical space and through existential time—with a lively air. Now the words came trippingly off his tongue: "I am here to appear before Congress."

A blonde tart in a bellhop's uniform leaned forward. Her lipstick was smeared across her teeth and chin. "Which Congress, cousin?" She handed him a thin translucent card. The list moved up from the bottom:

Congress of Moral Thrift

Congress of the Exalted Bomb

Congress of Meaningless Labor

Congress of the Supreme Insignia

Congress of Commoditized Food Syrups

Congress of Elite Precedence and Entitlement

Congress of Lasting Fear

Congress of the Present War

Congress of Alleviated Sovereignty

Congress of Elastic Logic

Congress of Grammatical Regression

Congress of Inveterate Multipliers

Congress of Meaningless Intercourse

Congress of Topographical Subdivisions

Congress of Congressional Amplitude

Congress of Automated Transactions

Congress of Equivocal Pronouncements

Congress of Everything and Brain Control

Congress of Zombies, Warriors, and the Last War

Congress of Enmity and a Bone through the Septum

Congress of the Splendid Light of the Flat Screen

Congress of Burning Cities

Congress of Useful Idiots

Congress of the Righteous Path to Self-Destruction

Congress of Personification and Revenues

Congress of Tears

Congress of Horror

Congress of Strife

Congress of Weariness

Congress of Despond

Congress of Despair

Congress of Persuasive Hand Gestures

Congress of Flying through the Air with Satan

Congress of Power, Mountebanks, and Usable Forces

Congress of THz Waves

Congress of Sharia and Corporate Organization

Congress of Transnational Possessions

Congress of Skulls

Congress of Cultural Surfaces

Congress of the Noble Lie

Congress of Poets, Rock Stars, and Mad Scientists

Congress of Social Pregnancy

Congress of Community Resources and Dependency

Congress of Colonial Repackaging

"Ah!" He handed the card back to the woman. "The Congress of Pharmacological Property, please."

"Sure, cousin." Her chin shook nervously as she spoke. "That's room 43,372. Follow your host, please." Before her bony hands was a keyboard covered in what appeared to be cobwebs. Upon looking more closely, however, the cobwebs resolved into a mere trick of the light, and Bronson patiently waited and tapped his fingers against his portfolio, somewhat relieved to be feeling so normal. She typed the room number into the keyboard. As she finished, a door opened in the front of the granite desk. A small black box running on three wheels shot out and moved across the floor toward the elevator. Its voice was crisp and mechanical: "Follow me, sir… follow me, sir… follow me, sir…"

Bronson stared with mild amusement as it moved off. "I would like to stop at a drugstore along the way." Remembering his manners, Bronson added, "Please."

The woman smiled up at him. Her left eyelid twitched. "No problem, cousin. Good as done." She typed the instructions into her keyboard.

"Thanks." He nodded and rapidly walked off after the host.

The elevator was one of those spherical turbo jobs, and as he stepped inside he anticipated a quick ride. There was a strap hanging from the ceiling. He grabbed it. The doors snapped shut. There was a hissing sound and the elevator lurched backwards. It slid horizontally a few seconds and then dropped seven floors.

It stopped to pick up a man in an astronaut suit who was pushing a gurney before him. There was a hissing once more and they were off. Strange green goo seeped through the sheet on the gurney, and for a moment Bronson wondered if he should attempt to collect a sample for Eddie.

But the elevator was once more shuddering to a halt. The door shot open and Bronson's little host wheeled out. The corridor was crowded with people wearing uniforms of every nation and service. Bronson couldn't help staring at those who wore the scarlet jumpsuit of the Submarine Science Patrol. Apparently they paid no attention to him. In fact, everyone was busy following their hosts, which ran to and fro like angry terriers, keeping the people moving in orderly columns and often scolding those who sought to exceed or fall below the prescribed walking speed of three miles per hour. Bronson was a tall man and he could not abide the midget pace. He picked up his host and pushed through the crowd at his own speed.

"Put me down, sir." The host's little voice was prissy. "Sir, violating Pentagon corridor speed limits is a court-martial offense."

Bronson drew his automag and used the handle to hammer the host's speaker. No one paid attention, and he walked swiftly along with the host softly buzzing in his arms.

They came to the drugstore. Bronson placed the host on its back and went inside.

He went directly to the aisle that contained the hemorrhoid preparations. A General's aid was there carefully reading box labels. Bronson watched him. The aid chose and left. Bronson stared after him as he walked away, and then Bronson casually turned a complete circle to make sure no one was watching. All was clear. From an inside coat pocket he drew a box of TT-21 suppositories and placed them on the shelf. The box was printed like the most popular preparation and carefully sealed and wrapped.

Bronson walked to the exit mumbling, "From thought to essence to substance to something else to *someone* else..."

Outside in the hall he placed the host on its wheels to see which direction it went. He picked it up after a few feet, then weaving his awkward portfolio between bodies, his tall form moved swiftly down the hall.

The numbers above the doors were in the 43,300s now, so he knew he was approaching his endpoint. He slowed his pace somewhat and got ready. He fully knew what to expect. There would be the Network agents and their cameras, a few bouncers, groupies. In the age of digital editing, it wouldn't really matter what was said, and the Spectrum, Hegemony and Network agents on the Patient Zero Committee would be pretty loose and talkative. There would be some bipartisan posing, but that coming only from the Network agents. As their paystream came from syndication revenues, it was in their interest to create a sense of drama that the average bearded lady and dog faced boy in the street could relate to. Otherwise, it was going to be a happy-go-lucky free-for-all. An Hegemony agent might get on his high horse and rhapsodize the new spirit of global monetization, or a Spectrum agent might call for a prayer or denounce as ungodly those who oppose the policies of President Bones, but all in all it was going to be a meeting of well-medicated politicians busy digesting their breakfasts. Hopefully, P. T. Bono wouldn't be there. Not that Bronson disliked P. T. Bono—they were quite fond of each other, or so it was rumored (falsely, of course)—but Bronson knew the committee hearing room would be too small to contain their combined expressions of sanctimonious indignation. He simply wanted to get in, win approval, and get out.

"Bronson! Bronson Bodine!"

Bronson looked up to see a tall blonde body builder in a zebra stripe bikini. She carried five-pound dumbbells in her hands. Sweat dripped from her chest and forehead, and big wormy veins crawled up and down her arms and legs.

"Well, well, well," said Bronson, "Jolly Jill Jalopy!"

She smiled an honest, friendly smile. Bronson wasn't just another man. He was a regular guy, just like the cats on the Strip she pandered and puked with back in Tinseltown. "They're all ready for you, Bron."

"Gave them a show?" He pumped his right arm back and forth in a pantomime of arm curls.

"I'm America's sweetheart, the last word in easy-greasy-pie-on-the-sly. And as your secretary—" she winked, nodded sharply and raised her thumb, "—you got your thumb on the power plum."

Bronson so loved showbiz talk. "A famous appetite is better than capped teeth."

"You've got clout." She glanced down at his host and spotted the broken speaker. She nodded and chuckled in recognition of his style. "Listen, my own box is pulling away. Ta-ta, Bron."

His eyes followed after her as she caught up with her host. But he wrinkled his nose when he became conscious of the ridiculous smile on his face. It was really best to center yourself as star in *your own* movie, and leave the showbiz types to foist *their* movies on the dazzled masses—and yeah, yeah, yeah, as far as that goes, every spy for himself!

He turned around. Room 43,372 was just ahead.

He placed the buzzing host down, squared his shoulders, and marched inside.

Cameras began flashing. There was some applause. Many in the audience wore freak-out bags over their heads. A few patriotic college students in the back of the room lifted signs and booed. The signs read:

Don't Cure Our Hero, Patient Zero!

and…

Germs Are Congenital, Who Needs <u>Free</u> Medical?

and…

Scab Doctor Go Home!

Bronson ignored the rabble (most were inflatables anyway) and went straight for the table. He set his portfolio down and undid the manacle. Television cameras rolled up and lowered to allow him a clear view of the congressmen at their desks. There were twelve of them sitting in two rows, one row behind and slightly above the other. Bronson recognized them all and knew their affiliations. The chairperson, Representative Joe Pinty of Wyoming, picked up his gavel and tapped the crowd into silence.

"Good morn'n, Doctor Bodine." Representative Pinty spoke with a laconic western warble.

"Sir." Bronson nodded as he watched through the corners of his eyes for a raised pistol, or a throwing knife coming his way. By the wall some joker wearing a Billy Bones mask lifted a noose.

"First," said Rep. Pinty. "We'd awhll like to comment on the testimony of your secretary, Ms. Jolly Jill Jalopy, which concluded some ten minutes ago." There were a few hoots and whistles, which the honorable chairperson summarily gaveled away. He continued. "You have a fine lady, sir."

Bronson clenched his teeth and cocked his head either way. His lips moved quickly, trembling, "Thank you." There was a glass of water before him and he gulped it down.

The chairperson took a deep breath. "Doctor Bodine." He took another deep breath. "Doctor Bodine, you bring with you in this affair of Patient Zero a unique vision of Americo medicine. It is your desire, is it not, to operate on, uh, Patient Zero?"

Bronson wrinkled his forehead. "Yes," he stuck his lips out, "and I'll do it for free."

A strange hush fell over the room and everyone could hear the chairperson rustle through his papers. "Uh, Doctor Bodine—" He was lost a moment in thought. "Doctor Bodine, before I turn the questioning over to my distinguished colleagues, I would like to ask you a question."

Bronson stuck out his chest. "Very well, sir!"

"It is a question that I think is on everyone's mind, or, uh, in the back of anyway." He sniffed and scratched his head. "You see, Doctor Bodine. We all 'preciate your credentials and respect you for your many years of service with the Air Force and your contributions to aerospace medicine."

"Thank you, sir."

The congressman smiled back. "Is what we were wondering—I'm wondering anyway—is why a young doctor like you isn't taking advantage of your situation. I mean, wouldn't you rather be transplanting baboon hearts into human infants, or perhaps be the president of a chain of franchised clinics for surrogate mothers? You see, it just plain confounds me to see a young doctor with your kind of talent," he paused and glanced down at the camera, "not take advantage of the prosperity Americo is dyin' to bestow upon you."

The room was still quiet. Bronson leaned up to the microphone. "Sir, those jobs are best left to all the pharmachemical executives parading around the NIH on the backs of unicorns and those winged ponies with the big eyelashes."

There was general uproar, more gaveling, and then the chairman recognized Representative Felix Franz of North Carolina.

"Doctor Bodine." Representative Franz shook his head and frowned. "Your secretary has described, with enthusiasm, your plans for a private, off-the-shelf medical organization that would conduct operations forbidden by the World Health Organization with funds generated from the foreign sale of proprietary Americo medical equipment, medicine, and body parts. Body parts taken from convicts, I believe, was the wording in your proposal?" Bronson stared down the representative, who, after a brief paranoid flush, continued: "Now, what I want to know, Doctor Bodine, is why this peculiar organization of yours has selected Patient Zero for its first case?"

Bronson raised his hands and moved his lips mechanically. He paused, folded his arms and rocked back and forth. "These are d-d-dangerous times," he stuttered slightly, caught himself, and at last spoke forcefully: "The threat of Omega certainly warrants the attention of every conscientious physician. And action must be taken, for Bones' sake! Unknown elite forces seek global depopulation in terms of billions. Imagine what would happen if 977-K fell into their hands!"

Everyone started laughing. Some of the newsmen stood up behind their cameras and looked around the room. People shook their heads, exchanged smiles. It took a few minutes for everyone to get back into character.

Representative Franz cleared his throat and answered the big agent: "There is always the threat of Omega, always has been. Since 977-K is known to Zero alone, perhaps it is wise just to leave him under lock and key down there in New Aristotle. Whatever. The bottom line is that it is illegal for anyone, even MDs, to enter Patient Zero's safety capsule."

Bronson knitted his eyebrows together and with dumbfounded indignation quoted Alexander Hamilton: "It is vain to impose constitutional barriers to the impulse of self-preservation." His eyes became teary as he spoke slowly and deliberately. "Nine-seven-seven-K is a threat to the entire human race. Saving the life of Patient Zero is the only way we can save ourselves. He alone created 977-K, and he alone can create the antidote."

The congressman raised his eyebrows and with his hand motioned at Bronson. He turned to the other committee members. "Has this man taken upon his shoulders the salvation of the human race? I wonder, if we allow him to operate on Patient Zero, and Zero is saved, 977-K destroyed... I wonder, what happens then? It is a short step, as I see it, from operating on Patient Zero to socialized medicine!"

The crowd grew angry and Bronson turned to give them a dirty look. His only chance was to dominate them, establish the sadomasochistic relationship Vitaly had suggested back in the helicopter. He turned around once more and stared into the cameras. He knew how to use his blue eyes. "Right now, right this very second, even as we happily smack our lips and snorggle up our cheesepuffs and buttsteaks, our tacos and Moo Goo Gai Pan, our chitlins and our lumpy gravy—there is a man alone, in pain, and this country is doing nothing to relieve that pain." Bronson's fist hit the table when Representative Pinty tried to gavel him. "No, Congressman. No, Congressman. Just a minute, Congressman." Bronson pointed at him. "It is our duty as human beings—even more, it is our duty as entrepreneurs—to provide Patient Zero with every comfort our medical technology can provide."

"Whether this is or is not the case, Dr. Bodine." Representative Hugo Peters of Ohio shook his pen quite forcefully. "Can we allow you to risk your life, and let you risk incurring criminal status upon yourself by allowing you to operate on Patient Zero? Believe me, Dr. Bodine, we on the Select Committee admire your distinguished medical record, your taste in secretaries, and your sincere desire to perform surgery. But when the performance of that surgery violates the law—!" The distinguished Representative from Ohio shook his head.

Bronson screwed up his face and dangled his jaw as he anticipated his next line. He acknowledged their attention with a nod: "Any law which prohibits the saving of a human life isn't a law of humankind, but rather an idol of barbarians."

Many in the crowd were turning on to Bronson's sincerity. One by one the protest signs lowered at the back of the room.

Representative Franz spoke again. "Do you maintain—" he cleared his throat with irritation, "—do you maintain that Congress has no meaningful role to play in making medical policy? Are you secure in the belief that the World Health Organization will approve a diversion of funds for this clandestine operation?"

"No." Bronson sensed the crowd was with him. With a ripping motion he un-zipped the portfolio and pulled out a poster-size enlargement of Patient Zero's face. He placed the image in front of his desk so the cameras and Committee members could see it. "No," he said again. "I simply maintain that I will meet with Patient Zero alone, and operate on him anywhere in the world!"

A single tear hung from Bronson's eye, and when it fell the reporters had already begun writing: "It was so quiet in the room that everyone heard the good doctor's tear hit the table."

The crowd, reporters, groupies, everyone went out of control. Bronson drew his .52 caliber automag, racked the slide, raised the gleaming weapon above his head, fired—and the exploding ammunition blew craters in the ceiling. The sudden cheers were deafening. "Bronsonmania" had swept the committee chamber. People ran forward to hoist the good doctor on their shoulders.

The room was alive with talk of a new doctor series, Bronson haircuts, and the caduceus replacing the field of stars on the Americo flag. In the ensuing weeks, ninety-two Americo universities added premedical programs to their curriculum. Medical schools themselves fought tooth and nail for new faculty. The so-called "germ stocks" rocketed to historic highs on the Nuevo York and Americo exchanges, and playing "doctor" spread like an epidemic among children of all ages.

Everyone wanted to operate on Patient Zero.

3. Descent into Ascension

"MISS SWEETONION, DID you say?"

The young luscious round-bottomed brunette softly pressed her lips into a delicious smile. She began repeating herself, but Bronson couldn't hear over the howl of the shining Dornier 31 VTOL jet lifting above them into the bright Pacific sky. And at this point he did not care. It was enough to gaze at her pretty face. The wind from across the sea blew her thick dark hair around her head, and she seemed to delight in again and again pulling it around her back and letting it fly. Each time she released the thick tresses they streamed up at Bronson, giving off the scent of strawberries and mint. She was a slim woman with a pert round bottom, perfect tummy, hard breasts, and straight, attractive shoulders. Her blue jeans were faded and worn, but clean, close-fitting, and neatly frayed around the tops of her tan feet and the little daisies that ornamented her flip-flop slippers. Her blouse was a pale yellow smock and Bronson could see the brown of her nipples through the irregular weave. He looked from her nipples to the dark blue of her eyes, which coolly smoldered above high, slanting cheekbones. Her gaze was virile, defiant. Her nose was handsome, and she held it up like a proud Castilian; but the natural ballerina pout of her lips suggested Eastern Europe, and perhaps Belorussian was part of the mix. "And there is a sweet onion behind this rose," thought Bronson. He took her by the arm and struck off for the small superstructure at the end of the platform. The hovercraft she had arrived on was just then pulling away across the shining swells, a cloud of swirling mist obscuring the stern as the eye-catching craft accelerated and slipped quickly away.

The platform was two-hundred feet long by fifty wide, held in position by softly-purring stabilization motors. The floating structure faintly lifted and receded with the swells, resilient against the slapping waves. The sun was bare and white, blasting through the sky with its radiance. Rows of bright clouds drifted over every horizon, purpling with distance.

Bronson and Miss Sweetonion were inside now, climbing down a metal stairway.

"You have come over from Guam?" he asked. He took off his Ray-Bans and his blue eyes blazed upon her. She waited for his glance to fall to her figure but instead he watched her face. Nothing was conveyed by his expression but ease and professional friendliness.

"No jets for humble researchers," she said. "I make the trip twice a year. The hovercraft from Guam is the worst part. Shakes my teeth loose."

"Then you've been down to the labs before. Where are you from?"

"Santa Cruz. Took three days to get here. Can you believe it?"

Bronson smiled. "I left Washington twelve hours ago."

"Military priority." She sounded skeptical. Bronson thought it was probably his uniform. Evidently she had not heard about the operation.

"I've never been to the labs," said Bronson. "Let alone seven miles down." He shifted his doctor's bag as they walked along the hall. Just ahead was a door.

"New Aristotle," she said frankly, "is a nut house. There are people who've been down there so long they are afraid to come back to the real world." A delightful look came across her face. "I give them something real to wonder about."

"News items?"

She wondered if she was being too obvious, too comfortable, but she liked this mission. "Oh," she was matter of fact, "the worst part is the helium-oxygen atmosphere. Makes everyone sound like a chipmunk when they talk."

Bronson opened the door and followed her. The compartment they found themselves in was long and narrow. At the end was a heavy steel hatch with a wheel handle. Near it, standing behind a green counter, was a swarthy man wearing the scarlet uniform of the Submarine Science Patrol. He saluted with two fingers raised to the back of his ear.

"Miss Sweetonion. Ah, and Colonel Bodine!"

"Hi ya, Gomez." From the large bag over her shoulder she took her papers and handed them to the official.

He looked them over. "Everyone will be happy to see you again, Miss Sweetonion." He handed them back and took Bronson's papers. Everything was in order.

The somewhat officious but altogether pleasant Submarine Science Patrol officer moved from behind the counter and led them through the hatch at the back of the room. On the other side was a large compartment with an opening in the floor the size of a small swimming pool. In it the ocean pushed up and slid together, washing occasionally over the sides and across the floor. Floating in the center was a short yellow conning tower. The hatch was open. *Aqua Zeppelin* was written in black letters below the rim.

"It's like a dirigible," explained Miss Sweetonion, "but filled with gasoline instead of air. There are ballast tanks along the sides of the hull to make it go up and down. The passengers sit inside a metal sphere that dangles from the bottom."

"About five hours," added Gomez. "Seven miles is a deep dive."

Bronson gazed innocently into the woman's eyes. "Do you enjoy going down on the *Aqua Zeppelin*, Miss Sweetonion?"

She pressed her lips together and looked the other way. "I rather like the ride."

A gangway began lowering from the ceiling, and as the line played out it swung freely. With not a little effort at the winch, Gomez wrestled the gangway in place. Bronson and the woman crossed over, mounted the little conning tower, and climbed down the access tunnel that led through the gasoline tank to the sphere of the bathyscaphe. Following the tall agent, Ms. Sweetonion closed the hatches as she passed through them. Once inside the sphere, she switched on a light.

Bronson looked around. "Cozy."

There were no windows. A half-moon dinette dominated a good part of the wall. The rest of the sphere was divided between a sink, a small refrigerator, and a walled-off water closet. She opened the door and looked in at the head. "Yuck. I don't think it's been cleaned since the last time I was here."

Bronson set his bag down and picked up the microphone.

"Here, give me that." She took it. "All right, Gomez, we're in. Let her go."

Motors started humming and there was a bubbling noise. Gas started hissing into the room. "Oxygen and helium," she said. "Say 'good-bye' to your sexy baritone."

There was a low-pitch metallic *chung* and Bronson could feel they were lowering. She opened the refrigerator and pulled out two cans of Yucca Cola. The tops were dusty and she wiped them on her blue jeans. She sat down at the dinette and opened them. "*Salud.*"

Bronson took one. "To the blue-eyed."

"The paragon of the species."

"Where matter meets spirit."

She lowered the can from her mouth and licked her lips. "So tell me, man who likes our eyes." She chuckled once with a shrug. "You're no Air Force wonk. Why is it so important you get down there?"

He wiped his mouth. "Don't you watch TV?"

A laugh.

"I am," he lowered his voice and looked both ways, "on a secret mission."

"Not too secret if it's on TV."

"I appeared before the Congress of Pharmacological Property yesterday, but perhaps you thought it was a docudrama?"

She whipped a rope of hair back over her shoulder. "Yeah, that must have been it."

"I had hair like yours once. Long, thick, wild." He nodded at her.

"You don't look like the biker type."

They both laughed because when she said "biker type" her voice had become shrill. Then they both laughed again because their voices sounded like chipmunks.

"No—he, he, he, he, he, he, he, he! My big sister kidnapped me when I was a little boy and took me to live on a Buddhist commune in up-state New York. Then, with the Karma Squad hot on our heels, she took me off to live with an up-market witch coven in Wales. I didn't get a haircut for three years."

Miss Sweetonion's eyes glittered. Her squeaking voice made her sound more excited than she actually was. "What happened?"

Bronson sighed—it was a shrill whistle. He was startled for a moment and then continued: "The diet of chutney, hemp seed paste, and lentils nearly stunted my growth, but before any real damage could be done I was rescued by the group leader of a nearby Swiss monitoring station. Afterwards, he was my benefactor. In fact, he helped me get into espionage."

"Awwww…" she tilted her head. "That's awfully sweet."

"But he was too late in one respect. There I was, an eleven-year-old with all manner of wonderful posh witches to nurture me." He looked up as if to behold the image, then looked at her. "My CIA file lists only one weakness."

"Oh?" She was intrigued.

"Yes. Beautiful women in blue-jeans, with resplendent Pre-Raphaelite hair."

She shook her head, glowing. "You are a silly man, Colonel Bodine."

"Long flowing skirts will do also."

She was struck by his assertiveness. It was quiet for a few moments. He looked around the sphere. "Too bad there are no windows. I would like to see outside."

She silently marveled at his versatility, his confidence. "You can't see much below two-hundred feet anyway. Here—" She pressed a button on the wall and a small screen flickered to life. A circle flashed in the lower left corner of the screen. From it a series of "L" shaped bars, increasing in size, traced a pattern to the center of the screen. "This is like a window looking straight down. We will follow the path framed by these lines to New Aristotle, here at the circle." She watched him study the screen, then he quickly glanced at her and smiled cruelly, or so it almost seemed. His mouth, she thought wistfully, was absolutely brutal. He had seen enough; she switched off the screen and picked up her Yucca Cola. "It's a dark, cold seven miles, Colonel Bodine, the very bottom of the Mariana Trench, the deepest point in the ocean. Thinking about it gives me—I don't know— empty feelings."

Bronson leaned back. "I like it. Even unable to look out to gaze at the surrounding ocean, just knowing where I am makes me feel alive, safe, where I am supposed to be. I like being away from the society of my species,

Miss Sweetonion. I am not misanthropic, you understand. I just have other things, ahem, going on."

His allure was like a whirlpool, and she moved closer to him. "What are you going to do down there?"

"Save a man's life," he sniffed. "I'm a surgeon."

"What's so secret about that?"

"I don't know. No one else wants to, I suppose."

She pulled back. "Patient Zero?!"

"Ah, so you have heard something."

She looked concerned. "You will be going back in the tubes."

"The tubes?"

"You will find out. An outsider being allowed back in the tubes." She shook her head and lifted her can of Yucca Cola. "You really are a heavy."

"Tell me about the tubes."

"For such a big shot—never mind. The tubes are—well, you know how New Aristotle is made out of five Trident submarines welded together, four side by side and the fifth across the top?"

He nodded. "The labs are in the bottom four."

"Right. But the most dangerous experiments are in the tubes—the missile launch tubes. Those fools are investigating stuff so dangerous they conduct their experiments on top of Trident ICBMs. Anything goes wrong and they launch the experiment into space. Patient Zero is kept in the tubes. You will have to operate standing on top of a missile while some funny looking scientist holds his finger over the launch button."

"You've seen the tubes?"

"No. I calibrate and maintain the seismographic recording instruments housed in the top section." She shook her head. "Patient Zero. You ever pull any crazy stunts like this before?"

"No," he said quietly as he studied her.

She raised her eyebrows. "Honey, I thought we might... I mean, I'm not sure you're ever coming back now." Her chipmunk voice added a touch of farce to her doubt.

Bronson was lost in a bizarre calculation that sought to integrate their ridiculous voices, her changing mood, and his growing lust. He downed the rest of his Yucca Cola, and then took two more cans from the refrigerator.

"Here." She took them and wiped off the tops on her jeans. Her spontaneity impressed him.

They drank quietly. The conversation about Patient Zero combined with the effects of the helium had certainly spoiled the moment. Then Bronson thought he might try tempting her with his physique. He took off the Air Force suit coat and rolled up his sleeves. He watched her stare at his arms—his unusually hard and minutely-defined musculature took her by surprise, as he had anticipated. Then she stared at the bandage on his left arm. He saw the bandage was appealing to her maternal instincts. He pulled his tie away and dropped it across the table, then he unbuttoned the top three buttons of his shirt. As she watched him unbutton his shirt she bit her lip, then looked rapidly away. The quiet was full of questions. Miss Sweetonion was now staring straight ahead like a sphinx, her thick dusky hair falling down to the small of her back. There could be only one way to get the mood back. Bronson turned her head with his hands and then lowered his mouth to her blooming lips.

Their mouths met. They drank each other's thirst.

She pulled away, "We've only just met!"

"Sweetonion." He brought his teeth under her ear, pushed them across her neck. "We've only just been born."

The *Aqua Zeppelin* plunged deep into the Mariana Trench. Solitary in the vast waters, the bathyscaphe was a steel splinter piercing eternal darkness. The sperm whale and the giant squid alone shared the abyss, locked together in mortal combat, soulless forms of an angry twisting might. Currents carried through the trench, fingers of warm and cold that reached out to wind mysteriously through the sunless void. The bathyscaphe slipped over and between the currents like a mercury drop as it sank to depths deeper than the very bottoms of the seas.

New Aristotle stood across the throat of the trench at Challenger Deep, 35,800 feet below the surface. Sealed in a luminous carbon composite, the station was like a glowing nest of giant sea cucumbers, that most offbeat of pulsating marine good fellows, and a fitting bed upon which the Kraken might be found, as Tennyson says, "battening upon huge sea worms in his sleep." The weight of 1,118 atmospheres pressed against the reinforced hulls with a force of 15,662 pounds per square inch. Light itself was refracted by the pressure into oblique curves. The illuminated walls of the trench appeared to bend up and curve over the laboratory complex like the walls of a black cavern, while the narrow floor of the trench bent down in either direction like the slopes of a steep hill.

Inside the control center of New Aristotle, technicians monitored the progress of the descending bathyscaphe. As the craft approached a level 200 feet above the laboratories, they switched on the floodlights and the closed-circuit television. A voice over the intercom announced yellow alert and guards wearing the scarlet uniform of the Submarine Science Patrol beat to quarters.

Major William Shears of the SSP watched the compressed image of the *Aqua Zeppelin* lower out of the darkness. He turned to one of the technicians. As in the bathyscaphe, here voices were chipmunked by the oxygen-helium atmosphere. Shears sharply barked at the man: "Have Professor Budgie meet me outside the airlock." He checked his watch. "Tell him Dr. Bodine will arrive in approximately ten minutes."

The *Aqua Zeppelin* lowered steadily and was soon settling against the hydraulic cradles mounted amidships in the upper hull. Clamps swung into sockets and the cradles lowered into the section of the submarine that had formally carried missiles, now converted into a dock for the *Aqua Zeppelin*.

Professor Budgie arrived shortly after Major Shears, who was standing by the main hatchway with two of his men. The professor was a middle-aged man with pale skin and the wrinkles of one who worried excessively over trivial matters. Perhaps this was why he got along so well at New Aristotle; the trivial distracted him from the actual. Most people equipped with his considerable intellect would have figured out what was really going on here and left long ago. As it was, Professor Budgie had been down in the labs for six years without once visiting the surface. Besides a few incidental thoughts concerning Patient Zero, now he was concentrating on Major Shears, thinking how any policeman, no matter what his position, was a ridiculous, wind-up martinet. What an absurd uniform, and that salute! Why didn't everyone wear a nice white lab coat like him? He wiped his wrinkled mouth, raked his short fingers through his salt and pepper hair, checked his glasses for fog, and rocked nervously on his heels as machinery clanged and hummed on the other side of the hatch.

The bolts knocked out to the side and the hatch swung open. Major Shears and his two men raised their right hands and tapped the back of their ears.

Bronson stepped in with the big .52 caliber automag level in his hand. Miss Sweetonion followed toting his medical bag.

Bronson motioned for Shears and his two men to back up. He looked at the professor. "Are you Budgie?"

The professor considered the question. An abrupt flush of consternation appeared across his face. "Yes," he stammered. "Yes, yes, of course I am. Who else would I be?"

Miss Sweetonion's voice was absolutely shrill with helium. "Who would you like to be?"

Bronson caught a sparkle in her eyes he hadn't noticed before, or perhaps misinterpreted. But he filed this away as he motioned at the Submarine Science Patrolmen. "Gentlemen, I will thank you to unholster your sidearms and place them on the floor, please."

They did as he directed, Shears objecting, "Dr. Bodine, sir. After all, we are here to assist you."

Bronson chittered back. "First, you can stop squeaking. That will do me a world of good. And now, if you will excuse me, I have a patient waiting."

Major Shears put his hands on his hips. "One moment please, Dr. Bodine."

"What?"

"Your I.D."

"Why?"

A pause. "For your own protection."

Bronson pulled it out and handed it to the Major, who slid the thin card into a small box attached to the front of his belt. After a few seconds the box emitted a soft tone. A look of relief came over his face.

"You're a good egg, Dr. Bodine. Slick with a pistol."

The two men immediately warmed to each other. Bronson took the I.D. back and holstered his automag. He had made a good show of it. He was now sure of Shears' identity.

"What now, Dr. Bodine?"

Bronson suggested that the I.D. cards of all non-SSP personnel throughout New Aristotle be confiscated. "Just to keep everyone in their rooms while I'm here."

"But not mine!" The professor grabbed the little box hanging from the front of his belt.

"Of course not." Bronson smiled sportingly as Shears handed Bronson a box of his own, which he clipped to the front of his belt. A look of relief appeared on the faces of the second and third SSPs as Bronson slid his I.D. into the box.

Major Shears went to the intercom and ordered the I.D. confiscation. A few minutes later reports started coming back, and Shears gave Bronson the thumbs up.

"Well then, Professor, shall we?" Bronson nodded at the submarine patrolman, discreetly winked at the woman, and then he and Budgie left the compartment.

The narrow winding corridors of New Aristotle were lined with pipes and conduits. Electrical equipment hung from racks in positions of seeming irrelevance. Components were connected arbitrarily. Wires hung out everywhere, some evidently arcing to produce the faint odor of ozone that everywhere tinctured the atmosphere of New Aristotle. Shelves were placed in every convenient gap in the walls to hold spare parts, tools, instruction booklets, even brown bag lunches. As they moved along they passed SSPs who demanded to "plug-in" to Bronson's and Budgie's boxes for a quick check. To do this the SSPs would draw a coiled wire from their own boxes and insert the USB jack at the end into the sockets of the boxes worn by Bronson and the professor. The procedure always concluded with a neuter smile appearing on the faces of the patrolmen. But they never smiled at Bronson's or Budgie's faces, instead always at their boxes.

After the third check they turned into an empty corridor. Bronson closed the hatch behind him. "What's Zero's condition?"

The professor exhaled a studied sigh. "Stable. As yet he refuses to divulge any details of the 977-K antidote."

"I might do the same in his position." Bronson checked his watch. "Has anyone volunteered to assist?"

A shrug.

"I suppose I understand that too. What is it you do here?"

"Launch Supervisor."

They started walking again when two SSPs came down the ladder at the far end of the corridor. "I will be depending on you." Bronson followed Budgie through a hatch. "How is the capsule sealed?"

"There is an airlock in the side of the launch tube, then a hatch in the side of the capsule. A field of ionization keeps the air inside the capsule. The capsule itself is ten feet across, and sits on a fifty-foot missile. But what you really want to know is if I will order a launch if it becomes necessary?"

"No," Bronson said flatly. "What I want to know is how far you will go to prevent a launch?"

They had come to a stairway leading down. The professor paused at the rail. "We've never had to launch in the past. I don't know why it should become necessary now."

"Neither do I, Professor. Still, I have my concerns. Can you use a pistol?"

The professor scratched his head, examined his fingernails. "There might be a way around all this."

They moved down the stairway discussing their options. At the bottom of the stairs they found themselves in a long compartment running nearly the entire length of the hull. The scarlet form of a solitary SSP was at the other end, three-hundred feet away. He stood stiffly with arms akimbo and stared at them.

Set into the floor at seventy-foot intervals were four shinning round hatches that suggested the doors to a massive bank vault. Each led down to one of four hulls housing the laboratories. The professor led Bronson to the hatch at the near end. A stylized numeral "4" hovered above it, a hologram.

Bronson watched the professor work the hatch control. Suddenly it occurred to him that the professor was one of those people who never left New Aristotle. "How long have you been down here?"

"Just six years."

Bronson felt a vague need to be chummy. He looked down the long compartment and nodded at the hatches. "How are things organized down here? What is the classification system?"

"Energies. Final causes." A motor whirred as the hatch began rising. "Our subjects are reduced to theoretical paradigms that are determined by the ways the subjects interact with each other."

"The potential and the actual. Stasis and kinesis?"

The professor nodded. "The dialectics of energies realizing their full capacity: how they encounter and interact with one another."

"With a psychosocial and political emphasis?"

The professor looked down; a lunatic intensity tugged and ticked his face as he contemplated the culture of self-promotion in the knowledge industry to which he belonged. "Ostensibly. Ha, ha, ha. Ostensibly!"

The hatch was now fully raised and the two men glanced into the disquieting opening. Below it was pitch black, interrupted by the periodic flash of a strobe.

The professor explained. "The strobe will flash once every second. It slows people down. Among the tubes we take only a few steps at a time, secure in the calm of our motions."

They went down the stairway and the hatch closed over their heads. They were in complete darkness; the strobe suddenly flashed. Bronson drew his automag. A second later the professor saw the weapon. He chuckled, and Bronson caught the frozen image of the professor's mouth open in mid-guffaw. "The strobe makes you feel uncomfortable, my friend? But not to worry, come…"

Bronson saw several "pictures" of the professor with his mouth open in various ways, and then the back of the professor, then the professor several steps ahead.

Bronson followed—slowly at first to gauge the professor's stride. Then he moved steadily behind him, every second getting a picture of the professor's body leaning one way or another; and with each flash the walls of the compartment completely changed. Moving through such conditions demanded absolute patience and calm. In this way perhaps it was a good system, though Bronson did not think it was necessary.

"Turn on a light."

The professor suddenly stopped, darkness, then faced him. "Really, Dr. Bodine. I prefer it this way. Soon you will be accustomed. You won't even notice the intervals of darkness." Bronson didn't see the professor's mouth open during the flashes.

The professor was half-turned at the next flash, then several feet off. He walked more quickly now. "Relax, Dr. Bodine. It is easy. When I was a teenager I used to play with a strobe light in my basement. Didn't you?"

Bronson felt the desire to put him off. "I come from a dimension where people are never teenagers."

The professor was quiet for a moment, then he chuckled. "Ah! To a certain degree, so do I."

They moved on through a series of hatches and corridors, passing through compartments occupied by technicians who stood at their stations patiently waiting for the flashes that allowed them to manipulate their equipment. There were no SSPs down here but sometimes Bronson caught the frozen image of a pit bull running up and down the deck.

They moved on, finally stopping before a triangular hatch. Floating just below the ceiling a hologram rapidly flashed:

THE TUBES

Professor Budgie pulled a lever. The hatch split into three sections and drew apart. On the other side scenes from *The Exorcist* were shining on the curved walls. They stepped through and the projectors shut off as the hatch slid together behind them.

"The projections deter unauthorized personnel from entering this area alone," explained the professor with his heliumized voice. The strobe illuminated a mischievous smirk.

Bronson squeaked back: "Terror is an efficient means of maintaining order. There are no ambiguities, and it is easy to administer, particularly in a high-tech environment."

The professor agreed. "And we have very strict sexual taboos down here, too, as you might imagine."

To either side in the smooth round walls and receding in perspective were niche openings, twenty-four in all, which provided access to the capsules that stood atop the missiles.

"You do have, "Bronson asked, "the facilities to synthesize the 977-K antidote?"

The professor took a few moments to answer. "Were you aware that the formula for 977-K, like the antidote, is known only to Patient Zero? In fact, no sample of 977-K exists outside of Zero's body."

Bronson grunted, wondering what the professor was getting at.

"Would it not be more easy simply to—" The strobe caught the professor in a shrug.

"Launching Zero will not work." Bronson had already considered that option. "It would be too easy to send a spacecraft to pluck him out of space."

"Of course," said Budgie, "I—I am not a callous man, you understand?"

"Of course." Bronson grinned sarcastically and waited for the flash. "Who besides you can launch these things?"

"It is all done from right here: each missile has a launcher sub-station. Only I can do it." On a chain around his neck the professor wore a key. He pulled it out now, held it up to Bronson and waited for the flash. "You need this key to initiate a launch. Now, there is also a master station in the main hull, and Major Shears also has a key, but he is not authorized to use the equipment. Moreover, he doesn't know how to use it."

"He also has a key?"

"He is a Major in the Submarine Science Patrol, after all. Do not worry. It is taped to his chest. You would have to get his shirt off to get at it, assuming you knew it was there."

Bronson did not respond so the professor turned and led him into the niche that stood before Patient Zero's missile. A turning hologram hovered before the hatch:

BIOLOGICAL HAZARD
NO ENTRY

Bronson watched it rotate. The letters adjusted each half-revolution to face forward.

"You are very brave," said the professor, who stood by a small panel on the wall. Bronson decided this must be the launch control. He reached out and grabbed the professor's shoulder. "Come in with me."

The professor took several deep breaths. The strobe caught him in a series of pitiful expressions: confusion, fear, anger, loss.

"Professor Budgie?"

"Have I a choice?"

"Look at it this way," Bronson noticed their chipmunk voices were strangely feminine. "You really haven't been alive the past six years anyway."

"I—" Budgie winced as Bronson squeezed his shoulder. "I can't argue with that."

The grip relaxed and Budgie opened the hatch, which slid aside to reveal a small airlock. They stepped inside and the hatch closed. Bronson rubbed his eyes; finally, the confounded strobe was shut out. The second hatch opened with a hiss. Before them, illuminated in red, was the missile's nose cone. They looked down into the dark silo. About seven inches separated the curving wall from the polished metal skin of the missile.

The professor rubbed his hands together nervously, then grabbed the handle on the hatch before them. He twisted and there was a soft hiss. The door pushed open and they stepped into the dark capsule. The air inside was sour.

A circular fluorescent light flickered to life at the peak of the conical ceiling. Below it, Patient Zero lay unconscious on a soiled gurney. Bronson set his medical bag on the floor and began examining him.

Patient Zero was approximately six feet tall, hairy, and pear-shaped—his hips were considerably wider than his round shoulders. He was partially bald and the one-inch scar under his chin told Bronson that the man was in fact Zero. His pulse was very weak, and a cold sweat covered his forehead, chest and genitalia. The scrotum was inflated to the size of a softball, packed with intestine.

Budgie waited as Bronson completed his examination. "How is he?"

"Alive, barely. Hand me my bag, please."

The professor picked it up. Somehow the catch came undone. The bag burst open and CD boxes fell across the floor. Bronson and the professor looked at each other. The professor pushed his hand through the bag. "It is full of CDs. No instruments?"

Bronson put his hands on his hips and frowned. "My instruments must be in my CD case. Of all the luck." He sighed. "Is there a player inside the bag?" The professor nodded and pulled it out. It was a simple affair, twelve inches long with a four-inch speaker at either end.

"Don't let the size of the speakers fool you." Bronson selected a disk, *The Twelve Dreams of Doctor Sardonicus*, and handed it to Budgie. The professor put it in.

The music got things moving. "Those speakers do sound good," yelled the professor.

"What?" Bronson couldn't hear over the music.

The professor cupped his hands around his mouth. "What are you going to do without instruments?"

Bronson shook his head and yelled. "I don't play an instrument; I'm just into the music."

The professor gave up trying to talk, but then tugged at Bronson's shoulder when the tall agent pulled a fourteen-inch long bowie knife from under his suit coat. "What are you going to do with that!?" Budgie stared at the angry-looking knife.

"Don't worry." Bronson hefted it and eyed the edge of the blade. "I've successfully cut cataracts out of peoples' eyes with this thing. Got a lighter?"

The professor patted his pockets. He shook his head.

Bronson pursed his lips in thought and then rubbed the knife a few times under his arm. He set it down on the gurney and drew a felt tip pen from his pocket. He poked carefully at Patient Zero's abdomen and then began drawing esoteric symbols, occult diagrams, Hebrew letters, and, just to be on the safe side, a few formulae from the integral calculus.

The professor folded his arms. "Will that help?"

Bronson was rubbing the knife under his arm again. "Can it hurt?" He winked. The ink in the pen, like the fluid in his deodorant pads, was a disinfectant. "You don't happen to have a tarot deck on you?"

"Is that scientific?"

"No, I just thought if you got bored..." Bronson pinched a flap of skin over Patient Zero's abdomen and pushed the blade in. He tensed his arm and the knife moved rapidly back and forth. The skin sprang apart like rubber. There was surprisingly little blood.

The professor cocked his head at this. "Why doesn't he respond to the incision?"

Bronson said, "Pinch yourself."

The professor did. He felt nothing. "How is this possible?"

"The music player emits ultrasonic tones which depress the hypothalamus and amygdala. As well, the music suppresses the anxiety centers of the prefrontal lobe." Bronson continued cutting. The incision slowly dilated as the knife cut an opening in Patient Zero's abdomen. Soon the peritoneum was exposed. Bronson manipulated the shiny yellow sack, softly pushing on the intestines inside. There was extensive strangulation. He pushed his hand down towards the groin to locate the tear in the peritoneum. He found more knots, then found the spongy shaft of intestine that ran into the scrotum. He pulled his hand out. Things were going to get tough.

"Is there something the matter?" asked the professor.

"I'm going to have to repack the peritoneum." Bronson picked up the knife and began cutting the sack open. It was a tough incision demanding extreme control. One unintended slip or twist could cause the sack to rupture like a water balloon and send dozens of feet of springing intestine across the capsule. Bronson took quick sharp breaths. "There!" He put the knife down. "Not bad, if I say so myself."

He reached inside the peritoneum and tugged at the intestine where it poked through at the bottom. The scrotum moved back and forth, and then began shrinking as Bronson pulled the intestine free. When he had drawn it all the way out of the scrotum, he reached in with his other hand to feel around the intestines and the peritoneum. "I require your assistance, Professor."

Budgie moved around the gurney and stood opposite Bronson, who drew out a long coil of intestine and handed it to him. "Now walk back with it, slowly, as I feed you more slack."

The professor did as he was told and was soon doubling the intestine around his hands and arms like yarn. When it was all out, all fifty feet of it, and the professor's arms looked like they were wrapped in massive spaghetti, Bronson began putting the intestine back into place. He worked quickly but methodically, untwisting knots, massaging compressions, loosening impacted stools; in less than ten minutes the intestines were back in place and free to function properly.

Professor Budgie sighed happily, but grew concerned. "We've surely been infected with 977-K by now!"

Bronson shook his head. "We inhaled it when we first entered the capsule. But have no fear. Patient Zero himself will supervise the synthesis of the antidote—within the hour."

After what he had seen so far, the professor had no reason to doubt this. And there was of course no anesthesia for Patient Zero to recover from. In most cases, that alone was eighty percent of the post-operative recovery process.

Bronson looked satisfied. "Find the *Procol Harum* CD." The professor sifted through the bag and held it up. Bronson had the Professor stand in that same position as he unscrewed the handle of his knife and shook out the needle and suture stored inside. Bronson noticed Budgie had lowered the CD and was waiting for instructions. "No, no, no," said Bronson with mild reproof. "Hold that CD up and stand still until I say so."

The professor nodded obediently and raised the CD once more. He stood very attentive in this attitude as Bronson prepared the needle and set to work.

Bronson exhibited remarkable energy and self-assurance. The hole in the bottom of the peritoneum was sutured first, then the larger incision in the front of the sack. Bronson tore open the lining of his suit. Sewn inside was a quilted patch made of a white crystalline material. He placed this on top of the peritoneum. It began foaming around the edges.

"What's that?" asked the professor.

"Antibiotics, nutrients, amphetamines, vitamins, you name it." Bronson finished by sewing the main incision. It was done, and he shut off the music player with a snap. "*Voilà!*"

Professor Budgie was struck dumb for a moment; then suddenly realizing the miracle that had transpired before him, he began waving the CD with animation as he expressed his congratulations, "Bravo, Dr. Bodine, bravo!"

Bronson's lips twisted up in a nervous smile. He raised his hands to examine his fingernails. For a split second he saw Eddie Allan's approving glance, heard his happy laugh.

"All right." Bronson rolled his massive shoulders. "Let's move him out of here."

The professor was quite willing. "Can I put the CD down now?"

Bronson shook his head and directed the professor to follow with the CD raised. The professor complied as Bronson pushed the gurney out the hatch and into the air lock. The door behind them closed and the other opened. Once again they stood in the staccato world of the strobe light.

"What's in this tube?" said Bronson. He pointed at the hatch opposite. Rotating before it was a hologram reading:

POLARIZED SEXUAL CONTRARY

"Ah," said the professor. "Gnats."

"Gnats? Is that all?"

"Simple gnats." The professor nodded forthrightly, still exhibiting the *Procol Harum* CD.

"Let's get him in then. And you can put that down now."

The professor, hesitating slightly, at last slipped the CD into the pocket of his lab coat. For several moments he remained somewhat confused by Bronson's little joke; moreover—and he puzzled over this with some concern—he had after all remained attentive to following instructions. The assortment of conflicted emotions at last produced a momentary flush of anger; nevertheless, he just as quickly reasoned that if a man with a Robin Hood beard could leap through the political hoops and make it down to New Aristotle—no less wearing an Air Force Colonel's uniform—and then perform emergency surgery on the most dangerous patient in the world, then it was the least he could do to indulge that man's quirky sense of humor.

Budgie had operated the doors and Bronson was now pushing the gurney forward. Inside the missile were ten or twelve gnats bobbing rapidly up and down near the ceiling in a kind of mating dance. Bronson shook his head. "Gnats. You've corrupted the innocence of simple *gnats*?"

The professor kneaded his hands together. "New Aristotle was created to separate, study and catalog 'the energy' in all its guises."

Bronson thought a moment about what this meant for modern science. Could it be the vanguard of knowledge existed at the edge of—what was it?—at the edge of something comparable to a ZR-7-12 reverie? And what could check and balance this dream of pure ideas? Could it be the mental prophylactic of a TT-21 perception wipe? "Well then," Bronson sighed with intense reflection as he considered the dozens of cutting-edge experiments in the missiles around him, and at last pronounced the word, "Abracadabra."

Professor Budgie blinked his eyes at this, but there were more pressing matters. Bronson raised his hands to his mouth and exhaled as he considered his next move. At last he said, "It is time to inform Major Shears of our success."

Several minutes later they were sitting at the communications station near the entrance to the tubes talking to Major Shears over the videophone. They didn't tell Shears that they had moved Zero to the second missile. Shears himself was full of admiration and congratulations. "I will inform Washington that Patient Zero is recovering and the antidote for 977-K is forthcoming."

The screen went blank and the professor turned to Bronson. The strobe caught him with his mouth open. "Now we will see if your hunch is right."

Less than a minute later it happened. A shudder ran through the hull. There was a muffled bang, a pit bull barked once sharply, then they heard the creak and ting of steel under stress. Patient Zero's missile had been launched.

"And so, Dr. Bodine?" The professor steadied himself against an instrument panel. There were more creaking sounds.

"Come on," said Bronson.

Bronson and the professor moved through the stroboscopic corridors as rapidly as possible. In a few moments they stood beneath the heavy hatch leading to the upper hull. The professor moved the control lever back and forth. It clicked impotently. The door remained sealed.

Bronson spoke flatly, "Locked from the other side."

On the ceiling a blue warning light began flashing. "Well that cuts it," hissed the professor. "The *Aqua Zeppelin* is leaving the station."

Bronson cleared his throat. "At least we've still got Zero. Let's get back to the communication station and find out what's going on up there."

But back at the videophone they didn't get Major Shears—Bronson lowered his brow in a deep and dreadful frown—it was Miss Sweetonion. Her dark blue eyes glowed with a deranged passion. Often between her words she would press her lips together and let them spring softly apart. "Bronson," she began, "the seasons of love approach and pass with a pressing haste. As arms embrace they too must push away and reach out for new worlds. What I did was out of no spite for you. You were merely a tree caught in my Autumn." She pressed her lips together. "This is a recording." The screen went dead.

The professor was the first to speak. "A mere discharge of energy my friend, expending potentials, water seeking its own level. Do not let this trouble you."

Bronson ignored such trifling. She was one of *them*. He affirmed his authority, his rightness of action. "Ah! But we still have Zero. They will find an empty missile." Bronson envisioned a clandestine spacecraft rendezvousing with the useless Trident. "All right," he broke from his reverie. "Let's get back to Zero and cure this disease of ours."

They piled all the necessary equipment and materials on a two-wheel hand truck and went back into the tubes. They paused outside Patient Zero's hatch to listen to the creaking hull.

"Will it hold?" asked Bronson.

Budgie looked nervously around; each strobe flash framed a different expression of concern. "It should," he squeaked. "It is supposed to."

"Supposed to," echoed Bronson. It was both an appeal and a curse.

They turned and went through the series of hatches. When the last swung aside, Patient Zero turned his head and blinked his eyes at them. "Am I?"

"Alive?" Bronson chuckled as he wheeled the equipment up to the wall.

"Are you the doctor? I feel strange."

"Too well, perhaps?" Bronson reached down to check his pulse.

Zero picked his head up. "Then I've been operated on? Goodness. Thanks, Doc." Notwithstanding the distorting influences of the helium, he didn't sound like a geneticist.

Bronson scrutinized his face. There was something adolescent about his manner. "Don't thank me yet. I know you're tired, but you've got to help us synthesize the vaccine for 977-K. We all have it now."

"977-K?"

"Of course!" insisted Professor Budgie.

"But—" Patient Zero fought to hold down a smile—and then gave up. He grinned broadly. "There is no 977-K."

Neither Bronson nor the professor could answer him.

"You see," Zero explained, "977-K is, well, like a placebo. You know the old saying, 'The threat of Omega keeps the peace'? I'm not even a geneticist. I'm a computer programmer. It's my job to fill computerized information reference systems all over the world with little hints and suggestions—you know, little clues that the scientific community picks up on, becomes alarmed about. And before you know it the public is living peaceably under the threat of 977-K and the mysterious Patient Zero. It's really easy. You just grab a reference book, throw some fancy terms around, and *voilà!*"

The professor diverted his eyes from Bronson's knitted brow, and then pointed at Zero with stern accusation: "But it backfired on you."

"Yeah, did it." Patient Zero whistled. "When I got sick with the hernia and nobody came to operate on me—wow! Was I scared. But then thanks to you, Doc, you're the cat's pajamas. You saved me. You got guts. I wish there was something I could do for you. Maybe I could invent a disease and name it after you, then tell the world you cured it? I could pack the medical bibliographies with dozens of publications with your name on them. Or maybe I could get you another degree, or create a department for you to head at some major medical school—hey?!"

Bronson and the professor turned and made for the door. It slammed behind them. More confused than annoyed, Patient Zero shrugged, and then began sniffing his fingers.

"We have to get that hatch open somehow," said Bronson. He and the professor left the tubes and moved rapidly down the strobe-lit corridor.

"We could call again on the videophone?"

Bronson shook his head. "*They* are too thorough. Miss Sweetonion has most assuredly liquidated everyone in the main hull.

"Gas?"

"Perhaps."

Professor Budgie shook his head. "Poor Major Shears. I'll try to call up anyway.

The hull shuddered.

"It's worth a try," said Bronson. But then he had another idea. "Do you have any diving gear down here?"

"Not, er—"

"Well?"

"There is." The professor's mouth was dry. He sounded like a cricket. "But there is a failure coefficient of about sixty percent. We're seven miles down, you know. Without warning," he snapped his fingers, "you're flatter than a gingerbread man."

Bronson sniffed. "Let's just do it."

They found a technician who was certified in the Emerson DK-5. It resembled a medieval suit of chain mail impregnated with rubber. The helmet was egg-shaped; the large end was transparent and fit over the wearer's face, while the small end trailed back over the shoulders. An oxygen/carbon dioxide exchanger was strapped to the back and connected to the helmet by a thin hose. The texture of the suit felt uncanny between Bronson's examining fingers. The technician explained the suit was of a fractal design: the larger links were connected to smaller links, which were in turn connected to still smaller links, and so on all the way down to molecular scales. It was a tough material, but most of the suit's strength actually came from the ability of its interlocking surfaces to utilize the water's own pressure as reinforcement.

It was a bit small for Bronson but he managed to squeeze in. The professor regarded the way his muscular build distended the suit at the shoulders, and he wondered if this might disturb the suit's ability to properly distribute the pressure. The technician did not think that it would.

"How long do I have?" Bronson watched the technician smear an orange jelly along the helmet's flange.

"You have a good exchanger there." The technician nodded. "Is three days enough?" He and Bronson chuckled to break the tension.

The professor rocked back and forth nervously, his flashing profile shifting with each blaze of the strobe. "Enter through the bathyscaphe berth," he advised. "You shouldn't have any problems with the airlock."

"Can I swim in this thing?" asked Bronson. The helmet came down over his head. The squeaking voice of the technician was muffled. "Certainly not below 20,000 feet, which is the level of the abyssal plane extending east from the edge of the trench, while to the west the continental shelf rises to the surface. Throughout the region, the water is far too dangerous. There are currents that stream down and through the trench like windstorms. Divers who dare swim the open waters invariably disappear, dashed against the walls of the trench, dragged hundreds of miles over jagged cliffs and sharp pinnacles. In your left hand glove at the tip of the ring finger is a small wheel that controls the swim bladder. Keep it turned all the way clockwise. Don't swim off the bottom, and stay close to New Aristotle. You will find a ladder on either side of the top hull, between lab hulls three and two."

Bronson nodded and they led him to an airlock. He stepped in. A strobe flash froze Professor Budgie with his shoulders bent over; another flash caught his worried face gazing up as he searched through the darkness; the next flash froze his face in an expression pinched with doubt, while his right hand was raised in the initiation of a wave good-bye. Then a final flash revealed the professor smiling playfully. Both hands were raised, one waving, the other holding the *Procol Harum* CD. The hatch banged shut.

The water flooded in and warmed as it expanded in the chamber. But as the chamber filled, the water compressed and cooled once more. The helmet lights turned on automatically upon contact with the water, and Bronson could see folds pressing into the suit. To the upper left in his field of vision the head-up display showed time, temperature, pressure, depth, and compass heading.

The hatch above his head was swinging upwards into the open water.

He climbed out and stood on the long deck. The entire mass of the New Aristotle laboratory complex glowed a lurid green, illuminated by the phosphorescent material that was poured like concrete over the five hulls that stood alone here at the very bottom of the world's oceans. To either side, the walls of the trench curved up and around until they almost formed a roof, while the floor of the trench seemed to bend off and down, as if New Aristotle was built upon the summit of a steep submarine hill. And the strange refractive property of the water had its effects on Bronson's immediate vicinity as well. He looked down at his hands. They appeared a foot across, curving up at his gloved fingertips like the petals of a flower. His boots seemed tiny and far away. He had the uneasy impression that he was fifty feet tall. But most disturbing of all was New Aristotle. The five trident submarine hulls appeared distended and curving. The glowing concrete enhanced the effect, and Bronson found himself feeling dizzy.

Another shudder went through the hull. Through his feet he could feel the shock wave go back and forth as it dissipated. He turned and moved along until he found a place where the glowing concrete ramped down at a shallow angle. He walked down to the sea floor, which he discovered to be hard smooth rock. It was barren, sterile, seemed almost scrubbed—the swift currents, no doubt. He plodded across the smooth rock, concentrating on his breathing. It was an effort to lower his diaphragm. "Keep moving," he thought, "Keep moving."

He was near the stern of the hull, glancing up at the stumped fins, when it imploded. At this depth there was no suction. The enormous weight of the water snapped into the volume that had been the submarine hull. Bronson had heard a soft click, and before him now was a flattened stretch of black metal and glowing concrete wreckage fifty feet wide by four hundred feet long; just above, a large cloud of effervescence ascended into the darkness. It was so sudden and matter-of-fact that it made him gasp—and then with a wrenching sense of loss he thought of Professor Budgie.

The implosion of the hull wasn't without its effect upon the others. It took less than fifteen seconds before the upper hull imploded. A web of black cracks appeared instantaneously in the glowing concrete, and then the hull crumpled together into a jagged and broken wreck of black metal that dropped against the remaining three hulls. Blocks of glowing concrete tumbled and rolled to a halt as the sparkle of ascending atmosphere quickly dissipated in the darkness. The other hulls went quickly, one after the other, suddenly flattened against the sea floor like the first. A few pieces of glowing concrete had scattered, but most of it pressed softly to the sea floor, tracing with pale-green rubble the silhouette of the New Aristotle Abstraction Laboratories.

Bronson turned away. He felt remorse, but only a little. Because he had kept moving he had survived. The thought strengthened him. "Three days," the technician had said. Bronson had plenty of time. Without once looking back he marched to the side of the trench and began the seven-mile climb.

He knew that far above someone would meet him when at last he reached the edge of the continental shelf, activated the swim bladder, and kicked up into the glowing aura of the surface of the sea.

COLD ECHOES

TO TOWER AGENT NABNAK Tornasuk there was nothing so stirring as the sight of the two submersible hydrofoils beached on Nuku Hiva's black sands. Their forward manipulator arms were splayed out to brace the cylindrical hulls upward, as if the *Acrobat* and the *Stranger* were a cozy pair of prehistoric monsters that had crawled forth from the sea to pause in awe of the blazing sky. The surf rolled up and with a mighty grace crashed against the twin craft. The afternoon sun glared in the transparent spherical bows. The air rippled above the cooling exhaust hoods. Atop both conning towers sleek radar antennas rotated with determination.

Tower agents Vitaly Yurchenko and Bronson Bodine stood before the hydrofoils splashing sunscreen on their pale white hides. Both men were tall and powerfully built. Vitaly looked like a television wrestler, broad and bullish with a blond high-rise crew cut. Bronson, with a thick mop of black hair hanging nearly to his shoulders, a pointy Robin Hood beard and mustachio, and the slim waist and broad shoulders of a swordsman, vaguely suggested the image of a Renaissance mercenary whose ruthlessness had made the fortune of many a city-state.

Chief Lonetree was standing in the surf tying back his shining hair. He had been experimenting with the waves, testing their force, learning their timing, enjoying the psychic release of being tossed about by the earth's liquid skin. Nuku Hiva has no barrier reef and the ocean throws her trembling edge directly against the shore. Now the lanky warrior wiped the water from his eyes and positioned himself for the next curling wave, which came as if drawn up by a spirit, mounting higher, rearing. Lonetree threw himself forward and knifed into the wall of water. His body disappeared into the moving crystal, then he shot up behind the crest and bobbed there as the wave passed beyond him and threw itself at the beach.

Nabnak stared down at the crashing wave, feeling the cool water swirl and withdraw around his square feet. He listened to the foam sputter as it drained through the course black sand. He folded his arms and kicked at the water. Within him vague emotions rose and fell and rose again. "Waves," he softly said to himself. "Is this Einstein's cosmos of quivering gelatin? And what is this role I am playing? Me, in a world that never sees snow?"

"Nabnak!"

The Eskimo turned to see Bronson Bodine offering sunscreen.

Vitaly was running into the water. Bronson stared at him for a moment. The big Russian launched himself forward and disappeared into a wall of water. Bronson cheered, "Are you bathing, friend Nabnak?"

Nabnak was splashing on the lotion. "Think it's okay to take my glasses off?"

"With your brown eyes?" Bronson nodded. "For a few hours." But Bronson did not remove his Ray Bans from his frost-blue eyes.

Together they ran at the ocean as if they meant to beat it with their fists.

They hurdled the first breaker and the second. Five foot tall Nabnak sprang and careered, his thick legs propelling him over the breakers like a bullfrog. The third breaker caught Bronson and flipped him over, but Nabnak managed to clear it, and also the fourth. When the bottom was too deep to spring from, he swam about like a seal, banking around the curving surf, kicking up so only his calves were in the water, and leaping like a dolphin over his friends as they reached out to grab him. Vitaly caught his ankle and yanked him back into the water. Sweeping down in a fluid motion, Nabnak placed his hands against the bottom, cocked his legs against Vitaly's chest, and then snapped all his muscles at once so the big Russian heaved from the water and flipped backward.

Freckled surfers and finely-tuned Olympians have their moments, but you have to be a spy to really have fun in the water. The agents of the Invisible Tower splashed for an hour, diving through the waves, body surfing, exploring and practicing different techniques for drowning an adversary. Then they went for a six-mile endurance swim. They swam on their bellies with their hands firmly clasped behind their backs.

They were three miles out in the open ocean when overhead came an albatross, the tips of its long, narrow wings gently oaring the wind. It was five feet above them when Nabnak shot from the water and plucked a feather from its tail.

"Nabnak!" shouted Bronson. "Shame on you. Don't you remember the Ancient Mariner?"

The Eskimo stared blankly at his friend. Suddenly he remembered. His eyes bugged out. "With all my heart I wish I could give it back!"

"Nonsense," insisted Vitaly. "Are you feeling *guilty*?"

Nabnak looked unsettled.

"It's all right." Bronson watched the great bird disappear behind the waves. "It's forgiven you, I'm sure."

"Forgive!" Vitally spat a stream of water from his mouth. "Forgotten, maybe. How could a bird forgive?"

"Because it's the nature of life to forgive," said Bronson. Wanting no more to do with this conversation, he began kicking toward the shore; the others followed as if drawn by magnetic attraction.

But Nabnak felt he needed to do penance of some kind so he swam back to shore with the stem of the feather pinched between his upper lip and his nose.

As they crawled onto the beach Bronson suggested they scale the three-thousand foot cliff that followed along the shore. The other agents, panting from the swim, turned slack jaws toward the cliff, which draped down from the sky like an emerald tapestry. Ropes of steaming vegetation, vines, twisting palms and lush carpets of ivy and shrubbery clung to the cliffside. Jagged red rock cut forth from the jungle to form slanting pinnacles.

"Tell you what," said Nabnak, spinning the feather between his fingers, "Let's eat now and climb the cliff in the morning." He checked his thirty-two function spy watch. "It's almost six-thirty."

It was a popular proposal. A few minutes later they were reclining on their blankets, enjoying a delicious stewed salmagundi that included shiitake mushrooms, cauliflower, broccoli, royal jelly, and an olive-green ocean grape that Chief Lonetree had collected along the beach. There was an occasional cough as they gobbled down the healthful food, and a great *slurp*

slurp slurp and smacking of lips as they washed down their throats with subterranean salamander phlegm.

"You know, I really am sorry I plucked that feather," said Nabnak as he picked his teeth with a fourteen-inch-long Bowie knife.

"Consider the matter lost, immersed forever in the ocean of time," quipped Bronson. "But you have to learn to temper your enthusiasm." And he showed everyone how he could take a vitamin by sucking it down through his nose.

By now the sun was oozing down the west side of the sky like a sticky glob of orange oil. At a latitude seven degrees south of the equator, the sun sets rapidly. Soon its glow was reflected in a shimmering path across the sea. Bronson was using what was left of the light to read from *1001 Places No One Will Ever Find You*, a tour guide published especially for agents of the Invisible Tower.

"Listen to this." He sat up on his blanket and read aloud: "'Nestled in the lush Taipivai Valley stands beautiful Lemuria, visionary recreational development created by music industry illustrator Jon Yesterday.'"

I remember him," said Vitaly. "He did all those cover designs for Cough Casual, about twenty years ago. His subjects were space arks, mysterious obelisks, naked blonde faeries—that sort of thing. Not a bad artist, really. And he wasn't without integrity. He certainly came out against Self-Induced Slogan when they recorded 'Does Anybody Remember Laughter?' And Yesterday's goals were noble enough—"

Nabnak moved his hand with a flourish as he recited Jon Yesterday's famous mission statement: "'All the trials of excess and loss will be won if I may but create a cultural heritage for my species.'"

Bronson smacked his lips equivocally. "Now it seems he's developed his concepts into some kind of community." He continued reading: "'Begun as a single fiberglass amorphous egg-hut in 2019, fifteen years later Lemuria is a ninety acre, two-hundred room resort with facilities for scuba diving, sailing, surfing, rock-climbing, spelunking, hang-gliding, Reiki massage, improvised group drumming, interpretive dance, meditation, astrological investigation, past-life channeling, spiritual healing, and vegetarian dining. A psychedelic dungeon equipped with chains, whips, ropes, exotic oils, manacles, passion swings, rubber sportswear and blindfolds provides an elegant venue for progressive soul work—'"

131

"Soul work!" Nabnak started at the phrase.

Bronson glanced up briefly, "Sounds dreadfully psychological," then continued reading: "'Three world-class hydroponic gardens provide guests with state-of-the-art fruits and vegetables that have been genetically engineered for human digestive and nutritional requirements.'"

"I like it out of the ground," said Nabnak. The other three nodded.

"There is," continued Bronson, "'a theater called the "Dynamicon," spinning centrifugal booths for meditation and yoga, a sweat lodge, sensory deprivation chambers, and a disco with a computer-controlled light show.'" Bronson turned the page and looked up. "It's about ten miles from here."

"What's it look like?" said Vitaly.

There was a sketch of the resort in the book. "Sort of like a cluster of diatoms and vertical noodles," said Bronson. He passed the book to his friends.

"This is worth looking into," said Vitaly.

"It seems innocent enough," Bronson nodded, taking the book back, "but it's also the sort of place where our particular kinds of *friends* might be found."

"What else is on the island?" asked Nabnak. He wasn't in the mood to go looking for trouble.

"Well—" Bronson quickly skimmed across a page. "There's the 1,137 foot Vaipo Waterfall, but that's on our way to Lemuria."

Nabnak forced a smile. The horizontal orange rays from the sun enhanced his gentle manner. "Why don't we just make this an R and R trip? We could try some rock climbing up and down that waterfall?"

"Maybe," said Bronson, "but let's check out this resort, too. Who knows who might turn up?"

Nabnak shrugged. "Wouldn't it be possible to interrogate a plump tourist or a government official, and be done with it?"

Bronson and Vitaly exchanged a quick glance and looked away.

The surf rolled and hissed along the beach. A few birds straggled in, rising and dipping on the wind, and several winged silhouettes fell across the sun before passing overhead and disappearing against the face of the cliff that was now painted in glowing red. Bats were beginning to come out.

The four men looked to the setting sun, felt its dying warmth on their faces. Soon the big red orb pillowed against the horizon and sent aloft refracted after-images—a series of orange crescents that lifted upward and thinned to nothing as the sun fell behind the tense plane of the sea.

The stars winked in as rapidly, playing tag with their eyes.

"Let's build a fire," said Vitaly.

They combed the beach for wood. Nabnak found a hoard of dried palm stems packed beneath the brush that ran along the base of the cliff. He carried them to Vitaly who took charge of building the fire. Tearing the fibrous palm stems into strips, he set them together in a teepee, then held his lighter beneath the mass. A few fibers began glowing and he fanned them with the guide book. As the embers grew he fanned harder.

"No," said Bronson, walking up with an armful of wood. "You have to start with a tiny pile, get it going, then build it bigger."

"The wind's dying down," said Vitaly. "Have to fan it."

"No," said Bronson. "If you had a tiny fire you'd simply blow on it."

Vitaly bluntly said, "This works!" The fire began blazing in surges as Vitaly fanned.

"True enough," said Bronson. "But it's the principle. It's our campfire, our hearth. It has to be built with care and knowingly tended."

"It's just a fire," said Vitaly. He fanned at it sloppily.

Bronson grew irritated. "It's a matter of aesthetics, I suppose. How much you care."

Lonetree scratched his chin while Nabnak shook his head. Why did everything have to boil down to an aesthetic issue? And what had aesthetics to do with "caring," as Bronson put it, or right and wrong?

But the controversy was forgotten as the fire was left to its burning and everyone settled down on their blankets. The Invisible Tower was restored. Chief Lonetree produced his banjo and they entertained themselves singing songs like "Sun Watcher," "Crawl Out of Your Pupa" and "A Brief History of Religion in the West."

Overhead a billion stars rolled slowly across the sky. The cooling air was so fresh that each star in the Milky Way was a clear and distinct point, a single individual messenger obscured not so much by the multiplicity of whispering voices as by the sheer galactic vastness from which they spoke. Brighter stars could be seen for their colors, and silver-blues, coppers, violets and greens bedazzled the infinite heavens. The big white stars shone in the mirror of the sea, and the entire universe was a wheel that turned slowly to drop the stars behind the suspiring waters.

2

WITH THE DAWN CAME rain.

During the night a cloud bank had gathered against the cliff. Now as it slowly ascended with the morning wind it cooled and released its pent up moisture over the four agents rousing on the beach. They pulled their blankets over their heads and hurried to their vessels—Vitaly and Lonetree to the *Stranger*, Bronson and Nabnak to the *Acrobat*.

It was still raining twenty minutes later when the men emerged wearing camouflage ponchos and matching sombreros. They climbed down and waited on the beach as the mechanical arms came to life and dragged the submersible hydrofoils back into the ocean. When the two craft were fifty yards from shore air began hissing from the ballast tanks. The water churned up around them as they submerged. They sank rapidly to the bottom where they could dig themselves in and obscure themselves against the offhand chance an aircraft might spot them in the shallow water. In a few moments black sand churned up to the rain-spattered surface.

Satisfied the two hydrofoils were concealed, the agents turned and marched indifferently through the rain, which was steadily increasing. The clouds swirled gracefully above like themes in a meaningless epic. Against the mountainous cliff, the clouds took on the murky hues of bruises—brown, purple and dark-green. Further out they became olive-green and gray. The wind picked up and sheets of gray rain rose and fell and shot sidelong against the cliff, where in running waves the vegetation anxiously tossed back and forth.

The agents eagerly assaulted the cliff and made rapid progress. They found it unnecessary to traverse the narrow ledges, and rather ascended straight up the cliff face that in places pitched to an angle of eighty degrees or more. The many vines and branching trees provided excellent hand-holds, and Nabnak was neither bluff nor boasting when he observed, "Climbing a ladder couldn't be easier."

The murky illumination became a kind of twilight as they climbed into the clouds. The rain muffled to a hum. Everywhere sailing shapes of mist grew and turned and folded and sank out of sight. The vines and twisted trees appeared dark and alien in the dim light, while the red rock of the cliff was dark and shiny with rain—a color like spilled blood beneath the black-green of the vegetation.

Higher within the clouds the wind spun wildly. Sometimes it felt as if they might be sucked off the cliff. The rain spattered the vegetation like gunshot and occasionally the rain fell up. Once a shrub tore away beneath Lonetree's foot, but as he started to slide Vitaly caught his boot and shoved him upwards. The agents grouped together in a narrow concavity where they locked their arms in the vegetation.

"We climb the crumbled side of a volcanic caldera," said Bronson, shaking water from his brow. "All the Marquesas are of volcanic origin. Cliffs like this are common."

"You mean we're going to climb more cliffs?" Nabnak wasn't complaining so much as measuring the day ahead. Water had penetrated his clothing and was running down into his boots.

Bronson tilted his sombrero against the slashing rain. "These islands are made up of valleys separated by steep ridges that radiate from the center like spokes of a wheel. Once we're at the top we'll move along the ridges." Vitaly reached out a hand and Bronson gave him a pull up.

"This rain is ridiculous," said the big Russian.

Bronson was thinking the same thing. "The east side of the island is arid. When we get out of this we will dry out fairly quickly."

"A stroll along such brave ridges should prove a spectacle of rare beauty to the eyes, as well as a fount of cleansing wind most vivifying and wholesome to the lungs," said Nabnak in a facetious tone. Chief Lonetree, playing it coy after his own fashion, grunted several times in agreement.

The rain had slowed by a noticeable amount and they resumed their ascent. The conversation turned to the topic of mountaineering. Vitaly observed that climbing in the Himalayas was more trouble than it was worth, adding that the Andes were more beautiful. Bronson and Lonetree agreed. Peeling a twelve-inch centipede from his trouser leg and discarding its writhing form, Nabnak wrinkled his nose and said, "I like it wherever it's cold."

The rain abated to a light drizzle and the cliff rounded into a steep but negotiable slope where the vegetation thinned abruptly and gave way to forms fit for an arid environment. Spiny bushes, succulents and even a few cacti were scattered across the rocky slope. Suddenly they emerged from the clouds and above them was the vast, blue vault of the sky. They paused to gaze behind them. At their feet the clouds followed along the cliff in either direction to form an endless cotton pathway that was cut flat across the top by a stratum of warm, dry air. Beyond the clouds, the surface of the ocean spread out like a broad shimmering floor. The sea and the sky and the great expanse of the atmosphere formed a shining spectacle of space and light that lacked any apparent definition beyond what could be ascribed to such exploratory flights as find expression through the free and shifting imaginations of poets and painters.

The blazing sun was suddenly vaulting over the ridge before them. The agents put on their Ray Bans.

"It's nearly eight," Nabnak said as he looked back and forth between the sun and his thirty-two function spy watch. The others walked past, and he followed them up the slope.

As they moved along they stripped off their ponchos and rolled them into little wads they poked into their utility belts. Under their left arms gleamed stainless steel .52 caliber automags. Bronson passed sunscreen around to smear on their arms and faces. He was delighted to have completed the first leg of their trek across Nuku Hiva. He shook out his sombrero and replaced it. "Polynesia, gentlemen. We have arrived." His handsome teeth flashed in the sun.

For a moment Vitaly experienced those melancholy pangs of satisfaction known only to hermits and rovers. He slowly clapped his hands. "Polynesia," he said in tones measured and even, but not without animation. "So it is."

Just ahead was the round top of the ridge.

Bronson was marching before them and was the first to reach the top. Suddenly his tall form halted. His shoulders slumped somewhat. His arms dropped to his sides as he stood without motion in the wind.

The others reached him and discovered the source of his disappointment. Before the travelers were a fast food restaurant and a modern paved road. To the left, across two miles of desert scrub covered with goats and condo development signs, was a double runway jetport. A sleek Boeing 787 Dreamliner was just then buzzing in for a landing. The goats, intent on tearing away what little was left of the vegetation, ignored the big aircraft.

A wedge-shaped automobile whispered by. Another. Three more.

Subdued, scratching their heads, they started off down the road. Another car, this one a taxi, roared past them. The driver's face turned around and the taxi screeched to a halt. The driver hesitated a moment then backed up to the agents.

He poked his head out the window. "*Bon'our, messieurs.*" He spoke with a thick accent.

"*Bonjour,*" Bronson said. "*Taipivai?*"

The cab driver nodded, smiled. "*Votre argent Francais?*"

"*Non.*" Bronson pulled out a ten-thousand dollar bill and snapped it proudly with his finger. "*L'American.*"

The driver got out. "*Bon bon.*" He sprang around and opened the doors for them.

They piled in and the taxi sped off.

After banging up through the gears the cabby announced, "*La Terre a un axe incline.*"

"What'd he say?" asked Nabnak, whose linguistic knowledge included only a smattering of ancient Near-Eastern languages.

"The earth has an inclined axis," answered Bronson. He nodded at the driver. "*Comment cela?*"

The driver held up a well-worn pocket atlas. "*La Terre est rond.*"

"*Non, non,*" said Bronson, playfully leering. "*La Terre est la femme.*"

"*Ah!*" exclaimed the cabby. "*Vous desirer vahine a' Taipivai?*"

"What did he say?" said Nabnak, still unable to make sense of the conversation.

"He wants to know if we are meeting our girlfriends at Lemuria," said Bronson.

"Ah, 'soul work'" quipped Nabnak ironically, then revealing some knowledge of French after all, he smiled and cupped his big hands over his chest. "*Oui, my companions and moi voyage du la Source du Cosmos!*"

The taxi roared on, filled with ambivalent laughter.

The road followed the edge of the desert plateau. In the distance green ridges stood tall like the spines of giant reptiles.

The driver held nothing but contempt for the hundreds of goats foraging along the road, and he complained the time was coming to do something about the problem. He and other businessmen on the island were organizing a hunt to cull the goat population. They were destructive animals. Four of the ten islands in the Marquesas, he explained, had been completely stripped bare by the goats. But he was confident that this wouldn't happen on Nuku Hiva. He frequently turned back to face his passengers as he spoke, and, not a few times, nearly drove off the road. Though a Marquesan, in this way he shared much in common with his brother chauffeurs in Paris.

He became excited when Bronson pressed him with questions about the Taipivai Valley and Lemuria, and his pidgin grammar became too convoluted to understand. Vitaly then asked him about Herman Melville, Paul Gauguin, and Thor Heyerdahl. Did he know who they were? Did he know they had lived for a time in the Marquesas?

"*Ah! Oui!*" exclaimed the driver, and in French he went on to say, "And it would please you to know, sir, that these three gentlemen had often relied on this very taxi during their visits!"

He pointed out a mountain on the right. "*Tekao,*" he said, "*1,183 metre.*"

"Impressive," said Bronson. "*Impressionnant.*"

"That's about three and a half thousand feet," observed Vitaly.

The cabby turned to Chief Lonetree, who was sitting in the front seat with him. "*Marquesa?*"

Lonetree showed his bottom teeth.

The cabby pointed with his nose at Lonetree's hair and glanced back at Bronson. "*Vahine?* Ha, ha, ha." He faced forward again, shaking his head at his little joke.

Bronson was touched by this bit of irony. Here was a descendant of head-hunters—people who tattooed their entire bodies, grew long bushy hair or shaved it off completely—laughing at a lonely Indian's ponytail.

"Hey," said Nabnak. "While we got a cab, why don't we go check out Vaipo Falls. We'll make it to Taipivai in plenty of time."

"*Vaipo?*" asked the cabby. Bronson nodded. "*Oui!*" And the men flew forward as the chauffeur slammed on the brakes.

The car slid sideways to a stop on the narrow road, backed, and then roared off once more in the direction from which they had come. Soon they turned off the road and picked up a gravel route that followed a rocky ledge curving back and forth between the cacti. They shook along for a quarter-mile or so before turning onto a track of red dirt. They sped along it. To either side stood tall yellow grass with blue-winged blackbirds darting all about. Tekao Peak was still to their right. In five minutes they had driven half way around it. Turning then, they left the peak behind.

Soon the taxi was rolling off the road. It skidded to a halt at the edge of a deep twisting valley. The men pushed the doors aside and spilled out.

The valley was an enormous sculpture of color and space painted in a thousand shades of green and red. The shining blue of the sea and the glowing sky brought out the valley's depths and details. Frigate birds with blazing tomato throats and cormorants with flashing speckles floated in the updrafts, where they effortlessly shifted to and fro and lazily turned. From where the men stood they could not see the waterfall, but they smelled it as a cool sweetness in the dry wind.

"*Ah, ici,*" said the chauffeur as he pointed down a path between tall prickly bushes that waved in the wind. They started down it.

Bronson walked beside the chauffeur, the others following. They moved along quietly, feeling the wind and hearing it comb through the bushes.

From ahead came a flash as of sun on metal. Then a snort.

Bronson might have disregarded the flash, or interpreted the snort as coming from a boar, but together they made something click in his memory. He made a hand signal the others instinctively followed. Silent as cats, they dived into the bushes. Bronson cupped his hand around the chauffeur's mouth and dragged him into the undergrowth. They crouched silently, every sense tingling.

Then up the path stalked a ghoulish spawn more hellish than any of the devils that haunted the imaginations of Dante or Milton. They were horrible pink things garbed in ragged loincloths and threadbare tweed jackets with suede patches at the elbows. They were shoeless and were covered with barbaric ornamentation: shark teeth necklaces, rodent bone earrings, decorative scars. One even wore a Montblanc pen through his nose. They were four in number, and yet all seemed possessed by one common mind and spirit. Blood covered their forearms and ran dripping from their fingers as they pushed angrily forward. Evidently these four were an advance party. From behind them down the path came more snorting sounds.

Bronson estimated this second party of ghouls would remain out of sight for fifteen or twenty seconds. He made another hand signal. He, Vitaly, and Lonetree drew their fourteen-inch Bowie knives, while Nabnak yanked on

139

the stem of his thirty-two function spy watch and out zipped a thin steel strangle wire.

The first group of ghouls shuffled before them on the path. The Tower agents sprang from the bushes and straightaway thrust their knives into the monsters' backs. Nabnak's ghoul clawed the air as the Eskimo yanked the wire around its neck, pressed the thing into the ground, and then broke its backbone with his boot. It was over in the space of a breath. The agents silently dragged the dead ghouls back into the bushes.

The Marquesan chauffeur was crawling away in the opposite direction, his fine bronze complexion turning quite pale.

Bronson made another signal. The agents drew ammo clips marked with red from their utility belts and slid them into the handles of their stainless steel automags.

Up the path came the second group of the fiendish hell spawn. Blood was running down their arms; some raised their hands to their mouths and licked with ferocious abandon. Like the others, they gave a peculiar impression of being possessed by one common mind and spirit. There were nine of them.

Then the Tower agents rolled out. Bronson and Vitaly fell prone while Lonetree and Nabnak kneeled behind them. Together their guns roared and bucked up, dropped, and roared again. More than fifteen pounds of depleted uranium shot pumped into the ghouls' bodies and they flew back with a startling abruptness. Almost instantly they were a writhing heap on the dusty path.

The four agents stood up and mechanically holstered their weapons. Bronson shook his head with disgust. The sharp edge of loathing raised the pitch of his voice as he considered the urgency of the situation. "We've got trouble, Vitaly." The tall Russian didn't answer. "Well?" insisted Bronson as his gaze measured his friend's responses.

Lonetree and Nabnak looked up at Vitaly whose anxious eyes glared at the pile of ghouls. He inhaled. His massive chest heaved nervously.

"Well, what the heck are they?" demanded Nabnak.

Vitaly seemed to come out of a trance. There was a resolved loathing in his voice. "Paps."

"Paps?" asked Nabnak.

Vitally nodded. "Acronym for Provincial Academic Philistine: P. A. P."

Bronson stepped closer to the pile of corpses. He kicked his boot under one of the creatures, and as he rolled the thing on its back its mouth fell open to reveal filed teeth. "They seek out remote places such as this," explained Bronson, "places where they can remain undisturbed as they practice their abominable rites. Look at the way the shark teeth on this fellow's necklace have been threaded." He glanced up at Vitaly. "Through the *tip* of the tooth. And the blood on their arms—indications of a sacrifice."

"The Celebration of the Persistence of Tenure," Vitaly said softly, mournfully. "I've seen this before."

Nabnak peered nervously into the bushes. "Did we get all of them?"

Bronson nodded. "I think so—not that I want to go looking for more."

Nabnak pointed down the path. "Maybe one of their victims is still alive. We better go check."

Bronson bit his lip in dark contemplation. He stared down at the pasty-faced goons with an expression of profound revulsion. "No, they didn't leave anyone alive." Then he remembered their chauffeur. "Come on; let's get back to the car."

A few moments later they found him lying ten feet from the taxi, keys in hand, U-shaped teeth marks covering his body. Chunks of flesh had been torn from his face and neck.

Bronson thought he heard something. He drew his automag and fired into the bushes.

"Let's get out of here," he hissed. He snatched up the car keys.

They lifted the chauffeur and tossed his limp form into the trunk, then piled into the car and sped off with Bronson at the wheel.

"They travel in prides of between seventeen and thirty-five," explained Bronson. "They don't stray far from each other, so we'll be safe once we're out of the area."

Nabnak was counting on his fingers. "That leaves four to twelve. Let's hunt them down." Lonetree shook his fist to indicate he was ready.

"Negative," Bronson said flatly.

Nabnak tensely scratched his head, then pushed his fingers back through his hair. "What exactly are they?"

"Provincial Academic Philistines?" Vitaly smiled enigmatically and with disdain. "Knowledge of their natural history is not for the squeamish. I've been present at their sabbats. I've seen them gathered, rolling over on their backs like wolves exposing their bellies to the pack leaders. They're remarkably cruel to their initiates, bite them, starve them, rape them. They use a big metal rasp—" Vitaly held his hands two feet apart "—to file the initiates' teeth when they go through their various ceremonies. The process tears up the lips and gums. As time progresses and they become fully indoctrinated—and if they survive—all humanity is driven from them and they become the mindless brutes you've just seen. 'Dreadful' is an understatement. You might have noted their pasty complexions, their bleary eyes." He shrugged. "Comes from their nomadic existence, but it's also a consequence of their subverted humanity, which itself is the single basic principle of their collective psyche. Reports vary, but there is some consensus that their culture is characterized by ostentatious displays of respect, a barter system of esteem and emulation, ostentatious adulation, expressions of fanatical loyalty and undivided admiration, and the rehashed recollections—celebrated in their ghastly sabbats—of past triumphs and attainments reaching back into the dim twilight of collective human memory. The Invisible Tower has decided the best course of action when dealing with them is to use deadly force when encountered but otherwise avoid them. They are effusively erratic and unpredictable." Vitaly looked out the corners of his eyes as he slid a new clip into his automag. He hefted the steel weapon, fingered the cooling vents in the slide. "Hard to believe they once had human mothers." He shook his head and slapped the weapon into its holster. He stared out the window with vital introspection.

The taxi raced down the road heading toward the east side of the island. The road rose and fell, winding around cliffs and in-between bizarre formations of eroded rock. Soon they were driving among jagged green mountains and turning along the richly vegetated ridges that zig-zagged above the valleys. Some of the valleys were narrow and winding; others were deep and wide and afforded stunning views of the sea.

After driving for twenty minutes the taxi pulled off the road. "We walk from here," said Bronson as he stepped from the car and folded his map.

They followed him as he produced his Bowie knife and slashed a path through the thick invasive shrubbery that grew along the road. On the other side of the brambles was a thirty-foot drop off. Spreading below was a broad, flat ravine, walled-off at the other side by the heel of a steep, block-shaped massif. The ravine was dark and still, shaded by a variety of trees—banana, mahogany, balsa, pandanus, cypress, banyan, mango, kapok—all raising their leaves together to form an impenetrable forest canopy. Vines hung along the tree trunks and dangled in the air. Here and there gracefully curving palms had pierced the canopy to hold their gently waving fronds toward the tropical sun. The agents climbed down and moved quietly along the ravine, admiring the shafts of sunlight slanting through the leaves. A rich, musky scent made them dizzy, or was it the wonderland they strolled through? Ferns spread ten and fifteen feet across. Some were old and yellow with dry brown stems; others, bright green and silver-blue, were newly curling up from the loam. Large broad-leafed weeds, like giant tobacco plants, thrived especially in areas of dampness. Many of the vines bore a moss that hung sweeping overhead like torn draperies. The jungle floor was carpeted with a spongy material that was neither alive nor dead. Covering it were tree trunks in various stages of decay, smooth orange mosses, pale fungi, tangled weeds, brilliant orchids, and rain-washed networks of elevated roots. In places termite mounds rose like miniature mountains. There were spider webs five and six feet across. Red centipedes and green and brown iguanas clung to tree trunks. An occasional butterfly fluttered aimlessly through a sunbeam. Ants, beetles, walking sticks and roaches scrambled over each other in the endless chore of presence. And it all happened upon a topographical plane of reality that joined the surfaces of the trees and the leaves and the weeds and the rocks and the ground into one unified blanket of life.

Soon the agents came upon a little stream. The water in it was as clear and pure as the air. They kneeled to drink. It was cool, sweet.

"Hunh?" demanded Lonetree. He pointed to what looked like a mummified rat. It was dry, shrunken and covered with a thin beige film—not much more than bones in a fur sack. The legs were tucked in and the tail was curled tightly around it. Vitaly examined it, turning it over with a stick.

"What is it?" asked Nabnak.

"It's a Pap pellet," explained Vitaly, "Undigested organic matter coughed up by a Provincial Academic Philistine. It looks several days old."

Nabnak looked around nervously.

"Do not worry," ordered Vitaly. "They don't remain long in one area."

Bronson splashed water into his face as the others stood. "I wonder what kind of mischief the Paps could cause in a place like Lemuria?"

"How far are we now?" asked Vitaly.

Bronson played his hands through the water. "Where there's a stream in the Marquesas, there's a valley. Not far."

They got moving again and followed along the stream. Like children on a picnic outing, Nabnak and Lonetree ran ahead and pointed out Pap pellets as they came across them. About a quarter-mile further up, the stream was joined by a second that curved in from the other side of the ravine. The water began flowing noticeably faster and the Tower agents became aware of an incline. They picked up their pace. Blue sky shone through branches ahead, and then the trees suddenly parted where the little stream burst forth into space and plummeted down eight-hundred feet in a froth of mist and vapor, at last disappearing from view beneath the tops of the jungle trees.

Here then was Taipivai. It was a deep, ancient-looking valley with tall, rugged walls surrounding a stillness that went back to the beginning of time. In places the walls opened into narrow hollows, each sheltering a lonely silver waterfall. Slanting knolls raised over each other at the head of the valley, while further down across the floor reared strangely sculptured formations of rock sheathed in vegetation. And standing among these formations was Lemuria.

The settlement was built around the theater dome, the "Dynamicon" described in Bronson's tour book. Around it were a dozen main buildings connected by transparent tubes and swinging bridges. Some of the buildings were cubes, some were spherical; others were like mushrooms and sat above the ground on gracefully formed pedestals. Toward one side was a leaning tower built to resemble an abstract organic form. It was perforated with pore-like openings. Around the tower were crystal-shaped gazebos set in a half circle, while throughout the valley were little cottages with walls that curved down and flowed out around their elevated foundations like melted wax.

Beyond Lemuria was a long, narrow bay flowing in from the ocean. It curved gracefully between the valley's walls like a smooth watery promenade. Bronson let his gaze follow along the bay to the boundlessness of the Pacific. The sky was clear and he could see for many miles, but atmospheric conditions were such that the ocean melded into the sky without a horizon line. Floating out in the vague blue mass was a small, dark spot.

"A ship," said Bronson. The faces of others turned up from the wonders in the valley. Their eyes swam through the blue.

144

Bronson pulled a round ring from his utility belt. About the size of a quarter, the ring was a magnetic field lens, a device that combined a telescope's objective and ocular lenses into a single miniature unit. He held it a foot before his eye. The image was fuzzy. He flipped it over. "It's losing its charge," he said.

"When they go, they go quickly," said Nabnak. He handed Bronson his own.

Bronson raised the lens and turned it to focus the tiny image. He saw a cargo ship with a long, yacht-like bow and, at the stern, a tall streamline superstructure rising like the sail of a submarine. It was well out in the shipping lanes, but definitely on course for the island.

"Heading for Lemuria?" asked Vitaly.

Bronson shrugged. "It's too far away to tell, but it will make the island by nightfall." He trained the lens on the valley, slowly turning it to focus. He gazed over the buildings, the walks, identified what he took to be the administration center and the low translucent roofs that housed the hydroponic gardens.

"Have you noticed something?" he asked.

They understood at once. There were no people. Lemuria was deserted.

"Do you think those things got them?" asked Nabnak.

"The Paps?" Vitaly considered it, shook his head. "No. They wouldn't attack a settlement as large as this."

Bronson handed the magnetic field lens to Nabnak. "I wonder," said the tall, angular agent as he considered his next move. He seemed to turn over a doubt or two, and then looked up. "Shall we proceed, gentlemen?"

He led them over the edge where they discovered an easy climb. The vines and shrubbery provided ample handholds, though several times they found themselves lowering onto bare rock faces that forced them to re-climb sections of the ridge and find other routes of descent. But even this problem was overcome when Lonetree discovered a stairway carved into the side of the valley wall. They flew down it, taking two steps at a time, leaping over those not infrequent sections that had eroded and crumbled away.

At the valley floor the vegetation was much the same as it had been above, but here the sun reached everywhere with its rays. The leaves and fronds glowed with a luminous green and were edged with golden brilliancy.

In comparison to the heights of the ridges, the ground was sandier. There were noticeably fewer insects.

Bronson drew his automag and the others followed suit as they stalked toward the resort.

Along the way they came to a great stone platform thickly over-grown with vines, grasses and shrubs, and obviously many hundreds of years old. Bronson explained it was an example of a *paepae*—one of the foundations upon which the great ancient Marquesan families had built their wooden palaces. There were hundreds of them scattered throughout the valleys, and most had remained occupied until the end of the eighteenth century. Before the coming of the Europeans, each of the valleys had been a separate and independent kingdom. Protracted war had been carried out between the peoples of the neighboring valleys, with the various royal families sustaining grudges for hundreds of years, passing on wars, head-hunting and cannibalism from generation to generation—proof that the cold may echo even beneath an equatorial sun. Conditions hardly improved when the Spaniards arrived in the sixteenth century with their contagious diseases and their jealous religion. Though in deference to the Spaniards, the positive influences of these first contacts is proven today by the fact that the Marquesans are no longer warring with each other. Historians, and perhaps theologians, are best equipped to decide which contribution of western civilization—cross or disease—has exerted the benign influence over these islands. Over the course of the first half of the nineteenth century alone, the population of the Marquesas dropped from 50,000 to 20,000. When the French took over in 1842, the population plummeted by 1925 to a mere 2,000, who have since managed to triple their number, and who represent a splendid source from which to draw hotel staff.

As the agents padded deliberately forward across the sandy soil the bloody history of the place seemed to hang in the air, despite the gentle breeze, the swaying palms, and the fruit which fell so bountifully from the trees that it could rot on the ground undisturbed.

"A man could settle here and slam his door on the world," said Vitaly as he gazed up at a cluster of bananas.

Bronson had a moment ago noticed an appetizing land crab. He nodded. "I never put much stock in Genesis, but here it is: Eden. And it's a garden beautiful beyond the imaginations of the old Hebrews who wrote that book—but a garden that's seen as great a fall.

Lonetree frowned on all this, while Nabnak, wearing a knowing smile, made this observation: "The fallen state is just a state of mind. Do you think you're part of a cosmic conflict? Love the Earth and she will love you, even on the knife-edge of the unforgiving ice, as I can tell you. Really, Adam's problem was he didn't know how to negotiate with women. And so it is with such men who tragically dismiss all humanity from their women as well as from themselves, and who make the poor girls into interplanetary gateways, and moreover the unwitting subjects of their—if you will excuse my coarse expression—*soul work!*"

Bronson turned to his friend. "You are right, of course." His voice was strong, clear. "And you are a true American."

Nabnak straightened his shoulders and stood back. To hear such praise from Bronson Bodine!

They moved along between the trees, padding quietly, staring ahead, guns floating in their clutched fists. They were like four grim tyrannosaurs beneath the dazzling sun. Soon they were at the edge of the resort. The buildings were molded in PVC and fiberglass, materials that took readily to the exotic forms into which they had been molded. Upon close examination, they could see the Lemurians were very thorough in their attention to detail. The agents moved beside a mushroom house covered with clear vinyl veins that throbbed with pumping liquid, evidently a cooling mechanism.

"Looks kind of cheap, though," observed Vitaly. "Like a movie set."

Bronson nodded and pointed at the leaning tower angling above the tall and voluptuous palms. "Lonetree, Nabnak: please make your way to that tower and fix yourselves at the top."

"Anything else?" asked Nabnak.

"Yes," said Bronson. "Keep an eye on that ship."

Nabnak and Lonetree quietly sprang off and disappeared among the buildings.

"I saw the administration center from the ridge," said Bronson. "Let's find it."

Vitaly wiped perspiration from his upper lip. Concern tugged at his face as he looked about. "Strange. So quiet. So lonely. Empty of people, it isn't the artsy utopia described in the guidebook. More like a disturbing dream."

"But not yet a nightmare." Bronson smiled ironically and motioned forward with his automag clutched easily—but ready—in his fist.

They moved quietly, stepping deliberately, keeping low. Soon it became obvious the buildings were completely vacant, and so they came out from the shadows and strode upon the plastic paths that were molded and colored to resemble running water.

All the paths in Lemuria radiated from the domed theater, which architecturally as well as culturally represented the central hub of the resort. Next to it was the administration building. This strange structure looked like a lopsided Swiss cheese from which a large sundial sprouted fantastically upon slim tapering buttresses that undulated across the roof and down the walls. Not altogether stiff plastic, these extrusions pulsated with irregular motion, evidently the action of a pneumatic system of some kind.

The two agents circled the structure to survey it, and then entered by crawling through two of the many holes in the building's walls. Inside they found the roof was translucent. The shadow falling across the sundial was visible and the dial's numbers were molded into the ceiling. It was nearly four o'clock. Before the agents was a transparent table that bent down at the far end to thrust into the bright purple gravel that covered the floor. At the floating end was a touch sensitive keyboard molded inside the acrylic. The agents stepped up to it.

Bronson watched as Vitaly activated the keyboard. Very quickly something came up. Projected inside the table was a menu display listing all aspects of Lemuria's administration: finances, requisitions, guest lists, electronic mail and communication logs, and the production reports from the hydroponic gardens.

Vitaly looked up. "What do you think?"

"Let's have a look at the guest list."

Vitaly tapped a glowing line. An alphabetized list appeared and began scrolling across the table's transparent mass. The two agents recognized many of the names. Among them were famous musicians, artists, film-makers, writers, dancers, publishers, architects, and the charismatic heads of titular religions. Following each of the names were letters—either A, B, AB, or O. Some of the letters were followed by a minus sign.

"Blood type?" said Vitaly.

"Evidently." Bronson narrowed his forceful eyes. "But why should that information be listed here?"

Vitaly shrugged. "Medical background?"

"Perhaps." Bronson folded his arms. "But which of the guests have allergies? Which are diabetics? Why aren't these things listed?" He filed this puzzle away and suggested Vitaly try the reports from the hydroponic gardens, see on which date they ended. In this way they might discover the date the Lemurians disappeared.

Vitaly began—then Nabnak's voice was calling.

"Carry on," said Bronson. He pushed through one of the holes in the wall. Once outside he called, "Nabnak!"

"Here!" The Eskimo appeared running around the side of the theater.

Bronson drew his automag and paced forward to meet him. "What's up? Where's the Chief?"

Nabnak hooked his thumb over his shoulder. "He's back at the tower. We were watching that freighter. But it isn't a freighter, at least not below the waterline. It's a hovercraft. It's heading straight for the valley and will be here within the hour."

Bronson wheeled around and glared at the sundial atop the Swiss cheese.

3

CAPTAIN AHRIMAN AMBER stood fingering his oiled curls as he surveyed Nuku Hiva from the roof of the hovercraft's bridge. There was an air of dandified anger about the man, a presence of agitation, haughty indignation, a cozy familiarity with dissatisfaction. Occasionally, a broad, square grin appeared on his face, although it was as much a measure for admitting cooling air to circulate around his grinding teeth as it was a means for radiating mirth. Suffice it to say he was inebriated with himself. He was tall, gaunt and hawk-like. He wore a long and flowing coat of faded black leather, billowing silk breeches and python-skin jackboots. Around his waist was a scarlet sash that matched the ribbons in his long and shiny goatee. His mustache was shaved away beneath his nose, leaving two inch-long shafts that were wound tight with wax and rigidly fixed to curve out strikingly from his face. In his left eye was a large yellow cataract; but he couldn't be bothered by it now as he shook his head with exuberance and satisfaction.

He liked the wind blowing through his shoulder-length hair. He liked his big ship, the *Caprice Beyond Folly*, and he liked the spray that flew out from beneath the rubber skirt as her three-hundred foot length swept at fifty knots toward the jagged dark mass of Nuku Hiva.

Stuck in the sash about the captain's waist were two flintlock pistols with baby alligator head grips. His left hand lightly tapped one of the toothsome heads, while his gaze—as if following the movement of a falling leaf—left the island and settled on the beautiful red-haired woman sunning herself at his feet.

She was in her way a female Proteus, stubborn but easily malleable, and exceeding in that quality of being all things to all men. To the captain she was the saucy, lacquered lairhen, Jess Flatback. To the world she was the runaway wife of seventy-one-year-old Geoffrey Lamb-Baste, 6th Lord Tinkle. To Lord Tinkle, she was a shrug and a smile as he clipped a cigar. To herself, she was whatever she could get away with at the moment. Around her breasts and hips she sported a scant black bikini that was stretched tight over such fruits as only King Solomon knows how to praise. Her hair was thick and tangled and lay scattered around her shoulders like flames curling inside a furnace. Her face was like a sail, a bit weathered but fair in the sun, and fit for its purpose. Her lips were blood-gorged and pursed in a wicked smile. Beneath her wrap-around sunglasses her eyes were large, jungle-green and witchy. Amber thought of her eyes now, how he liked to be close to their half-open encouragement while locked together they played witness to the star-blown ancients of creation.

Now a sailor was crawling up the ladder at the rear of the bridge. His bare feet stomped heavily on the deck. He wore white silk breeches and, around his waist, a flowing black sash. Like his feet, his chest and head were bare, and his skin had the appearance of cadaverous leather. The steel cutlass at his side gave an impression of mechanical vitality, though the beast in his eyes was natural enough. Did he have a soul? Some principle of will or intellect? A raw landsman might believe there was something worthy in that wreck of a being who stood illuminated in the blazing sun, but Amber knew that man, like all his crew, was little more than a void of passionless hunger vaguely pressed into human form.

"Ar!" growled the captain when the sailor's eyes fell upon the woman. "What be your business, my little son—to get your *prince* cut off?!"

The sailor fixed his gaze on the captain and tapped his oily forehead. "The cargo haves the fever, Cap'n Amber. Mr. Trick sends me up ask'n wot's t'do?"

Amber snorted. He'd be damned if he'd lose money on this voyage. "Tell Mr. Trick, 'Hose 'em down!' That's wot's t'do."

The sailor tapped his forehead again, "Aye-aye, Cap'n," and slid down the ladder.

As the woman leaned up her red hair fell behind her shoulders like the folding wings of some Mesopotamian locust god suddenly materializing atop a ziggurat. She drew the sunglasses down her nose. Her green eyes shone with cold appraisal.

Drawn to the eyes, Captain Amber raised his booted leg and straddled her so his knees were at either side of her hips.

She slid the sunglasses back to cover her eyes. In ringing Sloan Square English she snooted: "Right. It's no wonder they're sick."

"Aye. That delay in Guinea might turn out 'spensive." He reached toward her face to remove her glasses. Her eyes were gates hiding something… keeping something out of reach. It had nothing to do with beauty or lust. Her eyes gave those things freely. It's what her eyes didn't give that so fascinated him. Perhaps because he possessed—or had smashed—everything else he had ever desired.

She reached up with her fingers and delicately touched the stands of bright red that blew across her brow. "I don't think the Lemurians will be here to collect the cargo. They said they were leaving by the fifteenth of the month. That was two days ago."

"They best wait," he said. "No one cheats Cap'n Amber and is left with blood for hearts to pump!"

Phrased melodramatically, she thought, but it was the truth. He was a deft and efficient killer. That's what this man was about, how he brought order into the world. She loved order.

"And what will you do if they have departed?"

He stepped away without further betraying his intentions. "We're calling land inside this quarter-hour. You go below and rest for my return." He adjusted the pistols in his sash and turned to leave. "By dark, there-abouts, I shall be back. Have me a duck roasted. Perfume well and freshen thy breath with butter."

He swung to the ladder, placed his hands and boots outside the frame, and then slid down the opening that led to the bridge. His predatory form suddenly presided over a wide rectangular compartment bordered by forward-slanting windows through which the glare of the sun's rays, cut off by the overhang, dazzled the floor and lower walls. Like animated skeletons dancing obliviously to the tune of accustomed habit, two dried-out sailors worked calmly with their equipment. One stood over the helm as he monitored the autopilot. The other stood over the chart table towing a pen carefully and slowly along the line of the ship's rapid progress. Mounted above in open racks were radios, direction finders and satellite navigation equipment. Amber strode to the chart table and examined the sailor's black line—the thunderbolt of Amber's intention striking at the underbelly of the island. He nodded and marched to the ladder. "Through the bay and straight up the beach, my children!" He gave them a nod and began descending.

"Aye, Cap'n." They spoke under their breaths, intent on their business.

Below the bridge was the attack center housing the ship's radar, communications, and fire control equipment.

"Lookout!" barked the Captain as he slid down the ladder.

The radarman turned his crooked nose at the captain. A gold hoop swung in his ear. "Aye, Cap'n. Clear seas."

Amber nodded. "And the sky?"

The radarman twisted a dial on his set. The screen altered, displaying a single contact. As the computer analyzed the contact, more specific data appeared in the corner of the screen. The lookout read it off:

"Aircraft at thirty-seven-thousand feet, twenty-one miles to the south, heading sou'-by-sou'west at five-hundred knots." The computer made a cross reference check. "Koala Airlines flight 221 bound for Sydney."

Captain Amber nodded and continued down the ladder.

Below the attack center was the engineering systems monitoring deck. The captain called to a large-boned Chinese with a sloping forehead and a cleft pallet: "Yak!"

The Chinese spun instantly from the panel he was watching, grunted "Yo-ho!" and thumped across the floor. He rolled like an ape as he walked, his ponderous arms swinging from round and powerful shoulders.

"Yak," ordered the captain, "Pump shotguns and cutlasses. Five of each." He continued down the ladder with Yak following. Once down two levels, they separated. Yak moved forward to the armory, the captain moved aft for the chapel. Their boots banged purposefully on the grate decks.

The chapel was dimly lit by tall candles standing to either side of the black marble altar. Displayed upon the alter was an inhumanly-large human skull. Behind it on the wall was a copy of the official portrait of the Reverend Billy Bones, the eye-patched jelly-jowled President of the Unlimited Corporations of North America, or Americo. In the center of his eye patch was a shining silver cross. One side of his mouth was drawn up in a folksy grin, while the other remained pressed together in a bloodthirsty grimace, the president's usual expression.

The captain saluted the portrait as he entered the chapel. There was a sea chest in the corner which Amber eyed angrily, and then he bent down before the altar. As his knees settled upon the patch of rug set forth for the purpose, a switch was activated and milky incense smoke began curling up through the skull's eyes and teeth. The effect was pure bunk and the skull itself was a meaningless idol—notwithstanding rumors it was an *Annunaki* relic— but such fabrications were things Amber could pray to without feeling like a hypocrite.

"Great Navigator of my soul," he began. "Hear my petition! I seek a great treasure beyond Earthly wit or ken, for which I beseech thee: steer me to my filled-in hole. Be it upon yellow sandy isle or gray city canyon, I have a powerful craving to dig it up. My arms are thy shovels. I butcher men for thy glory. My soul tops off the bargain. Thou art a measuring God. Give me high marks. Put me down in thy log for a hefty share. Deliver unto me a bright treasure: golden crowns, pearls, rubies, a mirror of blazing platinum rotating above my bed, and the respect of the community. Amen."

He held up his thumbs to display the scars that marked his blood oath.

The sea chest in the corner rattled once. The lid slowly raised and a robbed and hooded figure slowly stood to face the captain. "Amber," it whispered.

As his indignation began boiling, the captain slowly raised his knees from the rug and stood. A dagger slid from his sleeve into his hand. He well recognized the figure that was stooping slightly with its feet still inside the chest. Amber gestured with the dagger. "You," he growled. "Dost thou not know better to stalk up on a man in his prayers? One day I'll learn ye manners, monk."

The robbed figure raised his arms, his hands winnowed out from the sleeves. The hands, white as bone, reached up and pulled the hood back to expose a noticeably asymmetrical bald head. The monk's face was pale, mottled, and webbed with tiny ruptured blood vessels. Strangely enough, there was something youthful about his features, and in fact the man had not yet reached thirty. His voice suggested a distant wind: "I am having difficulty balancing my loyalties to you, Captain Amber, and my loyalties to the Synod. We are two days behind schedule. The success of this voyage—which is vital to the experiment being undertaken by the people of Lemuria—is of prime concern to Spectrum's highest echelon."

Amber was red in the face. "I was with William Bones when he ran a fifty-seat tent off the side of the midway; before you could genuflect, my little son. Damn you and damn the Synod if they thinks a better Cap'n can be found what runs this ship!"

The monk smiled thinly. "Your association with Billy Bones gives you powerful leverage, it is true. But know there are other elements within Spectrum, powerful elements, and they aren't so readily impressed with the recent success of Billy Bones or his maudlin Old Time Revival."

Amber spat and stepped forward. "I've killed men fer less'n that." He slammed the monk against the wall and raised the dagger. "I'll learn ye manners."

There was a strange passivity in the monk's eyes that made the captain hesitate, and then his murderous lust was gone—but not his anger.

Amber dropped the knife and pulled the monk forward. Again and again he pumped his fist into the monk's stomach. The monk became strangely limp as he accepted the abuse. Then his legs buckled and he fell forward from the chest.

"The Lord is with me, and don't forget it!" sneered Amber, and leaving the monk gasping on the floor he stormed from the chapel.

Yak stood waiting outside in the open air, his arms burdened with shot-guns and cutlasses.

"Come along!" barked Amber. They marched forward to find Mr. Trick.

At that moment the mate was at work on the deck supervising two sailors who wrestled with a fire hose. They had just sprayed down the cargo, and the hose was heavy with water. Big metal doors were sliding over the opening in the deck.

Mr. Trick was a pink-skinned Scotsman with a jutting chin and an angry forehead that angled forward from deep brutal eyes. His build was sailor-like and square, with long, hard arms that gave the fifty-six-year-old man a formidable appearance.

"Trick!"

The mate turned and leveled his indented brow at Yak and the captain.

"Bring two men, Trick." The captain didn't pause as he marched past the mate.

Trick followed Amber with his cold eyes, then looked past the captain at mountainous Nuku Hiva, now less than a mile away.

The *Caprice Beyond Folly* slowed as it approached the island. The stern yawed, carried by the ship's momentum. Damper jets shot hot gasses to the side to steady her course, and she rumbled smoothly into the long bay leading into the Taipivai Valley. Sea birds lifted from the water and swirled around the ship. In a few moments she was gliding her bow over the beach, where she halted.

The ship's six turbofan engines began whining down. At the same time, the flexible rubber skirt around the waterline deflated. Doors swung aside in the bow and a ramp rolled out to bang down on the beach. Two backhoe-equipped Humvees with Jolly Rogers painted on the hoods burst forth and roared for the valley's interior.

Standing in an open window atop the leaning tower, Bronson, Vitaly, Nabnak and Lonetree watched the approaching Humvees with disbelief.

"Piratemobiles?" Bronson said with affected wonder. The others registered his humor and gazed on.

The Humvees sped into Lemuria, their roar growing louder as they wound along the plastic paths. They looped once around the theater dome and stopped. Amber and his men jumped out with their shotguns swinging level. Amber hurried into the administration building.

"What do you think?" asked Vitaly.

Bronson shifted his large shoulders. "Wait and see. This is the first time I've observed Spectrum agents in the field."

Elsewhere in the valley other eyes—eyes not so civilized—watched Captain Amber and his men.

Moments passed and the captain crawled out of the administrative building. He dispersed his men. They walked cautiously through the resort, shotguns raised.

Nabnak wondered what they were looking for.

"Let's ask," said Bronson. He raised his voice. "Ahoy, shipmate! Proud captain there!"

Amber looked up and caught sight of the men in the leaning tower. Amber's men stopped in their tracks and looked up.

"Ahoy yourself!" called the captain.

"You'll not find a soul in the valley," said Bronson. "If that's what you're looking for."

Amber narrowed his eyes at this. "What else might I be looking for, thou tower-perched loon?"

"I am called Bodine, sirrah!"

"And your business, Bodine?"

Bronson laughed. "Presently, my business is yours!"

"Ar!" Amber lowered his shotgun and set his free arm akimbo. "Is thy business bloodshed and murder?"

Bronson cried back, "Aye!"

Amber pointed accusingly. "Is thy business terror and blackmail?"

Again Bronson cried, "Aye!"

"Thievery and torture?"

"Aye!"

"Rape and rapine?"

"Aye!"

"Lying to the ignorant masses, mind control and evanjackelizing?"

"Aye! Aye!"

Amber nodded smartly. "Then we are men not unalike. I be Cap'n Amber, the boldest human force in the Pacific. In yonder bay lies my proud ship, *Caprice Beyond Folly*. Come down from thy high tower and we'll draw articles."

"I'll hold you to 'em!" warned Bronson.

Amber boomed with approving laughter. "Aye, thou hast my affy'davy. Hasten down, me buck-o, and we'll splice hands on it!"

Nabnak expressed his doubt.

"It's all right," said Bronson. "He's as curious about us as we are about him. But you and Lonetree remain here and cover us. Vitaly, come with me."

Bronson and the big Russian climbed down from the tower. They marched toward the theater mindful of keeping themselves within sight of their friends standing at the tower window.

Bronson removed his Ray Bans and he pulled his sombrero back to hang at his shoulders. Shoving his black hair over his head with a proud swipe, he sauntered like a fearless cock as he approached Captain Amber. It wasn't difficult to conclude that Amber was a rash and explosive man. The best way to handle him would be through an overt display of confidence and command.

Amber had drawn much the same conclusion about the tall agent. He reached out boldly. "I said we'd splice hands."

Bronson took his hand. With narrowed eyes he motioned at their surroundings. "Strange how empty it is. I had anticipated a good trade here."

"And thy trade?" asked the captain.

"I have with me a cure of sorts, a device that heals the harmful side-effects of kundalini awakening." Bronson showed his teeth. The big blond Russian was like an unmovable wall behind him.

The captain narrowed his eyes at this, expressing both curiosity and skepticism. He nodded. "Aye, with such a device thou wouldst have done profitable trade with the exotic folk of Lemuria, who is plagued by their astral flights, kaleidoscopic nightmares, and such other grim fallouts of Godless meditation. But there's no custom here, d'yer observe? They is gone. Try Club Med on Bora Bora."

Bronson nodded. "My precise intention. Still," he glanced round, "can't blame me if I'm curious. I've been in these islands for three months and—" he paused "—forgive me." He nodded back at Vitaly. "My business partner, Vitaly Yurchenko."

Amber narrowed his eyes. "Russian, eh?"

Vitaly said, "American as any."

"That so?" said the captain skeptically. "Dost thou know who be the president?"

"Sure," said Vitaly. His accent was convincingly American. "Do you?"

Amber gestured with a mild flair. "Bold Bill Bones, I'm proud to say."

"And I'm proud to hear said." Bronson narrowed his left eye and snapped a big wink.

Amber laughed and smiled at Bronson. "Thou art a trump." And then cocked his head at Vitaly and lowered his voice. "But thou art a Russian, no doubting it, and an atheist."

There was no telling how Amber's mood might swing. A shark was more predictable.

"Never mind him," said Bronson.

Amber picked up his chin. "I never mind nothing. Have you business to discuss?"

"Yours."

"How be it so?" Amber had a dirty look in his right eye; his left eye—rather the clouding yellow star that had been his eye—stared blindly but held as much venom.

Bronson was biding his time, feeling out Amber. "My business? A proposition. The hire of your ship. That's all. Is it empty now?"

"What have you to put in it?"

"Something I found."

Amber appeared receptive. "Big, is it?"

"Yes. I'll need winches, tractors. I'll also need five of your men."

Amber was half-amused and half-impatient with Bronson's skylarking. "What is it?"

"I know I can trust you." Bronson pointed toward the interior of the valley. "An archeological treasure, worth millions."

"Treasure, eh?" Amber's long fingers slowly stroked his goatee.

Bronson was nodding. "A stone donkey with an eye patch."

Amber hesitated a moment. Was this an insult? He spoke slowly, "I know not where such an item could be profitably circulated."

"But I do," said Bronson.

Amber's fingers were slowly tapping the little knotted ribbons in his goatee. "Perhaps some other time, when my present business is completed."

Bronson raised his hands, feigning regret. "Another empty business dream, I suppose. I guess I side-tracked. You were about to tell me where the Lemurians were?"

Amber softly brushed his moustache forward. "No," he grinned mildly and appeared indifferent, but just the same Bronson could tell this was the issue that concerned Amber. The pirate took his fingers off his moustache. "I wasn't about to say a thing either way."

"Either way, you've said enough." Bronson's tone was deliberately taunting. It was time to wind up the situation, see what he might learn from that.

Amber was thinking much the same thing when he called out, "Yak!"

The Chinese with the cleft palate appeared around the edge of the theater and leveled his shotgun at the two agents. He was well hidden from the leaning tower. "Ah," said Bronson casually. "Your brother-in-law?" Then Bronson nodded back at the tower. Nabnak and Lonetree stood in the open window studying the situation with their automags in their hands. They had a clear shot. "Stalemate, as they say in chess. Could it be you met your match?"

Amber frowned, frustrated by the draw, but impressed, just the same, with Bronson's resourcefulness. Given a long leash such men could return profits.

Bronson studied Amber's face closely. He wondered if might ask the pirate if he could join his ship. He was satisfied that Amber was somehow the key to whatever had happened to the Lemurian people.

Then shots rang out. Amber and Bronson called for their men to cease fire. But when they saw two snarling Paps leaping onto Yak's back the reason for the gunfire became obvious.

Paps were suddenly everywhere swarming up the paths and over the roofs of buildings. They came howling, beating their chests, spitting like cats.

Bronson and Vitaly drew their automags and the big weapons blasted like cannon. Paps fell quivering, their filed teeth snapping up and down. Captain Amber cried "Ah ha!" as he blasted limbs off the ghouls with his shotgun. From the tower Nabnak and Lonetree picked off the Paps at long range, but they soon had problems of their own. Two of the ghouls had clawed up the underside of the tower and were lunging at them through the window. The Paps managed to vice their teeth down on the automags. Blows to their temples and eyes couldn't make the ghouls release the guns, so the agents lashed out with their knives. But the sharp blades merely taunted the Paps, who clamped their teeth more tightly around the automags and violently shook their heads. Nabnak jammed his knife blade into a Pap's mouth and attempted to wedge the jaws apart. Lonetree lost his knife and resumed beating the Pap with his fist, his knuckles scraping against the Pap's filed teeth.

By now Yak had thrown off the two fiends who had jumped him. They had ripped off his shirt and had torn great red gashes across his back. Bronson caught sight of Yak's bloodied form slash out with the cutlass and quickly hack down and behead the two Paps.

Mr. Trick came running past, a hoard of Paps padding after him like two-legged ants. His scalp was torn loose above his forehead and flapping back as he raced along. The other two sailors had died immediately when the fight began, having been silently pounced upon by the Paps as they had stalked toward the theater.

Bronson exhausted the last of his ammunition and began fighting the Paps hand to hand. He stood solidly, crouching low with his feet well apart. As the Paps rushed him he swung out with his fists to smash their jaws, crack their ribs and crush their eyes. His tall form moved with amazing speed. Several of his blows were instantly deadly, the Paps going completely limp as their flying bodies crashed against the ground. One of the ghouls howled with such vicious abandon that Bronson laughed as the thing leaned forward and charged. Bronson shot forward as it flew at him, throwing the entire force of his fist into the thing's forehead. The crack of its breaking skull was nearly as loud as a gunshot. The thing's forward motion was immediately halted and its arms and legs flew out in a reflexive spasm—it froze in place as the life force was knocked clear from the animal. Bronson spun away even as it crashed into the dust. Whirling and cracking a whip, a curiously squat Pap sprang off a roof, rebounded off the ground, and charged at Bronson. The sinewy agent drew his Bowie knife and dodged the whip as it snapped at his face and shoulders. The Pap's expression was pure desperation, and Bronson was revolted by its dismal character. Clenching his teeth, he stepped forward and explosively released the knife. The blade flashed, split through the ghoul's brow, and stuck. The whip slipped from the thing's hand. For a moment the squat figure struggled to straighten tall, then it stiffened and fell back against the earth.

Vitaly and Amber were also out of ammunition. Vitaly grabbed a Pap by the neck, squeezed its throat shut with his hands—compressing the thing's wretched neck nearly down to the vertebrae—and then swung the body furiously side to side to club the ghouls away with its flailing legs. Amber slashed out with his cutlass, sweeping it back and forth like a baton, tearing open their bellies, clipping their skulls, hacking at the sides of their arms and shoulders. Amber was particularly adept at snapping his cutlass to fling the crimson gore into the faces of the charging Paps. Before the theater was an undulating scene of mad fury, shrill cries, death shrieks, ripped flesh, flying blood.

Mr. Trick managed to climb to the roof of a gazebo. He was turning around at the pinnacle of the steep round roof as he lanced his cutlass down at the Paps and fed them steel. He would last for the time being, but his survival depended on the success of the others. With his free hand he wiped the blood from his eyes. He discovered the extent of his injury and reached grimly to clutch his scalp in place, meanwhile swinging the cutlass at the Paps as they spit at his face and clawed up the roof.

Now Nabnak and Lonetree were throwing dripping red torsos from the tower. Catching their breaths, they stared down with satisfaction as the two Paps impacted the ground and remained still. Then once more the two agents were picking off Paps at long range. The roar of the automags echoed like thunder across the valley.

The gunfire from the leaning tower was directed at the gazebo and the Paps began dropping off. Mr. Trick was clutching his torn scalp with a curious sort of indifference. With much satisfaction he viewed the Paps' bodies disfigure in cruel ways as the bullets slapped into their bodies and exploded.

The cooling sun lowered as the battle raged. The shadow of the western ridge rose across the opposite wall of the valley. To the men who fought, the shadow seemed to climb up the valley wall almost instantly.

The worst of the fighting—and the realization came like a dull shock— was over. Bronson saw his hands were torn and bleeding. There was a warm trickle on his face, and Vitaly, Bronson could see, was missing a piece of his ear. Captain Amber still swung out with his cutlass, but not so ferociously as before. His chest heaved. The left side of his face, the side of his blind eye, was crossed with jagged scratches and lacerations.

Nearly all the Paps had fallen. Over eighty of the ghouls lay scattered across the ground surrounding the theater. Glittering strands of crimson blood dangled from their hissing mouths, and some had strength to clutch at the gore spilling from their jagged wounds, or to howl to each other in some strange tongue that was nearly indistinguishable from the cries and groans of dogs. Some pounded their heads at the ground to hasten the inevitable oblivion. Some wretched and vomited as they crawled dragging their intestines behind them until they suddenly froze in the snap of death. Others quivered automatically, their stomachs pushing in and out as they panted away their dying breaths. Yak, limping and using his cutlass like a cane, made it a cold business as he stood over the Paps that still lived, raised the dripping blade, and hacked violently into their faces.

Bronson was pushing his hand against a cut on his forehead as he gazed around at the carnage: the absurd faces locked in the throes of death, the twisted limbs thrust into the air, the blood-soaked tweed jackets. With revulsion he realized that not a single Pap had retreated from the battle. They had all fought to the death!

Scientific curiosity seemed at that moment to have possessed Vitaly, who had placed a cyanoacrylate patch over his ear and was otherwise indifferent to the devastation around him. He drew a caliper from his utility belt, unfolded it, and began measuring the Paps' heads. The others limped along aimlessly, stupid with fatigue.

Bronson called up to Nabnak. The Eskimo waved and with a weary voice cheered, "All clear!"

Bronson waved back and then turned to Captain Amber. "That is that."

The captain was squeezing his leg to slow his bleeding. He nodded. "I feel damned—damned alive!"

Bronson drew a tourniquet from his utility belt, tied off the captain's leg, and then caught Vitaly's attention. "If you are done with your scientific admeasurements, Mr. Yurchenko, I'd like to get back to that tower."

Vitaly sniffed amusedly, folded up his caliper, and moved off with Bronson.

As they retreated, Captain Amber, Yak and Mr. Trick limped to one of the Humvees. They piled in and drove off toward the ship.

Beyond the western ridge of the valley the sun was sinking below the waves. Framed by the near-black walls of the valley, the sky was fading into bands of gray and deep navy. The wounded agents said nothing to one another as they strode painfully through the gloom. Bronson and Vitaly glanced at one another, their battle rage dying into a sense of ambivalent camaraderie.

162

Nabnak and Lonetree met them at the base of the tower.

Bronson sat down and leaned back between two of the many pores molded into the tower. From his utility belt he drew a handkerchief that he used to wipe his face.

"This is my plan," he began.

"Plan!" said the others with amazement.

Bronson knew what he was about. "I want you to climb out of here and make your way back to the *Acrobat* and *Stranger*. You will have to move quickly to keep up."

"Keep up?" Their jaws hung slack.

"Yes," said the big agent as he appraised the amount of blood in his handkerchief. Nabnak produced an adhesive bandage and applied it to Bronson's cut. Bronson brought the handkerchief back to his head. He continued: "I want you to catch up with Amber's ship. I'm going to get aboard. It's getting dark, so it shouldn't pose much of a problem."

"Shhh," said Vitaly. "Listen." From the beach came an airy whine. It grew louder. The *Caprice Beyond Folly* was starting its engines.

"You'll never make it," said Nabnak. "They're leaving."

"Then I better run," said Bronson as he tossed the bloody handkerchief aside. He rolled to his feet and was off.

4

WHEN CAPTAIN AMBER shimmered into shallow wakefulness the morning after the battle with the Provincial Academic Philistines, something was missing. It wasn't a feeling he could fully grasp, not immediately. Instead, his predatory imagination leapt swiftly from vantage point to vantage point like some hungry cat stalking its prey. Who was this Bronson Bodine and his strange companions? They had fought with a murderous ferocity that went far beyond a pack of sea tramps claiming they possessed—what was it?—a device that cured the after-effects of kundalini awakening? Aye, Amber recalled, that was a likely reason to seek the Lemurians, who were a people dedicated to strange and diabolical accelerations of the spirit through astral travel and out-of-body sensuality; indeed, hastening the advent of metempsychosis before death itself. And what was that about an ancient archeological treasure in the jungle? Bodine had spoken of a stone donkey.

Clearly a provocation considering how the symbol of the sacrificial donkey figured in Spectrum's pantheon of deontological archetypes. But what was that blasted sense of... what was it? He couldn't place the feeling, and it gnawed at him as much as the mystery of Bodine and his men, or his even more pressing concerns over the missing Lemurians and that blasted cargo he was anxious to be rid of. Alas, he could not leave the cargo at the settlement in the Marquesas but now must carry it to the south... far to the south where Jon Yesterday was... And what was that damned thing that gnawed at him?!

Beside him in bed, Lady Tinkle looked as exquisite as a watercolor rose. She was fast asleep, breathing softly with her thick red hair fanned out over the pink and lemon pillows: a cool, splendid, sylph-like spectacle of such fantastic beauty and exotic excitement that it shocked him into a clearer mode of thinking.

He sat up and looked around the cabin. Everything was as it should be—books, charts, weapons. A portrait of Billy Bones glared down at him from behind his desk. Everything was still, quiet.

"The engines!" he realized. The ship was dead in the water. He flew out of bed and began dressing.

"What's the matter?" sighed Lady Tinkle, and her large green eyes opened slowly, joyfully, and they were glittering with such witch-light as the caldera of smoking volcanos could rightly envy, and to prove his divinity Empedocles might leap into her eyes instead of smoldering Etna. She sat up heedless of the covers sliding off to expose her superb, moon-white breasts. The room filled with her radiance, and indeed the spirits of other stars might find themselves comfortable in the luminous assurance of her bright and extravagant aura.

"I know not," Amber hissed, pulling on his boots. "The ship is stopped. D'yer not hear?" From the night table he snatched the flintlock pistols with the baby alligator head grips, glared at her quickly with his one good eye, then left the room. He latched the door behind him and Lady Tinkle thrilled to the sound of the chains rattling against the door and the snap of the padlock.

He went directly to the engineering monitoring room. Yak was there speaking through the intercom with Mr. Trick, who was working in the engine room.

Amber took the microphone. "What be the problem, Mr. Trick? Why 'ave we stopped?"

"Sar!" barked the mate. "Engine temperature passed the red line and the computer shut them down."

"All six turbines?" Amber couldn't believe it.

"Aye, sar. I never seen the like. I tooked off the inspection plates and found nothing."

"How long before re-start?"

"One, maybe one and a half hours." The mate hesitated. "That's assumin' they 'ave fer a fact or'eated."

"Aye." Amber understood. The problem might lie in the monitoring system that had shut down the engines.

Following this, Yak had already removed the panel covering the thermo-static bay. He stuck his head in and checked the little two-prong plugs that formed the system's logic circuit. He grunted. They had been rearranged. He put them back in correct order, then pulled his head out and nodded to the captain.

Amber raised the microphone to his cruel mouth. "Trick," he growled, "get things together back there. Restart as soon as possible. Yak," he added, replacing the microphone, "check every system running through this room." He went up the ladder.

Passing through the attack center he called to the lookout: "Yo-ho! Report!"

"Sea and sky all clear, sar!"

Amber grunted and continued moving up the ladder.

The bridge was brightly lit by the morning sun beaming through the port windows. The captain surveyed the deck stretching out below and then took up a pair of magnetic field lens binoculars to scan the glittering Pacific.

The intercom buzzed.

Amber snatched up the microphone. "What?!"

"Sar!" barked a sailor. "I'm with the supercargo. 'is neck is broke."

"Where?!"

"In 'is office, sar."

"Stay right there."

165

Amber slid down the ladder. Someone was loose on his ship. Perhaps one of the cargo had escaped? But who among those savages could have reprogrammed the engine shut off? Likely the monk was up to something.

Amber found the supercargo slumped back in his chair with his head shoved over the top of the backrest. The captain felt his jugular, turned to the sailor. "When did you find him?"

"Just now, sar. I was bringin' 'is tea."

Amber looked around the room. A large, gray cat was sleeping atop one of the cabinets. There were no signs of a struggle. On the supercargo's desk the computer was on, evidently. Amber shook the mouse and the screen flashed to life. It displayed an inventory of the cargo. Why on this particular morning would the supercargo be going over such things?

On the screen were six columns showing data on the people in the cargo hold: I.D. number, origin, sex, age and blood type.

The captain reached over and shut it down. "Go find someone and haul that stinking carcass out'a 'ere!"

The sailor barked, "Aye, sar!" and ran off.

Amber stared at the dead supercargo, the distended neck. It must have been a powerful man to snap the head back in such a fashion. The cat was awake now, twitching its tail at him. Then the sailor returned with a companion.

"Forget the supercargo," growled Amber. "Stay with me."

Amber looked caught in a dream; his eyes slid back and forth in their slits. The glistening yellow rondure in his left eye admitted a mere blur of light, but it would be no exaggeration to say his eyes together looked through the bulkheads and decks as his imagination crawled through every corner of the ship. He grabbed a walkie-talkie from the supercargo's desk and led the men forward.

A warm breeze was blowing across the deck when they stepped out through the hatch at the base of the superstructure. Four stories above, the Jolly Roger snapped angrily from the top of the radio mast.

Amber marched for the two giant cargo doors amidships and depressed the foot lever that activated the motors. There was a grinding sound as the doors abruptly lurched and slid aside.

It was dark down in the hold where the eyes of the members of nearly a dozen aboriginal races flickered curiously. Among them were Australian

Aborigines, Maori Polynesians, Micronesians, Melanesians, Yanomami from Brazil, cannibals from the jungles of New Guinea, Hmong mountain folk, and Bushmen from south-central Africa—fifty-seven beings caught in a spell of physical deprivation and rising apathy. In a world shackled together by giant corporations, it had been difficult collecting these "stragglers," as Amber called them.

He stared down at their miserable forms, indifferent to their coughing, their hushed moaning, the pleading garble of odd languages. He grunted. Things seemed in order here. It was just a hunch, but he had to make sure none of them had slipped away. As he counted their faces the breeze shifted and a foul stench wafted up from the hold.

"Hose 'em down!" he ordered the two sailors. He lifted the walkie-talkie. "Mr. Trick, how much longer?"

Static poured from the walkie-talkie and the mate answered. "We're ready now," he paused, "but there's a new problem, sar."

"Out with it, man!"

"We've lost eighty-seven-thousand pounds of fuel, sar."

"Acht! Are you sure?"

"Aye, Cap'n. We've no more than twelve-thousand pounds—le'n two day at cruisin' speed, sar."

The captain growled. "I knows how far we may ramble on twelve-thousand pounds of fuel, Mr. Trick! Have ye got the leak corked up?"

"Aye, sar. But that be it. T'is not a leak. Someone's been a'monkey'n with the dump valves."

Amber wanted to dash the walkie-talkie against the deck. Cursing, he called the attack center and demanded the distance to the nearest oiler.

A few minutes later the radioman called back to report a Russian oiler some nine-hundred miles to the northeast. Amber cursed again. South was the direction he was headed. But what choice had he? He made a rough calculation. With the available fuel the ship would have to be slowed to near thirty knots if they were to make the nine-hundred mile detour. That would take thirty hours; then add refueling time—almost three days lost. And he was already running three behind. "It's that blasted monk!" he cried. "It's sab-ee-tage!"

The two sailors hosing down the cargo looked up at him.

Amber stared them down and they quickly looked away. He called the bridge and ordered the appropriate course change.

A few moments later the six JP-7 turbofans spooled up and ignited. The flexible skirt inflated and lifted the ship from the water, then the hovercraft moved off to the north-east. Grimy exhaust flew from the six exhaust ports in the rear of the superstructure. Then the air intakes at the sides of the superstructure closed slightly, adjusting as the engines down-throttled and lowered in pitch.

Amber regarded their slow progress, then he turned his back on it and marched off to find the monk.

Could it be the monk? It made no sense. The Lemurians were considered top-priority by Spectrum. Amber knew the monk might try and destroy him, but the monk wouldn't go so far as to jeopardize a project Spectrum considered so important. Or was it all part of a power struggle within Spectrum itself? Doubtful. Billy Bones had his boot on the organization's neck, and that meant the monk's neck as well as anybody's. The more Amber thought about it the more it seemed impossible the monk was behind his problems. Still, a talk with the vexatious fanatic seemed the right course of action.

Before the steel door to the armory, Amber ran into Mr. Trick, who had initiated a search for the possible intruder. Trick and his men had completed their search of the superstructure and the aft section of the hull, and were moving forward to check the holds.

"And inspect the fuel tanks and the bilges," ordered Captain Amber. Drop a man down with'n air hose if'n 'ee 'aves to, but search every inch. I'm gonna 'aves a jaw with the monk."

Mr. Trick nodded. "Aye, sar. But I just been to chapel. Knocked on his chest, I did. Stubborn mule refused to answer."

"He'll speak to me," swore Amber, "or by the blood of Billy Bones I'll have cook serve up his gizzard for supper!" And with further oaths Amber stomped down the corridor.

As Amber opened the door he discovered a chapel that appeared darker than usual. Purple smoke poured angrily from the skull on the alter. He saluted the portrait of Billy Bones and then turned to the treasure chest the monk slept in. Amber went over and rapped on it. There was no answer, so he opened it.

It was empty. A couple of Bohemian Grove brochures were stacked in one of the corners beside a roll of toilet paper. Amber slammed the lid and sat down on it. He was thinking the monk was to blame after all. Then the mate was calling over the walkie-talkie.

"Aye," hissed Amber. "What is it, Mr. Trick?"

"It's the monk, sar!"

Amber sprang to his feet. "The monk!"

"Aye, sar. On the foredeck. He just jumped in the sea!"

5

BRONSON BODINE SWAM deep, his arms winding through the water while his legs pushed up and down together inside the monk's robe. He spread his arms and with a manly sweep curved up and hovered in blue space. He heard the growl of the hovercraft diminishing and pictured the ship moving across that same silvery surface that swelled and pulsed forty feet above him like a membrane of living light. He followed the sound as it circled once and then surged away. As the growl dwindled and at last merged with the hushed "OM" of the ocean, Bronson quivered like a truant schoolboy with an uncertain sense of victory. Then he thrilled to hear the echoes of whale song calling in the distance.

The monk's robe slipped off and floated away behind him. He reached down to spread the soles of his boots into swim fins and kicked up to the silvery light. As he ascended the water became clearer and brighter—and more likely to thrust down his windpipe.

He burst through the surface and breathed deeply. The hovercraft was a half-mile away and whistling faintly. The tall superstructure appeared like a giant chess piece sliding across the plane of the sea. Bronson was unsure if those aboard could spot his head among the rolling waves, so he quickly dunked his head, rolled to his back and lifted his lips through the skin of the water to breathe deeply of the life-giving atmosphere, and he felt an exhilaration known to drowning men, or maybe to gods. Then he thought in curious wonder at his own prowess, his independence, his obstinate ability to survive. Once more, afar off in the vast abyss he heard the rising chorale of the whales and wondered at his situation: his imagination touched upon outlandish impressions that exceeded the amazement of his senses, and he

169

conceived himself as a discorporeal being that was unified with the great expanse in which he drifted, a living cavern of visible sound and audible space. He righted himself once more and located the dwindling bridge of Amber's ship. All around shimmered the vast Pacific beneath a sky that appeared to glow more brightly and to fly higher than he had ever seen it before—all radiating around him as a sudden great impression that filled his senses as fully as, a few moments before, something of that same splendid sky had forked down into his straining lungs.

Beyond the hovercraft he watched a purple limb of cloud whiten as it reached around the horizon. It was a long curving band and he easily conceived it to be the arm of a giant octopus pulling itself over the globe; and at this time of year the head of that octopus would be the center of a whirling typhoon. Soon a second purple shadow crept over the horizon, brightening as it ascended, another reaching arm.

His thirty-two function spy watch included a miniature theodolite that he used to check the hovercraft's heading. North-by-northeast; the hovercraft was turning to avoid the storm. If only he were so maneuverable. The situation felt doubtful but he knew he would soon rejoin his friends, and a swim in the open ocean before an advancing storm was great sport, after all.

He rolled around and shoved off toward the empty horizon. His butterfly stroke was never in stronger form.

Sixty miles to the northwest the *Acrobat* and the *Stranger* were skimming across the waves. Water sprayed from their foils and their supercavitating propellers kicked enormous rooster tails through the air.

Nabnak sat alone in the transparent spherical bow of the *Acrobat*. Before him in the low uncluttered instrument panel, the speed indicator showed seventy-three knots. The fuel levels looked good, though at this speed he liked to keep an eye on the gauges. If for no other reason it was reassuring to watch them remain steady.

He also kept a sharp eye on the ocean. The passive Doppler radar had made contact with the hovercraft twenty minutes earlier. Obviously Bronson had succeeded in slowing the craft and it was likely he was floating around out there in the sea. Nabnak knew that Bronson would not linger on the hovercraft longer than necessary.

Nabnak tapped the throttle to keep abreast of the *Stranger*, a mile to starboard and closing. He thought back to the previous night. It was fortunate that he, Vitaly and Lonetree had made it across Nuku Hiva and back to the hydrofoils without any difficulties. Vitaly had said that the Provincial Academic Philistines were probably wiped out in the fight at Lemuria, but as they made their way in the dark up the narrow cliff steps it wasn't reassuring when Vitaly observed that so many Paps gathered together in one place was unprecedented, and thus his knowledge of Pap behavior was probably obsolete.

It was with some relief when they found the taxi and, in the relative security it afforded, set off across Nuku Hiva. The taxi took them to the west end of the island in forty minutes. After climbing down the cliff and recovering the *Acrobat* and the *Stranger*, the realization they were probably no more than four hours behind the hovercraft put them in good spirits.

So it was with a certain amount of gusto when Nabnak threw the throttle forward and sent the submersible hydrofoil across the waves with the light of the tropical stars all around him glittering in the sky and flickering in the sea. The 4,500 shp Rolls-Royce Proteus 15M/553 gas-turbines powering the two craft were rugged and reliable engines. Catching up with the large pirate hovercraft was certain.

After swinging to the south of the island, the *Acrobat* and *Stranger* picked up the chemical trail left by Bronson. During the night he had thrown into the hovercraft's wake tablets made of a chemical compound that registered in the olfactory equipment aboard the two hydrofoils. In this way radar was unnecessary and the bizarre, self-styled pirates were oblivious as Bronson revealed their position.

Soon after dawn, the agents picked up the radio communication between the hovercraft and the oiler. Through RDF triangulation they pinpointed the hovercraft's exact position. They adjusted their course accordingly. Now what remained was recovering Bronson, but as they noticed the arms of the storm reach around the horizon they began to wonder if he would risk the open ocean.

Nabnak was busy formulating Bronson's alternatives when a tiny green blip appeared on the passive radar screen. Ah! Bronson had activated his transponder. Triangulation figures from the *Stranger* beamed over via infrared laser. They had a good fix on him.

Sweeping in from starboard, skipping across the swells, dashing aside the smaller waves with its razor-sharp foils, the *Stranger* closed the distance between the two vessels. Long sheets of water flew to either side of the *Stranger* and several times she dipped and pitched precariously as Vitaly pushed the craft to its limits.

While more arms of cloud reached over the horizon, the two hydrofoils converged until they were running twenty yards apart. They tossed and bogged through the waves that angled in from the southeast. The sea grew heavier by the minute as the storm mass flared up into a blinding white cliff, a bright and gigantic mass towering against the azure. They passed beneath the mass and found a dark ceiling of shadow and emerging violence. With demonic exhilaration, torn patches of cloud chased across the tense sky, where higher aloft the dappled fabric of the cloud ceiling churned and boiled with exotic energies—a strange webbed mantle that recalled the glowing pre-dawn visions of lucid dreaming.

But it wasn't the churning clouds or heavy seas that prompted Vitaly and Nabnak to ease back the throttles and lower the hydrofoils into the waves. The radar signal from the pirate hovercraft showed it to be only twenty-one miles away. Best not to reveal themselves, and slower cruising would facilitate the task of making visual contact with Bronson. The particular type of transponder in his utility belt was good for long-range homing, but within a mile or so its signal, bounced back and forth by the waves, showed up on their screens as a shimmering patch with no distinguishable concentrations of intensity. Even now the little green blip on Nabnak's screen was growing, diffusing. Bronson was somewhere just ahead.

Through the pressure sphere Nabnak watched Chief Lonetree's head emerge from the *Stranger's* short conning tower. A light rain was beginning to fall and Lonetree held his hand over his brow as he brought a pair of magnetic field lens binoculars to his eyes. He quickly and methodically scanned the rolling swells.

Suddenly the rain was falling heavily against the *Acrobat's* pressure sphere. The world became a runny blur. Nabnak set the autopilot and crawled back through the access tunnel to the conning tower.

Water fell upon him as he slid the hatch back. The wind howled. He stuck his head out and rain whipped against his face. An occasional wave splashed over the hull and washed around him and down the conning tower. He pulled a plastic skirt from a pouch inside the hatch, poked his head and arms through it, then snapped the skirt around the coaming. Much in the same way his ancestors had sealed their waists and legs inside their kayaks.

The sky was now completely obscured by turning clouds and slashing rain. The tops of the waves were torn off by the wind, and occasionally the two craft dipped down into troughs twenty and thirty feet deep.

Chief Lonetree maintained his watch with the binoculars and fought to keep steady while the *Stranger* rolled and dipped beneath him. Pitching up sharply and then falling between the swells in the *Acrobat*, Nabnak gripped the coaming firmly as he leaned into the wind. He narrowed his eyes against the cutting rain. Five miles to starboard the sky was black as night. The world seemed turned on its side, poised as if to drop into the swirling darkness.

Odd notions creep into men's minds in times like these. Nabnak found himself looking down at his short, muscular arms. The knuckles on his big square hands were like steel knobs. A moment ago (a quarter century?) his arms had been the smooth delicate limbs of a boy. Those, it seemed, were his "real" arms and hands. Who did these massive grabbers, so long and thick, belong to?

Then Chief Lonetree was calling and gesturing. There was Bronson sixty yards away holding a green flare from which smoke streamed sideways in the rushing wind. Bronson slipped back into a deep trough of water, then up he shot. Jagged waves, sizzling in the rain, tossed before and behind him.

Nabnak noticed that Vitaly had taken on ballast so the *Stranger* rode several feet lower in the waves; Nabnak climbed through the tunnel to the cockpit and toggled the ballast levers to lower the *Acrobat*; the pressure sphere was cleared of the distorting rain. He saw the *Stranger* angle off to the right, and he twisted the control stick to follow.

The *Stranger* pitched and yawed as Vitaly compensated for the waves. From his perch in the conning tower, Lonetree called and waved to the unseen man in the water.

Suddenly Bronson slid around the *Stranger's* smooth transparent bow. Inside, a startled Vitaly stood up and searched the tossing surface to see the diving form of Lonetree rocket into the water, angle upwards, then dolphin kick in three robust bursts to catch Bronson under the arms. Aboard the *Acrobat*, Nabnak snapped the throttle back, blew several hundred pounds of ballast, then crawled to the conning tower. He thrust his head out the opening and spotted his two friends bobbing up and down in the water between the hydrofoils. Bronson was motioning for Lonetree to return to the *Stranger*. The Chief did so, while Bronson, heaving nearly clear of the water in four tremendous butterfly strokes and assisted by a wave, dropped across the afterdeck of the *Acrobat*. Nabnak sprung across the closed air intakes behind the conning tower and helped Bronson to his feet. As they met, the craft lowered beneath them. They grabbed a groove in the hull as a wave washed over. For a moment they were under five feet of water. Then the craft surged up to break through the surface. Water streamed down the *Acrobat's* sides. The men sprang forward for the conning tower and dropped inside. At the same time Lonetree lowered himself into the *Stranger*.

"I've seen calmer seas," snorted Nabnak ironically as they tore off their dripping clothing inside the pressure sphere. He switched on the heater.

Bronson was raising a towel to his head. A startled expression came to his face. "I feel like I could sleep for a week. Any problems last night?"

Nabnak shook his head. "Went smoothly. And you?"

Bronson turned abruptly. "Our friend, Captain Amber, carries an interesting cargo. But what has it to do with the people of Lemuria?" Bronson rubbed his back and arms with the towel, then gently felt the cut on his forehead.

"What's the cargo?"

"Human beings." Bronson threw the towel aside and pulled on a pair of shorts and a long-sleeved shirt. "Representatives, actually, of the few remaining aboriginal peoples still living according to their ancient modes of life: African Bushmen, New Guinea tribesmen, Maori from New Zealand, Australian Aborigines, Yanomami from Amazonia, Hmong mountain people from Laos…"

"Slaves, you think?"

Bronson smiled. "Amber certainly fits the role of blackbirder." Through the transparent sphere he caught sight of Vitaly waving inside the sphere of the *Stranger*. Vitaly held a microphone in his hand.

Bronson took up his own microphone and switched to the hydrophone circuit:

"Yes, Vitaly, go ahead."

"How's the water?"

Bronson was scratching his beard. "Would you think ill of me if I said 'wet'?"

174

There was a pause at the other end. Then Vitaly said: "Forgive me if my question sounds dry, but did you have any doubts out there?"

"Worldly or metaphysical?" quipped Bronson.

A pause, then one mocking guffaw. "Our wit is tiresome. Lonetree is rolling his eyes with disapproval."

"Tell him thanks."

"My goodness, now he's smiling."

"The Chief smiling? I'd like a picture of that."

"Not any longer," said Vitaly. "The smile has vanished. The moment is lost."

Bronson passed his hand back through his hair. "I suppose that means we need to return to business."

There was a pause, then Vitaly said, "That was a smart move, dumping the hovercraft's fuel."

"Fuel?" asked Bronson.

"Of course," said Vitaly. "We ran into a slick about three hours ago. Then a little later as we monitored the pirate's transmissions we learned they were going to rendezvous with a Russian oiler to refuel."

"Refuel?" Bronson narrowed his eyes at this.

"Yes! Isn't that how you slowed them down? That's why they changed course."

Bronson thought a moment. "I re-circuited the thermostats for emergency turbine shutdown. I didn't go near the fuel."

Vitaly grunted. "What's this Amber character up to?"

Bronson looked over at Nabnak. "Why would Amber dump his fuel?"

"What's that?" Vitaly asked.

Bronson spoke into the microphone. "I asked Nabnak why Amber would dump his fuel."

"Doesn't make sense." Vitaly hesitated as he thought. "Amber's heading had been due south. Now it's north-by-northeast."

Bronson was gazing down at the weak and oft-interrupted blip on the radar screen. "Right now I think the best we can do is make sure we don't lose him."

Nabnak unrolled a chart and indicated the rendezvous point the Russian oiler had broadcast earlier that morning.

"Bronson?" Vitaly asked.

"Yeah, right here. Nabnak is showing me where this oiler is supposed to be. We can assume that's where Amber is headed; but we must also assume that Amber is aware his communications might be monitored."

"A diversion, eh?"

"I don't know," said Bronson. "But I'm going to glue myself to that hovercraft until I find out Captain Amber's game."

"I'm with you."

Bronson put up the microphone and took the controls. He worked the stick and throttle together and coaxed the craft through the heaving waters.

The *Acrobat* gathered speed and raised up on its foils, the *Stranger* followed close behind. The two craft moved deliberately like a pair of lions raising their alert heads as they stalked a beast in the distance. Long, slender sensors ran out of the hulls of the two craft. Like insect feelers, the sensors provided information about the rolling waves. Trim computers used the streaming data to adjust the foils as the two craft skimmed up and down the mountainous swells.

Inside forty minutes they had caught up to the hovercraft, which was making little progress through the heavy seas. The rear of the streamline superstructure raised straight up from the stern like a cliff. Halfway up the superstructure were six exhaust openings arrayed in two horizontal rows. The openings were each eight feet in diameter and from them the angry wail of hot gasses poured into the swirling wind.

Pulling the throttle back to belly the *Acrobat* into the waves, Bronson dared approach quite close to the stern of the hovercraft. For some reason his eyes focused on the exhaust openings... something around them. Then his mouth dropped open.

When he first saw them he had the distinct impression of bats clustered together against a rock wall. Then as he drew closer it dawned on him. The sinewy limbs, the loincloths, the threadbare tweed jackets—clinging near the warmth of the hovercraft's exhaust ports were thirteen Paps. One by one they twisted their heads from the cliff-like superstructure and snapped their filed teeth at the tossing *Acrobat*.

6

CAPTAIN PADORIN RUCHKOV of the fleet oiler *Boris Chilikin* skeptically eyed the pirate hovercraft as it shrank towards the southern horizon. Captain Amber had left a bad taste in his mouth. There was something unclean about the flamboyant buccaneer with his scented hair and his half-naked crew. Captain Amber tainted even his view of the lovely cumulus clouds sweeping like a fleet of tall ships behind the typhoon, now hundreds of miles to the northwest.

It was with some amusement then when Captain Ruchkov saw the two submersible hydrofoils spring from beneath the waves and shoot off in pursuit of the hovercraft. Somehow Ruchkov knew that the men in these exotic craft would mete out the justice that must soon catch up with Amber.

"But next week, Comrade Captain, they could come after us," proclaimed the first officer, Commander Mikhail Bakunin. He read well his captain's thoughts.

Ruchkov turned his round face at his executive. "You think so?"

Bakunin carried himself with the ease of the old world playboy military officer. "The men in those craft hold no quarter." He nodded confidently as he brushed his finger along his suave mustache. "We might be sinking now, but they believe the American is a bigger fish."

The captain wrinkled his nose. He was disappointed—but just as glad—that he was not a "big fish." He didn't question Bakunin any further on the matter. His executive officer was—he knew positively—a former KGB agent, and probably much more besides.

The two men stood quietly on the bridge and watched the hydrofoils, the bright spray fanning to the sides and blowing behind as they skied into the glare of the southern horizon. The water pulsing from the craft glimmered brightly in the sunlight; at last the burning spray (for such it began to seem) dwindled into bright sparks as the craft drew distant and then somewhat theatrically vanished. The five officers and seamen who shared the bridge with the captain and the first officer worked quietly at their stations. But the stillness of the scene was short lived.

"Comrade Captain!" announced the officer monitoring the damage control panel. "Trap number seven—a red light!"

Captain Ruchkov raised his eyebrows at this. "A trap? Are you sure?" He brought his palms together and squeezed nervously.

The damage control officer nodded earnestly. "Indeed, Comrade Captain. Trap number seven."

Commander Bakunin was eager, like a man anticipating an afternoon sport. "Shall I see?"

The captain stuck out his lower lip; he was still squeezing his palms. "Both of us. Let us arm ourselves." He spoke evenly but forcefully at the damage control officer, "Alert security detail," and then he and Bakunin left the bridge.

Trap seven was in the aft hold. Along the way they stopped at the armory and equipped themselves with AK-47s.

"What do you think?" said Bakunin. He lowered his cap across his brow and struck a jaunty pose with the automatic assault rifle.

The captain shook his head. Spies were always clowning around. "You look like American gangster."

"Ah! In the uniform of New Soviet Restoration Corporation, Comrade Captain?"

Ruchkov pursed his lips ironically. "I am too careful to acknowledge your amusing distinctions."

They struck off for the aft hold in good spirits. Through their jesting they assured each other of their mutual trust. The situation was extremely dangerous, requiring each to place his life in the other's hands.

They soon reached the hold. Bakunin pulled the hatch back and, with weapons leveled, the two men stepped quietly into the semi-darkness. The captain's finger shook over the trigger, and Bakunin softly but firmly reminded him to lift the finger off the trigger and extend it over the guard. The left side of the compartment was cluttered with piled casks, containers and lumber. To the right were large spools of transmission line. Suddenly lights came on overhead.

"Who's there!" called the captain. He wheeled around with his rifle. Three sailors were stepping in through the hatch. They carried hinged bludgeons. By some unvoiced mutual consent everyone froze and listened.

Save the monotonous humming of machinery below decks, all was quiet.

"Comrade," hissed the executive officer to the captain. "Trap is in far corner."

The captain nodded for the sailors to follow.

They advanced through the center of the hold and then, hesitating for a moment, moved cautiously around a stack of casks. They stared down in wonder.

There on the floor, caught in a giant mousetrap six feet long, the heavy steel bar pinching down across its chest, was a quivering, half-dead Pap. In shock and nearly unconscious, but somehow sensing their presence, it began growling. Its fists tightened. Its toes flexed and curled. The bar was pinched deeply into the ribcage and blood seeped steadily from the Pap's lower jaw, which was hanging open and fixed at a fiendish angle.

Captain Ruchkov extended his tongue. "Yeach!"

Shaking slightly, Commander Bakunin stepped forward and raised the butt of his rifle. He was about to strike… then the Pap's eyes sprang open.

Pinned fast by the heavy bar to the wooden base of the trap, the Pap picked up its head and took in the scene. In reaction to the sight of its chest pinned down by the bar, its tongue flicked the air rapidly. Its eyes suddenly turned up at the staring men. It hissed reflexively, then looked sidelong into a corner of the hold, evidently taking stock of its situation. Several times it gasped in reaction to the disclosures of its black thoughts. Suddenly it turned to the captain and Bakunin and began speaking in a hushed gravel whisper that seemed hardly of this earth: "You must tell the Dean—" the Pap shook in the frenzy of near-death; but in facing its own final mortality it settled back into the fearless menacing form of its devilish self: "Tell the Dean— Yesterday has gone— Yesterday has gone— the next phase—"

Bakunin swung the gunstock down against the Pap's forehead. The crack of the blow was as sharp as the sound of a snapping bough; the creature shook fiercely at the assault, then gasped into fast and absolute stillness. The men could almost feel the draft of the brutal spirit falling into its personal underworld, and whatever black and hellish hole that was they surely could not fathom, and they stood there unthinking as if in a daze, by their own life force mercifully blocked from peering further down into that grisly and final pit of ignominy. So sudden, violent and definitive had been the death blow that the captain had forgotten his curiosity about the obscure meaning of the Pap's last words.

The sailors looked at each other and discovered in each other's faces a new respect for the executive officer's steeliness.

"Is… Is dead, Comrade?" asked the captain.

Bakunin nodded, amazed with himself. "Utterly. The lamp is out. The long day is done. The desert sands sigh no more."

"I was hoping for something more exciting," observed the half-bewildered captain as he turned to his executive officer, pursed his lips, then shrugged with something like disappointment.

"Oh," said Bakunin encouragingly. "They don't travel alone. There's sure to be more."

The captain sniffed. "It was filthy pirate. He brought them aboard. Like rats."

"Indeed." Bakunin licked his lips. "They are clever. I wouldn't be surprised if they had boarded the hovercraft and drained its fuel, knowing they could transfer over to our ship, and then on to their destination."

"Filthy," was all the captain could say.

Then the intercom was scratching on. The damage control officer announced trap number twelve in the forward bilge had sprung.

"Let's just leave it down there," said the captain. He shivered. "Yeach!"

But Bakunin was already running eagerly for the hatch, his weapon raised. "Tally-ho!"

7

"MONEY!" SANG CAPTAIN Amber as he admired the flapping bills in his fist. "Money! I do loves it. Like you my sweet." He gave Lady Tinkle a kiss on the cheek and thrust his fist over the windscreen. The blue hundred dollar notes, each with an eye-patched Billy Bones in the center, fluttered and clicked in the wind.

The pirate hovercraft *Caprice Beyond Folly* flew across the waves at fifty knots. Spray wound up behind her in a spinning cloud. They were on course again and Amber was once more his usual blustering self. Fresh and scintillating after the storm, the ocean was a sight too pretty, and Amber could scarcely bother with such problems as had plagued the voyage. So he was delayed a few days? He'd find Jon Yesterday, he'd get paid in the end, and that's what mattered. And the loss of the monk? Amber decided that was the work of Providence. If questioned about it later, he could truthfully say the monk had drowned himself. Meanwhile, the ship was better off without the scurvy dog. The men sang and danced on the deck. Even Lady Tinkle,

180

usually aloof and reserved, was poking and squeezing her captain playfully as he clutched her to his side.

"Before the orders of the Heavenly Cap'n," bellowed Amber, clasping his lover's waist, "all was darkness and men sought out heat. Then mankind built him ships and liberty was hailed. Liberty, my darling—'tis like a distant island riding the sea's round rim, an island all covered by dumb donkey-people that the Sky Cap'n put on this Earth to let us give 'em what fer! Aye! Let the donkeys of this Earth do what's work, and I'll tell 'em so. That's why today we dress and sing and sport as we do, my lass. Give us a kiss! Mmm! And another!" She really planted one on him and he pulled away crowing. "Trust in the Heavenly Cap'n's orders writ down right here on Billy Bones' articles-a-faith: 'Create Thy Own Reality'!" He shook the money in his fist. "Flesh follows the funds. Man cannot live by bread alone, but goeth and seeketh out the paths laid down by blue-ooo-ooo money. We reach for it, stretch our bellies out upon the course it lays, bathe in it, love in it. I tell you—money. Ah, it makes me want wine!"

"Ouch!" she shrank away from him.

"What's this!" he said.

She was looking down between them, holding her bright red hair off her face. She bit her lip theatrically, feigned astonishment and poshly intoned, "Your pistol jabbed me."

He leered. "Tha'tweren't me pistol, thou sweet hen!"

Down on the deck, Mr. Trick—with a line of black stitches across his forehead—waved merrily from among the throng of dancing sailors. The captain signaled back with an upraised fist.

"Yo-ho!" cheered Mr. Trick, and he crossed his arms once more and fell in with the dance. Yak stood nearby banging pans together as Parson Pete the blind charlatan and Naughty Ned Neptune scratched their fiddles, while little Emmanuel, the club-footed Pueblo, blew springing melodies from his ocarina.

"This is a happy ship," hissed Amber and he shook his curls in the wind. Lady Tinkle reached her hand around his neck and clutched the tossing locks.

"I'm growing cold in this wind," she said.

"Cold you should be in these latitudes," said Amber. "And it shall grow crisper still, by and by. He looked down at her, into those eyes that at once shone like green caves of ice and temples of howling love-making.

He stepped before her to block the wind even as he drew her tightly to his hard, battle-scared chest. "I will cover thee."

Forty miles behind, streaking the sea with white ribbons of foam, the *Acrobat* and the *Stranger* maintained their forceful advance. The agents busied themselves with conversation, music, and plenty of sleep. The high-performance systems aboard the craft were in constant need of monitoring and maintenance: fire control recalibration, engine adjustments, bolt tightening. Chief Lonetree was particularly fond of crawling into the many narrow access tunnels that wormed around the *Stranger*. He could spend hours on his back pulling himself along the handrails as he examined service plates, dipsticks, electrical connections, pipe insulation. Vitaly often wondered about the Chief when he disappeared for these long periods, and he imagined all manner of bizarre psychological reasons for Lonetree's "maintenance fixation" and "tinker reclusiveness." Vitaly was content to spend an entire afternoon at the controls, practicing the vowels and regional dialects of the dozen or so languages he knew, or singing the last movement of Beethoven's Ninth, or quarreling aloud with people he hadn't seen in years—and vocalizing both sides of such arguments. He spoke with clarity that was like life. Another form of this idiosyncrasy was his habit of drifting from accent to accent, idiom to idiom, as he spoke with the memories of his friends. Vitaly had been a child star of the Moscow Circus, the adopted son of a Brooklyn boxing promoter, a teen-age chess champion, a Cambridge astronomy student and, during a brief infatuation with the writings of Nicholas Roerich, a Tibetan holy man in the Manjushri tradition. The combined influence this diverse background had upon his speech sometimes made him sound as if each individual syllable he enunciated was voiced with a declension or an inflection that had nothing to do with the mood he was trying to convey. Bronson once suggested that listening to Vitaly talk was the aural equivalent of attempting to pick one's way through an emotional collage, or reading one of those kidnapper's notes pasted together with disparate letters and syllables clipped from newspapers and magazines.

"I wonder what's going on over there?" said Nabnak. He was looking across the thirty yards of water separating the two craft and studying Vitaly sitting alone in the *Stranger's* transparent bow with his mouth chattering away and his arms gesturing expressively.

Bronson looked over. "Haven't you ever seen a mad Russian talking to himself?"

Nabnak shrugged. "Is that a Russian trait?"

"Russian Aristocrats." Bronson nodded. "They have strange tempers. Vitaly is a relatively tame example of the species. They consider themselves artists and act like prima donnas. Their capacity for conspiracy is matched, probably, only by the English, and Vitaly has lived in both societies. It becomes absolutely insufferable when he begins affecting the air of an Oxbridge don, peppering his conversation with boring puns, stale epigrams, literary allusions and terms like 'wipe out' and 'gnarley'."

Nabnak cocked his head. "'Wipe-out' and 'gnarley'?"

"Sure," explained Bronson. "He dropped out of Cambridge for a semester and became a surf bum."

"In Southern California?"

"No. Outside London. He leased a film studio sound stage, imported forty tons of sand, set up a sun lamp, and hired a voice teacher from the Royal Shakespeare Company to coach him in the lingo. I'm not quite sure what was behind it. Wanted to picture himself with the ocean reflected in his sunglasses, and the rushing clouds forming a backdrop for his grinning, wedge-shaped head."

"Pretty eccentric, I'd say."

Bronson agreed. "And he took it on with real zeal—that old unimpeachable Russian conviction."

Nabnak shook his head with amazement. "One righteous dude."

"Righteous!" Bronson chuckled. "Oh, his Oxbridge-don-beach-boy trip pales in comparison to his übermensch-Led-Floyd-martyr. He combs his hair over his eyes, falls in love at first sight with women who look like Mariska Veres, spends all afternoon in his room with the curtains drawn reading the Bible and astrological almanacs, daydreams about gaseous nebulae, formulates elaborate plans for leaving society and moving to a forest—and the next thing you know he's going through a crisis—thinks he's become a bag lady or something. He combs his hair out of his eyes, brushes his teeth, then throws away his music recordings as he declares, 'I will never *care* again!'"

Bronson kept a steady hand on the stick as the *Acrobat* swept on. The sea was a dark metallic blue that mirrored the slight trace of haze in the sub-tropical sky. They were thirty degrees below the equator now, almost twelve-hundred miles south of the Tuamotu Islands, where several years earlier Bronson and Vitaly had brought a pair of French officials who, in their youthful frustration, they had sought to make an example of.

It happened on the island Moruroa, "place of the great secret," which in the latter half of the former century had been a French facility for testing nuclear "devices." Despite official denials, radioactive fallout spreading from Moruroa had contaminated the South Pacific food chain and increased the incidence of leukemia among the Polynesian peoples. Even as they moved their facilities from island to island, the French denied their tests were dangerous—just as the civil and military health ministers for French Poly-nesia at Papeete claimed that cancer rates in the South Pacific were quite normal, while at the same time (with the collusion of international health authorities) denying journalists access to Polynesian medical statistics.

In response, Bronson and Vitaly identified a pair of energy ministers in Paris, tracked them down to a fashionable café in the Place Des Vosges, followed them into *les chiottes*, tittering brightly and slapping the backs of the ministers, whereupon, amidst many buffoonish gestures and curses of shocked outrage, they abruptly thrust the ministers through the alley window of *les chiottes*, ushered them into the back of a lorry, fastened them inside oxygen-mask-equipped travel trunks, flew them by commercial airliner to Moruroa, unpacked them and brushed them off, then locked them inside a shark cage (meanwhile apologizing profusely in polite and obsequious terms that became increasingly ghoulish as the crime reached its climax—"*Mais, ce garçon est incroyable!*"—itself the vilest part of the episode, at least to Bronson's recollection) and lowered them down through a crack to the island's poisonous core.

"I'm going to miss Polynesia," said Nabnak. He was busy with his sketchpad trying to capture the energy and speed of the *Stranger* skimming across the water beside them.

"I guess I will too." Bronson happily perceived the bubble of Moruroa burst from his memory. "I love the palms and the warm ocean. But we're more creatures of the cold, you and I. You were bred for the tundra, and I would best make my home in a Norwegian pine forest, or on the side of a heather-covered hillock standing at the abrupt end of a deep and curving glen."

Nabnak agreed. "The tundra is beautiful—in summer. It's like Mars or something. But I have no illusions about the cold. It eats men."

Bronson thought about this. "I suppose you're right. But humanity—I mean the mythic vision of an ultimate communal consciousness—that comes from the colder latitudes, don't you think? What did the warmer latitudes ever give us? Agriculture? Writing? Monotheism? Stratified civilization? Empire? Law codes? Science? Philosophy? Medicine? Tsk. The seeds of all our unhappiness."

Nabnak shrugged and kept drawing.

"You belong in your igloo," Bronson gushed in rapturous tones, "greasing yourself down with seal fat, anticipating a six-month night of communal wife-swapping, or maybe saying 'good-bye' to grandma as she cheerfully crawls out the door for the last time. And me, too. Don't you see me up on the side of a glen, painted blue, bare-chested, a plaid blanket flowing from my shoulders in the merry wind, accompanied by my baying hounds, swinging an axe over my head, running down some poor soul who happens to be smaller and more frightened than me?"

"Well," said Nabnak with dubious earnestness, "doesn't Marx promise that eventually history will restore us to the natural state?"

"We can only hope, friend Nabnak. We can only hope." Bronson scanned the displays on the *Acrobat's* instrument panel. He found himself thinking about their quarry. "What do you make of this *aficionada* we're following, Captain Amber? Is that really his name? He has the emotional depth of a Spanish conquistador, and an inquisitor's sense of right and wrong. It makes me ill to think of his kind taking over the United Corporations of North America."

"It takes more men," observed Nabnak, "than Billy Bones and his crew to run the UCNA. He's just a trend—like The Beatles or public water systems—something tangible for the white-collar proletariat to cling to."

Bronson saw the reason in this. "I wonder how Amber fits in with the people of Lemuria? That cargo of his? What do the world's richest and most influential artists want with a shipload of aboriginal peoples? Why are they interested in their blood types?"

"I've been thinking about that." Nabnak set aside his pencil and sketch-pad. "Maybe they're dabbling in genetic engineering?"

"Could be. But the ideals of the Lemurians just don't jibe with something like that; not experimenting with humans, anyway. I remember the CD covers painted by Jon Yesterday, who is after all Lemuria's leader. They were fantasy-oriented, gentle, benign. They embraced a wildly optimistic view of nature that promised a future of bright and startling beauty. Quite humbling, actually. I absolutely cannot see Jon Yesterday condoning the kidnapping of aborigines and bushmen."

"Well," said Nabnak. "Artists are pretty ambitious types. One thing leads to another. They change. The Lemurians are mixed up with Captain Amber, and that means Spectrum. Something's gone seriously wrong."

Bronson nodded absently. His gaze was fixed beyond the waves. "I remember a little poem printed inside one of the album covers that Jon Yesterday had designed; the words sung by the Welsh bard Taliesin when he set foot upon Ireland. Penniless and unsure of his course in life, Taliesin reached down to softly brush his hand through the bracken and contemplate his poetry, thus:

I am an estuary into the sea
I am a wave of the ocean
I am the sound of the sea
I am a powerful ox
I am a rowan of the cliff
I am a red hawk in azure
I am a dewdrop in the sun
I am a gorse of yellow beauty
I am a boar for valor
I am a salmon in a pool
I am a goose flying free
I am a lake in a moor
I am a shower in the wind
Of this artfulness I sing
As in this craft I live
And I breathe

8

THE NEXT THREE DAYS brought remarkable transformations. The sky grew gray, the ocean became leaden, and the sun flew lower along its daily path. On the fourth day they crossed the Antarctic Circle, the sun was left behind, and the ocean and the sky fused together into an immense, starless darkness animated by nothing more tangible than the vague play of ghostly forms.

Broad flat tables of ice extended into the night. The ice was pale in the darkness, as indefinite as something glowing in a dream. Upon it seals and birds squealed like lost souls beckoning the humans to join their uniform and unthinking ranks.

Occasionally in the distance clouds broke apart and faraway peaks stood as indistinct silhouettes against the silver stars.

The three sea craft cruised off the Pacific coast of the continent on a course paralleling the Ross Ice Shelf. Above the islets of table ice that shifted slowly in the thick and nearly-frozen sea, the sloping surface of the Rockefeller Plateau could be descried; and then the heights of the Queen Maud Mountains, sloping up to the brooding mass of Mt. Erebus, a twelve-hundred foot volcano sheathed in ice and scattered over with the frozen forms of torn boulders and broken rock which had previously vaulted skyward from the mountain's angry interior. Above the steaming mouth of the caldera, like a blot of dark grayness in a darker gray vision, a giant lenticular cloud was slowly oozing over the vast desolate expanse of cold and ice.

Not far from the foot of the mountain, a temporary base had been set up beside the sea. It was a dismal and squalid hamlet made up of depressed and wind-blasted buildings, heavily-stained fuel and water tanks, and the inevitable dump of ugly, frost-blistered refuse. Yellow lights shimmered around the compound, and slopping down from their vague glow into shadow was a long shallow ramp cut into the ice and leading to the sea. The *Caprice Beyond Folly* roared up the ramp and abruptly shut down its turbines after the long voyage from the equator.

As the flexible skirt deflated and the hovercraft lowered, Captain Amber was in his cabin drawing a tiger skin parka over his energetic frame. He had been in contact with the base for several days now, but the person he had spoken to was unable (or was refusing) to discuss the cargo and their

187

arrangements. Amber had come half way around the world. It had been a long voyage, and he expected to be paid for it.

Slipping his pistols under his parka, Amber called to Lady Tinkle to hurry. They made their way forward through the vessel; Lady Tinkle's boots clicked rapidly against the deck as her legs shuffled. Her patent leather parka was accented across the shoulders with fox tails, and her rabbit skin mittens were studded with glittering diamonds. Yak, wearing a parka of wolf skins (complete with a cape!), joined them, and altogether the trio made a fashion statement doubtless not matched since in the annals of Antarctica society. As they marched down the ramp in the hovercraft's bow the yellow glow of the base appeared unnaturally weak and distant.

They trudged up the ice ramp. Beneath their boots the frozen path was as hard and dry as rock. Like devils in the darkness, seals barked and growled and a million penguins squawked at each other in cryptic strains. The cries of the beasts joined in a forlorn paean of melancholia disabused of sentiment; it was a revelation of eroding neglect, a lingering sense of loss, the final abandonment of false hope. Altogether the diabolical rapture swirled in a wavering pulsation that rose and fell and swept side to side with the wind. But while the wind blew lightly across the ground, from far above amidst the black skies transcending the peak of Mt. Erebus came a dull hollow roar that was sometimes fluted by the jagged rim of the volcanic caldera. Amber and his companions paused to listen to the mountain's call. It was a lonely wail—a voice of yearning emptiness that sent cold echoes up their spines.

They stood transfixed as the wailing sound died down to mix with the groans and cackles of the wildlife. They continued walking toward the central building and went inside.

It was a multi-purpose community center, mess hall and movie theater. A sickly frost, here and there green with a creeping mildew, covered much of the ceiling. In the back was a battered kitchen. Two rows of tables were set up along either wall, with a broad aisle running between them. Sitting at the end of one of these tables was a lanky, athletic man with thin blond hair. A long corncob pipe was set firmly in his teeth, and as he puffed on it his eyebrows ticked involuntarily. Without using his hands he slid the pipe from side to side in his teeth, his tongue working the pipe stem like a hand on an oar. He smiled with narrow eyes as Amber's boots banged across the wooden floor. "I'm Cahstairs," he said with an Australian accent. "You're Captain Amber, I reckon?"

"Aye." Amber nodded but his arms remained at his sides when the Australian offered his hand.

"I suppose y'want to get dan to business?" Carstairs said, unperturbed, smiling.

"Aye," grunted Amber. "Where's Jon Yesterday? 'E's who I 'ave business with, unless you be his mate?"

Carstairs nodded. He was very aware his smile was annoying Amber. "Mr. Yesteh'day has taken the Lemurians to the interiah. That was four days ago. They were disappointed you failed to arrive on time with yeh cah'go. But they insisted on beginnin'. Their timetable was most strict. There were certain—astrological alignments, shall we say—that could not be disregah'ded. But I have been authorized to take delivery of yeh cah'go, and that's all you're really interested in, eh?"

"Indeed," said Amber. And his eyes widened slightly and then narrowed sharply as Carstairs drew a thick blue roll from inside his down vest and lifted it slowly toward the seaman. As Amber took the roll and began counting, Carstairs smiled engagingly at Lady Tinkle and exchanged a few words on the subject of Mt. Erebus, whose fluted wail was again calling. Yak looked on quietly, several times wiping away the wet that glimmered on his cleft upper lip.

Amber grew more cheerful as he finished counting. "Very good, Mr. Carstairs. I knew Mr. Yesterday wouldn't be going back on our arrangement. Be sure to tell him I was powerful sorry I was late. It ached me heart, it did, to think I might slow up his project."

Carstairs snorted smoke through his nose. "Tell me," he said, "will Brother Mezereon be join'n us soon? He's to accompany the cah'go to the interior."

"Ah," said Amber, shaking his head. "The poor monk met with a tragic mishap. The perils of the sea."

Carstairs winced slightly. "How's that?"

"Aye. He fell overboard whilst studying the pretty light of the sun shining against the wavy water. Hypnotized, he was, by the beauty of it all. Alas, he'll see the sun no more. The sharks done dragged him down to Davy Jones.

It was the saddest day you might tell about." Amber drew a handkerchief from his sleeve and dabbed his eye with a dainty twist. "Rest in peace."

Carstairs put out his pipe in token respect. "You cared deeply for the man?"

"Like a brother, he was. We prayed together on every spare occasion. A treasure of a man." Amber brought the handkerchief to his nose and blew like a foghorn.

They all stood quietly with bowed heads. Amber's eyes flashed back and forth as he slipped the money under his parka. "But done is done. Where do ye want me to be putting the cargo? I must depart. Aye, and with haste. I haves a valuable medical consignment to drop off with the good sisters at the Convent of Juan Fernandez in Valparaiso. Sick orphans, don't you know, need'n vaccine, Gawd bless 'em."

"Right," said Carstairs. I have a release I want you to sign, and a receipt. Then we can begin—" Carstairs looked up. "Do y'hear something?"

Amber glanced back and forth then spun around. Outside there was a faint whistle. "Ar!" he cried. "'Tis the *Caprice*!"

They ran out of the building to see the hovercraft lifting on its skirt. Seventeen men—the hovercraft's crew—were scattered over the ice ramp, some unconscious, some moving slightly and moaning. Very quickly the hovercraft was backing down the ice ramp and raising a cloud of mist from the water. It curved around in the darkness and, engines opening up, roared out to sea.

"Thunder and lightning!" cried Amber. "By Bones I'll cut off their heads and feed their black hearts to the devil!"

Amber was so angry that Carstairs caught him completely off guard. There was a thud and Amber saw stars. A few moments later, he and Yak were waking up on the ground.

Amber growled and shook his head as he came to. Then he felt inside his parka. "Blast! That dog took my sweet money!"

They stood up rubbing their heads. Lady Tinkle pointed into the darkness. "He ran that way." Almost at the same instant an engine revved up and headlamps flashed on. Amber drew his pistols and fired, but the tractor drove on and quickly lost itself across the ice field. Soon its headlamps winked out in the darkness.

"Carstairs!" hissed Amber. "Remember that name. I'll rip his throat out! I'll use the jaw bone of a dog and cut off his head! With me own bare hands I'll drag out his rotten heart and smash it against the ice!" Amber continued pronouncing oaths as he led his companions to the prostrate forms of the crewmen scattered across the ramp.

Most of the men were moaning, bleeding, in shock. Many had broken bones after having been thrown from the hovercraft's sides. Mr. Trick was among them, unmoving. The fall had broken his neck.

Leaving Yak and Lady Tinkle to examine the men, Amber marched among them barking his puzzled anger. The cargo of aboriginal outlanders had somehow managed to escape from the hold, surprised the crew, and had taken over the ship.

"Aye, and did the savages work their way free, or did someone let them out of the hold?!" No man could answer. The cacophony of the groaning crew, the complaining wildlife, the wind, and the dwindling whine of the hovercraft reflected the confounded situation. Was the Australian Carstairs behind it? Amber looked every way into the darkness and mulled things over.

They spent the next half hour carrying the crewmen to the main hut. Lady Tinkle put a pot of broth on the stove as Yak and Amber broke chair backs to make splints for the broken bones. They worked quietly, their emotions overwhelmed by the completeness of the disaster. Amber glared suspiciously at everyone and everything.

Suddenly the door swung open. All activity stopped.

Two hooded figures entered. One was tall and pantherish; the other short, but as broad and sturdy as a bear. They wore utility belts around the waists of their white jumpsuits. Large stainless steel automags gleamed in their shoulder holsters. They lowered their hoods.

"It is very good to see you again, Captain Amber," said Bronson Bodine. Beside him, Nabnak Tornasuk studied the situation.

"Ar!" growled Amber. His eyes shook in their sockets. On the table beside him was a large meat cleaver he had been using to cut bandages. He snatched it up and hurled it at Bronson.

Bronson caught it easily with a curving motion that was as subtle as it was disarming. He hefted the cleaver significantly, eyed Amber coolly, and then casually set the weapon on a table. He and Nabnak unzipped their jumpsuits and sat down. They had hard, businesslike expressions on their faces. "I would have approached you earlier," said Bronson, "to help with your men, but then I thought it would be prudent to wait for you to cool down. I won't try and convince you that I have had nothing to do with your recent misfortunes, though I think it would be hasty of you to make any conclusions before considering that we once fought side by side and prevailed together against a common enemy; and, indeed, it was the Paps, who seem to be the scourge of this enterprise, that once more join us together."

Amber wrinkled his forehead at mention of the Provincial Academic Philistines. It hadn't occurred to him that it was they who had released the cargo. It seemed plausible. "Avast! You can belay that fancy talk, Bodine. I'm belly up."

The tall agent took a moment to admire Amber's flamboyant figure, and it occurred to him that they were like a pair of twined snakes, heads raised to glare at each other with equal measures of wary familiarity, total suspicion, and predatory contempt—they saw each other as little more than means to an end. In the flat brutality of such cynicism, Bronson found something refreshing, like the thrill of handling a fabulous cobra, at once ready to softly stroke its spread hood, or, if need be, to drive the thunderbolt of oblivion through its ghastly being by snapping its neck like a whip.

As if reading the younger man's mind, Amber boldly hacked and expectorated against the floor. "We'll murder each other later. What's thy proposition?"

From his jumpsuit Nabnak produced a map and unfolded it on the table. Their eyes lighting up, Amber and Yak moved in to examine it. They fingered the edge of the map with something like reverence, rubbed it with their thumbs, tapped it, gave it a careful pinch. Did they believe the thickness and texture of the paper had something to do with the quality of the information printed upon it?

The map showed a section of the continent including the Pacific Coast of Antarctica, from the Bellingshausen Sea to Wilkesland, and a broad section of the interior. A few of the larger science stations were indicated, but the most prominent feature was a Maltese cross at the South Pole labeled "Lemuria Two." Circling it at a fifty-mile radius was a thin gold line labeled "Magnetic Defense Zone."

Amber fingered his goatee, eyeing the cross at the pole. "No one ever made no map that didn't lead to no treasure. Where'd ye get this?"

"While you were carrying your men in," said Bronson, "we were going through the other buildings to check for Paps, and found this. There was also a radio. We tried to make contact with the Lemurians. Either no one is there or they're not answering. We were certain we were calling on the correct frequency. It was written down in the log. But as you say, maps aren't made for aesthetic reasons."

"Thou dost not think treasure is aesthetic?" asked the Captain.

Bronson shrugged absently. "The problem is this Magnetic Defense Zone." He tapped the gold circle around the pole. "What is it? And how do we get through it?"

Amber chuckled. "Aye, and so you comes to thy old mate, Cap'n Amber, to fetch up this treasure?"

Bronson straightened. "Why are you so sure we're going to find a treasure?"

Amber gazed slyly at the men around the table. "Ah, whatever it is, it's more interesting to you than nightmare relics, kundalini orgasms, or whatever you was going on about back in the Marquesas."

As they discussed logistics, Lady Tinkle brought them cups of steaming broth. In the flurry of activity her dark red hair had become disheveled, and the steam at the stove had made her wipe away her make-up. Bronson took note of her loveliness, how it was delightfully enhanced by the disarray of her toilet.

Amber noticed Bronson's wandering gaze and altered the course of the conversation in mid-sentence "—the quality of a man's appetites says as much about 'em as 'is actions."

Bronson caught his meaning—and something of his manner. "Aye, we'll get along."

9

THEY OUTFITTED THEMSELVES from the abundant stocks of supplies the Lemurians had abandoned when they left for the pole. Bronson questioned Amber as they loaded the snow tractor and was satisfied the captain knew nothing about the Lemurian's project; nor did Amber express any interest.

When asked about the Lemurian's requirement for a group of aborigines, Amber matter-of-factly answered, "Knowing they was artists and such lot, I took it they needed me cargo for a vampire orgy."

"Are the Lemurians vampires?" asked Bronson.

Amber shoved a box into the snow tractor and shrugged. "Whatever they take a fancy to: voodoo, faeries, weird foods. People withouts a religion do strange things. Their money's good, however, so I suppose it's the orders of the Cap'n Up Above." He lifted another box and shoved it into the tractor.

Bronson gave the appearance of agreeing. "Cap'n, why is Spectrum interested in the Lemurians?"

Amber glanced up at Mt. Erebus. "Aye, that has crossed my mind." But he would say no more. He walked back to the building.

Bronson exchanged glances with Nabnak who was cranking a fuel pump at the rear of the tractor. "I don't know," said Nabnak as Amber walked out of earshot.

"Don't know what?" asked Bronson.

"I don't know if it's a good idea mixing in with him. The tractor is loaded. Let's shove off."

Bronson shook his head. "No. We might need them at the Magnetic Defense Zone, for diversions if nothing else."

Nabnak pressed his lips together as he drew the pump from the fuel drum. He slid the pump into another drum. "I'd guess Amber's thinking the same thing."

"I know he is," Bronson said flatly. Something caught his attention. "Look at this—"

Yak and Lady Tinkle were approaching. Yak had found a mortar in one of the huts; he raised it to show Bronson as he approached. Lady Tinkle was carrying a .308 caliber AR-15.

Bronson hefted the mortar into the tractor. "Well done, Yak."

The Chinese nodded. Bronson impressed him as an able leader, and he was wondering if a shift in allegiance might be a shrewd move at this point. "One box mortar rounds," said Yak. "I get." And he went back to the buildings.

Lady Tinkle set the butt of the rifle on the ice. "Yak is thinking you might be able to keep him alive better than Amber."

Bronson cocked his head. "I'm going to do my best to keep all of us alive."

"I won't tell Amber about Yak. That's Yak's business. But I'm sticking with Amber, you understand?"

"Why tell me?"

She moved her head in a way that drew his attention to her haunting eyes. "Because when I pick a man it's because he's true and able. I shall stand by him."

Bronson shrugged and turned toward the tractor. "Okay."

Nabnak worked the pump stoically as he wondered about her.

Soon Amber and Yak approached with the last of the equipment. Amber helped Lady Tinkle up into the tractor and then climbed after. Yak handed up the crate of mortar rounds and followed. Nabnak was just completing the fueling. He closed down the cap and went to the front of the tractor. He gazed across the great waste before them. Even in the darkness he was experiencing symptoms of snow blindness. The ice plane looked like a photo negative desert. The overcast had thinned somewhat to admit the starlight.

Bronson was in the process of starting the turbine engine when Nabnak pulled open the cab door and jumped in.

Nabnak pulled his hood down and glanced at the instrument panel. "This is simple enough." Then he looked back at Amber, Yak and Lady Tinkle. They sat across the top of a long bench that covered an equipment box. Amber looked characteristically impatient as he gazed forward through the broad windscreen. The engine whined to life and the tractor lurched forward.

Nabnak spoke to Lady Tinkle. "Would you like my seat?"

She gave every appearance of wanting it, but hesitated. In fact, she did everything in her power—little glances, expressions of discomfort and condescension—to make Amber tell her to take Nabnak's seat.

Nabnak smiled as they passed each other, and it doubly amused him when she averted her eyes. Amber also sensed her defection, but was not so amused. For the past several hours he was turning over doubts about Yak, and now this. It was beginning to seem the only person in the tractor he could depend upon, ironically, was Bronson Bodine!

The tractor drove smoothly across the ice shelf. The treads growled against the snow. The tractor burst through the occasional drifts without the slightest check on its speed. Bronson discovered infrared goggles beneath

195

the seat and put them on. He switched off the white headlamps and activated the infrared lights that were clustered around a mast on the tractor's roof. They illuminated everything inside a surprisingly broad radius. The others saw pitch black through the tractor windows, while Bronson saw a deep purple plane stretching beneath a crimson sky in which the stars appeared suspended in concentric auras of cadmium, cerulean, lavender, sangria, and amethyst.

To Bronson's right, Lady Tinkle appeared to have copper skin and emerald hair. It startled and amused him to see her in such colors. She was in her way a supernatural being, a glowing archetype in some tragic myth about her own lack of self-regard. Thinking deeper on it, he wondered at his own tendency to reflect on beautiful women in unusual and exotic ways. Unsatisfied with the insight, he turned to the business of driving.

The pole was still over two-hundred miles away when Bronson called their attention to the strange green cube to the left.

"Where?" asked Nabnak.

"There," Bronson said, and he pointed into the darkness.

"It's the goggles," said Nabnak.

"Of course." Bronson activated the headlamps and turned slightly to the left of their polar heading. "Do you see it now?"

"Something," said Nabnak. There was a tiny reflection of light, about two-thirds of a mile straight ahead. "A cube, did you say?"

Bronson throttled up to full power. "It's a tractor."

"Avast!" growled Amber. He leaned forward. "A tractor, you say? Moving, is it?"

"No," answered Bronson. It looks shut down; maybe for some time. I don't see any heat." Bronson removed the goggles. His eyes blinked a few times. "Were you expecting someone, Cap'n?"

"Not expecting," said Amber in his angry, energetic way, "But hoping! Upon my soul, hoping!"

Bronson throttled down as they drew near the tractor. It appeared deserted. "You want to zip up, Nabnak?"

They circled the tractor and dropped Nabnak behind it. Bronson drove in a half circle and turned to direct the headlamps at the front of the other machine. There was too much frost inside the other's windshield to see inside.

"There's someone in there," Bronson said, pulling his hood up.

"I'm coming with 'e," growled Amber.

Bronson, Amber and Yak dropped into the snow and trudged up to the other tractor. Nabnak waved at them from the rear, and with hand signals indicated he was going to open the door. Bronson went to the front door on the opposite side and started banging. At the same time, Nabnak threw open the back door and leaped inside.

"Bronson!" called the Eskimo. "There's an unconscious man in here."

The big agent yanked open the door and thrust his head inside. Nabnak was kneeling over a half-frozen form wearing advanced polar gear not unlike their own.

"Is he alive?" asked Bronson.

But Amber had forced his way in before Nabnak could answer. He pulled the hood away from the stranger's face. It was a familiar face, topped with thin blond hair. "Avast! Lads, it be Carstairs! Me prayers is answered, mysterious like." He rifled through Carstairs' snowsuit and pulled out a roll of blue notes. "Ah, the sweet money which is by rights mine. Justice is done." He grinned at their startled faces—his teeth set edge-to-edge—and crammed the roll into his parka.

"He's half asleep," said Nabnak. Bronson crawled back through the cab.

"Aye," growled Amber. "Halfs asleep n' halfs dead. He's got a leg in both the blacker worlds. Leave him, and let the blackest world take all!"

Bronson glared angrily at Amber. "Captain Catastrophe, can you put the swashbuckling, seventeenth-century personality big top on hold! It's become a frightful bore!" Bronson lowered his voice in strange emphasis. "A frightful bore."

Amber wrinkled his lips and looked at Nabnak.

Nabnak shrugged.

"Come on," said Bronson, who was feeling Carstairs' pulse. "Let's move him back to the tractor."

Nabnak jumped to the ice and Bronson and Amber handed down the stiff form. Yak, who had been waiting outside, helped the Eskimo carry Carstairs to their tractor. Once inside, they undid Carstairs' snowsuit and began rubbing his limbs. Lady Tinkle held a rag over his frostbitten mouth.

"Mind you," said Amber in an false apologetic tone. "I don't wish 'em to die. It's just 'e and 'is mates is what's to do with me stolen ship. Things been done to me crew's what's I'm in vinegar about. I'm a charitable man. So whats if 'e kicks me in me 'ead when me back's turned and steals me money?!"

Bronson viewed Amber like he was something coiling around. "Sure, I understand, Cap'n."

Amber nodded. "I just don't wants to appear ungentlemanly, eh? That reflects poorly on President Bones, we being mates 'n all."

"What happened to the other tractor?" asked Lady Tinkle.

"There were a couple of bullet holes in the rear," said Nabnak. "It ran out of fuel."

Carstairs became conscious then and stared at the people around him. He said nothing, but with his expression acknowledged he was now safe. He closed his eyes again and went back to sleep.

Bronson was taking his pulse. "He'll be all right." He set the wrist down and went forward.

"Aye," said Amber. "He'll be all right. We'll fix 'em up good for he can stands trial." The captain banged himself down in the front passenger seat.

Bronson put the tractor into gear and slid the throttle forward. "Stand trial?"

"Aye, we'll finds 'em guilty and make 'em walk the plank."

Bronson was about to put on the infrared goggles, but instead he placed them on the dash. "Weren't you saying something about charity a moment ago?"

"Walk'n the plank's very humane, me thinks," said Amber "Ain't cruel, and it certainly ain't unusual."

"Thaw him out and make him walk the plank?"

"Aye. Just so."

Bronson thought a moment. "What if he had a cataract in his eye? Would you take it out before you made him walk the plank?"

The captain raised his hand over his own bad eye. He was mildly angry. "What's this then! A parable?"

From out of nowhere (his sleeve perhaps?) Bronson produced a fourteen-inch Bowie knife. "A parable, as you might say. Aye." Bronson turned the blade slightly and it reflected the glowing lights of the instrument panel. "Cap'n, why don't you let me remove your cataract."

"With that?!"

"Sure. I've done it before."

Amber lowered his hand. "What? Takes away what the Lord puts there? Nay. Besides, President Bones has no left eye a'tall."

"Ah, but don't you understand," said Bronson. "That cataract is preventing you from beholding the Heavenly Admiral's true orders."

"What dost thou mean to say?"

"Well, what you were saying about Billy Bones. It sounds like the half-blind leading the half-blind. You know deep down that the industrialists Bones is in cahoots with caused your cataract, don't you? They're polluting the atmosphere. Sure. Their industry has destroyed the ozone and let in the ultra-violet rays that gave you that cataract. All those hours staring across the sea—it ate out your eye. Even right here, even though we're in the middle of the six-month darkness, even here there's a hole open out to space and letting in the ultra-violet that by rights should be reflected back into infinity."

"Ah," said Amber. "Thy faith is weak. Dost thou think the Heavenly Admiralty would allow us to destroy ourselves? And even if it's so, would the Admiralty log it against us if we was just to ignore it? They wouldn't put it upon simple sea fare'n folk like myself to fix the sky."

"Are you so sure? It seems to me, Cap'n, that once you set your mind to accomplishing something, you do it."

"Alone against the universe like the fallen First Mate? Nay." Amber shuddered with revulsion.

Bronson was amused by the allusion. "No, not alone. I represent an organization of sportsmen and enthusiasts who think fixing the sky isn't out of the hands of individuals. We have extensive facilities, laboratories, libraries, aircraft, submarines, computers, satellites—we have infiltrated the government, the military, industry—it's only a matter of time before we take over. As a Spectrum agent you must have heard of Eddie Allan, the inspiration of our movement."

"Ach!" cried Amber knowingly. "So it's clear to me now. Thou art an agent of the Invisible Tower. Aye, I've read the dossier on your organization. And that crazy manifesto, b'gosh! I know all abouts Eddie Allan and Mikhail Bakunin. There's another one. Reilly. Syd Reilly."

"That's interesting," said Bronson. "I would have expected you to know Allan's and Bakunin's names, but not others. Maybe you're misinformed?"

"Nay. We learn more about thy activities every day." Amber shook his head. "You're a bunch of mad scientists that don't know what's what. No religion. No rituals. What kind of world is it you'd build? Yer stumbling into dictatorship and you don't even know it. Bah! You don't recognize inequality betwixt men. You don't believe in riches nor treasures. You don't believe that the Heavenly Admiralty looks out for men what looks out for themselves. Tsk-tsk-tsk. Now Spectrum—my crew—we sees what's going on and what goes to who fer doing what. Aye, pious action it is to do what's best for thyself. It means you understand where the Admiralty 'as puts you in this blasted universe, and yer doing yer best to look after yerself. Thou art a blessed child of the Heavenly Cap'n, who helps them best what helps themselves. Take care of that child. Aye, and we got a trump of a leader in Bill Bones. We're the ones what's taking over, my little son."

"Says you," Bronson said with a touch of clever affect, but at the same time he sensed Amber's thinking was less extravagant than his manner might suggest.

Amber cocked his head and out of the side of his mouth spoke with sure and steady accusation: "You're a bunch of ivory tower control freaks what's read too much Plato. Moreover, people knows how yer flim-flam works, portrayin' Gawd-fear'n Christians as un-edycated Bible-thump'n swabs 'n money-grub'n frauds. Aye, I can 'magine how someone like you would describe *me* if this tale was to be told. But it's all a decoy. Technocrat propaganda 'n psychedelic toad piss! Aye, an' where'd *you* get *yer* money, eh? As sure as eggs is eggs, we're sailing the same seas thar, me buck-o; aye, if sense sarves me wrong, and the other waren't. Pah! Truth burns but lies consume! Nature's God and nature's laws! You can't change 'em with public relations, mysterious artifacts, squatting up and down in yer yoga hornpipes, stickin' peculiar thangs in yer arifices, nor weave'n childish tales 'bout revolutions in consciousness."

"Maybe I'll show you different," said Bronson. "Let me remove that cataract." He fingered the knife blade. "No charge."

"Gad!" Amber shook his head. "*No charge*? Thems two words haves a blasphemous ring! I ask you, man to man, not to use such language in front of Lady Tin—"

"What's that!" called Nabnak. He leaned forward and pointed at the windshield.

"What?" said Bronson. He turned to discover the source of Nabnak's bewildered cry, and immediately braked the tractor. He was surprised the objects—figures, rather—were so close, of a sudden dominating the scene before them. There, standing like statues on the icy field, literally frozen in place, were three Provincial Academic Philistines with their limbs held in odd configurations, like semaphores of some kind.

The first, standing perfectly straight, held his arms out in a "T". The second pointed with his right hand to the sky and his left hand to the ground. Deeply squatting, his legs were broadly splayed. The third stood upon his left foot. His right was just off the ground, the toe pointing downward. His arms were raised at either side and bent at right angles, forearms vertical, like a Whirling Dervish; but of course his "whirling" form was frozen in space and time. All three figures glistened with rime ice.

Bronson winced as he realized the Paps had evidently assumed these positions while a fourth had poured water over them. They had sacrificed themselves in these positions, freezing themselves to serve as a sign for... for their fellows, perhaps? or for posterity? There was very much an ancient and tomb-like feeling about the scene. Compare statues standing before the entrance to a necropolis, though here little more than empty fields of ice waited beyond.

Amber growled knowingly.

"Can you read those postures?" asked Bronson.

Amber stroked his goatee as he pondered sharing his interpretation. But the meaning of the Paps' "signal" was so obscure there seemed no reason to demure. "Aye," he said at last, and then slowly recited the following:

> Passing from what was into spectacle
> A frozen moment awaits, outlasting all others
> Ahead, all that is to come

Amber's voice was well-tuned to deliver the cryptic lines. The significance was a true mystery, but the barbaric nature of the Pap's self-sacrifice was plain enough; their ice-covered forms, their discipline, their indifference to their own suffering—what a lurid scene of self-abasement! Feeling himself nearly hypnotized by the sight of the—what?—foolish puzzle, Bronson threw the tractor into gear and roared around the frozen Paps. The grotesque scene was left behind.

At last Nabnak said, "Evidently, Jon Yesterday has made an impression on the Paps."

After some hesitation, Bronson agreed. The others were mostly silent. Lady Tinkle observed they might do well to turn the tractor around and return to the coast. Amber balked at this, and then, a little later, several times hummed knowingly. Yak appeared indifferent, Carstairs remained oblivious.

Then once more Nabnak was leaning forward and pointing out the windscreen. "There!"

Bronson sought to follow the direction of the pointing hand. "What?"

"A big circle—something—rolled across our path, moving fast."

"Circle?" said Bronson.

"Yes. A disk—I think." Nabnak gestured eagerly. "Put on the goggles."

Bronson switched off the headlamps, switched on the infrared lights, and donned the goggles.

Once more he saw the eerie purple plane, the crimson sky, and the auras of the stars. In the distance he could make out the edge of the ice shelf and the black outline of the Queen Maud Mountains. There was nothing else. Then, abruptly, a salvo of green disks flew out from behind the mountains, seven or eight of them and moving fast. They shot overhead. There was a series of sonic booms.

"What is it?" said Amber. Yak and Lady Tinkle pushed up beside Nabnak and together they gazed into the blackness beyond the windshield.

"Projectiles of some kind," explained Bronson. "Here come more."

He watched them fly out from behind the mountains. They were lower this time. They hit the plane a half mile ahead. Some of them skipped and rocketed up once more through the darkness. Others embedded themselves in the ice or rolled across the plane like giant coins; they appeared perhaps ten feet in diameter.

"Are they shooting at us?" asked Nabnak.

"Evasive maneuvers!" ordered Amber.

Bronson pushed the throttle forward and turned to the left.

Then he saw the ornithopter.

It swooped in low across the ice, dipping and rising, banking and darting, coasting and surging forward as its wings reached and pulled back. Never before had Bronson seen such a craft. It seemed as much fish as it was bird.

Long metal spines supported the wings and the long, forked tail. Much of the craft's mechanism was exposed; the back of the machine and the cockpit-head were sheathed in bright metal.

Now another salvo of green disks streaked in from the mountains. The ornithopter was clearly the target. It jerked almost to a complete stop and pulled up. The disks shot before the nose of the craft. It backed slightly and then dipped forward and swooped down toward the tractor.

"It's an ornithopter," said Bronson, who continued to be very much amazed. "A big one." He switched on the headlamps. It was coming down at them. The tips of its wings turned up and the tail twisted diagonally. It abruptly slowed, and then cleanly flared as landing gear with tank treads lowered from its belly. Then, its massive wings slowly back-flapping, the ornithopter settled down tentatively and gracefully. And there it stood sixty yards before them with its wings half-folded and held menacingly over the fuselage.

"Theories?" asked Bronson.

"Maybe it's the Lemurians?" suggested Nabnak.

"I says we drive under it so we're out of them guns' line o'fire." Amber pointed at the cannon muzzles in the craft's blunt nose.

"Perhaps we're expected," said Lady Tinkle. "Turn on the radio."

Bronson did so—and revved up the turbine to full power. His hand rested on the transmission lever.

The lights on the radio flickered as it scanned the frequency bands. It locked onto something: "This is Sky Watch. Ice Snake, do you read? Do you require assistance, Ice Snake?" There was a pause for several seconds. "Ice Snake, hold on. We're coming out to get you."

A ramp began lowering from the belly of the ornithopter.

Bronson turned to Amber. "Are you Ice Snake?"

Amber frowned—then there was a bang. Carstairs had slammed the door open and was jumping from the tractor.

Yak and Nabnak turned to follow him, but Bronson called them back. Then Carstairs came to view in the front window.

"He runs pretty well for a sick man," growled Amber vengefully—then he was knocked back in his seat as Bronson shoved the tractor into gear.

Two men with machine guns were running down the ornithopter's ramp. They opened fire on the tractor. At the same time the ornithopter's cannons went off, but the tractor was too close. The shells bit into ice.

Amber drew his pistols. "Good-oh! Drive, lad! Right under the bird. We'll board 'er! Let the devil take the hindmost!" He scrambled across Yak's back and crouched ready by the open door.

"No!" ordered Bronson. "Nabnak, close the door!"

The cannons fired again. Bronson turned to the right and raced behind the ornithopter.

Yak sat quietly as Nabnak pulled Amber back and slammed the door.

"Avast, thou monkey!" Amber raised his pistols—but Nabnak snatched them away. Amber sat there startled, blinking. He looked at Yak. "Lubber, art thou content to see thy cap'n treated so?"

Yak averted his eyes.

Amber sighed, and then looked up at Lady Tinkle. She quickly turned away; then, composing herself, she turned forward to watch Bronson drive the tractor.

Bronson was adjusting the periscope mirror, turning it to fix on the ornithopter. He had just framed it in the viewer when suddenly it spread its wings and leaped into the air. It gained altitude rapidly, and then shot off in the direction of the coast. From behind the mountains more disks appeared and chased after the ornithopter. With an uncanny mixture of mechanical and life-imitating movements, the flapping craft dodged the disks and was soon lost in the darkness.

Amber sat in the back of the tractor with a philosophical look on his face. "Well, Bill Bones is still me friend. True as 'is word, old Bill is. A gentle-man. Upon my soul, a man of the cloth. Aye, I remember that old tent beside the midway. He'd pack 'em in, ol' Bill would. Have 'em hootin' and hollern' about such things as a body can only point to and wonder. Bold Billy Bones and 'is Old Time Revival... Oh, them was the days. He had a way of fixin' on you with that one eye a'is. Shazam! Makes you think it was St. Vitas Dance to see 'em jump'n o'er chairs and roll'n in the aisles..."

The tractor continued on. In another hour it was angling across the lower slopes of the Queen Maud Mountains. The machine zigzagged, steering around cliffs of ice and black rock as it climbed higher. The atmosphere began taking on a solid, glassy appearance. The stars grew into crystalline figures that refracted prismatically, while the cool blues and greens of the Aurora Australis glimmered over the mountains like stage curtains drawing aside to reveal the wreck of the world.

They passed through the mountains and found themselves creeping onto the plane of the great glacier that capped the interior of the continent. It sloped up gradually. Before them—seventy miles away, five-thousand feet higher in elevation—the pole awaited.

10

BRONSON STOOD SHIVERING on the million-year-old ice. His snowsuit was barely a match for the wind that was gusting now to forty knots. Nabnak, Amber and Yak stood huddled against the side of the tractor. At the rear of the vehicle a plume of white exhaust trailed horizontally.

The tractor had been stopped at the edge of the Magnetic Defense Zone, repelled by the electromagnetic field radiating from the dark brown ceramic material that everywhere covered the plane before them. Lemuria Two was out there in the darkness, fifty miles further on.

Bronson stooped at the edge of what was surely the largest machine ever built by human beings. It seemed to have been shoveled into place like asphalt and then rolled level. He wondered at the financial resources of the Lemurians. How could any group, save a government, afford to cover almost eight-thousand square miles of Antarctica with superconducting material? He stood and walked on to it. He felt nothing, though the idea of stepping into a magnetic field strong enough to repel the tractor made him uneasy.

He turned and looked at his companions huddled by the tractor, then stared back in the direction of the pole. If not for the wind they could walk the fifty miles to Lemuria Two. He took the infrared goggles from his pocket and put them on. The superconducting plane appeared maroon. At a point along the horizon was a faint yellow glow. It was surely their destination. He stared at it for a few moments and then rejoined his companions.

"What do you think?" asked Nabnak.

Bronson shook his head. "I'd say walk, except for this wind. Perhaps the snow tractor could be modified; we might be able to connect the frame to the generator and degauss it. That might work."

Nabnak agreed.

"D'ye hear something?" barked Amber.

They all wheeled toward the pole. There was something coming at them. A shadow flashed by. There was a great slamming thud and the ground vibrated.

They ran behind the tractor. Twenty-feet away, a metal disk—eight feet in diameter by a foot thick—had embedded itself in the ice. It was solid cast and curved on one side to form an airfoil. Nabnak compared it to a giant Frisbee.

They heard the noise again.

"Lady Tinkle!" exclaimed Amber. He ran up to the tractor and threw the door back. He called for her. She jumped out as the tractor was hit.

The disk blasted the tractor into the air, flipping it over and over. It landed in a heap of twisted metal, completely smashed out of shape. Turbine fuel spilled out across the ice.

Bronson, Nabnak and Yak had been knocked over by the concussion. They got up and ran to Captain Amber and Lady Tinkle who lay together in a heap.

Bronson began feeling the woman's limbs for a break. "You're lucky," he said as her head cleared.

"Luck, bah!" bellowed the seaman. "'T'was the wits of Cap'n Amber what saved 'er."

Lady Tinkle was without her parka. Amber gave her his own. Meanwhile, Nabnak and Yak went through the tractor's wreckage. They found her parka, but it was soaked with turbine fuel, as were the tents and sleeping bags. Yak wringed out the parka and brought it to Amber. With shaking fingers the buccaneer put it on.

Bronson was standing behind them examining the first disk. "Nabnak!"

Nabnak came up and they began pushing the disk back and forth. Yak joined them and the three men managed to break it free. Bronson estimated it weighed nearly a quarter-ton. With difficulty they wheeled it across the ice toward the superconductor.

"Now push it over," said Bronson.

The disk fell toward the superconducting surface and miraculously rebounded against an invisible force—it sprang up to rest at a thirty-degree angle. They stooped to haul up on the bottom edge of the disk and then slid it over the edge of the superconductor where it flattened out and floated four feet in the air. Bronson steadied it against the tendency it had to move toward the ice. He turned it left and right. "It may rest at equilibrium further inside the perimeter," he suggested.

It was worth a try. They pushed the disk to a point thirty yards from the edge and, just as Bronson had predicted, it stayed put.

"It's completely frictionless," he said. "If not for the wind we could send this to Lemuria Two with one good shove."

"Now if it wasn't for the wind." Nabnak rapped the disk with his gloved fist and marked a slight resonance.

Bronson pushed the disk so it rotated slowly. "So it will take ten shoves, or maybe fifty. It doesn't matter. We will ride on it, huddled together to keep each other warm. One of us will push. We can take turns. Yak, get the captain and Lady Tinkle, then help Nabnak bring whatever provisions you can salvage from the tractor."

Nabnak and Yak ran back to the ice to tell the others what was to be done. The combination of fuel, fumes and cold had made Amber unwell; Yak had to carry him to the disk. It lowered a fraction of an inch as the captain was laid upon it. Yak ran back to help Nabnak.

"Will this work?" asked the woman as Bronson helped her onto the disk.

"I told you I'd try and keep us alive." He nodded at the wrecked tractor. "And I think Captain Amber has especially succeeded in keeping you alive."

She gave up any hopes she had about Bronson then and there. "And I said I'd stand by my man." She took off her gloves and turned to warm Amber's face with her hands.

Bronson's eyes dropped and he pushed lightly on the disk, gauging its inertia.

Then Nabnak and Yak came bounding up with the provisions.

"I'll push," said Bronson. The others climbed on the disk.

He lowered the goggles over his eyes and could see the heat from their bodies radiating and rushing off with the wind. He leaned into the disk. Initially it almost seemed to push back, but once started it was easy to keep moving. It accelerated before him. Soon he was sprinting behind it and if it wasn't for Nabnak's out-stretched hand he would have been left behind. He caught the hand and Nabnak pulled him aboard.

"About thirteen miles an hour," said Bronson, huddling into the warmth of their bodies.

Every few minutes he lowered his legs from the edge and kicked at the plane to get them back on course for the pole.

"This would make a good sport," said Nabnak.

Bronson agreed. "But how would you play?"

Nabnak thought a moment. "Make the disks smaller and ride lower to the ground, then race around on them like skateboards."

"I don't know," said Bronson. "I kind of like cruising along like this. It's like a little pleasure tour. How about a snack?"

Captain Amber burst out with an expletive. "Ar! Pleasure tour! By thunder, it must be sixty below!"

Nabnak passed Bronson a cheese sandwich. "Anybody else?"

"May I, please?" asked Lady Tinkle.

Nabnak handed her a cheese sandwich. "Captain Amber?"

"Unless you have something what goes with the smell of fuel!"

Yak seemed to want something, but he shook his head. "I no wanna eat in front of my cap'n."

Amber pursed his lips proudly when he heard Yak express these sentiments, then he growled at him: "Good lad; 'bout time that ugly head of yearns come to 'is senses. Rub my legs for me. They is cold. Chop, chop!"

After the sandwiches were swallowed and they were done rubbing their teeth with their tongues—which was nearly impossible in the cold—Bronson handed the infrared goggles to Nabnak. "Look where we're headed."

Nabnak put them on and stared at the horizon. About five miles away was a large yellow dome. It looked perhaps fifteen stories tall, a perfect half-sphere. A quarter mile from the dome was a pillar of hot gas—a white flame, actually, and at least fifty feet tall. The goggles made it possible for Nabnak to see how the heat trailed away as a long curving smear through the sky. The trace of heat became yellow, orange, then a progressively deeper and deeper red until it was obscured in the crimson sky.

"Take the goggles off," suggested Bronson.

Nabnak did so. Now knowing where to look, he could make out the faint emerald glow of the dome. Nearby, the column of flame appeared shorter, and it was blue now with a bright violet cone at the base. Nabnak compared it to the flame of a Bunsen burner. "Evidently the exhaust from their power plant."

Bronson took the goggles and put them on. "We'll go there to warm up and rest before we meet the Lemurians. He turned to dangle his legs off the edge of the disk. With one kick he adjusted their course.

Soon he was lowering his feet once more—this time to slow their progress. Yak followed his example and dragged his feet as well. Nabnak stood up on the disk to take in the scene.

The flame loomed larger and larger before them. It buzzed deeply, evidently the exhaust of a large, slowly-moving turbine. Beyond it was the dome, easily 150 feet tall and raising above the plane like the bald head of some ruinous genius.

They began to warm rapidly as the disk slid within seventy feet of the flame. Without the super-cold, the superconducting material lost its effectiveness, and the disk descended until it slid into the ground. They dismounted. Amber tore off the damp parka and angrily cast it aside as the others stomped their feet and began shedding their outer garments. They stretched their arms and legs, turning round and round to warm themselves against the rushing flame.

"My bones are cold inside me," Nabnak said with wonder. "I can actually feel my bones are cold inside me." He nodded at something. "Who's that?"

A solitary figure was walking toward them, meanwhile keeping to a circle about fifty feet from the flame. It appeared to be a woman with shoulder-length red hair, garbed in blue jeans shorts and a tie-dye T-shirt. Then they could see it was a young man. He stopped to wave when he was about thirty feet away, and then he came up to them.

"Welcome to the witches' meeting on the edge of nowhere."

This charmed a little levity out of Bronson, which was never very difficult. "Gee, witch boy, we must have made a wrong turn somewhere. We were looking for the Lost Empire of the Lumurians."

The stranger didn't seem to mind being called "witch boy." He pointed at the dome. "The Lemurians are inside the phalanstery. You are welcome to join them if you wish… that is if you have an appetite for freaking the mind fantastic."

"Not your cup of tea?" Bronson asked.

The witch boy had a charming manner, but his acute intelligence was tinctured with cynicism and immaturity. He smiled up at Bronson like an insincere keeper of mystical secrets. "I've overstayed my welcome, that's

all. Come with me. I've got some milk crates we can sit on, back this way."
He hooked his thumb over his shoulder. "And lots of beer."

They began walking. Nabnak and Yak carried the provisions while
Amber, naked from the waist up, wiped the oily fuel from his body with
Yak's parka.

Bronson asked the witch boy how he came to Antarctica.

"About six months ago," he began, "I got a ride on a yacht. You know,
one of those deals where you wash the dishes and now and then give the
skipper's wife a little attention? We left Santa Cruz and went to Hawaii,
stayed there a couple of weeks, and then went down to the Marquesas. But
along the way we were becalmed for about a week at the equator. Not only
the skipper's wife, but the skipper started pinching me, too."

"Yachties," grumbled Captain Amber with disdain.

"Yeah, anyway," continued the witch boy. "When we got down to Nuku
Hiva I ran away. I wandered around the island for a couple of days. I met a
taxi driver, and I almost convinced him the world was flat. Eventually I
stumbled into the Lemurians' valley. It was free, so I hung out there, sipping
pina coladas while the wives of all these old broken-down rock stars and
comic book artists ran their fingers through my hair. They asked me to go to
Antarctica with them. 'Why not?' I thought. So we flew down here. But I
wouldn't go into the phalanstery with them." He glanced over at the dome
with mixed contempt and frustration. "No way."

They had reached the witch boy's little encampment. There was a big
cooler and four plastic milk crates set in a semi-circle. Bronson, Amber,
Lady Tinkle and the witch boy sat.

"Beer?" said the witch boy. He began passing around the longneck
bottles.

Nabnak wrinkled his nose as a bottle was passed his way. As an agent of
the Invisible Tower, the thought of taking depressants repulsed him.

"Go ahead," said Bronson. "One or two is a good idea in this cold."

Nabnak reluctantly opened a bottle, sniffed, tasted. He stuck out his
tongue.

Yak swallowed the contents of his first bottle in one gulp. The next he
nursed, kissing and sucking at the bottle's mouth.

"Tell me about the Lemurians," said Bronson. "What are they up to?"

The witch boy gazed over at the dome. A bitter expression came over his face. "No way." He spit with loathing. "I ain't going in there."

Bronson stared up at the tall blue flame, watched it lick at the stars. "Were you ever inside the dome?"

"For about two seconds. Then—wham!—I was out of there." The witch boy shook his head. "Were you ever asleep on a stormy night in July when suddenly you were awakened by an exploding transformer and thought they dropped the bomb?"

Bronson smiled. "Yes, as a matter of fact. That happened to me once." He sipped his beer.

"Then you know," said the witch boy, and he glanced over his shoulder at the dome and shuddered.

Bronson mused on this, then found his thoughts turning to Jon Yesterday, the leader of the Lemurians, the visionary who had brought so many people—including himself—to this strange outpost at the bottom of the world. He asked the witch boy what he thought of the great artist.

"He's a strange man." The witch boy cocked his head as he sifted through the many ambiguities. "He is certainly a visionary, but rather childish when it comes to judgement. He doesn't seem to see a difference between his paintings and the real world. He is very likeable, the way a little kid is likable. You can tell he was charismatic when he was young, and it shapes the way he thinks about everything, including the creations of his own mind." The witch boy looked up at the big agent and was impressed that Bronson was a man of many talents, not all of them benign. "Anyway, what do you think of him?"

"I'll let you know after I meet him." Bronson appraised the situation. "Is there a way to shut down the Magnetic Defense Zone?"

The witch boy nodded. "Yeah. On the other side of the flame there's a manhole cover. Leads down into the power plant. I thought about shutting it all down. But it would kill the Lemurians." He narrowed his eyes at the dome. "They're so vulnerable, so weak; but they're also hungry. They want to eat you. Use your soul. Absorb your energy."

Bronson set his beer down on the superconductor plane. He stood. "This shouldn't take long. Nabnak, will you join me, please?"

Together they moved off.

Yak sat down on Bronson's crate. "I no like the looks of that dome too."

Captain Amber agreed. "I gots my money. I wants no more to do with them Lemurians. Aye, they be a strange lot."

Lady Tinkle undid her shirt, exposing the top of her black bikini. "I'd like to know how we're getting out of here."

Amber grunted, "Aye."

"Why do you talk like the president?" asked the witch boy. "You don't go for that pirate malarkey, do ya?"

Amber returned a cold stare. "President Bones is my mate, I'm proud to tell."

The witch boy laughed contemptuously and opened another beer. "Why don't you go choose a real act. I mean, that Billy Bones is like right off the side of a cardboard cereal box.

"What knows you about it, thou cheeky, cream-faced son of ignorant fancy?"

The witch boy belched. "Yeah. I know all about it. Billy Bones, high priest of the guilt-ridden leach. He keeps all the working-class stooges entertained with the commandments of Complex Beef Chief—the TV Admiral who holds the keys to a great treasure chest full of hamburgers. I'm not uneducated, you know."

"Aye." Amber nodded sadly. "But thou lacks a proper sense for it all. Accept how it's all laid out for a slick hell spawn such as yer ugly and vile self. Take it upon yer rotten shoulders to choose a better treasure than what's on the TV. Let them that's donkeys donkey, if they wants to you. You and I know what's fer." Amber winked. "Aye, and mum's the word."

But the witch boy wasn't swayed by Amber's wise counsel. He went on: "And the donkeys set their alarm clocks to pop off good and early so they can get out there and find the great housewife in the sky before the pins work out of their tails and they become lonely old men cast adrift on cold wet streets with Ebola zombies picking through their empty pockets. Spooky. Keep a stiff upper lip!"

"Hast thou not heard the affy-davy of Cap'n Jesus?" said Amber earnestly, and not without compassion.

"Yeah." The witch boy belched. "He died to give us something to think about during our leisure hours."

Yak grunted in such a peculiar way that the witch boy burst out into crazy guffaws. Amber pronounced them all damned, and then himself deeply chortled at their lost state. Lady tinkle waved her hand dismissively as she musically declaimed, "Silly men."

Bronson and Nabnak returned just then.

"What's everyone laughing at?" asked the Eskimo.

One after the other, the witch boy tossed the agents bottles of beer. "Sinbad and I were exchanging old treasure tales."

Amber ignored him. "Dids't thou shut down the Defense Zone, Bodine?"

With much hearty gusto the big agent opened his beer. "Aye, Cap'n. Nothing for it now but to wait."

"That's what this place is all about," said the witch boy. He twisted his mouth to the side as he sat staring at the flame. He quietly mused: "Somehow I wonder if life is where we prepare ourselves to escape from our identity."

"I always thought it was the other way around," said Bronson. "Life is where we prepare ourselves to accept identity."

"How about a place where we outgrow our personality?" retorted the witch boy.

"Isn't that what I just said?" Bronson could feel his tongue inside his mouth, all the way down to where it smoothed into his throat.

Overhead the aurora turned red and streamed like threads of lava across the sky. The glimmer of the stars darted through it, arrow-like.

"Does anyone feel deranged?" asked Nabnak.

Everyone nodded.

"The Lemurians are giving off some kind of force from the phalanstery," explained the witch boy. He looked beyond the flame at the dome. "I'm never going back in there. Never."

"I'm going to march right in," said Bronson.

"Why?" asked the witch boy.

Bronson opened another beer. "Because when I'm afraid of something without knowing why, it makes me angry." He took a slug. "And when I'm angry I do something about it. You got to overcome fear, overcome it with the solitary resource of your own resolution."

The witch boy nodded at the pirate. "You're talking like Sinbad."

Overhead, the flapping shadow of an ornithopter moved against the aurora.

"Avast!" called Amber. "They's back."

Everyone looked up and watched the ornithopter as it soared by. It continued in a straight and unswerving line, it's long membranous wings slowly pulling the craft through the black Antarctic night. Bronson put on the infrared goggles. Soon the ornithopter was out of sight. "It's gone," he said.

"Can I see those goggles?" said the witch boy. Bronson handed them over and the witch boy put them on.

"Ar!" grunted Amber. "My turn next."

"I wonder who that ornithopter belongs to?" asked Nabnak.

"Yeah," the witch boy said, blinking his eyes as he removed the goggles. "And what's it doing here?"

"Most obviously reconnaissance," said Amber as he took the goggles and put them on. "Hey-ho! This be a wondrous trick. Sell them to me, Bodine!" The pirate took them off and gave them to Lady Tinkle. "Try these on, my love. Well, Bodine? How much? What says you?"

But Bronson was looking out across the superconductor plane. Another aircraft was approaching. The others followed Bronson's gaze and found the aircraft's winking navigation lights hanging in the sky. Soon they could hear the whistling craft and then its silver form was illuminated by the flame.

"Our friends!" exclaimed Nabnak as he recognized the sleek outlines of the Dornier Do-31E VTOL transport. It hovered in with deliberate intent, yawing slightly as it slowed. Gasses sputtered from control nozzles. It lowered to a precise touchdown one-hundred feet away. As the engines began whining down, the cargo ramp at the tail smoothly lowered. Invisible Tower agents Vitaly Yurchenko and Chief Lonetree emerged dragging two large crates down to the artificial ground. Bronson and Nabnak ran up to help them.

"What do you have?" asked Bronson.

"Special equipment." Vitaly held a crow bar and with it began pulling nails from the top of the crate. "Eddie Allan suggested we bring it along."

"Eddie knows what's going on down here?"

Vitaly stopped drawing nails. "Everyone knows what's going on down here: MI-6, CIA, NSA, the Invisible Tower, Network, Hegemony, Spectrum, *L'Aliénation Internationale*, United Dictatorships; even *they* do. *They* have one of their best men snooping around, an Australian named Carstairs. Eddie says to watch out for him."

"I think he just flew by. What is it, Vitaly? What are the Lemurians up to?"

The big Russian shrugged. "Either Eddie didn't know, or he wouldn't say. I have the feeling he wouldn't say because if we knew—"

Bronson finished the sentence "—because if we knew we wouldn't go near them. What's in the crates?"

"I don't know." Vitaly heaved the crowbar and began drawing nails. "Special equipment. It's been a fast two days."

"You got the hovercraft to the proper authorities?"

Vitaly nodded. "And Amnesty International is seeing to it that the aboriginal peoples are returned to their homelands."

Bronson nodded. "Listen, Vitaly. Keep that under your hat. I've got Amber with me here."

Vitaly glanced up at the silhouettes sitting before the rushing flame. "Who are the others?"

"His girlfriend, one of his sailors, and some kid who followed the Lemurians down here."

"What is this!?" Nabnak exclaimed. He and Lonetree had gotten the lid off the other crate.

Then Vitaly was pulling the lid off his crate. Bronson looked inside.

"Prehensile tails," said the big agent, betraying less surprise than Nabnak. He reached inside and pulled out a plaid skirt. "And kilts!"

They all looked at each other.

Each crate contained two kilts, two Tam O'Shanters with matching tartan bands, and two prehensile tails. The tails were six inches thick and eight feet long with furry tentacles at the base. The tentacles were curled up, and they were lined on the underside, like the arms of an octopus, with suction cups. The tails were hairless, muscular, and the veins bulged everywhere beneath their pale white skin. They were not pleasant to look at.

"I have one question," Nabnak said, pulling down his trousers. "Why are we doing this?"

No one answered. It was an eerie feeling bringing the tails up to their naked backsides and feeling the tentacles coil around their waists, the suckers attaching themselves.

"Ouch! Hey! This thing stung me!" cried Nabnak.

"No it didn't," said Vitaly. It stuck a needle into your spinal column to join itself with your nervous sys—ouch! Ow-ow-ow!"

Nabnak laughed. "I told you!"

They became dizzy as the genetically engineered prehensile tails acclimated themselves to their nervous systems.

"How long before they have to be fed?" asked Bronson as he slipped his legs and tail through his kilt. He pulled it up around his waist and put the bonnet on.

"You don't feed them," said Vitaly. "These are the disposable model. They should be good for about a day."

Bronson made a face like he had bitten into a lemon. "Disposable! I disagree with that on principle. Who did Eddie buy these from?"

"So is disposable," Vitaly said, shifting into his impatient Russian accent. "Who is caring, anyway?"

"Well, I am!" insisted Bronson.

Nabnak spoke quietly to Lonetree. "Why does everything have to be a moral issue?"

Bronson began lecturing Vitaly. "Disposable tails? I mean, what's next? Disposable hearts, disposable brains, disposable feet, disposable pets, disposable friends?"

"Is everybody in readiness?" asked Vitaly. He shook his head impatiently and put his bonnet on.

"Yeah," said Nabnak. "Except I don't want to wear this funny looking hat."

"Put it on!" gasped Bronson. "Why do you always have to be so contrary?" And with his tail twitching impatiently behind him he marched back to the fire.

"Did anyone ever tell you that you have perfectly handsome legs, Mr. Bodine?" Lady Tinkle looked Bronson up and down as he approached.

He smiled shyly at her, wondering what the tail looked like hanging down beneath his kilt.

Vitaly and the others joined the group.

"Well," said Bronson. "We're going in. Anybody want to come? How about you, witch boy?"

The witch boy shuddered slightly and chuckled. "No, that's all right. Tell you what, though. I sure could use a ride out of here when you come back… if you come back."

Bronson assured him. "No *ifs* about it. We'll get you out of here."

The four Tower agents drew their automags to check the magazines.

"What do you think?" asked Vitaly.

Bronson suggested Nabnak and Lonetree load up with exploding rounds, while Vitaly use armor piercing. Bronson himself would use depleted uranium shot.

They walked off toward the dome, slapping magazines into their pistols. Once they were away from the flame the wind cut through them.

"My legs!" complained Nabnak. His teeth chattered.

Bronson nodded back at him. "Aren't you glad now I told you to wear your bonnet?"

As they drew closer to the translucent dome they could make out curious shadows moving within. Some of the shadows seemed to quiver, others snapped back and forth violently, while some were very still, expanding and contracting every few moments as if something inside was breathing.

"We're being reckless," said Nabnak.

"Not reckless," insisted Vitaly. "Insane!"

They approached the side of the dome. It appeared to be made of an organic material, like the chitinous exoskeleton of an insect. They pressed their hands against it and felt a slow, throbbing reverberation, like the beating of a giant heart, or hundreds of hearts beating in synchrony.

They continued walking around the dome, at last coming before the entrance. It was a large and stately archway, without doors, fully thirty feet tall by ten feet wide. Through it came a brilliant emerald light. Their tails began shaking with expectation. This was it, the demesne of Jon Yesterday, as much a realm of mind as it was a location in space. The agents stared at each other with grim resolution. Then they went in.

Once inside the entranceway they halted and glared into the emerald light; the brilliance of bio-luminescence radiated all around them. As their eyes quickly adjusted they saw the Lemurians had joined their bodies together into one great organism. It was stretched across an aluminum scaffold that ascended to the top of the dome. The flesh stretched and coiled over the scaffold like animated putty, hanging by hooked claws that grew from the tips of bony tendrils. At the top of the thing was a massive lung turned inside out. Mucus foamed around it as it jiggled and breathed. Below the lung was a knotted core from which emerged the tendrils that wound through the structure and from which hung a bony maze of living curtains—draperies of sweaty pink flesh that folded back and forth like a living maze, scattered with faceless mouths that shrieked and laughed and cried and howled and sang and conversed in a dozen different languages.

The Tower agents gaped at it, watching it undulate and quiver. Then Vitaly was calling out in alarm.

Specialized defense tendrils covered with barbed thorns were reaching down at them. Bronson raised his automag and fired, but the tendrils were swinging in from every direction—except directly above.

The agents reached for the scaffold with their tails and pulled themselves away as the tendrils curled around to seize them.

"To the top!" called Bronson, and he sprang through a closing loop of tendril.

The agents followed Bronson up the scaffold, leaping, swinging, reaching. Beneath them the spasmodic tendrils screwed up and around the aluminum poles. The tendrils moved swiftly, forcing the agents to dodge and pivot. The men ran across the poles like tight rope walkers with arms raised outwards, balancing with their tails; they leaped and climbed higher. They kept moving, swinging around poles, diving through the air.

Once Nabnak was at the juncture of six poles with tendrils coiling at him from every direction. Vitaly reached down with his tail, grabbed Nabnak's tail, and swung him over to Lonetree, whose tail was raised to provide Nabnak with a step. The Eskimo leaped off on one foot, caught Bronson's tail in his hands, and then he swung over to a pole that he caught with his own tail. He swung half way around the pole, caught the pole with his hands and feet, and raced up it.

But there was no time to appreciate acrobatic marvels. They kept climbing for the top.

Once near the curved ceiling they ran recklessly across the poles, knowing they could catch themselves with their tails if they fell. Below them the thorny tendrils raised through the scaffolding like angry pythons. But in following the winding courses of the darting agents many of the tendrils had become tangled. Many were backing to free themselves.

Bronson drew his automag and fired at the few tendrils that were still advancing. Nabnak and Lonetree swung down below the lung to the knotted root of the tendrils and selectively fired at the bases of those tendrils that had thorns. Far below, the feverish voices of the Lemurians shrieked, caterwauled and laughed.

Lonetree and Nabnak worked quickly and deliberately, their automags exploding as they aimed at their targets. Bronson stood near and covered them, occasionally he fired. Vitaly was quietly perched fifty feet below. It was clear to him that his friends were adequately dealing with the tendrils. He holstered his automag and pulled a camera from his utility belt. As he began photographing the scaffold he realized it was arranged in a pattern that exactly inverted the ten-fold mandala of *Kṣitigarbha*... suggesting what? Vitaly thought he beheld some new form of transcendence, but its significance—if there was some significance—was completely unfamiliar to him.

Soon his friends swung down to join him. They sat quietly catching their breaths.

"What do you make of it?" said Bronson finally.

Vitaly replaced the camera. An expression of fear-repressing intensity drew back the corners of his mouth. "They've joined their bodies together. Can you believe it? The tendrils and this lung thing were either grown from genetically engineered DNA, or human flesh—or maybe created surgically from the flesh of people such as Amber had in his hold. There is yet lots of space here. Room to grow in—or to add more people."

"But what's the purpose?" wondered Nabnak. With his tail hanging down behind the bar upon which he squatted, he looked quite rugged and manly.

"Knowing the Lemurians?" Vitaly shrugged. "It's some kind of psychological experiment. Perhaps an attempt to achieve higher consciousness."

Bronson slapped a new magazine into his gun. "Why don't we ask?"

They climbed down slowly, wary of meeting the minds that could conceive such a bold affront against nature. For surely that's what it was: an attempt to join what the universe in its wisdom had kept apart, separate, and independent.

On uncoiling tails the men lowered themselves to the floor. Before them hung the tapestries of flesh. There was a regular pattern of bone and veins, as if each of the Lemurians had been stretched out, their sides sewn together to form the hanging walls. But their physical features were gone. Their limbs were indiscernible, as were their faces, sexual organs, ears, hair, nipples, blemishes. All had been leveled into one smooth homogeneous drapery of life. There were no eyes, but as the Tower agents came to the opening leading inside the folds they felt a massed presence looking out at them. And they heard the voices of the Lemurians speaking through the round, mouth-like openings which miraculously opened in the flesh—each like a pore stretched open to hundreds of times its normal diameter. To either side the talking walls formed a living corridor that went on for many yards before finding obscurity in the glowing bioluminescence.

As the agents passed into the corridor a pore expanded and spoke to them in a voice more authoritative and determined than the chattering voices further down the passage. As it spoke more pores opened around it, speaking with it in unison and with the same determined voice. Occasionally the outlines of a chin or forehead, or the form of a brow ridge and cheek bones would appear around the speaking pores, as if a face behind the fleshy wall was pressing out from behind.

"I am the Prime Aspect," said the voice. "I am the will of the Lemurians. Who are you to invade the ecstasy of our endless realization?"

"We mean no offense," said Bronson. "We are from the world you left behind. Our purpose is simply to observe. We come in peace, offering friendship. We wish only to learn."

"There is nothing to learn," it said. "Men age but they do not grow. All that is worthwhile are the combinations of aspects, the endless realization. Is this what you have come to learn, autonomous one?"

Bronson thought a moment. "Are you Jon Yesterday?"

"That being and less and many more. His aspects have been diffused. His will and the will of the Lemurians have been synthesized into my fleeting sense of identity. I am the Prime Aspect."

"Prime Aspect," said Vitaly. "May we walk among you and speak with the other aspects of Lemuria?"

"You will learn nothing," it said listlessly. It seemed already to be losing interest in them. Many of the pores that had been speaking with the Prime Aspect's voice were once again contracting and closing. "Enter if you will. You have removed our means of preventing you. But hasten, your autonomous forms are repellent to us, and you confuse the process of our realization."

"What did you intend to do with the aboriginal peoples you hired Captain Amber to gather?"

Several screams echoed out to them from inside the labyrinth.

"Their loss has condemned us," said the Prime Aspect. "Their primal emptiness was to be the key factor in the ultimate achievement of our vision. Alas, the echoes of civilization resound too deeply within us. We haven't the space. We haven't the emptiness. And thus we no longer seek the barren force, and so proceed through endless realization. But our will remains intact; the original vision impels us still." It paused, evidently conversing with itself. "Unless *you* can bring the aborigines to us?"

Vitaly shook his head. "Its thought processes are severely compart-mentalized."

Bronson answered the Prime Aspect. "No. We prevented it. We could not allow you to use people against their will. But perhaps we can still help you."

"If you mean what you say—" gasped the Prime Aspect against the background music of more screams "—then leave us!"

"We wish to respect your privacy," said Bronson. "But it is necessary for us to understand if we are to keep the outside world from destroying you."

"Are we a threat?" asked the Prime Aspect, dwindling.

"Perhaps," answered Bronson.

It paused as if to communicate with itself. Then it said, "Our work shall eventually be carried out through the interactions of the autonomous ones. In time humanity itself shall unfold along the course we have…" It dwindled out completely.

"What was that?" asked Nabnak. "A prophecy?"

"Apparently the Lemurians have a very mechanistic view of history," said Vitaly, "despite—or maybe because of—their emphasis on person-ality."

"Explain," said Bronson.

"Vitaly shrugged and then nodded toward the emerald glow that became brighter the further they gazed into the labyrinth. "It would seem the explanation lies ahead."

Bronson gazed down the corridor of flesh. The voices of the Lemurians were combined in a wavering buzz that at once expressed horror, chaos, dissolution—yet also a strange elation.

"It reminds me of a slaughter house," stated Nabnak.

Bronson nodded grimly but was resolved nonetheless. He led them in.

Vitaly attempted to speak with the pores lining the fleshy walls, but they were as listless as the Prime Aspect. They were more intent on speaking with each other. Some of their conversation resembled the maneuverings of children and parents seeking to gain psychological leverage over one another. They argued over domestic problems, infidelity, money, and time and effort lost on unfulfilled dreams. It was a play of passions, a display of fear, contempt, hopelessness, loss.

Other aspects engaged in bizarre debates concerning academic sophistries like classicism, romanticism, globalism, impressionism, modernism, vorticism, cubism, futurism, imagism, realism, naturalism, surrealism, existentialism, cultural relativism, post-structuralism, capitalism, Hegelian idealism, post-modernism, post-colonialism, new-historicism, materialism, empiricism, intersectionalism, social-constructionism...

In the vicinity of these debates, Vitaly raised a flap of skin and found an unconscious Pap partially melded into the fleshy fabric. Evidently something was preventing it from fully joining with the Lemurians. Vitaly suggested that a bullet in the head would take care of the simple parasite. Bronson observed that provincial problems required better than provincial solutions. Acting on impulse, Nabnak grasped the Pap's shoulders and drew the thing out so they could view its face. The revelation produced a startling effect upon the agents.

"Bob Dylan!" pronounced Bronson. The other agents stared in disbelief.

"It cannot be," insisted Vitaly.

Indeed, the half-digested Pap did resemble the venerable world-class poet, who in many ways was the generative impulse that had made possible the phenomenon of Jon Yesterday, who was also, ironically, the great poet's antithesis. Perhaps in the barren psychic void of Dylan the ever-sunny Yesterday had found the loam from which sprung the exquisite ever-opening flower of his gorgeous vision. But Vitaly again insisted it was impossible, and he explained that most Provincial Academic Philistines bore a close resemblance to the poetical icon. As if to conclude his assessment, Vitaly reached down with his powerful hands to snap the Pap's neck.

"I wonder how that thing got in here?" asked Nabnak, and he stuck out his tongue as Vitaly lowered the flap of skin over the lifeless abomination.

Vitaly shook his head and pulled a pocket psychoanalytic calculator from his utility belt.

They continued moving between the tapestries, listening to the voices of loneliness, inspiration, tenderness, guilt, anger, despair, exuberance, regret, faith, cruelty, logic, indifference, lust, hope, vanity, caprice, wonder....

"It's like everything that ever happened to these people and all their thoughts and feelings are echoing around in here," said Nabnak.

Chief Lonetree nodded. "All these voices speak at once for the Manitou."

"That's very interesting," said Bronson. He turned to the Russian. "And have you a theory, Mr. Yurchenko?"

Vitaly shook the pocket psycho-calculator at Bronson. "I've identified textbook cases of mental disorder, neurosis, psychosis, phobias, fetishes, hypersensitivity, neural deterioration, hypochondria, disorientation, in-civility, perversity, autism, anorexia, anal-retentiveness, abusiveness, acrimoniousness, repressed affect, narcissism, psychopathology. And it's as if these conditions are crossbreeding with one another, creating new pathologies. In time these new pathologies will themselves diffuse, but only to appear again after several generations. And so it goes cycle after cycle *ad infinitum.* It is logical to assume that other personality traits are separating and combining like the mental disorders. I wish I had the equipment to test for them. But based on my sample of mental diseases, it is not unreasonable to assume that every aspect of the Lemurians' collection of personality traits will aimlessly reflect and rebound inside here incessantly, without purpose and without growth."

"The Prime Aspect said something about an endless realization," offered Nabnak. Chief Lonetree, lost in his own thoughts, nodded to himself.

Bronson stood thinking with his tail curling through the air. "Don't throw the baby out with the bath water," he advised. "Just because mental disorders echo around aimlessly doesn't mean positive traits aren't positive. Besides, personality isn't that important. What really matters is character." He smiled as he arrived at some kind of resolution. "And you have to be autonomous to possess character, don't you?" He looked around him at the collage of personality and wondered at the categories that had been identified by the sober tyranny of the Prime Aspect. Bronson's own identity depended upon none of it. His tail hit the floor.

"Come on," he said. "Let's take the witch boy home."

"And Captain Amber?" asked Nabnak.

"Ah!" Bronson mused, striking a mighty pose in his kilt. "He is home."

The tall agent of the Invisible Tower twitched his tail playfully as he pictured Amber anchored firmly and forever outside the Lemurians' dome, his piratical form outlined by the slowly-turning flame in the Antarctic night, his indignant voice endlessly railing against the stars.

CIRCUMSCRIBING CIRCUMSPECTION

"OH GOD, LOOK HOW steep it is." With her blue purse swinging from her elbow, the fat lady leaned forward and looked down the steep gravel roadbed of the inclined railway. Stomping behind her on the wooden platform were three mischievous teenagers with long dark hair and scruffy black trench coats—and these young men were her sons. They moved forward suddenly and banged their feet against the platform as if to shove her down the rails. The father, supporting a brown paper grocery bag on the handy shelf of his belly, shook his head and scolded them with a fatherly, "Hey hey hey, now." But his eyes were twinkling happily. There was something very familial about the boys' pantomime.

The fat lady stepped back and held her arms against the tent of her yellow smock as the empty carriage clicked up to the sunny platform. She eyed the carriage dubiously, aware her sons were studying her every movement, her every gesture, every aspect of the mysterious picture she presented before them. Behind her were poplars that raised around the platform from the cliffs below, and further off were the dully roaring American and Horseshoe Falls with the crumbling cliff face of Goat Island between them.

"Mom," the oldest boy glared wide-eyed at the roofless carriage, "do you think it's stress-tested for hauling hippopotami?"

The fat lady turned around and—face screwed together with sarcasm—mocked him with a squeaky voice, "Mom, do you think it's stress-tested for hauling hippopotami?" She turned her bulk sideways and sat down in the carriage with a resounding thud.

"Better check the suspension!" cried the youngest son.

"Wise guy," she said. "Why don't you crawl under the wheels and check the suspension—after we start moving." She slid her enormous bottom across the bench.

They climbed aboard and sat around her like the disciples of some great sage prophet. She was their Socrates, their Buddha. The middle son pointed down the toothed rails. They lay at a steep angle, forty-five degrees or more. "I hope this thing stops when we reach the bottom."

"We might just keep going straight and carve a new tunnel under the falls," said the oldest son. He lit a cigarette.

The carriage jolted and began clicking down.

"Oh! Jesus Christ!" cried the fat lady. She lifted her hands in front of her with exaggerated, but lazy, surprise. "Why don't they give some kind of warning? A person could have a heart attack!"

The oldest son reached to feel her pulse but she swatted his hand away. "I mean it," she said in a very grave and sober tone. "One of these days someone is going to have a heart attack on this damn thing, and I don't suppose it's insured." It was going *kik kik kik kik*... "Sure is awfully loud," she continued. You'd think the Canadian government could afford to put a rubber gear on the crazy thing. I don't know why we didn't take the elevator…"

"Look at the view," said the father, unheard. He gazed with satisfaction at the Horseshoe falls, seeing a small submarine teeter for a moment at the edge, then he glanced across the gorge, at the trees, the cliffs, and finally down at the gravel passing beneath the carriage as it shook along. He cocked an eyebrow with a sudden doubt, and again looked up at the falls, but the submarine, if that's what it had been, was gone.

The youngest son glanced up along the moving rock wall. "If I had a hang glider I'd jump off this cliff."

"You mean go over the falls in a barrel," corrected the mother.

"Maybe I would consider it for one-million-nine-hundred-fifty-thousand-three-hundred-forty-seven-dollars-and-forty-nine-cents," said the middle son. "And not one penny less." He started to light a cigarette but the mother snatched it away.

"Hey!" He pouted.

She looked at the brand name on the filter. "You can smoke when you can afford your own." She put it in her mouth, lit it, and took a long, luxurious drag. The father also lit up. He was imagining he was a famous tightrope walker who had crossed the falls many times, and found all this talk of petty barrels and cliffs amusing.

"Mom," said the oldest son. "Say we had a big lever—a really *big* lever—and we used it to shove you from here down into the gorge, *ker-splash!* How long do you think it would take the falls to fill the gorge back up?"

"Ha, ha, ha," she cackled in mockery of his wit, all the while training a rapid side-long glance at *whatever* strange distractions her extraordinary sensibility could perceive.

"He's just being sixteen," said the father, unheard. The brown paper bag crinkled as it shifted on his lap.

"Hey!" The oldest son stood up and pointed towards the bottom of the Horseshoe Falls. "Down by the rocks! A mud walrus!"

"A mud walrus!" The other two boys stood up. The mother and father craned their necks to catch a glimpse of the fabled beast.

And the dozen or so passengers in the carriage craned their necks also. "Where?" said a man in a checked suit.

The three boys sat down laughing.

The fat woman roared like a beast "Ah-hoooo-gahh! Ah-hoooo-gahh!"

The sons clasped their hands together and become very still. Angelic expressions lit their faces. The father, who up to this time had been sitting with his arm behind his wife's damp, billowy shoulders, sat forward and turned toward her. Expectation and joy and admiration filled his eyes, while little invisible fairies leapt on his lap and stuck out their tongues to catch the love dew dripping from tips of his eyelashes. Suddenly the moon moved across the sun and what had been sunbeams were extinguished in a wave of darkness that suddenly filled the gorge and climbed almost instantly up the massive curtain of the falling water. The three sons appeared suddenly owl-like in their trench coats, their faces glowing with an invisible light, while the other passengers in the carriage, struck by the impossibility of what they beheld, themselves appeared masked by a shifting green glow. And meanwhile the father, always a picture of solace and inner-peace, appeared almost saturnine in the deep umbra of his stillness and contentment. The fat woman grunted and swallowed to clear her throat—all precisely according to the formality the family had witnessed many times before. Her voice was strong and deep:

The Mud Walrus

Shake with bellow proud and hoarse
Oh, walrus of Arctic land
Combat foul clime, create!
Vast white waste escape
Find recompense, shake!
Bellow hoarse and bellow loud:

Farther up were seasons, changes
Which leapt the planet rim
Into a vault of forms, spaces
A universe vast and like a gong
Clanging countless deaths, the breaths
Sages sighs, singing songs
Of drawing wise the cosmic distinction
In what a man can and cannot do
And minting the stars' faint ring:
Golden circles, coins of the eternal realm
Spinning vibrant across the heavens!

For one precious moment larded with silence there was complete realization. The falls were cotton. Then as abruptly as it had descended, the shadow of the eclipse was lifted, and burning sunbeams once more poured into the gorge to race forward across the water and blast the falling cascade with all the dazzling excellence of our generous and selfless star. All around the carriage passengers took out palm-size electronic mirrors in which they watched their life stories unfold. Meanwhile, the father reached down into his bag and pulled out some paper cups and a two liter plastic bottle of Diet Pepsi.

"And here," he said with mild pride, pulling out a white bakery box, "I've got some doughnuts."

THE CATHEDRA OF
EUDEMONIA

BRONSON BODINE SAID: "There is absolutely nothing like a visit to Eddie Allan's secret base beneath Niagara Falls. One over-awed agent, after having been shown the genetic menagerie, the physics laboratories, the aircraft hangers, the submarine pens and the great garden-cavern, was moved to proclaim: 'It is the moral breast of the universe in that it suckles the will to better Mankind.' In the conversation that followed, Madame Geoffrin's illustrious salon was brought up and offered in comparison. 'Ah,' observed the agent, 'but that was the eighteenth-century. And besides, those *philosophes* were a bunch of gigolos anyway.'"

Bronson Bodine raised his index finger. "Eddie Allan's base isn't a promise of some future enlightenment that's to be arrived at through method, dogma and rote procedure, or through dull and tedious application. It is a renaissance taking place *now*. And, indeed, at no time in history has the rose of scientific and psychological knowledge had better soil in which to thrive: here free thought is tolerated. Where else may philanthropist and mis-anthrope better combine their energies and walk together upon so common a road? The universities are extinct! United Dictatorships makes you cut your hair! *L'Aliénation Internationale* is full of control freaks! The government is owned by Hollywood, and vice versa! Is it any wonder the nation turns to the 'moral breast', to the grand menagerie, the physics laboratories, the aircraft hangers, the submarine pens, and the garden-cavern? Here bold experiments are fearlessly dared. Here stirring ideals are proposed and scrutinized and defended by Mother Earth's bold champions. Here the mighty and terrible forces of the universe itself are called and challenged and conquered."

Bronson Bodine lowered his index finger. "And what is more: beyond all this important, ennobling, Humankind-forever-expanding-into-the-cosmos type stuff," he concluded, "whenever I visit, Eddie has some neat new gadget or genetic mutation to kill some time with."

He was sharing an elevator with his faithful Eskimo companion, Nabnak Tornasuk, and a tall, handsome Mountie. Neither had been paying much attention to Bronson. In fact, Nabnak seemed bothered about something. Perhaps he felt intimidated by the presence of the good-looking Mountie who had given the short, muscular Eskimo a funny look when they boarded the elevator? Poor Nabnak was so ugly, so pitifully squat. And what made it even worse was his kindheartedness. Nabnak didn't resent the Mountie, he was rather ashamed about his own self. All the fashionable occult prop-aganda about people creating their own realities had gotten to him. He thought it was his own fault he was so ugly. "New Age guilt trip" was the phrase Bronson used to describe the syndrome.

Bronson's own good looks, his brilliant blue eyes, rakish Robin Hood beard and Apollonian physique somehow escaped Nabnak's sensitivity to what nature had denied him. As often happens in good friendships, a sort of osmosis had taken place. Bronson thought himself a member of the Eskimo race, while Nabnak imagined that Bronson's good looks belonged to him. Nabnak was sometimes even vain about it. When they were out together and the women turned their shameless, longing faces to Bronson, Nabnak always thought, "Ah! You see but his shell, the clay of the man. Come over here and learn of his true beauty. Know him for his noble deeds, the wars he wages, his furious strengths and his surprising weaknesses. And then know Nabnak, his friend, his brother in battle and his companion beneath the sun. Know Nabnak, and know that Nabnak is beautiful too!"

But for all his concern over his poor appearance, Nabnak always did well with women. Attracted by Bronson's winsome gaze, after they approached they invariably turned to Nabnak, who was a sensitive, intelligent and witty conversationalist. Bronson, they found, was too moody. He could only speak of esoteric scientific theories, awkward childhood memories, or the shifting nature of human identity. A ravishing member of the Royal Shakespeare Company once remarked, "He's quite nice playing kissy-face, but even just one sentence coming out of that man's mouth is like three acts in a Greek tragedy!" Quite understandably, Bronson never had any girlfriends. Nabnak, on the other hand, was constantly making new acquaintances, whom he took roller skating, go-cart racing, or off to play miniature golf. Bronson's love life amounted to little more than a series of explosive collisions with exotic spies—beautiful women, it was true, the most beautiful in the world (once Nabnak lost his breath when Bronson, shaking his head, pointed out some stunning gazelle on the cover of a fashion magazine), but what did Bronson have to show for it?

The elevator eased to a halt and the door slid open. The odylic scent of minerals, herbs and flowers flooded around them. Beyond the doorway was the garden-cavern, where the lights of a thousand glowing mushrooms scattered through the darkness like stars. Rugged stalactites, webbed with mineral luminescence, hung from the ceiling in dreaming majesty.

Nabnak and Bronson nodded to the Mountie and stepped out onto the wooden platform that was elevated fifteen feet above the floor. They stood among the stalactites and gazed down at the rich foliage that was specially adapted to the darkness. They allowed themselves to be hypnotized by the spiraling stream that circled the cave five times before drawing their eyes to the whirlpool in the center of the floor. It made a quiet, civilized sound, a faint "wsssh" that harmonized with the wavering insect drone of the Eastern instruments a group of Mounties strummed and bowed at the other side of the cavern. Bronson took a deep satisfied breath and exhaled whatever concerns he had about anything. This was a home of sorts. During his career he had been on many important and exciting missions, but the best were those that began in this cave.

Weaving between the stalactites was a network of winding tracks, part of the unique mechanism Eddie Allan had devised to move his broken, limbless body through the subterranean base. There were many rumors, but Bronson knew Eddie had lost his limbs, and most of his skin, because Eddie's own stepfather, notorious spy master John Allan, had boiled him in oil. It was an admission about himself Eddie withheld from most other agents of the Invisible Tower. Many did know that Ed die was John Allan's stepson, but

231

Eddie thought it best they didn't know how really depraved John Allan was and have it reflect poorly upon himself.

But why Eddie had confided in Bronson is even more interesting. While Eddie suggested it was because of Bronson's great intelligence (Bronson was the only person who could beat him in chess) it was more probable he did so because in Bronson's persona Eddie saw himself. While never as robust as Bronson, Eddie had memories of himself with raven black hair, the handsome forehead of a poet, bright, knowing eyes, and, like Bronson, Eddie had excelled in swimming. Eddie (and Nabnak also, it might be stated) saw Bronson as a being who was unconquerable by either nature's cannibalism or the schemes of evil men. But Bronson's most admirable quality, and this they only partially realized, was something greater than a shrewd intellect or an athletic physical form. He let them inside him. He gave them shelter.

"Ah, Bronson Bodine! Friend Nabnak!" The voice was unmistakable, electronic. Emerging from a tunnel in the sloping ceiling was Eddie Allan. He glided toward them from the far side of the cavern suspended on four thin wires. A little wheeled frame holding motors and pulleys whirred above him as it rolled along the tracks that curved between the stalactites. Across his mouth he wore an amplifier the size of a pocket radio. It was secured around his scarred, bald head with rubber straps. His torso was stumped from the bottom of his rib cage to the tail of his spine, and a variety of tubes, filters, bottles and plastic sacks hung in the open cavity. They jiggled when the little cart hit bumps in the tracks. He called the artificial organs his "sleigh bells." The pulleys squeaked and the wires unwound as he lowered to meet his friends, who were climbing down from the wooden platform.

"You look well, Eddie." Bronson waited until Eddie swung to a stop and then smiled.

"Thank you, friend Bronson—*cgh*." Eddie's dull eyes, straining up, shone like old pans.

Nabnak folded his massive arms and leaned back slightly. This was a meeting of men. Real men. "It is never a long voyage to Niagara Falls, Eddie."

The suspended ash-man was quiet for a moment. The pulleys squeaked. Finally he accepted and acknowledged the Eskimo's warm greeting. "But long are the days between your visits, friend Nabnak."

Bronson thought this was a little much. Sentimentality bored him. "Eddie," he asserted. "Am I mistaken, or do you have that 'up-to-something' look?"

Nabnak sensed this too. "Something's cooking, huh?"

The pulleys squeaked as Eddie rose to a vertical position. He laughed mockingly. "*Cgh-cgh-cgh-cgh-cgh...*"

An amused smile crept across Bronson's face. He turned to Nabnak. "What do you think?"

Nabnak nodded. "It's a biggie." He took in Eddie's outlandish giggling form and glanced back at Bronson. "Yes, definitely a biggie."

"A mission?" asked Bronson.

Eddie kept laughing.

"No." Nabnak studied Eddie. "That's a genetic mutation laugh."

"*Cgh-cgh-cgh-cgh...*"

"Perhaps," Bronson said evenly.

Nabnak shrugged. "Has he captured someone?"

"*Cgh-cgh-cgh-cgh...*"

"Well," observed Bronson. "It is definitely nothing serious. If it were an international crisis or an ecological catastrophe of some kind, he wouldn't have been laughing this long."

"*Cgh-cgh-cgh-cgh...*"

Nabnak threw his hands into the air. "I give up."

Eddie lowered to the horizontal once more and, still laughing, turned 180 degrees. Abruptly the laughing stopped and he swung off through the air. The pulleys rattled overhead as the motorized cart clicked through the switches and picked up momentum.

Bronson and Nabnak looked blankly at each other and then set off after the little imp.

He disappeared into a tunnel. Bronson didn't recall seeing this particular tunnel during his last visit. He fingered the rock by the entrance. The rock was marked with fresh cuts and was covered with a light powder. Apparently it had been recently cut. "A new project," he said, and he smiled archly. Nabnak rubbed his large hands together.

They moved quietly through the dark tunnel. A lamp mounted on the motorized cart cast a curving yellow light across the ceiling. Ahead on the tracks, blind lizards picked up their chests and scrambled for the shadows.

The tunnel gradually curved and then straightened and angled down for several hundred yards. In places water dripped down the walls. It flowed to the bottom of the incline, where a long, shallow puddle had collected. Eddie buzzed over it while Bronson and Nabnak splashed through in their knee-high combat boots. Then the tunnel angled up once more. They could see light ahead and they picked up their pace.

"Ah, Eddie!" exclaimed Bronson as they stepped into an immense, brightly lit cavern.

It was a spherical cavity, perfectly smooth, nine-hundred feet in diameter. Shivers ran up their backbones as Eddie explained it was carved, or rather *melted*, by a small atomic blast. They stood at the tunnel opening, finding themselves about sixty yards from the center of the curving, bowl-shaped floor. At their elevation, and ringing the sphere at regular intervals, were an additional seven openings. Catwalks spiraled up along the continuous rock wall of the sphere. In the center, hanging from chromium chains, was a doughnut-shaped fusion reactor. Great dynamos were supported around it on massive steel girders; while other girders, two-hundred feet above, supported heavy-lift cranes, massive mechanical arms, spherical tanks, a tangle of pipes and ducts, gleaming steel pincers, and mobile control cars.

A Mountie approached and handed Bronson and Nabnak hard-hats. Awe-struck by the magnitude of the machinery above them, they donned the hard-hats automatically. Extending below the dynamos were long, scissoring arms of steel, buttressed by mighty pivots that tapered to sharp points that pinioned against the naked rock of the cavern wall. Suspended from these arms and held in opposition above the floor were two gold-colored cylinders measuring thirty feet in length by three in diameter. They hung with their finely machined ends two feet apart, perfectly aligned. Between and just below the ends of the two cylinders was a massive articulated chair equipped with heavy steel cables, leather straps and electronic monitoring equipment. The chair was made of various materials including steel, chromium, titanium, carbon fiber, and the same gold-colored metal that made up the two cylinders. Four large bolts, fifteen inches in diameter, held the chair solidly against the floor. Before the chair, set on a rolling cart, was a rack of electronic equipment. Bronson supposed this was the control module for the enormous apparatus, whatever it was.

The Mountie returned pushing before him an ultra-high-speed photographic device. He eased it carefully down the gently sloping floor and set it up in front of the chair. Then, brushing his hands together, he walked back to one of the access tunnels.

Another Mountie was lowering from above. He was seated at the end of a jointed flexible boom six-hundred feet long. Directly below him, Eddie's pulley tracks—supported by inverted, L-shaped stanchions—extended from the tunnel opening to a point ten feet inside the sphere. The boom eased down and mated with the tracks. Eddie's pulley cart clicked into place at the tip of the boom and the Mountie swung down and disappeared into the tunnel.

Bronson lifted his hard-hat, scratched his head, and replaced it. "Eddie!" He raised his hand to indicate the grand scene before them. "What can I say?"

"Bravo?" suggested Eddie.

"Bravo!" echoed Bronson, nodding. With proprietary confidence he set his hands on his hips. "This enormous structure is one single apparatus devoted to a solitary purpose!"

"Just so," said Eddie.

"A solitary purpose." Nabnak put his hands on his hips and shook his head.

"Those cylinders," said Bronson, pointing in the direction of the chair. "Their color is very familiar. Are they are depleted uranium?"

Eddie harrumphed. "*Collapsed* depleted uranium. I call it nulltronium. The combined mass of both cylinders is in excess of six and one-half billion tons. If you were to put your hand up against one of them it would adhere to the surface. But it wouldn't be electromagnetic attraction that held your hand against it."

"Gravity." Bronson's voice communicated both awe and keen scientific interest. "What holds them apart in that position? The power of the fusion reactor?"

Eddie shook his head. "The nulltronium cylinders are polarized, and as you remember from your schoolboy experiments, like poles repel. But if you are thinking of magnetic polarization you are wrong. Gentleman, you are witnessing *gravitational* polarization: indeed, the first time the phenomenon has been created in the laboratory."

Bronson stared at the two nulltronium cylinders. He exhaled with a rumbling sound, and then with an expression fully reflecting the importance of the invention—indeed, with an expression not a little envious—Bronson stared up at is friend. "Polarized gravity?!"

Eddie's eyes widened and seemed to say, "And what do you think of that!"

The Mountie emerged again from one of the tunnels across the cavern pulling along with him a small wagon. On it was a cage containing a large, black monkey.

"*Celebes macaque,*" said Bronson.

Eddie nodded. "Come." Motors hummed overhead. The boom began gliding him down along the curving floor. Before him the chair loomed like the throne of some despotic technocratic emperor.

"Sleepies mac-a-what?" asked Nabnak as they followed.

"*Celebes macaque,*" explained Bronson. "It rhymes with 'curlicue.' An interesting species. They seem to have a more tractable disposition than the rhesus."

Nabnak was not altogether satisfied with Bronson's pronunciation, but he let it go. "Face like a baboon," said Nabnak as the various parties converged on the chair.

"Oh, it is a monkey," said Bronson.

They were together at the chair now. Bronson looked up at the dynamos and counterweights near the doughnut-shaped fusion reactor. He couldn't get over the size of the great levers which led down, crossed once, and held the two nulltronium cylinders slightly above and to either side of the chair. He could feel the mass of the nulltronium pulling lightly on his skin. He squatted down to inspect the four massive bolts holding the chair in place. And then Eddie was directing the Mountie to proceed.

"An interesting afternoon," said Nabnak as the Mountie pulled the monkey from the cage. The little hairy chap had a complacent, unassuming look about him. Nabnak smiled at him. "My, you're a friendly little fellow, aren't you?"

The monkey gazed around innocently as the Mountie strapped him into the chair.

"Just a little off the top," said Nabnak. "His mother will kill me if I bring him home with a crew cut."

The Mountie frowned at this and continued. The backrest was lowered just below the monkey's shoulders by means of a crank. Then four steel cables were wrapped across the monkey's chest and shoulders.

The Mountie walked over to the free-standing control console and flipped a switch. The cables contracted. The monkey began breathing more rapidly and gasped occasionally but otherwise was not inconvenienced.

"It is a shame *Celebes* cannot be taught diaphragmatic breathing," said Eddie.

"Yes, isn't it," agreed Bronson. He studied the nulltronium cylinders, not daring to get within five feet of them. They were perfectly symmetrical, perfectly aligned. The precision of the flatness at their ends was remarkable. "Were these machined?" he asked.

Eddie nodded up at the fusion reactor doughnut. "Grown, after a fashion, up there."

"I see," said Bronson, craning his neck. "And this system of levers and those dynamos up there, it's all set up to swing the two nulltronium cylinders through an arc and clap them together here." He pointed at the monkey's head.

"Correct!" exclaimed Eddie like a school master. "But this elaborate physical device produces a very spiritual, shall we say, effect."

"Spiritual?" wondered Nabnak.

"In a hypothetical sense," explained Eddie. "I am not suggesting extra-dimensional realities, or angels on a pin, or geometric conundrums, or anything occult—planes, sub-universes, polymorphic noises, or macrocosmic connections. Certainly music theory and the specific, crisp physics at our post-quantum scale-of-reality disprove the unworldly: the square-root of a negative number, synthetic co-ordinate systems, what have you. I'm suggesting, rather, something physical: not the *agenda* but rather the *muscle* of the soul, if you will."

"The muscle of the soul?" Nabnak wrinkled his forehead.

Bronson explained. "Eddie is using words hypothetically as he strives to develop a vocabulary we can use to discuss the phenomena that could be revealed by this experiment. You see, we have no hypothesis to test in this particular case. And we really can't learn any more about it until we proceed."

"Exploration!" Eddie added enthusiastically.

"Well," muttered Nabnak without satisfaction. "I'm not so easily convinced." He folded his arms, considering. "All right, but what are the knowns?"

Eddie made a throat-clearing sound with his amplifier. "*Cgh-zzt-cgh.* Primus: two three-point-three-billion ton nulltronium cylinders driven together by mechanically transferred electromagnetic induction. Secundus: the momentum of the clashing nulltronium cylinders is incalculable because of the tremendous masses involved, which will vary anyway because of the gravitational dynamics of the experiment. But I'm not curious about that anyway. Mostly, I wanted to build the thing. It's got to do something. Look how big it is!"

Nabnak rolled his eyes and shook his head.

"Well," said Bronson diplomatically. "It is certainly bound to do something."

"Right." Eddie nodded.

"Here hear," said the Mountie. He glared at Nabnak.

Nabnak shrugged defensively. "I dispute nothing."

Eddie gave everything a long scrutinizing stare. He asked the Mountie to check the position of the high-speed camera. Then they backed away and moved up the slope of the bowl-shaped floor. The Mountie pushed the control rack before him.

"I think this is far enough," said Eddie when they were forty yards away from the chair. "Ready?"

The Mountie nodded. Everyone looked at each other and then at the monkey.

Eddie said: "Throw it!"

A mighty hum began pouring out of the fusion reactor. The two nulltronium cylinders backed thirty feet apart and stopped. It was time. Sizzling purple thunderbolts struck out from the reactor and the nulltronium cylinders shot together like projectiles fired from cannons.

There was an ultra-low frequency thud.

Bronson, Nabnak and the Mountie were thrown to the floor. Their bodies were pressed down by a stinging static force that crawled over their skin. Then they were caught in a Euclidian grid of faceted monkey faces. A large purple diamond spit pink lighting from its center.

Then sputtering images of curved rock and machinery re-assembled around them. They were back in the spherical cavern. Only it wasn't spherical anymore. Everything was warped, folded together, distorted. The cavern was now shaped like a great prune. The nulltronium cylinders had remained unaffected, however, and were once again suspended in a position of equalized gravitational repulsion at either side of the monkey's head. The monkey was taking short, rapid breaths as the humans regained consciousness. They called to one another about the state of the altered cavern.

"But it looks like the distortion won't affect the operation of the mechanism," said Eddie. He still hung from the boom. Like the cavern, the boom had folded and warped somewhat. But it moved about now almost as effectively as it had before.

"That felt kind of relaxing," said the Mountie.

"Relaxing?" Bronson got up and rubbed the dust off his trousers. "That felt *great*."

Nabnak was twisting his finger in his ear.

Meanwhile, up on the surface, the Niagara River was rushing at Buffalo, New York, already flooding through the northern suburbs on its way toward the downtown office buildings.

"Let's do it again!" said Eddie.

"Hurrah!" The cheer was unanimous. The Mountie began checking over the control equipment.

"Wait," said Nabnak. "Let's look at the high-speed photographs."

Suddenly everyone looked at the monkey. It sat blinking at them, no worse for wear.

"I knew it!" crowed Eddie. "I knew it! The mass of the nulltronium cylinders combined with their rapid displacement and collision has distorted the gravitational-geometric infrastructure of the space-time continuum!"

"That might explain the warped walls," said Bronson. "I was wondering before if something like this might happen."

"The high-speed photographs?" Nabnak insisted, unheard—or ignored!

"You know what, Eddie?" said Bronson, beaming.

"Bronson?"

"Congratulations." Bronson bowed his head.

"Oh, now." Eddie allowed himself the exuberant luxury of rotating 360 degrees.

The Mountie stood up by the control rack. "It checks out. I don't know why or how, but it will work again. But let's check the pictures first," he added.

Bronson nodded.

"Okay," said Eddie.

Nabnak followed behind, waving them on.

The camera had escaped the warping effects of the experiment, perhaps because of its close proximity to the point of impact. The Mountie called their attention to this as he opened the back of the camera.

The camera had taken a series of pictures, each from a slightly different angle. It operated on the sliding-aperture principle. As the nulltronium cylinders came together, the camera's lens shot across a semi-circular strip of film emulsion to create a time sequence record of the high speed event. The Mountie peeled the strip from the back of the camera. It had already completely developed.

Bronson took it. Everyone gathered around him. The sequence of frames first showed the cylinders on either side of the monkey's head; then compressing the head; then the cylinders together and the monkey's head squeezed out like a two dimensional paper profile, with eyes, nose, ears, chin and forehead curved around the circle where the two cylinders met; but the rest of the sequence was obscured by strange grid lines and distorted magnifications of the monkey's features.

"When I see results like these," the Mountie pushed back his hat, "it makes up for having been sterilized by radiation when I was a little boy."

"Bronson, do you think the monkey went to another dimension?" asked Nabnak.

But Bronson gazed passed the Eskimo and fixed his eyes on the monkey. "Eddie!"

Bronson wanted to be the subject.

"Are you mad!" cried Nabnak.

"I think it will work," said Eddie.

The Mountie had already begun unstrapping the monkey.

Five minutes later the monkey was back in its cage and Bronson was strapped into the massive chair. The Mountie was just finishing up with the height adjustments. Then he draped the four steel cables around Bronson's chest and walked back to the controls.

"Bronson!" pleaded Nabnak, but it was pointless. He shuddered as the steel cables tightened around Bronson's chest.

"Really, Nabnak, ahem—" Bronson began taking shorter breaths. "Unlike the Monkey, I know how to breathe diaphragmatically."

The Eskimo sighed. "It worked on the monkey—once. But the entire apparatus became distorted in the process."

Bronson was confident, firm. "Eddie seems to feel the distortion hasn't affected the mechanism. Our tried and true representative from the Royal Canadian Mounted Police agrees. So come on now." He nodded Nabnak back. "We're at the threshold of an entirely new science. The freshly minted physics of gravitational polarization puts us at a Copernican moment in the history of knowledge; and, indeed, in our new physics does not history conclude forever upon the cusp of that very same non-stop moment? We owe it to our species to bring that moment to the fore, and I say shame upon those who would turn back now!"

Nabnak lowered his head and shook it slowly. He then looked up and forced a smile: "Thus speaks the man sitting brave upon the Cathedra of Eudemonia."

"Right!" cheered Bronson. "Now stand aside so we can set this thing off and advance humanity directly into the hellfire of the non-stop moment! Ah, and if indeed hellfire it shall be—which I do humbly doubt, dear friends, for I clearly see a goodly sparkle in yonder monkey's blinking eyes! I say, I want you to tell them: 'Bronson Bodine did not pass gentle through that yawning throat of flame, but gladly, fully game, and with meticulous determination!'"

The Mountie was adjusting the dials in the mobile cart. Above, the fusion reactor began humming.

Just as Eddie Allan had predicted, the two nulltronium cylinders swung back flawlessly. Then purple thunderbolts radiated from the fusion reactor. The cylinders shot together. There was a thud. A checkerboard lattice curved through the cavern. Exploding suns within exploding suns expanded from the center of nothingness to the void of eternity. An endless procession of naked Bronson Bodines danced across the stars.

Up on the surface, the river waters drained from the streets of Buffalo and surged back toward the Niagara Gorge.

Nabnak and the Mountie woke up on the floor with innocent, childish smiles on their faces. They sat up and began rubbing their eyes. Above them and still hanging from the boom (now more fully kinked and distorted) Eddie Allan made a buzzing noise with his amplifier. Then Bronson was crying out:

"Revelation! Revelation! Praise God!"

Nabnak and the Mountie sprang to their feet and ran down the sloping floor. Bronson's head whipped back and forth as he cried out: "Revelation! Revelation! I am alive! Oh! Oh! Oh! My heart! My heart! It gushes! It is pumping blood through my body! I am—! Alive!"

The boom creaked as it swung Eddie forward. "Friend Bronson! Friend Bronson!" He joined Nabnak and the Mountie, who both stared with open mouths at the sight of Bronson's head rapidly tossing to and fro on his re-strained shoulders. Bronson's skin seemed to ripple under his clothes.

"For goodness sake!" cried Eddie. "Get him out of there!"

They did so. Bronson sprang from the chair, raised his hands at his side, and began shuffling and tapping his feet—he was clogging! Just as suddenly, he stomped his feet to a stop. His friends looked at each other. Nabnak grabbed his shoulders.

"Bronson, what happened?"

Bronson cried out: "What is happening! *Happening*, you mean, friend Nabnak!" He hugged his own chest with his arms. His face was bright with light and inspiration. Then he snorted and pointed violently at the Mountie. He shouted: "Paper! On a big easel! And a magic marker! Hurry!"

The Mountie ran off to fetch Bronson's materials.

"What is it for, Bronson?" asked Eddie. "What are you going to do?"

"Oh, Eddie!" Bronson turned around in a circle and kicked his toes against the floor. He was quiet for a moment, looked up, and then burst forth: "Where's that paper?!"

"Coming," said Nabnak. "Good God, man! What happened?"

"*Happened?!*" cried Bronson. He narrowed his eyes and looked very angry. "*Happening*, thou man of inadequate knowledge. I! N! G!"

Eddie and Nabnak looked at each other.

The Mountie soon returned with the easel and Bronson straightaway set to work. He began sketching isometric cubes, triangles, cones, irregular solids. Then he began scratching down a complex system of hieroglyphs, abstruse mathematical formulae and columns of strange squiggles set up in the fashion of geometric proofs or tables of verb conjugations. He worked with impatient haste, tearing away the pages as he filled them and scattering them across the floor of the great cavern. Sweat beaded on his forehead.

"Eddie?" Nabnak turned his stunned face up to behold the limbless ash-man who had initiated these wonderful events. But Eddie just shook his head.

"I think it's something to do with what he saw *on the other side*," said the Mountie.

Nabnak exhaled, shook his head, saying with his motions, *Well that's obvious, isn't it?*

Bronson worked for thirty minutes with his friends gathered around him anxiously following his every move and commenting on the strange figures that he raced to put down on the paper. He was rapidly scratching down some curious jagged marks when, suddenly, he took a step back, turned around, and with all his might hurled the marker through the air. He shook his fists. "Finally!" he exclaimed. "I am done!"

The echo of his voice died away and there was complete silence.

Nabnak picked up one of the marked sheets of paper that had been tossed to the floor of the massive cavern. "Can you tell us what this is? What do these strange symbols mean?"

Bronson looked around at the scattered sheets. He shrugged. "Now that I am finished, I have forgotten what they mean. You can try to decipher this stuff if you want, but it looks like a bunch of scribbles to me." He gazed innocently at their anxious, staring faces.

"But Bronson?" protested Eddie.

Bronson shrugged. "Hey," he spoke to the Mountie. "I'm suddenly starving. Get me a sandwich or something."

The Mountie scratched his head, evidently reflecting on everything that had happened, then he slowly stumbled off to find Bronson a sandwich.

Nabnak found himself glancing over at the cage containing *Celebes macaque*. What had the monkey experienced?

243

SPY WEDNESDAY

"OH, MS. WANG, YOU dance divinely!" crowed John Allan as best he could with the rose between his teeth. His eyes were round and alert as he strained to hold his lips off the thorns. He wore white shoes, white flared pants, a white vest, and a black shirt unbuttoned to his navel. An Italian horn dangling from a gold chain set off his shiny tan. He spun around in the flashing lights. "Olé!" Hopped on one foot. "Woof!" Flapped his arms. "Ding! Ding! Ding!" Stomped and cracked his knuckles. "Hubba-hubba!" Jerked his head back and forth and walked liked a pigeon. It was all Ms. Wang could do to keep up.

"Come on, Wang, me lassie!" John Allan bounced his eyebrows up and down. "Let 'em fly!"

Ms. Wang tossed her head, sending her long golden hair through the air. The strobe lights froze her tresses around her face in a sequence of theatrical images. She had that distinctive order of charm that comes from an unsettling uniqueness, yet also she was rather broad-shouldered and straight through the hips. Her breasts were quite large, however, and she felt it necessary to hold on to them.

"They're quite secure," laughed John Allan. "Come on Wang, you sexy thing, let 'em fly!"

The music went thud-crash, thud-crash, thud-crash…

Around the dance floor articulated mannequins with distorted facial features clapped their hands. Up in the DJ booth, an eye-patched, jelly-

244

jowled Billy Bones look-a-like marched in place. He saluted each time the rotating floodlight flashed in his direction. He wasn't the President, though he had passed for Reverend Bones countless times on television, at supermarket openings, and in college lecture halls across the country. He looked and talked like Bones, but he wasn't the type to be bothered with problems of state or the politics of shovel-ready theology. Right now he was thinking how glad he was that he wasn't in Wang's place.

"'Atta girl!" cried John Allan. He paused, took out a coin and, with the girl bobbing before him, did what he considered to be a very witty impersonation of George Raft flipping a coin. He flipped it one last time and made a ridiculous attempt at batting it to the side with the rose.

Up in the DJ booth, the mock Billy Bones clapped and gave John Allan a big "Okay" sign.

John Allan looked up and saw him and shook an accusing but friendly finger that seemed to say, "Hey, wise guy, is this fun or what!?" John Allan's favorite gestures were those he picked up from a clique of retired Las Vegas entertainers he knew in Palm Beach.

The music changed to a Latin beat and John Allan took Ms. Wang and led her in a tango around the edge of the stage. The mannequins clapped and, jaws springing up and down, appeared to cheer them on.

The music suddenly stopped. John Allan cried "Do the Hustle!" but rather than the Hustle, he crammed the rose into the mouth of a nearby mannequin and began doing the Mashed Potato. Ms. Wang, growing fatigued by John Allan's impulsive capers, stood slowly stomping her feet back and forth, completely off beat. John Allan finished out the song playing air guitar. He made faces, tapped his toes back and forth, then spread his legs and wind-milled his arm through the air.

A new song began thumping but the mock Billy Bones quickly hit the pause button when it appeared the flamboyant dancer wanted to go into a soliloquy.

John Allan tugged at his collar and roughed up his hair. He walked up to the mannikin with the rose in its mouth while Ms. Wang quickly handed him a microphone. He cleared his throat and began: "And here it is, one week from Easter and I'm thirty-one. Thirty-one! It has a lonely sound to it, like train horns caterwauling in the distance. I am reminded of so many tired ages ago with my moon-struck wife and her darling lad, and me, me, me, me—a thirteen-year-old dad. And here I am at thirty-one, my rose in the mouth of a mannequin." He took a handkerchief from his sleeve and dabbed the mannequin's eyes. "Oh, don't take it so; let go of the past; listen to that boy-scientist within you. That's right. Would you like a hot dog?" He smiled tragically and lowered to his knees. "My friends around me are confused, wonder what winds I ride as I drift so. Ah—" He looked up to Ms. Wang, his eyes full of a sudden inspiration that was quickly lost to a wiser, more melancholy, but not bitter, expression. He reached out with his two hands, one toward Ms. Wang, the other toward the mock Billy Bones in the DJ booth, and waved them to his side.

The mock Bones jumped down, and together they all sat on their knees at the edge of the dance floor.

"My good friends," said John Allan, putting his arms around their necks. He crossed his eyes, tilted his head and wrinkled his lips like a drunk. "Youse guys," he faked a hiccup, "are like—*hic*—my family now. An—*hic*—'tanks for being so 'taughtful an—" he licked his lips, "—an so 'ery 'ery supportive —*hic*—on my turdy-furz birfday."

The mock-Bones grinned with skeletal sincerity.

"Ve do evewryting for you want, J.A." Ms. Wang's voice cracked a bit.

John Allan gazed at her. His eyes quickly sobered. "Would you terribly mind," he cleared his throat, glanced archly at the mock-Bones, then looked back at her. "Ms. Wang." He took her hand. "Would you mind—*for me*—changing back?"

The mock-Bones went "Eeeeeeee!"

Ms. Wang frowned and scratched her head.

"Good." John Allan put his hand on her large thigh. "I had the surgeon save all the parts."

2

TOWER AGENTS BRONSON Bodine and Nabnak Tornasuk were on their backs looking up at the stalactites and the orange and green bioluminescence that webbed through the rock. Their feet dangled in the narrow stream that spiraled around the cavern five times before draining through the whirlpool in the center of the lichen-covered floor. Not far away in a rocky recess, a

Royal Canadian Mountie was plucking a sitar that whizzed a cosmic *zzz-wranggg-a-zzz-dranggg-a-wranggg-a-zzz-drangggg*...

Nabnak stretched his arms up and then brought them behind his head. He yawned. The lichen carpet felt soft and cool beneath his back. "I think I could lie like this for about ten years," he said.

Bronson didn't respond. He folded his arms across his chest and pulled his feet out of the water. He was half-asleep, his bent knees the most conscious part of his body.

Around them blind lizards played. Overhead, ferns and trees with fanning leaves silently draped. Succulents and cacti grew from cracks in the cavern walls, and rings of luminous mushrooms tucked among the lichens cast a cool, blue glow.

"I—" began Bronson. He paused for ten minutes, "—am—" another ten "—rediscovering—"

"What?" said Nabnak with a jolt. Had his eyes slipped shut? He sat up looking confused. "You say something?"

Bronson twisted his head to face the Eskimo. "Social consciousness. An instinctive need for new unity."

Nabnak stared at his companion. "Sounds like you're dreaming."

Bronson hummed without meaning. His head rolled through clouds of semi-hypnogogic nonsense.

"You're nervous," said Nabnak, settling back down and closing his eyes. "Must be the war."

Bronson's eyes popped open. "The war? What war?"

"I don't know anything about it."

Bronson wondered for a moment if he had been dreaming. "Nabnak?" he said. "Did you say something about a war?"

One of Nabnak's eyes popped open. "Oh, it was just something I heard on the news. Probably nothing."

Bronson had never been a slow riser. He sat up and raked his fingers through his pointy beard. He twisted the ends of his mustachios. "Let's go find Eddie. Maybe he can explain what's going on."

They pulled their boots on, holstered their automags, strapped on their utility belts, then disappeared into one of the many tunnels that opened into the side of the cavern.

They checked the physics labs first, then the submarine pens, but there was no sign of Eddie. In the hanger a Mountie patching the airframe of the Dornier 31 suggested they look in the menagerie.

In the menagerie they found a Mountie giving a lethal injection to a hairy spider with a three-foot leg span. It had a very human mouth and a very human tongue that began sliding out as it died.

The Mountie told them Eddie was up at the wax museum.

"What's that thing for?" Nabnak pointed at the dead spider.

"Just a sculpture."

When they were out of earshot Nabnak said, "I don't know about that guy."

Bronson agreed. "Pretty artsy-fartsy for a Mountie."

"And creepy," added Nabnak.

"My point exactly."

They walked on, passing once more through the central garden-cavern and then into the three-mile tunnel that led to the wax museum. The paramilitary and scientific facilities were located under the Falls, where they had just been. Ahead at the wax museum there were interrogation rooms, recovery rooms, and information systems headquarters—the nerve center of the Invisible Tower. There were no rules or leaders in the Invisible Tower; no policies, goals or chartered missions; which is not to say they were nihilists or a group of hedonistic, or worse, ideological anarchists. To the contrary. They were a jolly association of gentlemen who cooperated with each other along lines they found implicit in the standards of sportsmanship and good taste.

Eddie Allan—because he lacked arms, legs, half his torso, and was thus unable to operate in the field—served in the Invisible Tower as *ad hoc* chairman of support facilities. But he in no way abused the obvious leverage this afforded him; and everybody invited him to their fruit juice parties because they wanted to.

Eddie was enjoying an Açai berry float when Bronson and Nabnak found him at the wax museum in one of the interrogation rooms. The non-spill cup was clipped to a holder sewn over the left breast of his little shiny Mylar sleeping bag—he called it his "fight suit." Attached to the suit were wires suspended from a motorized cart that ran on tracks hanging near the ceiling. Eddie was not insensitive to his limbless condition, but he didn't let it get him down either. Over his left breast was sewn an emblem reading "N.A.S.A." When he was alone with intimate friends he proudly went without the suit and let his strange artificial organs—contained in a cluster of plastic sacks and glass jars—swing freely beneath his truncated body cavity. But at present he had a guest tied in the chair before him.

"Ah, Bronson! Nabnak!" said Eddie through the little black amplifier strapped over his mouth. "May I present Dr. Alexander Concord Birthright the Third, Professor of Social Engineering and Ethical Systems." Eddie nodded at the man strapped in the chair.

Bronson smiled up at the good professor. "I would shake hands..."

"Quite all right," said the professor. "As you can see, my hands are presently, er, occupied. Your Mounties refused to leave me alone with Mr. Allan unless I wore restraints. Quite understandable, though I don't see why it's necessary."

"Well, they're in the habit of being thorough," Bronson said diplomatically, and he eyed the vat of hot wax bubbling beneath the professor's chair. "Are you one of *them*?" he asked.

"I do not think so," said Eddie. "He came to me with a story about the Teamsters trying to take over his university. You were saying, Professor?"

The professor, perspiration beading on his face, explained: "It all began when the graduate students presented a list of demands. Can you imagine such a thing? They wanted respect, fair play, academic freedom, a sense of dignity about themselves and their work. And that's not all: they wanted a living wage, and jobs when they graduated! The faculty's initial reaction was of course disbelief, and then outrage. We sought to bring them back in line by making them anxious about the future of their careers. I myself went so far as to give the students disapproving glances. I pretended to misunderstand them when they spoke to me. I even shook my head at them in the corridors. Initially we were successful, and it looked for a time like civilization would be maintained. This was, however, before the Teamsters entered the picture. The Teamsters want the scientific community to approve their mobile missile defense plan. You see, the Teamsters want to put ICBMs and their launchers on semi-trucks and play the old shell game with the Chinese. They claim it is the only sure method for Americo to preserve a retaliatory force in case of a Chinese first strike. Naturally, the academic community knows this is just more panda baiting. It's ridiculous—truck-based mobile missiles! Everyone knows rail is the best method for concealing a missile force."

"So what are the Teamsters doing at your university?" asked Bronson.

"Ah," said the professor. "It's not just at my university. The problem is all across the Academy. The Teamsters are unionizing graduate students everywhere. And the graduate students," the professor pursed his lips," are naturally supporting their Teamster brothers, tra-la, in their truck-based mobile missile charade. In return for Teamster muscle and protection, the students are creating a body of scholarship supporting the Teamsters' truck-based plan. Unfortunately, some of these students are clever, and with the Teamsters protecting them they are producing some very credible work disproving the rail-based missile plan supported by the Academy."

Eddie went on to describe how the Teamsters were fighting in the streets with the railroaders, greatly contributing to the chaos of the war.

Bronson made a dismissing gesture. "There's no war going on."

"People are killing each other!" insisted the professor.

Bronson shrugged. "People kill each other every day in automobiles. Just because some newsman calls it a war—" He shrugged again. Professors were so silly, he mused, living in their theatrical world with their abstract concepts labeling the cardboard scenery.

Eddie nodded. "It's a matter of semantics, I suppose."

"Or hermeneutics," added Bronson. He lifted his finger with stern indication.

Nabnak had a pen out and was doodling on his blue jeans. He pointed the pen accusatively at the air. "I say you're all dreaming."

Bronson and Eddie paused momentarily to stare at Nabnak, who raised his hands like a hypnotist and slowly intoned, "Sleeep, sleeep…"

They chose not to respond to his trivial antic.

Eddie asked for Bronson's appraisal of the situation, "Well, what do you think?"

"University professors? Disapproving glances in college corridors? ICBMs?" Bronson frowned. "Slumming." Bronson shook his head and then suddenly a light flashed in his bright blue eyes. "Humph!" he exclaimed, immediately fixing Nabnak and Eddie's attention. They scrutinized the professor carefully as Bronson continued: "Obviously, gentleman, the professor is one of *them*. At the end of the day it is immaterial to him whether the ICBMs are based in railroad cars or semi-trailers. The real issue is power and self-promotion. History is driven by such individuals: agents of Trans-global Corporate Technocracy."

From the ceiling hung a chain with a wooden handle. Bronson gave it a sharp tug and the mechanism for lowering the chair was activated. The professor began sinking.

The professor looked to either side at the wax bubbling below him. He was oddly stoic about the matter. "I know better than to struggle against the inevitable," he said. "So you better find some clown if you want to get your giggles."

Bronson shook his head. Nabnak and Eddie stared on with blank interest.

The mechanism shook slightly as the professor's feet lowered into the wax. He winced against the heat but otherwise seemed unaffected as the wax climbed over his ankles. He was surprised, however, to see the Tower agents were actually going to go through with it.

"You men are mad," the professor sniffed, apparently fully convinced of his authority in the matter. "Do you think my death is going to change the inevitable course of history? You have read too many comic books. Corporate social organization is mankind's ultimate destiny!"

"We'll put you up in the wax museum," said Eddie. "I think you'll go well next to Napoleon."

The professor scoffed. And then, as a measure to control the pain, he hissed as the hot wax soaked into his wool suit. He wrinkled his nose at the smell, and as the wax swallowed his hands he looked very cross. "Your sss-sssssssss-self-righteous values are rhetorical constructions lacking any refer-ences or authority! Idiotsssssssssss!"

Bronson tilted his head in resignation. "I can't argue with that."

The professor frowned with haughty disapproval, "All of you are in ssss-serious trouble! Sssssssss—I'm not going to let myself become angry. Ssss-ssssso— So knock it off! Sssssssss—"

"Ssssss-slumming," was all Bronson could say, and he dismissed the matter as the professor's hissing head was covered over by bubbling wax.

Except for the *gloop gloop gloop* of bubbles rising in the hot wax, there was complete silence in the interrogation room.

Eddie's weak gray eyes suddenly expanded. "How inhuman!" he exclaimed. "Did you hear what that bore said about mankind's ultimate destiny?"

"Napoleon?" said Nabnak with a huff. "I think he rather belongs next to Genghis Khan!"

"Theories of history, professors, bubbling wax—" Bronson rolled his eyes. "I mean *really*. Surely we can find something better with which to spend our time."

Nabnak agreed. "The professor had very poor manners. I am shocked. I am thoroughly shocked."

Just as Nabnak made his little joke, there was a tap at the door and in marched a Mountie with a very important message. Indeed, it was one of the most important messages Eddie had ever received. The Mountie held it up for Eddie to read. Eddie's dull gray eyes lit up. He made a "*Cgh-cgh-cgh*," sound through his amplifier.

"What is it?" asked Bronson.

Eddie winked at Bronson and then motioned for the Mountie to leave the room.

The door closed. Bronson was anxious to learn about the message.

"Well," said Eddie. "It seems Syd Reilly has picked up a clue that has led us to my stepfather."

3

CHANCES TO GET AT JOHN Allan were few and far between. He had always proven himself evasive, conniving, always one step ahead of Eddie. But now there was good reason for hope. Syd Reilly, *the* Syd Reilly was after John Allan this time, and judging from the message he sent Eddie, he was hot on the scoundrel's trail. Syd would get him, all right. Syd had the reputation of being the model agent in Tower. He was clever, dependable, brotherly in his loyalty; the consummate professional, he was completely devoid of animosity or prejudice. Bronson Bodine once said: "I deeply admire Syd. I have never seen him angry." Eddie Allan also singled out Syd Reilly for special praise: "Syd is who I want most to blow my stepfather's brains out." And Nabnak Tornasuk said: "Syd introduced me to my first girlfriend."

Syd Reilly was above all a sensitive and caring man, a humanitarian. It would be impossible to list his many charitable acts, but special mention must be made of the philanthropic institution he set up in the Smokey Mountains in an almost completely dry cave where he supported at one time no less than sixteen homeless mountain children, many scarcely into their teens. He saw to it that they received the very best medical attention, and personally provided them with an education that would rival anything found in Switzerland's most select boarding schools. And most of all he gave them his love, love of a kind which was denied to these unhappy young boys and girls by the uncaring system that had denied them homes with conscientious mothers and capable fathers. "I have only one regret," he once said as he reflected back over the affair, "and that is I ain't been able to share the good fortune the Lord has showered on me with more of His lost children."

We in the Invisible Tower take our hats off to ye, Syd Reilly. Bless you, wherever you may now be.

Setting out in the submersible hydrofoil *Acrobat*, Bronson Bodine and his faithful companion Nabnak Tornasuk made their way from Niagara Falls to Toledo where Syd in his message had specified the rendezvous point. It was just outside of town at the corner of Brint and Holland Roads in a quaint little bar called Pilgrim's Prognosis. It was an innocuous establishment, typical of the many humble but jolly watering holes that dot the Midwest. Inside it was comfortably dusty. Old, stained paneling covered the walls, which were decorated with beer signs and pictures of popular celebrities like Max Weber, Herbert Marcuse, and Charles Manson. There were also cardboard eggs, rabbits and tulips hanging on the walls in preparation for Easter, just four days away. To one side of the dimly lit room were a pinball machine and a scattering of tables. On the other side was a bar. Above the bar, up in the corner, was a big screen TV.

Bronson and Nabnak bought glasses of beer and sat down at a table against the far wall. Maintaining their covers, they pretended to drink, sipping their beers but then spitting out the noxious fluid under the table when no one was looking. Up at the bar, three fifty-something, grizzled, exhausted-by-life male citizens were watching the latest news about the war. By the pinball machine stood a joker with a Billy Bones mask hanging out of his hip pocket. An Ohio Blue Tip bounced around between his lips. It was a typical afternoon crowd.

"I was hoping Syd would be here when we arrived," said Bronson. He took a sip and bent down under the table. The beer left his mouth in a stream that slopped against the floor.

"Yeah," said the Eskimo as his friend sat back up. "These places always give me the heebie-jeebies. The sooner we get out of here the better."

"But the Easter decorations are kind of homey," said Bronson. He turned in his chair and looked over at the three men sitting at the bar. Beyond them, up on the screen, was a special report on the military crisis. Bronson wondered if the figure on the screen was really the President. On the good Reverend's shoulder was a green parrot with an eye patch identical to the patch worn by the President, even down to the little silver cross in the center.

The men at the bar started laughing over some bit of nonsense.

Bronson studied them for a moment, wrinkled his nose at them, and then called out: "You guys don't really think there's a war going on, do you?"

One of them turned and shrugged. "Reverend Bones himself is calling it 'The Conventional War.'"

"Aw, no way!" Bronson got up and joined them at the bar. Nabnak reluctantly followed.

On the screen Billy Bones was replaced by Dan Either, the infamous telecommunications conspirator.

"Now he's going to explain what the President just said." The man sitting next to Bronson shook his head and sipped his beer.

"I'll bet you five dollars there isn't a war going on," said Bronson. At almost the same instant the screen changed to show four marines standing on a Grumman hover platform. They were firing their rifles into the trees below them. In the background helicopters and more hover platforms skidded across the sky.

The man next to Bronson held out his hand.

"Oh no." Bronson shook his head, pointed at the screen. "That's no proof."

One of the other men at the bar leaned forward. "I call it circumstantial opportunist selection. Sort of like natural selection, but instead of survival of the fittest nation, it's survival of the leaders who are best able to create a crisis in the public imagination."

"Wrong," insisted the man next to Bronson. "Your analysis places too much emphasis on leadership. I call it the will of the post-industrial unemployed masses. The crisis gives them something to do."

"All right," retorted the other. "How about survival of the people dumb enough to follow their leaders?"

"But leadership is a fact."

"Then like I said, it's survival of the leaders!"

The third man sitting at the end of the bar knitted his eyebrows together. "What's all this talk of survival? You a Darwinian?"

The man in the middle stuck a swizzle stick in his mouth and nodded. "After five years serving as Envoy Extraordinary to Russia, you bet. It's a war for survival."

"Listen," grunted the man sitting next to Bronson. "I was Minister Plenipotentiary to China for eight years, and I am here to tell you that it all has to do with keeping your proletariat occupied."

"I think it's just a TV show," said Bronson.

"Oh, jeesh," said the man at the end, cringing. "Listen, son. I was Special Commissioner for Foreign Affairs during the last administration. I've been to hot spots all over the world, so I know what I'm talking about, see." He tapped his finger on the bar. "And I can tell you it's serious business. People are killing each other."

Bronson nodded. "And that's all they're doing. I wouldn't call it serious. Look at it scientifically. Why are they killing each other?" Bronson leaned forward across the bar. "I'll tell you why. It's because the experiment in survival of the dumbest isn't working. They're killing off each other because they are an evolutionary dead end. Look how they destroy the environment. They do it wearing the same blank expressions on their faces that they have when they shoot at each other from those flying platforms. Their minds are filled with flags and symbols and stupid slogans. They operate in a mythological world because the real world is over their heads. For heaven's sake, look at Billy Bones. How did he get elected? No. It's not a war. It's self-extermination. The experiment in compartmentalized technocratic civilization is a failure. Nature rejects it. And I say good riddance."

Back up on the screen now were scenes of more fighting. The Green Berets were taking a bad licking in the Mississippi Delta. In retaliation, the Governor of the city-state of Miami was dropping neutron bombs over

Havana. Then Vice-president Kidd and the Chinese foreign minister were shown together in a news studio, arguing over whether or not a weapon that destroyed people but not property was fundamentally capitalistic.

"This is giving me a headache," said Nabnak.

Several moments later an aspirin commercial flashed on the screen. Bronson and the former state ambassadors started chuckling.

For the time being the Special Report was over. A trembling old women in the last stages of senile decay appeared on the screen. She was wrapped loosely in a sheet like the Venus de Milo. A famous, well-groomed German media executive approached from behind and shaved her head. Then a very angry and self-impressed French chef advanced and plopped a fried egg on her bald pate. It wobbled to and fro because of the little old lady's chronic trembling. The media executive bent over her, extended his tongue, and used it to burst the sunny-side yolk. A caption appeared at the bottom of the screen:

SPEND AND ENJOY

Such sentiments prompted Nabnak and Bronson to exchange absurd, embarrassed smiles.

They waited a while longer, listening to Pasadena Polly, Billy Bones' own "Flamenco Filly" make a pitch for her new book on the President's sexual idiosyncrasies: *The Moral Spot.*

A hand fell on Bronson's shoulder. "Hey y'all."

The big agent turned to behold a tall lanky man wearing a mischievous smile on his handsome, heart-shaped face. Thick reddish-blond hair flowed down almost to his waist. It was Syd Reilly, all right. As usual he smelled like a campfire. He wore tennis shoes, blue jean trousers and a jean jacket that was faded almost completely white. In front of his right shoulder was a foam rubber pad held in place with duct tape. He held out his hand and Bronson took it and shook it righteously.

With Syd was a thin, hound dog of a man in his early twenties, ten years younger than either Bronson or Syd. He too was garbed in jeans but wore his dark brown hair in a short flat-top. Syd introduced him as Jimmy McClay, a new "occupant" of the Invisible Tower. Bronson coolly looked him up and down.

Like Bronson and Nabnak, Jimmy McClay carried a large, stainless steel .52 caliber automag under his left arm. The handle pointed forward to display a blue tape across the clip that indicated exploding rounds. There wasn't anything particularly admirable in Jimmy McClay's face, just a sort of hunger, a sort of wild intelligence that, Bronson wondered, might in some ways complement Syd's almost naive selflessness.

Syd went without a pistol. Instead he carried a 12-gauge pump-action blunderbuss. The depleted uranium shot in the shells Syd used (each weighing five pounds) was the reason Syd wore the thick pad on his shoulder. The "Old Mule," as he called it, packed one heck of a kick.

They bought beers and moved back to one of the tables. Jimmy drank his, but the others slowly sipped and spit out the slop on the floor.

"So you have a line on John Allan?" said Bronson, tugging his beard. He watched Jimmy McClay through the corner of his eye. Jimmy was the first Tower agent he ever saw actually enjoying beer.

"I'm here to tell ya," said Syd. He pushed a rope of bright golden hair behind his ear. "Y'see. One of John Allan's 'sisstants—a Chinese feller, I understand—is going in the Toledo Hospital for the Criminally Emotional for a sex change." He pursed his lips. "Now I'm pretty sure John Allan will be close by while the operation is going on, y'see, because this Chinaman feller is like John Allan's right hand man—er, in a manner of speakin'."

This gave Bronson an idea. "I'm no mean surgeon myself. With a surgical mask on I could waltz right into that operating room."

Syd shook his head. "I got it all figured, man. It'll be easier this way. I do want you and Nabnak to go in dressed up like doctors, but we'll wait till the operation is near over. I have your credentials all made up, along with your uniforms, back at the *Crow*." The *Crow* was a submersible hydrofoil identical to the *Acrobat*. "Jimmy," continued Syd, "will wait outside and be our wheelman."

Bronson glanced at Jimmy and then back at Syd. "Where exactly is the operation going to take place?

"Maybe the thirty-seventh or thirty-eighth floor," said Syd. "But we won't know fer sure 'till the day of the operation. This is the layout." From his pocket Syd produced a piece of paper and began diagraming the hospital's first, thirty-seventh and thirty-eighth floors. Tracing their movements with his finger on the diagram, Syd outlined the fine details of his plan. It was typically brilliant, typically "Syd Reilly."

"We've got John Allan." Bronson reached across the table and gave Nabnak a chummy nudge. "We've got *them*."

Nabnak nodded. "Are we going to take him alive, or maybe boil him in oil, like he did to Eddie?"

Syd looked up. "Imagine, a stepfather just a few months older than you. Phew. Them boys must'a been wild when they's young'ns."

"Playing Ali Baba," said Bronson. He suddenly remembered lowering the professor into the hot wax.

On the map Syd drew a cat waving its paw, his personal emblem. He handed it to Bronson. "As far as Nabnak's question goes, I think we ought just wait'n see. Whatch'y'think, man?"

Bronson nodded as he looked over the diagram. "What's your role in the plan."

Syd narrowed his eyes. "I want ya ta'turn me in."

"What?"

"Inside man," explained Syd. "It'll take about forty-eight hours for them to process me. Since the operation is scheduled for Friday afternoon, we ought t'get on wit'ch it."

Bronson checked his thirty-two function spy watch. "That's cutting it close, don't you think?"

Syd nodded. "Down t'th'bone. But havin' someone on the inside's worth the risk, don'cha think?"

"I don't know."

"Don't worry." Syd's head tilted as he winked. His golden hair framed a handsome face that was as angelic as it was rugged. "We'll be back in Eddie's cave by Easter."

4

BRONSON TURNED IN SYD to the Emotion Control Board and was awarded thirty dollars in brand new blue scrip. He felt odd taking it, but it was important to keep up appearances. As they put Syd in a straitjacket and hauled him away, Bronson gazed down at the money. Printed on it was Billy Bones' smiling, jelly-jowled face. The cross in the center of Bones's eye patch held his attention for a moment, then he folded the blue bills and crammed them into his pocket.

Bronson, Nabnak and Jimmy now had two long days to wait. To kill time they split up and covered the airport, the train depot, and the bus station. They knew it would probably be fruitless. John Allan was a master of disguise, but it was an agreeable enough activity that brought its own rewards. In the washroom at the bus station, Jimmy burst into a stall occupied by one Ibn Mahmud Al-Eichmann, a kingpin in the international human trafficking community, and executed him at point-blank range with his .52 caliber automag. At the train station, Nabnak poked around under the platform and found a terrorist bomb that had been made up to look like a sleeping pigeon. A terrorist disguised as a policeman attempted to interfere when Nabnak began clipping off the legs/fuse mechanism, but Nabnak prevailed in the fistfight that ensued and finished disarming the bomb in time to save the westbound Lakeshore Limited. At the airport, it was Bronson's good fortune to spot the notorious "Lady Godiva," a ruthless Hegemony agent who was in Toledo to promote the latest issue of the local electric utility's war bonds. Newsmen were waiting at the gate with cameras rolling. But when she stepped up to greet Toledo, Bronson pushed through, grabbed her by the shoulder and demanded she not abort his baby, completely dis-crediting her in front of hundreds of thousands of family-oriented viewers.

About this same time a military psychiatrist with a well-oiled Mohawk haircut was going over Syd Reilly's test results. "I don't understand," he said. "According to this you're calm." He waved the test papers.

"Well, yeah," answered Syd. "Too calm."

The psychiatrist thought a moment. "Would it bother you if I ordered your head shaved?"

Syd shook his head, sending waves of self-assurance propagating down his handsome mane. "It wouldn't be so long if I wasn't so calm. Do whatch ya want."

The psychiatrist shifted in his chair, cleared his throat. Syd's charming smile made the psychiatrist uncomfortable. "How would you feel about be-ing sent to the front?"

"And run the risk of someone's blood spattering on me?" Syd shook his head. "How 'bout you?"

The psychiatrist picked up his gaze. So, the patient had some hidden agenda. "Would you like to send me to the front?"

"Do ya wanna go to the front?"

The doctor smiled and tapped his pencil against the table. What was this now? "Tell me," he said, "do I remind you of my—I mean *your* father?"

Syd shook his head. "No, I liked my father."

"Ah, so you don't like me. In a sense, though, I am carrying out your father's role. As you were growing up he was the authority figure in your life. Whether you like it or not, that role has now been taken over by me. I am in complete control over you here. I could even order your stomach pumped if I wished."

"But my father was never an authority figure. He was a puppeteer's assistant. He never told anybody what to do, not even the puppets."

"Ah," the psychiatrist leaned forward. "You idolized him?"

"No. He never told me what to do, though."

"Then that's your problem," the psychiatrist said, wondering why he got stuck with all the hillbillies.

Syd thought a moment. "Hey, Doc."

"Yes."

Syd smiled. "To answer your question: Yes, I would like to send you to the front."

The psychiatrist nodded paternally. "Then we're making progress."

They shaved Syd's head and put him in an observation room with a two-way mirror. Syd sat quietly, occasionally feeling his naked head.

"He's hiding something," said the psychiatrist. He had his penknife out and was playing "chicken" with his assistant's hand. "I mean if he's okay, why did they admit him?"

"Perhaps," said the assistant, watching the knife jab down between his outstretched fingers, "I should go downstairs and check the admission officer's credentials?"

The psychiatrist shook his head. "Forget it. I'm going to release him."

The psychiatrist put his knife away and went into the observation room. He stood at the door and said, "Syd?"

"Yeah, Doc?"

"I'm going to release you. It sometimes happens that people turn in their friends and relatives to collect the reward money."

Syd nodded. "Or insurance."

"Is that what happened to you?"

"Oh, heck no." Syd knew he couldn't risk being released. "You see, Doc, the most evil man in the world is bringing his friend here Friday for a sex change operation, and I'm here to kidnap him."

The doctor cleared his throat. From his shirt pocket he produced a pack of cigarettes. He lit one as he stood thinking. "Who are you going to kidnap, Syd, him or his friend?"

Syd narrowed his eyes at the psychiatrist. "How do I know you're not one of *them*?"

They put Syd back in his straitjacket and locked him in a padded cell with a woman who thought she was vomiting up the sin and abominations that filled the cup of the Scarlet Woman of the Apocalypse.

Syd slipped out of the straitjacket easily enough. Now his problem was getting out of the rubber room. He looked down at the women. She was down on all fours, back arched, coughing over a bucket. He watched her gag. She spit into the bucket.

"Hey, darlin'." He bent down to help her. She pulled away. She appeared about fifty-five, her dry and pasty face was deeply creased and she had eyes like a wild animal.

"Easy girl." Syd patted her back and pulled her greasy graying black hair away from her face. She stunk—and then he caught sight of the bloody mucus in the bucket.

She had tuberculosis.

"My goodness!" said Syd. "Why don't they give you some medical attention? I mean, gosh, it's the twenty-first century!"

She looked at him, sensing his benevolent nature. "Y-you're not one of *them*?"

He pulled back from her rank breath. His straitjacket was within reach and he took it to wipe off her face. "Do you know who *they* are?"

She nodded. "John Allan is my husband."

Syd sat back to take it in. He shook his head. "You must feel pretty guilty?"

"But my boy, Eddie," she nodded. "He's a good kid." She took the straitjacket from him and finished wiping her face.

"I'm working for Eddie right now," explained Syd. "We're going to kidnap John."

"John's coming?"

"Friday."

"Then he will come by. He always visits me when he stops by, to torment me if nothing else. Unless—" She looked frightened.

"What?" Syd reached out and took the straitjacket from her.

She smoothed her hospital gown. "He might be too busy running the war and—and he won't come to see his Baby Cakes!" She started crying.

"Aw, now don't you fret," said Syd.

She screeched suddenly, "Wee-cheee! Wee-cheee!" and dropped on to her back. She screeched again "Wee-cheee! Weee-cheeeee!" and began sobbing and mumbling incoherently.

Syd threw up his arms and shook his hands. He couldn't bear to see another human being suffer. "Oh, you poor dear!" He clasped his hands around hers in a gesture of sincere and gentle empathy. "Is there anything I could do fer you?"

With much effort she swallowed her tears. Her lips trembled. "I need to feel loved."

5

AT NOON ON FRIDAY, Bronson, Nabnak and Jimmy McClay rumbled up to the Toledo Hospital For the Criminally Emotional in a 1971 Plymouth "Hemi" Barracuda.

Bronson and Nabnak climbed out. The hospital was a forty-story monolithic monstrosity with stained glass windows depicting a very Stalin-like Columbus discovering America.

Jimmy passed the blunderbuss to Bronson, who tucked it down a pocket sewn inside his lab coat. Nabnak looked on, casually turning his head and watching the busy street through the corners of his eyes.

Black helicopters were flying in overhead, bringing in the wounded from the field.

"Looks like we're taking a licking," observed Nabnak.

Bronson cocked one eyebrow. "Or is it *they* who are taking the licking?" He strode off toward the hospital doors. Nabnak followed close behind while Jimmy stared up and down the street before pulling off.

When the two agents entered the building, they found shot-up soldiers lying on the floor. The agents stepped over and between them. Signs on the wall cautioned against coming into contact with blood.

Bronson stepped up to the reception desk. "Dr. Magnum to see Patient Reilly."

The receptionist, a pale, bony woman with tattooed arms and a pierced eyebrow scrutinized Bronson's ID badge and then checked the registry. "Sorry," she said, "I have no Reilly listed. But that doesn't mean he's not here. With the war and all the wounded, everything's up in the air. Try the master-of-arms, twelfth floor. Sometimes they know."

Bronson tapped the desk and nodded. "Thanks." He and the Eskimo moved off, stepping carefully through the sea of wounded teenagers.

"It strikes me as a reflection," said Bronson. He regarded their ripped and broken bodies with both compassion and clinical interest.

"A reflection?" asked Nabnak. As he looked up at Bronson his heel slid across a pool of blood.

"A reflection of the past," Bronson said, catching his friend's elbow. "You see, the industrialization of information has rendered creative intelligence and originality obsolete. These people have no methodology with which to deal with the human condition—that is to say, the *post-human* condition. And since they can't come up with their own methods, they look to the past—a past that is overshadowed by conflict. I suppose it's the survival instinct. They look for what stands out most against the backdrop of history. If you're scared and survival-oriented, I guess that's war. So in response to twenty-first century problems, they conjure up the ghost of twentieth-century warfare.

"Monkey see monkey do," said Nabnak quietly. It seemed so fatal. He noticed his friend was showing signs of strain. "You okay?"

Bronson didn't answer immediately. They reached the elevator and waited. Bronson said, "I guess I'm concerned about Syd."

"Don't worry," Nabnak tried to assure his friend. "His creative intelligence is quite intact."

The elevator doors slid open and they marched in, pushing back a dwarf orderly who was attempting to walk out.

Bronson drew his automag from beneath his coat and pointed it at the dwarf's head. "You look pretty small for an orderly, especially in an emotion control hospital." He was wondering if the dwarf was one of *them*.

Nabnak also had his suspicions. "Be careful, he might have a net in his head." The Eskimo wrapped his forearm around the dwarf's head. The head twisted. He continued unscrewing it. "Just as I expected," said Nabnak.

Inside the plastic head was a net; and at the base of the dwarf's neck was an explosive charge set to blast the net through the brittle scalp. "They send them after runaway patients," explained Nabnak. "Their small size lets them fit anywhere; a ventilation duct, for instance. And the form of a dwarf is very appealing to people with emotional disturbances. Such people allow the dwarfs to approach them—and then *bang* they get popped with the net."

Nabnak turned the dwarf off with the switch inside its neck, and then began screwing the head back on.

There was a sudden thud overhead. Someone was on the elevator roof. The trap door in the ceiling opened and a familiar voice cried, "Hey, y'all."

Syd dropped down, startling them with his shaved head. His hospital gown was untied and hung like a cape from his neck. "Bald as an eagle, naked as a jay bird," he said. Then he spied the dwarf and bent down to pat it on the back. "Awww. Cute little feller, ain't he?"

Bronson and Nabnak looked at each other, and then they all scrambled up through the trap door.

On the roof of the elevator car was a woman Bronson somehow felt he knew. There was something strangely familiar about her. Like Syd, she was naked except for a loose hospital gown swinging from her neck. A shiny glaze of red mucus covered her chin, neck and breasts.

"Bronson, Nabnak," said Syd, "this is Eddie's mother, Mrs. Allan."

Bronson and Nabnak nodded, at once impressed to meet the mother of the famous spy, but also alarmed to behold her naked and diseased condition. Their expressions betrayed mute embarrassment. Bronson turned to Syd.

"No time to explain," said Syd. He looked up the dimly lit elevator shaft. The elevator was slowing, eased to a stop. "Have you got the Old Mule?"

Bronson pulled out the blunderbuss and handed it to Syd, who pumped it and set it down on the roof of the elevator. Then Syd gathered his gown up and tied it around his shoulder.

"We have to get you some clothes," said Bronson.

Syd shook his head. "No time. John Allan's in the building."

Mrs. Allan started coughing. "*Haugh haugh—haugh.*"

Bronson and Nabnak appraised the situation.

"How are we going to fit all these people in the car?" asked Nabnak.

"Oh—*ugh!*—*yeack!*—I'll ride in the trunk with Syd," said Mrs. Allan. "I don't mind. *He-uk! Gbt! Gbt! Gbt!*"

"Shh!" Bronson pointed down. It sounded like someone below them inside the elevator had found the dwarf.

The elevator started lowering.

"C'mon." Syd had everyone jump. They clung to the crumbly beads of mortar that ran between the concrete blocks lining the shaft. The elevator dropped away beneath them and disappeared into the darkness.

But Mrs. Allan had grabbed the counterweight cable and was shooting up the shaft.

"I'll get her," said Nabnak, and he scrambled up after her.

Bronson waited with Syd.

"So that's Mrs. Allan," said Bronson. She does have a kind of 'Allan' look about her."

"Don't she?" Syd wiped his mouth. "They threw me in the rubber room with her last night—after they shaved my head. This morning they sent in an orderly to clean 'er up on account of John Allan comin'. I jumped the orderly and we've been hiding in the elevator shaft ever since."

Bronson checked his watch. It was nearly one o'clock. "Have you found out where the operation is going to take place?"

"Thirty-seventh floor, operating room 'C'."

Bronson looked up. "Might as well have Nabnak and Mrs. Allan wait up there." Not wanting to raise his voice, Bronson took his gun and tapped instructions in Morse code against the brick. A few moments later Nabnak tapped back an acknowledgement. He had Mrs. Allan with him.

"Let's join them," said Bronson.

They climbed swiftly and caught up with Nabnak and Mrs. Allan at the twenty-ninth floor. Between hacks, Mrs. Allan said she couldn't go on.

265

Bronson had her climb on his back. "Try and cough the other way," he said, and they continued on. They made steady progress, climbing with their finger-tips and their sticky-toe spy boots.

Soon they were by the elevator doors at the thirty-seventh floor. Mrs. Allan was straining admirably against the urge to cough.

"How do you want to do this?" whispered Syd. He flexed his fingers. The blunderbuss was cradled across his elbows.

Bronson shrugged as he tried unsuccessfully to peek through the crack between the elevator doors. He hissed at Nabnak: "Climb to the top and pull the release so I can see."

Nabnak was up in an instant. He found the lever and tugged at it gently. The lever slid back without making a sound. Bronson pushed his fingers between the doors and eased them open. Right in front of him was a guard's blue trouser leg. Fortunately, the guard was facing the opposite direction and was unaware of the spy in the shaft behind him.

Bronson turned and held up one finger.

Syd pointed down the shaft.

Nodding, Bronson shifted Mrs. Allan's weight. He slammed the doors to the side, grabbed the guard by the ankle and yanked.

"Wha—!" As the guard fell back Syd smacked him in the head with the stock of the Old Mule. The guard tumbled quietly down the shaft.

After a few seconds a dull thud echoed up from below.

"Come on," said Bronson. He led them from the shaft into a white corridor. It was empty. Evidently John Allan had seen to it that the wounded were kept off the thirty-seventh floor. On the wall opposite the elevator was a floor plan. Operating room "C" was to the right.

Nabnak and Bronson drew their automags.

"Whatch'er packin'?" asked Syd.

"Tumbling dum dums," hissed Bronson.

Nabnak nodded. "Ditto."

They spread out and slinked down the hall. Every sense was awake. They stalked like cats, turned their heads to and fro, extended their necks and retracted them. They stayed loose, alert, cool. Syd's fingers rose and fell against the blunderbuss. The slightest sound chilled their spines. The air tingled. Just ahead the hallway turned ninety degrees to the left. Bronson lowered his automag and tiptoed ahead of them. He peeked around the corner.

Four men stood by what must have been the doors to the operating room. They were dressed in dark business suits. Little white wires led up to their ears where they wore earphones. Uzi's hung from their wrists.

Bronson pulled back and with his hands spelled out "four bodyguards" in sign language.

Syd nodded and crept forward to trade places with Bronson. He raised the Old Mule and tucked it firmly against the cloth around his shoulder.

He looked at Bronson and the others, then swung around the corner. The Old Mule flashed and kicked back with a roaring thud. The depleted uranium shot screeched as it swept through the passageway. The bodyguards flew back, perforated with hundreds of holes.

Syd ran down the hall with the others behind him. The walls were streaked from the depleted uranium shot, and the doors at the far end of the hall had been blown off their hinges.

The agents leapt over the bodies of the body guards and stormed into the operating theater.

Three nurses, an anesthesiologist and a surgeon stared at them with round eyes.

"Really!" said the surgeon. "This is unheard of!"

Sitting in the corner on a stool was—it could only be—John Allan. He wore a dunce cap on his head.

"My wife!" exclaimed John Allan. And then he did a double-take. "Really, darling, your modesty!"

Mrs. Allan pulled the hospital gown around her front.

"John Allan, I presume?" said Syd.

"You may," he nodded. "I see you are friends of my wife. She has recruited you, no doubt, to give me a much deserved heave-ho into the old doghouse?" He rolled his eyes. "I suppose I should thank you for taking it upon yourselves to remedy the haggard state of my family's private affairs. But as you can see—" He tapped his dunce cap. "I have already gone to the bother of setting myself up in the corner with this ridiculous *chapeau* on my noggin. Yes, I am a dunce: all the discomfort I've put poor Mr. Wang through. I admit it. I am responsible. And I really am ashamed." He gazed at the prostrate form on the operating table and bit his lip with mock concern.

"You're coming with us, John," said Mrs. Allan. "We're taking you back to Eddie. *Wheez wheeze wheeze*."

"Mr. Allan!" boomed the surgeon. "These people are filthy!"

John Allan nodded. "And rude." He pulled a small black box from his suit coat and pushed a button.

A blue light danced around Syd Reilly and he disappeared. A small pile of gray ash was left on the floor.

"God!" said Bronson and he fired at John Allan. But the dum dum bullet struck some kind of invisible shield and deflected, just missing the anesthesiologist's shoulder.

"An hypersonic repulser screen," sniffed John Allan.

"John!" Mrs. Allan's hands opened and clenched. "What happened to Syd!"

Her smug husband shrugged. "Who? The naked bald man? Oh, you see, darling, well—" John Allan widened his eyes for effect. "He is all gone."

She stomped her feet and threw the hospital gown back over her shoulder. "John! Lower that force screen this instant!" She put her hands on her pillowy hips. "This instant, John Allan!"

He stuck his finger in his nose and glanced off.

"Oh, you!" she cried. "Just like my father!"

He wiggled his finger. "Can't seem to get it out."

"John! You listen to me." She marched up to the force screen and narrowed her eyes. "To think of all those months I spent in bed waiting for you to become aroused. Flattering you with baby-talk, bringing you toast, indulging your neuroses—all for nothing. Ah! Why couldn't you have been like Eddie's father? Eddie's father was a real man! Eddie's father was a sexual hydrogen bomb! Eddie's father—" she turned around to show Bronson and Nabnak how very angry she was.

But they had run off.

Carter Kaplan has pioneered the application of poetry and fiction to the study of analytic philosophy, as presented in his book *Critical Synoptics: Menippean Satire and the Analysis of Intellectual Mythology*. In addition to a number of academic articles and reviews, he is the author of the Aristophanic comedy *Diogenes*, and a novel of intellectual life in trans-Atlantic culture, *Tally-Ho, Cornelius!* His Afterword appears in the International Authors edition of Nathaniel Hawthorne's *The Scarlet Letter*, and he led the translation committee producing the International Authors edition of Torquato Tasso's *Creation of the World*. He is editor of the annual literary anthology *Emanations*.

A consortium of writers, artists, architects, filmmakers and critics, International Authors publishes work of outstanding literary merit. Dedicated to the advancement of an international culture in literature, primarily in English, the group seeks new members with an enthusiasm for creating unique artistic expressions.

www.internationalauthors.info

29385887R00167

Printed in Poland
by Amazon Fulfillment
Poland Sp. z o.o., Wrocław